Pierced Lies

Marie Lefevre

Published by Marie Lefevre, 2024.

This is a work of fiction. Similarities to real people, places, or events are entirely coincidental.

PIERCED LIES

First edition. December 2, 2024.

Copyright © 2024 Marie Lefevre.

ISBN: 979-8230835875

Written by Marie Lefevre.

Chapter 1: The Piercing Encounter

The dock creaks under the weight of metal containers being shifted by the massive cranes above, the night air thick with the scent of oil and rust. I can't remember the last time I'd stepped foot here, and the sudden flood of memories nearly knocks me off balance. The harbor used to be a playground of sorts when I was younger—long before I realized how deep the family business ran or how ugly it could get. The carefree summer nights spent hiding behind old crates, trying to catch a glimpse of my uncle's associates as they went about their shady dealings, now seem like a distant, foolish dream. But tonight, I don't have the luxury of nostalgia. I'm here to play the role I've been assigned, whether I like it or not.

Luca steps forward, his dark leather jacket creaking as he moves, and for a moment, I wonder if he's even human or just some kind of shadow that has come to life. There's something almost predatory in the way he carries himself, the sharp angles of his jaw, the tightness of his expression, as though every moment is a calculated decision in a game he's already won. It makes me want to scream. His reputation precedes him, and it's not one of kindness. He is ruthless, a man of few words, most of them threats wrapped in a tight, efficient tone.

His lips curl into a smirk, the kind that feels more like an insult than a compliment. "Didn't think you'd actually show up, Vellano. Thought you were too busy in your perfect little world."

I don't answer immediately. Instead, I focus on the way the light from the nearby streetlamp glints off the edges of the shipping containers, reflecting off the slick concrete beneath my boots. I've spent years keeping a safe distance from this world, and now, for some cruel twist of fate, I find myself thrust into it, again. Only this time, I'm not the naive child who could be sent home with just a sharp word and a wink. No, now I'm a part of this—whether I like it or not.

"Did you?" I ask, turning slowly to face him, forcing my voice to steady despite the pounding of my heart. "Did you really think I wouldn't show up?"

His eyebrows raise ever so slightly, as though my words amuse him. "Oh, I was counting on it, sweetheart. The question is—how long before you get bored and go back to your little life in the city? People like you, they don't last long in places like this."

I roll my shoulders back, standing as tall as I can in my heels, suddenly aware of the fact that I'm far too close to the edge of the dock for comfort. The wind picks up, sending the scent of the ocean spiraling around us, tugging at the hem of my coat. I can feel the weight of his gaze, like a heat I can't escape. But there's a steadiness inside me, a new kind of resolve. This is my fight, my choice, and I won't back down because some dark-eyed enforcer is looking at me like I'm a puzzle to be solved.

"I'm not going anywhere," I say, my voice finally coming out more controlled than I feel. "And I'm not some trophy for you to toss aside once you're bored with me. I'll be here long after you've made your mark."

Luca watches me for a long moment, his gaze heavy, calculating. He doesn't speak for several beats, and I wonder if he's considering the same thing I am—that I've just stepped into a battle I'm not ready for. The underworld is no place for anyone with a conscience, and I've learned that the hard way. But what choice do I have? My uncle's dealings have a hold on my family, and I'm not naive enough to think I can walk away unscathed.

"I'm not worried about you," Luca finally says, his voice low and almost too smooth, as though he's waiting for me to crumble under the pressure. But I don't. I stand firm, even as the tension between us grows thicker, the unsaid words hanging in the air like a storm waiting to break.

He steps back, giving me a wide berth, and I can't tell if it's out of respect or simple disdain. Either way, it doesn't matter. The moment his attention shifts away from me, I can't help but notice the flurry of activity around us—the men unloading crates, the low murmurs of orders being exchanged. Everything here moves in a calculated rhythm, the hum of the harbor providing a soundtrack to the chaos just beneath the surface. It's a world where people survive on fear and loyalty, and I can feel the weight of both pushing against me.

The conversation fades into the background as my mind starts to race. I need to be smart, need to think ahead, but I don't know where to start. Luca's presence alone is enough to make my skin crawl, but there's something else. Something darker that I'm only beginning to understand. My uncle's empire isn't just built on muscle and intimidation. It's built on secrets, things no one is meant to know. And Luca Torelli? He's the keeper of those secrets. I can see it in the way he moves, the way his eyes never quite meet mine for too long—he knows things I don't, and that knowledge makes him dangerous.

I take a deep breath and turn away, not out of fear, but because I need to find my footing. It's not enough to just survive in this world. I have to be smart, strategic. If Luca thinks he can intimidate me, he's wrong. I'm not leaving without a fight, and I won't let him, or anyone else, define my place here.

The wind shifts, carrying the faint smell of diesel and damp wood, mingling with the acrid tang of saltwater. My boots tap against the slick concrete of the dock as I turn away from Luca, the metallic clinking of chains and the guttural commands exchanged between the dock workers ringing in my ears. This is all wrong—everything about this night feels wrong. The harbor, once a place of childhood memories, now feels like a cage. And Luca is the lock.

I try to steady my breathing, pushing aside the familiar gnaw of unease. My uncle's business, his empire, is built on shadows, secrecy, and blood money. I know this. I've always known it. Yet tonight, for reasons I can't explain, it feels personal. Luca's presence, his calm, calculated demeanor, rips through the veils I've so carefully draped over my life. He doesn't belong here. Neither of us does, not really.

I glance back at him, surprised to find him still watching me. His eyes narrow slightly, the corner of his lips lifting in a knowing smirk. I hate how effortlessly he slips into the role of intimidation, how easily he pushes all my buttons without even trying. His silence feels like a threat, heavy and suffocating. But I refuse to let him see how much it affects me.

"Do you always lurk in the shadows?" I ask, forcing the words out with as much bravado as I can muster. "Or is tonight just special?"

He tilts his head, considering me, his dark eyes never leaving mine. "I'm not the one hiding here," he says quietly, his voice a low growl. There's a sharpness in his tone that cuts through the air, a tension that seems to wrap itself around me like a noose.

I could punch him, I think, with an almost absurd clarity, but I know that would only add to the ever-present smirk on his face. What's the point? He would only see it as weakness. I fight the urge to respond, to fire back with something sharp and biting, but something inside me cautions against it. This isn't the time for defiance. Not yet.

My cousin, Nico, finally materializes from the shadows, his voice breaking through the thick silence like a lifeline. "Enough, you two. The boss wants to see you."

It's almost laughable how quickly he tries to diffuse the tension between Luca and me, but I can't fault him for it. Nico's got a vested interest in keeping things smooth, especially when it comes to his cousin and his unpredictable temper. Still, he can't hide the gleam of amusement in his eyes as he watches me, like he knows exactly what's been simmering between us since the moment I stepped off the cab and onto this cursed dock.

Luca doesn't take his eyes off me for a second, but finally, he steps aside, motioning for me to follow. "After you, Miss Vellano," he says, his voice as slick as ever. I can't decide whether he's being polite or mocking me, but either way, I'm not in the mood to test it further. I nod curtly and walk past him, trying not to feel the weight of his gaze on my back. I hate that I feel it. Even now, as I walk away, the lingering heat of his presence seems to follow me like a shadow.

The harbor is alive tonight, buzzing with the familiar hum of activity. The low growl of engines, the churning sound of loading cranes, the muffled conversations and commands drifting in the humid air—it's all part of the chaotic ballet that my uncle's operation runs on. I've never liked the place. It feels dirty, gritty, as though the world itself is holding its breath here, waiting for something to crack. Maybe that's why I've stayed away for so long. The darker side of the family business has a way of swallowing people whole, and I'd rather not get caught in its jaws.

As we walk deeper into the maze of containers and shadowed corners, I can feel the weight of every unspoken word between Luca and me. It's not just his eyes that bother me. It's the quiet way he moves, the predator's grace that hints at a past too messy to confront. The man isn't just an enforcer; he's a part of the machinery. He keeps the gears turning, the blood flowing, and the lies buried deep enough to never see the light of day. And for someone like me, someone who has tried so desperately to escape that very world, that's a terrifying thought.

Nico pushes open the door to an old warehouse at the edge of the pier, and the sudden rush of stale, cool air is a relief. The inside is dimly lit, filled with the scent of old wood and something far less pleasant—the sharp, metallic tang of oil and sweat. In the center of the room, my uncle sits behind a massive desk, his figure hulking in the low light. A glass of bourbon sits before him, the amber liquid catching the dim glow of the lamp beside him.

"Vellano," he greets, his voice gravelly from years of cigar smoke and too much scotch. "I trust you're here for more than just a social visit."

I resist the urge to roll my eyes. Of course, he knows why I'm here. My uncle's business isn't built on charity, after all. He's not interested in small talk. He's interested in one thing, and one thing only: loyalty. I step forward, ready to play the part I've been given, but before I can speak, Luca's voice cuts through the air like a blade.

"Miss Vellano has always been good at staying out of the family business," he says, his tone dripping with that same insufferable amusement. "I'm sure she has her reasons for being here tonight. But I'm curious—what's changed?"

I meet Luca's gaze, and for a moment, I wonder if he can see straight through me. If he knows I'm not just here because I'm family, not just here because I owe my uncle a debt. There's more at play here than I'm willing to admit, and I'm afraid that, somehow, he's already figured it out.

But that's a battle for another time.

My uncle's warehouse is dimly lit, the single hanging bulb above casting long shadows that stretch across the concrete floor like ghosts in a forgotten alley. The sound of footsteps echo in the space, sharp and steady as Nico and Luca trail behind me. My uncle's voice rings out, thick with the kind of authority that only years of ruthlessness can breed.

"I don't like being kept waiting, Vellano," Don Vellano says, his sharp eyes assessing me as I step into the room, trying my hardest to avoid his glare. The weight of his presence in the room is almost unbearable, suffocating in the way he commands attention without uttering a word. His face is a map of experience, lines etched from a life lived in shadows. He doesn't smile. He never smiles.

Nico leans against the doorframe, arms crossed, as Luca lingers near the back of the room, silent as ever. They make a silent wall of intimidation between me and my uncle, but I refuse to flinch. I'm not the same person I was when I left this life behind, all those years ago.

"I'm not here for the family dinner, Uncle," I say, crossing the room to stand in front of his desk, refusing to cower under his gaze. "You know why I'm here."

His fingers drum lightly on the polished wood, an idle gesture that somehow feels more like a warning. "Do I? Because last I checked, you've been too busy with your high society nonsense to care about what happens down here."

I hate that he's right. But it's too late to go back now, too late to pretend that the blood running through my veins isn't tied to this place. That's the lie I've been telling myself, the lie I've lived with for years.

"I'm not here for the nonsense," I say with a quiet certainty, my voice unwavering. "I need your help, Uncle. There's a problem."

The words hang in the air between us, thick with unspoken history. My uncle doesn't respond immediately. Instead, his dark eyes narrow, scrutinizing me, looking for cracks. It's like he's trying to figure out what game I'm playing, but for once, I'm not playing. I'm just here for answers, even if I have to drag them out of him.

"And what problem would that be?" he asks, his voice low and controlled, like he's already tired of the conversation. But I can see the shift in his posture. I know I've piqued his interest. He might not admit it, but this is what he lives for—the chaos, the power, the things that cannot be undone.

I glance briefly at Luca, who stands motionless by the wall, watching me with those eyes that feel like they're peeling away my every secret. His silence is unnerving, his presence a constant weight in the room. But it's not Luca that concerns me now—it's the problem that's been following me for weeks, the problem that's finally caught up to me.

"Someone's been poking around," I say, my words slipping out like a confession. I can feel the tension building, the room tightening like a noose around my neck. "Asking questions. About the business. About what you're really up to. I don't know who it is, but they're getting too close."

I watch the slow shift in my uncle's expression—his lips tightening, his brow furrowing, a hint of anger creeping into his voice. "Who?" he asks, leaning forward slightly. It's the first time tonight that I've seen him truly engaged. This is the side of him I've spent years avoiding: the Don Vellano who doesn't tolerate weakness, who doesn't let anyone get away with betrayal.

"I don't know yet," I admit. "But whoever they are, they're digging deeper than they should be."

The room falls into an eerie silence, broken only by the distant hum of traffic outside and the soft shuffle of feet from Luca, who's slowly making his way closer to the desk. The tension between us is palpable, a silent storm building just beneath the surface.

"I don't like not knowing things," my uncle says finally, his voice thick with a cold, unsettling calm. "And I don't like people who think they can get away with poking their noses into my business."

His fingers tap once more on the desk. "You're right to come to me, but this... you've put me in a delicate position, you know that?"

I meet his eyes with a steady resolve, not flinching this time. "I didn't want to come to you, Uncle. But I don't have a choice. I can't handle this on my own."

A smirk tugs at the corner of his mouth, his gaze flicking briefly to Luca before settling back on me. "Well, I suppose you'll learn something tonight, then."

His words hang in the air, cryptic, and for a moment, I wonder if I've just stepped into something darker than I expected. Luca shifts behind me, moving like a shadow, his eyes never leaving me. I can feel the tension building around us, and I can't help but think—what am I getting into?

"Luca," my uncle calls without even looking at him. "Take care of it."

I turn, eyes wide, but before I can protest, Luca steps forward, his movements calculated and precise. There's no hesitation, no questioning. Just that same cold resolve I've come to expect from him. I feel his presence behind me, like a looming storm, and I brace myself for whatever comes next.

"You're not going to like this," Luca says quietly, his voice a low murmur as he leans in close, too close, his breath warm against my ear.

I stiffen, feeling the sudden surge of panic in my chest. I glance back at my uncle, but his face is unreadable.

"Don't make it worse than it already is," Luca adds, his hand reaching out.

The next moment, the door slams shut with a finality that chills me to the bone. And then everything goes silent, too silent, as the weight of what's coming sinks in.

Chapter 2: The Vellano Code

The grand study feels more like a tomb than a place of discussion. Its vaulted ceilings loom overhead, pressing down with the weight of generations, their polished portraits staring back at me with hollow eyes. The chandeliers above, crystal and brilliant, cast cold, unforgiving light, their delicate chains tremoring with every word my uncle speaks. I can almost hear the ghosts of ancestors whispering through the stillness, but they're not the ones in control. That privilege belongs solely to my uncle.

His voice, deep and calculated, fills the space as he explains his vision for the Vellano empire. His words are smooth, confident, and suffused with an arrogance that grates on my already frayed nerves. He paints the future with promises of greater power, wealth, and influence. But beneath the surface, there's something more sinister—a quiet, insidious pressure, as though he's tightening the noose around my neck, one delicate turn at a time.

"You'll need to be more than just the face of the family, Alessandra," he continues, barely glancing in my direction as I stand rigid in front of the fireplace. "You're the key to winning over the Cavanagh Group, the only thing standing between us and global dominance in the sector. I expect your full cooperation, your charm, your finesse."

My fingers curl into fists at my sides, but I force myself to remain still. His words are a subtle weapon, a reminder of my place in this labyrinthine game of power. My charm? My finesse? He treats me like I'm little more than a decorative piece in a chess match. A pawn to be moved at his leisure, a mere tool to secure his kingdom. His empire. Not mine. Not yet, anyway.

I can feel the air thickening, suffocating me with the weight of his expectations. The familiar scent of polished wood, old books, and the faint musk of tobacco seems to close in around me. The room smells of history—of old money, old power, and old grudges—but it does nothing to comfort me. Instead, it makes me feel small, insignificant, a mere piece in his ever-growing collection.

From the corner of the room, Luca's presence is unmistakable. He's a dark silhouette, a shadow that blends seamlessly into the edges of the space. His cold, calculating eyes never leave me, though his face remains expressionless. He's always there—always watching, always waiting for me to slip. I've never quite trusted him, but I don't have much of a choice. He's my uncle's right hand, his enforcer, his eyes and ears in the world outside these walls. And he knows how to keep a secret. Or perhaps more accurately, he knows how to make sure no one is foolish enough to reveal one.

When I glance his way, his lips twitch, as though he's amused by some private joke that's meant for him alone. But then the sound of his voice, low and mocking, cuts through the tension like a knife.

"You're lucky he lets you sit at the table," Luca sneers, his words laced with venom. "After all, it's not like you're the one who built all of this."

My breath catches in my throat, and I feel my heart rate spike. It's as if his words had been a spark in a dry forest, and now everything in me is burning. A flash of heat rushes through me—anger, frustration, and a sharp sense of injustice that claws at my insides. But instead of responding with words, I step forward, fists clenched, and my voice rises, thick with fury.

"I'm not some puppet to be played with, Luca," I snap, my voice cutting through the heavy air. "You don't get to talk to me like that. You don't get to pretend you know who I am or what I'm capable of. I am not a tool in his game."

His eyes flicker with surprise for a moment, but the cool, calculating mask he wears never falters. He shifts ever so slightly, his posture leaning against the wall, as if waiting for me to say something more. But I don't give him that satisfaction. Instead, I turn back to my uncle, whose steady gaze never wavers.

"You expect me to help you expand this empire," I continue, my voice now steady but sharp, cutting through the dense air. "You want my cooperation? You want my charm? Fine. But don't think for a second that you can control me. I won't be your pawn."

The silence in the room is deafening. Even the clocks on the walls, ticking with the usual rhythmic precision, seem to have slowed, as though they too are waiting for the storm to pass. My uncle's expression remains unreadable, though there's a flicker of something in his eyes—something dangerous, a flash of irritation that makes the hairs on the back of my neck stand up.

"You'll do what's necessary, Alessandra," he says, his voice cool but tinged with menace. "You have no choice."

"No," I reply, my voice low but firm, my pulse thumping in my throat. "I do have a choice. And I'm not going to be controlled by you or anyone else. I'll help—on my terms."

The weight of his gaze bears down on me, and for a split second, I wonder if I've pushed too far, if I've made a mistake I won't be able to undo. But then Luca's quiet snort breaks the silence, drawing my attention.

"On your terms?" he mutters under his breath, clearly trying to hide a smile. "You've got a lot of fire for someone who's barely out of her twenties. It won't last."

"I'm not afraid of you," I snap back, meeting his eyes without flinching. The air between us crackles, charged with a kind of tension I can feel in my bones.

"Good," Luca replies with a smirk. "You'll need every ounce of that fire. You're going to need it."

The echo of my words lingers in the air, too sharp, too raw for the polished walls of the study. I can feel my pulse quicken, a rush of heat spreading through my body. Every muscle is taut, every breath measured, but I refuse to break under the weight of my uncle's icy gaze. He's used to this kind of tension—he thrives on it, feeding off the chaos that simmers beneath his surface control. But I won't let him intimidate me anymore. Not today.

Luca's snort, so quietly dismissive, cuts through the quiet like a blade. He's enjoying this, I can tell. He always does. His eyes gleam with amusement, as though he's waiting for me to crumble under the weight of my own defiance. He's used to seeing me as nothing more than a spoiled, pampered heir, a young woman playing at power. But he doesn't know me. Not really. Not yet.

"Why do you always have to be so... dramatic?" Luca's voice is low, almost a whisper, but it carries through the room with the kind of casual cruelty I've learned to expect from him. His words are meant to sting, to cut deep, but I won't let him see how much they affect me. I refuse to give him that satisfaction.

"I'm not being dramatic," I snap, turning to face him head-on. "I'm being real. Something you wouldn't understand."

His lips twitch with the ghost of a smile, the kind of smile that doesn't quite reach his eyes. It's the smile of a man who's used to seeing people squirm, used to watching others bend to his will. But I'm not about to bend—not now, not ever. If there's one thing I've learned in this family, it's that power is never given; it's taken. And I'm done waiting for permission.

"You think you can change things, Alessandra?" Luca's tone shifts, darkening, becoming more dangerous. "You're just like your uncle. You think you can play at the game and come out unscathed. But this isn't a game, sweetheart. It's survival."

His words rattle through me like a warning shot, but they don't land where he expects. I know exactly what he's trying to do—he's trying to intimidate me, to remind me of the stakes. He wants me to feel small, to cower under the weight of my family's legacy. But I won't let him. I won't be cowed by his cold, calculated demeanor or my uncle's endless demands. I've spent far too long feeling like a piece of property to be bartered over, but no more.

"I'm not afraid of you," I say, my voice quiet but steady. The words feel like a promise, a vow to myself that I'll no longer let them define me by their expectations. "And I'm not afraid of him either."

My uncle's eyes flash at my declaration, a fleeting moment of irritation crossing his face before he masks it with the practiced indifference I've come to expect. He's not accustomed to having his control challenged, especially not by me. But there's something else in his gaze, something I can't quite place. His lips curl into a tight smile, the kind that makes the air in the room feel suddenly colder.

"I see you're determined, Alessandra," he says, his voice now smooth, almost patronizing. "But let's not mistake stubbornness for strength. You can fight all you want, but in the end, you'll do what's best for the family. You always do."

There it is again—the family. The ever-present specter that looms over everything we do, every choice we make. Loyalty above all. The family motto hangs in the air like an invisible chain, binding me to this house, this legacy, this life I never asked for. It's suffocating, this constant reminder that my every action is meant to further their agenda, their vision of success. But what about my vision? What about me?

I can feel the resentment bubbling inside me, a pressure building beneath my skin. I've spent my entire life living in the shadows of their expectations, playing the dutiful niece, the perfect lady, the charming socialite. But it's all been a lie, hasn't it? A carefully curated performance. And now, for the first time, I'm not sure I can keep up the charade any longer.

Luca's presence in the room shifts, becoming more oppressive with every passing moment. His eyes never leave me, like a predator waiting for the perfect moment to strike. I want to lash out, to tell him to leave, to take his insufferable presence with him. But instead, I draw a deep breath, willing my body to remain calm, to steady myself.

"You don't get to tell me what's best for the family," I reply, the words slipping from my lips with a newfound strength. "I'll decide what's best for me."

There's a silence that stretches between us, thick and heavy, before my uncle speaks again, his voice dangerously low.

"You're not as clever as you think, Alessandra. You think you're some kind of renegade, a revolutionary. But in the end, you'll fall in line. You'll see it's inevitable. It always is."

I want to argue, to tell him that I won't be just another cog in his carefully constructed machine, but something about the finality in his words chills me to the bone. It's as if he's seen all of this before, every rebellion, every act of defiance, and he knows how it ends—how I'll fall in line, just like every other person who's ever tried to resist him. The thought makes my stomach churn.

Luca steps forward, his presence as cold and unyielding as the marble floors beneath our feet. There's something in his eyes—something dangerous, something that feels like a warning. He's not just my uncle's enforcer. He's a predator, and I'm the prey.

"You'll need more than just stubbornness to survive this world, Alessandra," he says softly, his voice almost a whisper. "You'll need power. And right now, you have none."

Luca's words, like a slap, hang in the air long after they've left his lips. They echo off the polished wood, ricochet off the century-old bookshelves, and settle into my chest like a weight I can't shake. I swallow hard, but the lump in my throat doesn't budge. I don't care what he thinks—what he all think. I refuse to be a mere accessory in my uncle's game of power, and no one will convince me otherwise.

But then, as if summoned by the heat of my frustration, my uncle's voice breaks the simmering tension with the chilling calm that only he can manage.

"You're right about one thing, Alessandra." His words drip with the kind of false sweetness that sends an involuntary shiver down my spine. "You're no pawn. You're the queen."

I bristle, my fists tightening again, though I keep my voice steady. "I'm not playing your game."

"Oh, but you are. You just don't know it yet." My uncle rises from his desk, slowly, deliberately, as though savoring the moment. He circles the room with the measured confidence of someone who's always been in control. "You see, this empire, this legacy we've built, isn't something you can just walk away from. Loyalty is the price of freedom in this family, and freedom..." His eyes gleam, dangerously. "Well, that's a very expensive commodity."

Luca watches us both, his expression unreadable, but I catch a flicker of something—amusement, maybe? Disdain? I can never tell with him. And that, more than anything, irritates me. I want to wipe that smug look off his face, to break through his impenetrable façade, but I know better. He's not the one I need to be worried about.

"I'm not a fool," I snap, taking a step forward. The floor beneath my feet seems to vibrate with the energy crackling between us. "You can't manipulate me with your threats, or your grand speeches about legacy. I'm not playing by your rules, and you can't make me."

There's a moment, just a moment, when I think I see something flicker behind my uncle's eyes—something that's not quite rage, but not far from it. Something that feels unsettlingly like fear.

"You think you have a choice," he murmurs, his voice dropping to a deadly whisper. "But in the end, Alessandra, we all have our roles to play. And if you're smart, you'll realize that yours has already been written."

I can feel my heart pound in my chest, the pulse of defiance pushing against the walls of my ribcage. I won't let him win. I won't let him turn me into the character he expects me to be. I won't be a part of his carefully crafted narrative, no matter how thick the plot gets.

"You'll see," I mutter under my breath, the words tasting bitter. "You'll all see. I'm not going to sit quietly in the background anymore."

Luca's low chuckle catches me off guard, and for the first time, I really look at him—really look at him. His features are sharp, his jawline a chiseled monument to the kind of discipline I'll never fully understand. But it's his eyes that hold me. Cold, merciless, and filled with a kind of knowing that unsettles me deeply.

"You're wrong, you know," he says, his voice taking on that unsettling edge again. "You don't get to choose when your story ends. Not in this family."

My uncle, sensing an opening, moves closer, leaning forward just enough that I can feel the weight of his gaze on me. "You'll understand soon enough, Alessandra. We're all bound by something far greater than our own wills."

I step back, my skin prickling with the suffocating realization that they've been preparing me for something—for a future I never signed up for. A future where I don't get to make the rules. The thought is like a cold gust of wind, creeping beneath my skin and making my entire body stiffen.

"You're so sure of yourself, aren't you?" I say, my voice trembling despite my best efforts to hold it steady. "You think you've got me all figured out. But you don't. None of you do."

The tension in the room is palpable now, thick enough to cut with a knife. For a long moment, neither of them speaks, the weight of what's unsaid hanging in the air like a thunderstorm waiting to break. I can feel the storm coming, the impending sense of something terrible, something inevitable, pushing its way toward us.

Luca finally breaks the silence, his voice soft but firm. "You'll learn, Alessandra. You'll learn that the Vellano name is a brand, not just a family. And there's no escaping it, no matter how hard you try."

My heart skips a beat. The Vellano name. It's been a weight around my neck since the day I was born, a legacy I didn't choose and couldn't escape. But now, as the words settle in my mind, a new thought emerges—one that's sharper than I expected.

Maybe it's not about running away from the name. Maybe it's about reclaiming it. Turning it into something they can't control.

Before I can voice the thought, a sharp knock on the door interrupts the moment, and my head snaps toward the sound. My uncle's eyes narrow, his lips pressing into a thin line as the door opens just a crack, revealing one of the estate's servants.

"Mr. Vellano," the young woman says, her voice shaky. "There's someone here to see you. They... they say it's urgent."

My uncle's expression tightens, and for the first time in a long while, something other than indifference flickers across his face. Curiosity? Concern? Something like it, but it's quickly masked by a stern glance toward Luca.

"See them in," my uncle orders, his voice clipped. He turns to me, his eyes cold again. "This conversation isn't over."

As the door swings open wider, a figure steps into the room—a man I didn't expect. A man whose very presence seems to pull the air out of the room.

Chapter 3: Dangerous Alliances

The rain beats relentlessly against the windows of the car, as though it's trying to drown out the tension in the air. The droplets streak down in frantic lines, obscuring the world outside. But inside, there's nothing to block out the sharp edge of Luca's silence. He doesn't speak unless he has to, and when he does, it's like a dagger wrapped in velvet. His hands, large and confident on the steering wheel, seem to know exactly where they're going, even as the city blurs by in a haze of gray.

We're headed into the heart of the city—the kind of place where the underbelly pulses just beneath the polished façade. The tall glass buildings gleam in the dim light, as if trying to convince anyone passing by that the city is a safe place to be. But I know better. I know the deals, the secrets, the shadows. I know that you don't belong here unless you're willing to sell a little piece of your soul.

"Why does he trust you?" The question spills out before I can stop it, my voice sharp, more of a demand than a curiosity.

Luca flicks a glance at me, his eyes as unreadable as the storm outside. "Because I get the job done," he says, his voice smooth, devoid of any emotion. "Unlike you, who's only here because of your last name."

The words sting more than I'd like to admit. It's a low blow, but it's true. I'm here because of my father's name, because of who I was born to. In a city like this, that's more of a curse than a blessing. People don't look at you—they look past you, expecting you to be nothing more than the sum of your family's reputation. That's why Luca hates me. I'm a reminder of everything he resents about this world, about this city.

I want to retort, to throw something back at him that will make him feel the same burn I do. But the words stick in my throat, the harsh truth sitting too close to the surface. I hate him for saying it, even more because it's the truth. I would have said something—anything—but my voice dies as I watch him grip the steering wheel, his jaw tight with an emotion I can't place. Maybe it's frustration, or maybe it's just the weight of whatever deal we're about to walk into.

The car slows as we approach the building—old brick, with the kind of history that makes the walls feel as though they've absorbed all the secrets they could hold. It's the kind of place that reeks of power, the kind where people come to meet in shadows, behind closed doors, to make promises they'll break before the night's over. A small group of men stands outside, waiting, their eyes cold, calculating.

"Stay close," Luca warns, his tone shifting to something more clipped, more dangerous.

I nod, my heart pounding in my chest. This is it—the moment I've been dreading. But as we exit the car, I can't shake the feeling that the real danger lies not within those brick walls, but in the space between us.

We're ushered into the building with little more than a glance from the men outside. I feel the weight of their eyes on me, as if they're already deciding whether I'll make it out in one piece. The lobby smells like stale coffee and old leather, the kind of place that's seen too many deals made and too many people broken. The elevator creaks as it ascends, the tinny sound of its cables straining adding to the unease that's beginning to crawl beneath my skin.

"Relax," Luca mutters, sensing my discomfort. But his attempt to ease the tension feels hollow. He's not nervous. He's not afraid. But I can tell—he's watching everything. Every flicker of movement, every subtle shift in the air. He's already calculating every angle, every risk. And that makes me more anxious than I've ever been.

The door opens to a small, dimly lit room. The man waiting for us is exactly as I imagined—a slick smile that doesn't reach his eyes, a hand extended too quickly, like he's expecting you to do him a favor before you even ask.

"Miss Devereux," he says, his voice oily and smooth, like the sound of a too-warm glass of wine slipping down your throat. "I'm pleased to meet you."

I force a smile, offering my hand. "The pleasure's all mine," I lie.

Luca steps forward, placing himself between us. He's always the one to lead these meetings. Always the one to set the tone. It's how he survives in a world like this—by being the one who makes the first move, even if it means making himself the target.

"I hope you've got something more than promises to offer," Luca says, his voice low, almost bored.

The man's smile falters, but only for a moment. "I'm a man of my word," he says, though I can see the flicker of hesitation in his eyes.

I know that look. It's the same one that every liar wears when they're about to make a move. I feel it, that prickle of danger in the air.

Before I can even take a step back, the door bursts open, and everything turns into chaos. The sound of gunshots is deafening. I freeze, my heart hammering in my chest. For a split second, I think I'm done for. But Luca moves, fluid and precise, pulling me behind him as he draws his weapon. He doesn't hesitate. He doesn't blink.

"You're not safe here," he says, his voice hard as stone.

I don't know what's happening. I don't know how he knows where to move, how to stay one step ahead. But in that moment, it doesn't matter. The world is a blur of noise and chaos, and all I can do is follow.

The staccato rhythm of my pulse reverberates in my ears as we sprint through the hallway, my breath short and jagged. The sound of gunfire has barely begun to fade, but Luca's movements are already a blur of precision—calculated, practiced. He doesn't need to think about it; he's been in this position too many times to count.

"Keep your head down," he growls as we reach a door at the far end of the hallway. I don't need to be told twice. My instincts kick in, and I crouch, pressing myself against the wall, praying that the dust in the air doesn't give us away.

For a moment, I wonder how he knows exactly where to go. The door. The hall. It's as if he's seen this scene unfold before, as though he's been walking these same halls his entire life, despite how little I actually know about him. I want to ask him, to demand how long he's been living in this world, but I don't dare speak. My voice would just give us away.

Luca's hand on my arm is firm and reassuring. He's got a way of being both a shield and a weapon in one. His thumb brushes against the bare skin of my wrist, a touch that would feel almost intimate if it weren't so loaded with urgency.

The door creaks open, just enough for Luca to slide inside first, his eyes scanning the dark interior. I follow closely, though every instinct screams at me to turn around and run. There's no backing out of this now, though. There's nowhere to go, no way to escape.

Inside, the room smells like wet concrete and bleach, the kind of sterile scent that clings to abandoned places, to crime scenes, to the aftermath of things that should never have happened. A dim light flickers overhead, casting eerie shadows across the walls. The only sound is the distant hum of machinery, and the soft shuffle of our footsteps on the floor.

Luca takes the lead, moving silently, his gun in hand, his posture one of complete control. It's unsettling, how calm he is.

"You've done this before," I say before I can stop myself, the words slipping out in a breathless whisper.

Luca's eyes flick to me, a flash of something—maybe irritation, maybe amusement—crossing his face. But he doesn't say anything. Just gestures for me to stay quiet, his jaw set. He doesn't need to explain. He never does.

There's something about his silence that both repels and pulls me in. The way he moves, the way he speaks (or doesn't), it's all like a puzzle that I can't quite put together. I've spent a lifetime trying to navigate my way through my father's world, learning how to smile, how to charm, how to make people believe I'm someone I'm not. But Luca? He doesn't need to pretend. He doesn't care whether you like him or not.

The door at the far end of the room opens, a soft click that reverberates through the space. My heart leaps into my throat, and before I can even process it, Luca's already ahead of me, pulling me behind a rusted metal beam, shielding me from whoever's about to enter.

Two men walk in, their figures large and imposing in the dim light. They don't speak—just exchange looks that are far too familiar. It's the kind of look people give when they've known each other too long, when there's nothing left to say. The kind of look that promises betrayal.

They don't see us, at least not yet. But I can feel the weight of their presence, the heaviness of the situation bearing down on me like a vice. I don't know how Luca knows this will be the moment they walk in. I don't know how he knows anything. But the way his body tenses, the way his eyes narrow, I know something's coming. Something bigger than either of us.

Then it happens. The floor beneath us seems to shift, a groan that echoes from the walls, followed by the unmistakable sound of a heavy door being kicked open.

Luca's reaction is instinctual. He pulls me into the nearest storage closet, the door closing with a soft click as he slides it shut behind us. My heart is thumping so loudly I can barely hear myself think, but I manage to force out a few words.

"Why are we hiding?"

"Because they've set us up," he says, his voice low and controlled. "This isn't a meeting. It's a trap."

I can feel the tension radiating off him as he stands just inches away, his hand pressed against the cool metal of the closet door. "You were never meant to walk out of this place," he continues. "But now, neither of us will."

I swallow hard, the weight of his words sinking in like a stone. "And you trust me to survive this?"

Luca doesn't answer right away. I glance up, but his face is unreadable. For a moment, I think I might have misheard, that I imagined the uncertainty I thought I saw flicker in his eyes. But then he meets my gaze, and the edges of his lips curl just slightly upward. It's not a smile, not really—but it's something. A small acknowledgment, as if to say, Maybe I do.

I open my mouth to say something, anything, but before I can, a loud bang splits the air, followed by the distinct sound of a body hitting the floor. It's all happening too fast now. Too many unknowns, too many variables.

Luca's grip tightens on my arm as he steps back from the door, his eyes darting around, searching for an escape, or maybe for a way to turn the tables. I feel a surge of panic. The trap is closing in, but he's calm—so much calmer than anyone should be in this kind of situation.

"What now?" I whisper, barely able to form the words.

Luca turns to me then, a slight smirk playing on his lips, and for a brief moment, I see something—a hint of respect, maybe even trust—in his gaze. Then his voice drops to a whisper, sharp and decisive.

"We make our own way out."

The moment we make it out of the storage closet, everything blurs into a mess of dark corners and frantic footsteps. Luca doesn't waste a second, already leading the way through a narrow back hallway, the smell of oil and mildew thick in the air. I can feel the thrum of his body, every movement so precise, so deliberate, like he's been in a hundred situations exactly like this. I hate the way he's so composed, like danger is just another Tuesday for him, while I'm struggling to keep up, to not trip on the jagged edges of my own thoughts.

"You think they've already contacted the cops?" I ask, my voice tight, laced with fear that I can't quite shake.

Luca doesn't respond right away, but I can see his jaw working, his mind calculating. "They won't," he mutters. "Not yet. This is their mess to clean up. But once they do... we'll have bigger problems."

The weight of his words sinks in like cold water, and I force myself to focus. Panic isn't an option now, not if I want to make it out of this alive. But the sheer weight of the situation—the betrayal, the lies, the danger—clogs my thoughts like smoke. How did we get here? How did I let myself get tangled in this world of shadows and violence?

I glance at Luca, my eyes tracing the hard lines of his profile, the set of his mouth as he moves ahead. There's a coldness to him, but it's not the kind I'm used to seeing. It's not the coldness of someone who's hardened themselves against the world. No, Luca's coldness is calculated. It's the kind of cold that wraps itself around you, a shield against a world that's out to destroy you.

I take a deep breath and move faster, trying to match his stride. I can't afford to hesitate. Not now.

We turn a corner, and Luca stops abruptly, his arm outstretched to halt me. His eyes narrow, scanning the area ahead. For the first time, I notice the faint tremor in his hands, the briefest flicker of uncertainty. It's subtle, barely noticeable, but it's there. And it makes me realize how much I don't know about him, about the things that haunt him, the things that scare him.

"You smell that?" he asks, his voice low and dangerous.

I freeze, my senses on high alert. The air is heavy with the scent of gunpowder, the faintest trace of something metallic. And then it hits me—there's a layer of something else beneath it. Something slick. Something wrong. The realization makes my stomach turn.

Before I can respond, Luca pulls me back behind a steel pillar, his hand gripping my arm so tightly I wince.

"They're coming," he mutters, eyes darting around. "They know we're here."

"What the hell are you talking about?" I whisper urgently. "How—?"

But I don't need to finish the question. Because suddenly, the sharp sound of footsteps echo down the hall.

My breath catches in my throat. There's nowhere to go. Nowhere to hide. We're trapped.

Luca looks at me, his gaze hard and unwavering. "Get ready," he says, voice tight. "Do exactly what I say."

He moves first, as always, his body a blur as he ducks into a small alcove, pulling me with him. His movements are instinctual, practiced. I feel a surge of panic, but I swallow it down. This is Luca's world, not mine. I'm just trying to survive in it.

The footsteps get closer, and the sound of muffled voices rises in volume. A quick flash of light—someone's holding a flashlight, searching the hall. We crouch lower, hearts pounding in our chests. The beam of light swings in our direction, and for one terrifying second, I think we're done for.

But Luca doesn't flinch. He's already positioned himself, already calculating the angle of attack. When the light moves just slightly to the left, he makes his move.

His body is a blur as he tackles the first man, a grunt of surprise escaping the guy's mouth. I barely have time to react before Luca spins, pulling me behind him, his gun already in hand. The second man is down before I can even register the movement, his body crumpling to the ground in a heap of useless limbs.

I'm left standing there, breathless, watching him work. It's a sickening, surreal kind of awe. I've seen this kind of violence on TV, in movies. But being in the middle of it, feeling the weight of it, the coldness of it—it's a different animal entirely.

Luca turns to me, his eyes flickering with something I can't quite place. Maybe it's pride. Maybe it's something darker.

"Move," he orders, his voice barely above a whisper.

We slip past the bodies, through the hall, into a room that's even darker than the one before. The only sound now is the rhythmic beat of my heart and the soft shuffle of our feet on the concrete floor. But I can feel the air thickening again, a new kind of tension wrapping around us like a vice.

Luca's grip on my arm tightens as we move deeper into the room. His expression is unreadable, but his eyes are sharp, scanning the corners, the shadows, every inch of space as though he's already predicting what's coming next.

I have no idea where we are now, what part of the building we're in, but the silence is louder than any gunshot, more suffocating than anything I've experienced. And then, as if the universe has decided to test just how far I can be pushed, the door slams open with a force that shakes the entire room.

Luca's head whips around, his body tensing, but it's too late.

There's a moment—a single, suspended breath—where everything seems to stand still.

And then, out of the shadows, a familiar voice cuts through the stillness, as sharp and unforgiving as a blade.

"Well, well. Look what we have here."

Chapter 4: Shadows of the Past

The mansion is a labyrinth of rooms and memories, shadows clinging to the walls like lingering ghosts. As I step onto the plush carpet in the hallway, the familiar hum of the estate's grand piano draws me closer, a magnetic pull that tugs at something deep inside. The music has an ethereal quality to it, soft yet commanding, as though it exists in a place just out of reach, somewhere between dreams and reality. I follow the sound, my heels muffled against the carpet, until I find myself in the lounge, where the dim light flickers from a lone lamp on the far side of the room.

Luca sits at the grand piano, his broad back silhouetted against the soft glow of the city lights filtering through the floor-to-ceiling windows. The sight of him, his fingers dancing across the ivory keys with such delicate precision, almost makes me forget the cold, calculating man I've come to know. There's a certain grace in the way he plays, a tenderness that seems entirely at odds with his usual demeanor. I hesitate, caught between admiration and curiosity, before I allow my voice to break the spell.

"What's a killer doing playing Mozart?" I ask, my words slipping out with more of a bite than I intended.

Luca's hands falter on the keys, the music halting abruptly as if the world has stopped for a moment. He doesn't turn around right away, instead letting the silence stretch, thick and heavy. When he does speak, his voice is low, almost too quiet to hear over the distant hum of the city.

"Not everything is what it seems, Miss Vellano," he replies, his words carrying a weight that hangs between us like an unspoken challenge. His fingers rest on the keys but don't move, as though they're somehow too tired to continue the song, or perhaps too afraid to.

I stand there, a few steps away, feeling like I've stumbled into something I wasn't meant to see. The image of Luca, the ruthless enforcer, sitting in the darkened room with nothing but a piano for company, makes my heart do a strange, unfamiliar flip. This isn't the man I've spent weeks trying to decipher, the man whose icy blue eyes seem to pierce through every façade I put up. This is something else entirely.

I cross the room slowly, my steps almost hesitant, as if I'm intruding on something private. The atmosphere is thick with unspoken words, and despite the quiet, I can feel the tension crackling between us, like static before a storm. I stand beside the piano, just close enough to reach out and touch the polished wood, yet too far to do anything more than observe.

"What do you mean by that?" I ask, my voice softer now, curiosity replacing the bite I had earlier.

Luca doesn't answer immediately, and for a moment, I wonder if he's even going to respond. The piano rests in the space between us like a barrier, as if the music and the silence it now creates are his way of keeping me at arm's length. He finally turns his head just enough to meet my gaze, and I catch the faintest glint of something—something guarded and raw—behind his eyes.

"You think you know everything about me," he says, his voice almost a whisper, "but you don't. You don't know the half of it."

I swallow the lump in my throat, not sure whether I'm being drawn into a dangerous game or a vulnerable moment. There's a truth in his words, a crack in the armor that he so carefully maintains, and I can't help but wonder what lies beneath the surface.

The room feels smaller now, the space between us charged with something I can't quite place. I take a step closer, just enough to feel the heat of his presence, but I'm still cautious, still trying to figure out the angle. He's a master at playing games, but for the first time, I wonder if he's the one who's been caught.

"What are you hiding, Luca?" I ask, the question slipping out before I can stop it. I want to take it back the moment the words leave my lips, but they hang in the air, thick with the weight of expectation.

His fingers twitch slightly on the keys, a subtle gesture, but it's enough to tell me that the question has landed, and he's not sure how to answer. He looks away, his gaze shifting to the window, where the city sprawls beneath a sky heavy with stars. For a moment, I'm not sure if he's seeing the same city I am, or if he's lost in some other world entirely, one I can't reach.

"I wasn't always like this," he says, the words so quiet I almost miss them.

I lean in slightly, my breath caught between the mystery of what he's saying and the fear that he might close off again. "What do you mean?"

Luca sighs, a deep, weary sound that seems to age him in an instant. "Before all of this... before the choices I had to make," he pauses, as if searching for the right words, "there was music. There was peace. I wasn't the monster you think I am."

His words hang in the air, fragile and raw, and for a moment, I see the cracks in his carefully constructed exterior. The ruthless enforcer, the man who had once been untouchable, becomes just another soul lost to circumstances beyond his control.

The thought lingers, and I find myself wondering how many others have crossed paths with him, only to walk away without ever understanding the man behind the mask. What would it take to truly see him, to pierce through the shadows of his past and find the man who still plays Mozart in the dark?

The silence stretches between us like a taut wire, and I can feel the weight of his words pressing against my chest. For a brief moment, the music that had seemed so gentle now feels like it belongs to a world apart—something fragile, almost sacred. The dissonance between Luca, the man I've come to know as cold and calculating, and the man playing the piano with such raw emotion, is unsettling. I'm not sure whether to be intrigued or terrified. Maybe both.

I can't bring myself to sit down. There's an invisible boundary between us now, one I don't want to cross, not yet. Instead, I linger in the space by the door, watching him as his fingers rest lightly on the keys, as if he's considering whether to play again or just leave things hanging in the air. He doesn't look at me, but I can feel his awareness, sharp and unyielding.

"What's your real name?" I ask, the question slipping out before I can second-guess myself. There's something about the stillness of the room, the intensity of his presence, that makes me want to break through the walls he's built.

He doesn't move. "Luca."

I raise an eyebrow. "Is that it? Just Luca?"

He finally looks at me, his expression unreadable, but there's a flicker of something there. It's too fast to catch, but I know I saw it. "What does it matter?"

"Because," I take a step forward, intrigued by the way his lips tighten at the challenge in my voice, "it matters if you're pretending to be someone else. If you're hiding behind a name that doesn't belong to you."

The tension in the room thickens, but this time, it doesn't feel like a barrier—it feels like a promise, something waiting to snap. I don't know if I want to break it or if I'm just daring him to do it first.

"I'm no one's hero, Miss Vellano," Luca says, his voice now colder than it was a moment ago, the warmth of the music gone, replaced by a hardness that sends a chill through the room. He rises from the piano bench with a fluidity that seems almost predatory, as if the man who'd just played Mozart is already slipping away, leaving only the enforcer I've come to know. "But I'm not the villain you think I am, either."

The room feels smaller suddenly, the walls closing in with the weight of his words. He walks past me, his shoulder grazing mine in the smallest of gestures, and I shiver, whether from the touch or the unspoken threat hanging in the air, I can't tell.

I watch him move toward the window, his gaze now fixed on the distant skyline of New York City. The lights stretch out before him like an ocean of secrets, each one flickering with the weight of untold stories. His hands are still, but I can see the subtle tension in his shoulders, the way his jaw tightens ever so slightly. He's not looking at the city anymore. He's lost somewhere in his own mind, caught in a memory that doesn't belong to this moment.

"Tell me, Miss Vellano," Luca's voice cuts through the silence, rougher now, like he's forcing the words out. "What do you think of when you look at that city? What do you see?"

It's an unexpected question, but it pulls me in. I move closer to the window, standing beside him but not too close. I'm aware of the space between us, and I wonder if I should fill it or just leave him in his thoughts.

"I see possibility," I say, my voice soft, and for the first time in a long while, I find myself speaking honestly. "The city has a way of making you feel like anything's possible, like every step you take could lead to something new."

Luca's gaze flickers toward me for just a moment, and there's a fleeting softness in his eyes. But it's gone before I can fully absorb it. He turns back to the window, his profile carved in the soft light of the room.

"And what happens when the possibility fades?" His question is quiet, but there's an edge to it, as if he's testing me.

"I don't know," I reply, my voice faltering slightly. "Maybe you make your own possibility. Or maybe you get stuck waiting for something that never comes."

He nods slowly, as if considering my words. There's a weight in the air, a heaviness that settles deep in my chest. It's not just the city he's referring to—it's something else. Something buried beneath the surface, a question that's always been there, hovering just out of reach.

Without turning to me, he asks, "What would you do if you were me? If you'd made all the wrong choices, if you had to live with the things you've done?"

I don't have an answer. Not one that makes sense. But I feel something stir within me, a surge of empathy that's both unexpected and unsettling.

"I don't know," I say, my voice low. "But I think you'd keep going. Because that's all you can do. You just keep going."

Luca's eyes remain fixed on the city, but there's something in the way his expression shifts that makes me think he's heard me, really heard me. He doesn't respond, but in that moment, something between us changes. The tension isn't gone, but it's different now. It's not just a game of power, of control—it's a shared understanding, something that's only just beginning to form.

The sound of a distant car horn breaks the stillness, and I glance toward the window, noticing that the streets below are alive with movement. Life, in all its chaotic beauty, continues on outside these walls. But inside, in this room, something new has been born between us—something unspoken, and yet more real than anything I've felt in a long time.

Luca doesn't answer, but the brief silence that follows feels heavier than anything he could have said. I take another step closer, daring myself to cross that invisible line. He's no longer playing, the room now filled with the echo of the last note that seems to hang in the air like a lingering thought. He keeps his back to me, his shoulders tense beneath the perfectly tailored suit that feels out of place in this intimate setting.

I want to push him, to find out more—about the man who plays Mozart in a mansion that smells of polished wood and secrets, about the life he hides behind those eyes that never seem to blink, never seem to soften. But I've learned enough to know that pushing Luca too far would make him retreat even further, and that's the last thing I want.

Instead, I lean casually against the piano, pretending indifference, though my heart is anything but. "You don't strike me as the type who needs to play the piano to unwind," I say, trying for lightness, hoping he'll take the bait. "More like a guy who hits the gym or throws back a whiskey, right?"

His chuckle, quiet but knowing, is like a dagger wrapped in velvet. "You think you know me so well, don't you?" His voice is smooth, almost playful, but there's an edge to it now, like he's teasing me just as much as I'm testing him.

I shrug, not backing down. "We're both experts in pretending to be someone else. I'd say that gives me some insight."

Luca finally turns his head, those eyes of his—cold, calculating—meeting mine. It's the same look he's given me a thousand times, but tonight it feels different. There's something more in them, a question or maybe a challenge, and I can't quite tell which.

"Maybe you're right," he says, his voice softer now, though it still holds a trace of that hidden menace I can't seem to shake. "But maybe you're not the only one pretending."

The words hang in the air between us, so thick with meaning that I almost choke on them. There's a weight to what he's saying, something deeper than the obvious implication. I wonder if I've managed to scratch the surface of the real Luca, or if this is just another game he's playing.

Before I can respond, the sound of footsteps breaks the tension. Both of us turn toward the hallway as the door opens, and a figure steps inside. It's not just any figure, though. It's Charlie, the man who runs the operations in this city—the man who, until now, I thought was just a shadow lurking in the background.

"Apologies for the interruption," Charlie says, his voice carrying that smooth, confident air that makes people listen. "But it seems we've got a bit of a problem."

Luca doesn't flinch, doesn't even acknowledge the shift in mood. "Go on," he says, his voice low and measured, his hands resting once again on the piano as if nothing's changed.

Charlie steps further into the room, his eyes flicking between Luca and me, noting the tension that still lingers. "It's the same thing. People are starting to talk. Too much movement in the streets. Too many eyes watching, and not all of them friendly."

I can feel the shift in the room, the way Luca's presence grows more menacing the longer Charlie speaks. The air is thick with the weight of their unspoken history, and I know there's more to this than just a few rumors circulating. But I can't afford to appear too curious, not now, not with Luca watching me like I'm some kind of puzzle he's itching to solve.

"How much time do we have?" Luca asks, his tone flat but intense.

Charlie hesitates, just long enough to make the tension unbearable. "Maybe a few days. Maybe less. They're circling faster than we anticipated."

Luca's jaw clenches, his hands gripping the edge of the piano like they're the only thing keeping him anchored. "Keep them off our backs. If anyone gets too close, take care of it."

I don't flinch. I've heard the same cold commands before. But something about the way Luca delivers them now—the way he doesn't look at Charlie when he speaks, the way his voice holds that ominous finality—feels different. It's like he's not just leading the charge. It's like he's preparing for something far more dangerous, something that could threaten not just his power, but the very thing he's built his life around.

Charlie nods and turns to leave, but not before casting me a quick glance. "You should be careful," he warns, his voice dripping with the kind of knowledge that makes my skin crawl. "People like him don't let things go easily. Not when they've got everything to lose."

I stare after him as the door closes behind him, the last words hanging in the air like a lingering echo. It's the first time anyone has ever spoken so openly to me about Luca, about the life he leads, and I can feel the walls around him tightening again.

Luca doesn't move at first, his back still turned to me, his fingers tapping lightly on the keys. I know he's not playing for me, not anymore. It's a nervous tick, a subconscious gesture, the only thing left to do now that the conversation has turned in a direction I wasn't ready for. I wonder if he's even aware of how much he's revealed—how much his actions have cracked open the door to a world that's far more dangerous than I ever imagined.

I take a breath, steadying myself before I speak again. "What happens now?" I ask, the words coming out far more fragile than I meant them to.

Luca's gaze flicks to mine over his shoulder, his eyes dark and unreadable. For a moment, the tension crackles between us, thick and suffocating, until he finally speaks, his voice low and almost resigned.

"You've got a choice to make, Miss Vellano," he says, his tone colder than it's ever been. "Stay in the dark, or step into the light."

And before I can respond, before I can even begin to process what he means, the lights in the room flicker once, twice—then go out completely.

Chapter 5: Fire and Ice

The ballroom glittered with crystal chandeliers, their light catching the edges of champagne flutes and the glint of diamonds worn by the city's elite, all gathered like birds of prey in their finest feathers. Manhattan had transformed into a playground for the power-hungry tonight, and I was just another well-dressed pawn in my uncle's carefully orchestrated game. The scent of expensive perfume mixed with the sharp tang of whiskey in the air, and a slow hum of jazz seeped through the grand room, faintly masking the tension simmering under the surface.

I walked the floor with practiced grace, my heels clicking against the marble like a rhythmic beat that kept time with my thoughts. Each step was calculated, my every movement curated to blend into the flawless image of the dutiful niece, the one everyone expected me to be. I forced my smile, flawless and practiced, like a mask I could wear until the night was over, but inside, I was already bracing for whatever my uncle would throw at me next. He had this knack for using me as a pawn in his endless power struggles, as if I were some fragile trophy to parade around—something to claim without ever truly seeing.

"Look at you," he had said when he'd invited me, his smile a little too sharp, his eyes glinting with some private joke. "Your mother would be proud of how you've turned out. A true lady of the city. Just don't forget who helped you get there."

His insinuations hung heavy in the air, as they always did. I hated him for it, but there was little I could do. Not while I was under his thumb, not while the family's debts and obligations loomed like shadows over my every move. So, I played the part, offering only the most graceful smiles and polite nods, and praying for an escape that wouldn't come.

The crowd parted, and I caught sight of Luca. Of course, he was nearby, always the silent sentinel, his tall frame looming like an immovable shadow against the backdrop of the ballroom. His eyes flicked over the crowd, calculating, watching for any sign of threat—just as he had done the first time he'd laid eyes on me. My pulse quickened at the thought, and I cursed myself for the way my body betrayed me even now, despite all the ways I had told myself I would never let him get under my skin.

Luca was as dangerous as he was enigmatic, with eyes that saw through everything, even the walls I had built around myself. His presence always seemed to pulse in the air around me, dark and magnetic, pulling my attention against my will. He wasn't here for the gala. Not really. He was here because I was, and when my uncle invited me, he knew that Luca would follow. His loyalty to my family was unwavering—whether I wanted it or not. I had tried, on more than one occasion, to convince myself that I didn't need him watching over me like a hawk, but it never worked. No matter how many times I tried to shake the idea of him, I couldn't seem to get rid of the feeling that his watchful gaze was a constant weight on my chest.

The music swirled in my ears as I sipped my champagne, careful to appear uninterested in the heated discussions around me. But then, I felt it—his gaze, sharp and purposeful, cutting through the crowd. I wasn't sure how he did it, but Luca always managed to find me, no matter where I was. I stiffened when I noticed his eyes fixed on me from across the room, a silent warning flickering behind his intense stare.

"Careful, you don't want to stand too close to him," a voice murmured beside me, and I turned to find Salvatore, the rival underboss my uncle had been so eager to show off. His smile was as thin as his words, dripping with an arrogance that I found both infuriating and predictable.

"I don't recall asking for your opinion," I snapped, meeting his gaze with a defiant tilt of my chin. I could practically hear the smugness in his voice as he took a step closer, the faint scent of his cologne mixing with the cloying sweetness of the atmosphere.

"You should be more careful who you trust in this city," he said softly, the threat veiled in politeness. His eyes never left mine, predatory, like a wolf circling its prey.

Before I could respond, Luca was there, a wall of pure menace. His hand brushed against my arm, pulling me back just enough to shield me from Salvatore's encroaching presence. His grip was firm, bordering on possessive, and I could feel the heat of his fingers through the thin fabric of my dress. A shiver ran down my spine, and I cursed myself for it.

Luca's gaze shifted from me to Salvatore, the subtle tension in his shoulders tightening like the draw of a bowstring. "You think you're untouchable, Salvatore?" His voice was low, dangerous, a growl that sent a ripple of unease through the crowd. "You're not."

I was still reeling from the electric charge of his touch when Luca tugged me away, not gently, but with the same ferocity he had used when he'd first appeared in my life, when I had thought I could escape the family ties that bound me. His fingers dug into my arm as he led me through the throng of guests, and I fought the urge to pull away, to snap at him, but the words lodged in my throat. He was right. I had no say in the matter—not with him so close, so insistent on making sure I was safe, even when it made my heart beat out of rhythm.

"You don't get to decide who I talk to," I bit out, frustration bubbling over as I faced him. The anger was thinly veiled, but underneath, there was something else—something I wasn't ready to confront.

Luca's expression softened, just barely, as he stopped. His gaze met mine, dark and unreadable, before it flickered down to my arm, still held tightly in his grasp. "I decide what's best for you," he said, his voice softer now, but still with that edge that made it clear there was no room for negotiation. "And I'm not about to let some snake like Salvatore get any closer."

I swallowed, my heart hammering against my chest.

The soft hum of the crowd around us suddenly felt deafening, each whispered conversation like an echo in my ears. My breath came in shallow bursts, caught somewhere between annoyance and... something else I wasn't prepared to name. Luca's hand didn't leave my arm, even after he'd dragged me away from the clutches of Salvatore and his serpentine charm. His grip was tight, but it wasn't unkind. It was more like a tether—secure, unwavering. For a fleeting moment, I almost wished he'd let go. Almost.

"Let me go," I snapped again, my voice cutting through the murmur of the room with the sharpness of broken glass. But my words lacked conviction, even to my own ears. The truth was, I didn't want him to let go. Not yet.

Luca's lips pressed into a thin line, his jaw clenched so tightly I was sure it would crack. He didn't even look at me. Instead, his gaze scanned the room, cold and calculating, the kind of look that made people step back without him having to say a word. I hated how effortlessly he commanded attention, how his very presence seemed to bend the atmosphere around him.

"We're not done here," he muttered under his breath, low enough that only I could hear him. The words weren't a threat—they were a statement. The kind that made your skin tingle with unease, like standing too close to a live wire and not quite realizing how dangerous it was until it was too late.

I tried to pull away, but his fingers only tightened around my arm, urging me forward with the same unspoken command. I wanted to argue, to fight, to tell him he had no right to control me like this. But as we pushed through the crowd, it felt like the space between us was closing in, and for reasons I couldn't entirely understand, my heart beat a little faster. My feet seemed to follow his lead, like some magnetic force I couldn't escape.

Finally, he stopped in a quiet corner of the ballroom, tucked away from prying eyes but still within reach of the sparkling chaos of the event. He turned to face me, and I couldn't help but meet his gaze head-on, though every instinct screamed at me to look away. His eyes weren't soft—not even close—but there was something about the intensity behind them that made me want to say something—anything—to break the silence.

"You don't get to do that," I finally said, my voice barely above a whisper, as if speaking louder might give him even more power. "You can't just swoop in and play the hero whenever it suits you. I'm not some damsel in distress, Luca."

He raised an eyebrow, the corner of his mouth twitching into the faintest of smirks. "I'm not playing anything, Miss Callahan." The way he said my name sent a shiver down my spine, and I hated how it felt. "You don't need saving, I know. But there are people who don't see it that way. And Salvatore? He's one of them."

I crossed my arms, trying to project some semblance of control, but it was slipping through my fingers like sand. "And you think you're the one who gets to decide who I talk to, who I—"

"No," Luca interrupted, his voice turning cold as his gaze swept across the room, over the people swirling around us in their lavish gowns and crisp tuxedos. "But I'm the one who makes sure you're not caught in the middle of something you can't handle."

I wanted to argue again. To tell him I was perfectly capable of handling whatever the city—whatever my uncle—threw at me. I had done it before, after all. But the way his words hung in the air, the way he seemed so certain of my weaknesses, made me pause. For just a moment, I wondered if he was right.

I shoved the thought away, unwilling to let him see that he could get to me. "I can handle myself just fine, thank you." The words came out more forcefully than I'd intended, but I didn't care. I wasn't going to let him believe I needed him. I didn't need anyone.

Luca's expression softened for the briefest of seconds, but it didn't reach his eyes. "I know you can. That's what worries me."

Before I could respond, my uncle appeared at the edge of our little corner of the world. His smile was wide, practiced, and entirely too eager as he took in the sight of us standing there. My stomach turned, but I pushed the feeling down. He had an uncanny ability to make every situation feel like a performance, and this one was no different.

"Luca, my boy, good to see you," my uncle said, his tone so overly cordial it made me cringe. His eyes flickered over to me, a flicker of satisfaction in their depths. "I hope you're taking care of my niece here. She's a treasure, you know."

I resisted the urge to roll my eyes. My uncle's charm was as fake as the diamonds adorning the necks of the women around us, and just as sharp. He knew exactly how to manipulate the room—how to pull the strings without ever showing the hand beneath the velvet glove.

"Always," Luca replied smoothly, his posture never shifting, never wavering. It was a skill I could never quite master—this ability to be calm, composed, unshakable in the face of the most ridiculous situations. "But I think your niece can handle herself just fine, as usual."

I didn't know whether to be offended or grateful. But I took a deep breath, willing my irritation not to show. "I'm fine," I muttered, directing my words mostly at my uncle, though I knew Luca was listening too. "Just peachy."

The corners of my uncle's lips twitched upward, a silent acknowledgment of the tension that crackled between us. "Good, good," he said, but there was something in his tone that didn't quite match his words. Something colder, calculating, as if he had already decided how the evening would play out. "Let's make sure the rest of the night goes smoothly, hm?"

He turned to Luca, offering him a look that was laced with all the meaning of a whispered threat. "We wouldn't want any... misunderstandings, would we?"

Luca didn't even flinch. "No misunderstandings, sir."

As my uncle drifted away, disappearing back into the crowd, I felt the familiar weight of his influence settle over me again. I hated it. I hated him. But there was little I could do, not when the game was still being played, and I was trapped right in the middle of it.

The room buzzed with a slow, suffocating tension that wrapped itself around us like a vice, but I couldn't shake the feeling that I was in the middle of something much more dangerous than the usual charade my uncle loved to orchestrate. The polished floors beneath our feet seemed to shimmer in the light of the chandeliers, and the laughter of the guests—light and carefree—was somehow louder than ever, though it all felt muted, like an orchestra playing out of tune.

Luca still hadn't released me from his grasp. His hand was heavy, though I couldn't deny the warmth of it. The ache in my arm where he held me felt more like a mark of ownership than protection. I'd told myself time and again that Luca was just a bodyguard, just a shadow in the background of my life, but the more I spent in his presence, the more that story seemed to unravel.

I wrenched my arm away from his grasp, finally gathering enough courage to face him. "You're crossing a line," I muttered, but the words felt weak, even to my own ears. "This isn't your fight."

Luca's eyes darkened as he took a half-step forward, closing the space between us with an effortless calm that unsettled me. "You're wrong," he said, his voice steady but layered with something I couldn't quite place—anger? Protectiveness? "It's always been my fight."

His words held a gravity that made the ground beneath me feel unstable, like the earth was shifting with every syllable he spoke. I wanted to argue, wanted to stand my ground, but something in the depths of his gaze made me pause. What was it about Luca that twisted everything around me into confusion? Why did the very thought of him close enough to touch make my pulse race, but the next moment, the thought of him hovering like a predator made my skin crawl?

Before I could untangle the mess of thoughts swirling in my head, I saw Salvatore again, this time across the room, lurking near the bar with a glass of whiskey in hand. He was staring directly at us, his eyes gleaming like a wolf in the night, and for all his bravado, I could see the undercurrent of caution beneath the surface. Luca's presence had unsettled him, just as it unsettled me.

"Stay away from him," Luca murmured, his gaze flicking briefly to Salvatore, then back to me. "He's trouble."

My lips curled into a smirk before I could stop myself. "Is that your professional opinion, or do you have some other, more personal reason to dislike him?"

Luca didn't flinch, but there was a brief flash of something dangerous in his eyes—something I couldn't fully decipher. "You're in over your head, Adriana. And you have no idea what kind of danger he poses."

I stared at him, momentarily speechless. There were so many questions racing through my mind, so many thoughts that I couldn't quite piece together. But before I could ask him to elaborate—before I could demand to know why his words felt like a warning wrapped in an unspoken threat—there was a movement to my right.

My uncle. The man who had been watching us from across the room, no doubt evaluating everything like some kind of puppet master, appeared at our side as if by magic, his smile as smooth as ever. But there was something different in his eyes now—something sharper.

"Well, well, isn't this just the perfect little family reunion?" My uncle's voice was low, but it rang clear across the room. "Luca, Adriana, looking cozy over here, away from the festivities. What's this? A private conversation?"

I fought the urge to cringe. The sarcasm in his voice was as biting as it was intentional. He wasn't here by accident, and he certainly didn't miss a beat when it came to exploiting my every move. His presence, though cold and calculating, seemed to suck the warmth out of the air, and the smile he flashed at Luca was all business.

"You're always so protective of my niece," he continued, turning to Luca with a knowing look. "I'm sure she's grateful for your... concern." His tone dripped with something insidious, as if he was privy to some private joke that I wasn't part of.

Luca didn't flinch. If anything, he stood taller, his posture stiffening in a way that made him look every bit the untouchable force he was. "I don't need gratitude, sir. Just a promise you'll keep her out of things she doesn't understand."

For a brief moment, I could have sworn there was a flicker of something in my uncle's eyes—perhaps something close to amusement, perhaps something darker. But whatever it was, it was gone before I could grasp it. His smile didn't fade. "Of course," he said smoothly. "You know, Adriana, I always thought you had more sense than to get involved with the likes of him."

I recoiled, instinctively stepping back, but my heart slammed painfully against my chest. The tension between Luca and my uncle, though polite on the surface, was unmistakable. There was history there, more than I could fully grasp, and for the first time that night, I felt the true weight of it pressing down on me. These weren't just two men with an obligation to my family—they were rivals, players in a game I hadn't even realized I was part of.

"I'm fine," I said quickly, the words sounding hollow even to my own ears. "You don't have to keep checking in on me like some prized possession."

Luca's eyes flickered to me, briefly betraying a hint of something—regret, maybe?—before he looked back at my uncle. "I'll make sure she's safe," he said, his voice cold and distant, as though the conversation was already over.

My uncle gave a low laugh, as if he were entertained by the exchange. "Safe? What's that supposed to mean, Luca? Safe from what, exactly?"

I opened my mouth to answer, but the words caught in my throat as my uncle's voice dropped lower. "Or are you afraid of something?" His gaze flicked to me then, his eyes narrowing as if a plan had just fallen into place. "I think it's time you understood exactly what kind of business your uncle is really in."

Luca's hand twitched at his side, and my stomach turned. My uncle's words were a spark, igniting a wildfire of thoughts I had avoided for years, and I could feel the heat rising—something wasn't right.

Before I could say a word, the lights flickered, momentarily plunging us all into darkness. A hush fell over the crowd, and the sound of hurried footsteps echoed in the distance. My breath caught in my throat as I glanced around, but when the lights came back, Luca was gone.

And I was standing alone.

Chapter 6: The Velvet Cage

I stand in the doorway of my uncle's estate, my fingers curled around the heavy brass handle like a lifeline, as if I could somehow pull myself out of this nightmare by sheer force of will. The air is thick with the scent of polished wood and old leather, a familiar mustiness that only makes the house feel colder. The sun is low, casting long shadows over the marble floors, but it's not the time of day that's making the hairs on the back of my neck stand on end. It's the heavy presence of my uncle in the next room, the force of his will pressing down on me from all sides, and the terrible truth that I'm trapped.

I had hoped for a moment of peace. A break from the suffocating grasp of my family. Instead, I find myself in the drawing room, pacing like an animal in a cage. My thoughts are chaotic, tangled together like a web too dense to untangle, and I have no choice but to turn to Luca, my unlikely confidant. Of course, he doesn't want my questions. He never does. His eyes, dark and unreadable, always seem to be calculating something. If anyone could see the storm brewing in me, it would be Luca. But that doesn't stop me from walking straight into his office. I'll drag the answers from him if I have to.

"You're not going to like it," Luca says as I sit across from him, his voice low, each word carefully measured, as though he's trying to steer me away from something I can't yet see. "You don't want my advice."

His words strike a chord, a jarring note in the quiet room. I'm not sure if it's because he's right, or because there's something more to his warning that I'm not ready to face. But this marriage—this disgusting farce of an alliance—isn't something I can stomach. My uncle's plans for me, neatly laid out like a business contract, are suffocating. A man I barely know, tied to me by nothing more than power and obligation. The idea of it twists my stomach.

I want to scream at him, tell him to stop hiding behind that impenetrable mask of his, but something keeps me in check. Maybe it's the calm way he leans back in his chair, a silhouette of quiet authority, or maybe it's the unsettling realization that Luca knows me too well.

"What if I don't want to follow through with it?" My voice is soft, barely a whisper, but it feels like a declaration. A line I've just crossed. I didn't mean to say it, but now the words are out, hanging between us like smoke.

He doesn't flinch. His gaze flickers to the window, the light of the setting sun dancing across his face. For a moment, he seems miles away, caught in some distant thought. "You've always been good at hiding, at playing the part." His voice cracks just a little, a rare vulnerability breaking through the otherwise cold tone. "But there are paths you can't come back from."

The weight of his words hits me harder than I expect, but I don't back down. I can't. "I don't care. I can't do it, Luca. I won't do it."

His eyes snap back to mine, sharp as ever. For a brief second, I wonder if he sees the depth of my desperation, or if he simply reads the stubborn set of my jaw. He doesn't speak immediately. Instead, he stands, crossing the room with a fluid grace that almost feels predatory. His presence fills the space in an instant, and I'm suddenly aware of how close he is.

He lowers himself onto the arm of my chair, leaning in just enough that I can feel the warmth of his body. There's something about the way he looks at me, something that sends a shiver racing up my spine, but I don't pull away. Not this time.

"I can't promise you anything," he says, his voice steady, but there's a hint of something darker behind it. "But if you're serious about finding a way out, I'm the only one who can help you."

I want to argue, to point out that asking Luca for help is like asking a wolf for protection from a bear. But the truth is, there's no one else. No one else I can trust to get me out of this mess without condemning me to a fate worse than a forced marriage. I swallow hard, the tension in my chest refusing to ease.

"Just don't make me regret this," I whisper, my voice barely audible.

His eyes lock onto mine, and for a fleeting moment, I think I see something—something almost like understanding. Or maybe it's just the weight of his gaze, the intensity of it, that makes it hard to breathe. Either way, I don't look away.

"You won't," he says quietly, his words steady but laced with a warning.

I take a deep breath, trying to steady my racing heart. My uncle's plans may have already started to unfold, but there's still a way out. With Luca at my side, I'll find it, no matter the cost.

The next morning, the city seems unchanged, as though nothing could possibly be amiss, and yet everything is different. My uncle's voice echoes in my mind, his words as tight and calculating as the silk tie he always wears, as if his carefully curated world is something I could simply slot into, like a piece of furniture in a space meant for it. But I am not a piece of furniture, nor do I intend to fit into any corner he decides for me.

As I walk through the streets of downtown, my heels clicking against the concrete like a metronome counting down the minutes to a decision I cannot make, the city feels alive in ways I don't remember. The air smells of fresh-baked pretzels and the distinct scent of summer rain about to break free. It's as if New York itself knows something I don't. The summer heat has softened overnight, but there's still a sticky humidity that clings to your skin and curls at the edges of your hair. It's the kind of morning that makes you want to grab an iced coffee and forget all your problems, except the coffee would only stain your dress and you're more likely to think about what Luca said last night—the way he stood so close, his voice like sandpaper against my nerves. I try to push it from my mind, but it lingers like an itch I can't quite scratch.

I find myself standing in front of a café I used to frequent, its windows steamy from the warmth inside. The familiar buzz of conversations, the clink of spoons against ceramic cups, the rhythmic hum of life being lived—it should comfort me. It should make everything feel normal again. But all I can hear is the echo of Luca's words, and the deeper, more pressing question that follows them: What am I really willing to do to escape this cage I'm in?

The question stabs at me, a cold reminder that there are consequences to every decision, and the path I choose may take me further from my own skin. For a moment, I wonder if I should walk into that café, order my usual, and pretend that everything is fine. But the idea of pretending, of slapping a smile on my face and carrying on like nothing's wrong, gnaws at me until I can't stand it.

Instead, I turn and head toward the park, looking for some kind of sanctuary in the shade of its old trees. The park, with its winding paths and quiet corners, is an oasis in the heart of the city. A place where I can walk alone and think, where the chaos of the world can fall away for just a little while.

The sound of birds flitting between the branches above me drowns out the hum of traffic, and for a moment, I am alone with my thoughts, and the crushing weight of the decision that looms. I can't go through with the marriage my uncle has planned. I know that much, but how can I escape without breaking everything around me? How can I escape without losing everything I've ever known?

It's in the midst of this tangled mess of questions that I hear his voice behind me. "You're not supposed to be here."

I freeze, feeling my pulse quicken at the sound of Luca's words. I don't turn to face him right away, because somehow I know that if I do, something will change. We'll cross a line that can't be uncrossed. But I can't keep pretending either, so I take a deep breath, steady myself, and turn to face him.

"Maybe you're not supposed to be here either," I say, my voice sharper than I intend. There's something about him—something that both unnerves me and draws me in. He stands just a few feet away, the sunlight filtering through the leaves above casting a dappled pattern across his face, making him look almost... otherworldly. Like he's part of the park itself, a fixture in the landscape I didn't realize I had grown used to.

He raises an eyebrow, the faintest hint of a smile playing on his lips. "You're angry." It's a statement, not a question, and the way he says it feels almost like a challenge.

"I'm furious," I admit, my words coming out in a rush, as though the pressure that's been building inside of me for days is finally finding a release. "My uncle—he's making decisions about my life like I'm some kind of pawn on a chessboard. Like I don't have a say in anything." I meet his eyes, feeling something raw and unspoken pass between us. "I don't even know the man I'm supposed to marry."

Luca doesn't flinch. He never does. Instead, his gaze shifts to something in the distance, his hands shoved deep into the pockets of his jacket as if to hide a restlessness I know he doesn't want me to see. "The world doesn't always give us choices," he says, his tone unreadable, like he's speaking from a place I can't quite reach. "And sometimes, you have to make your own path, even if it means walking through fire to get to it."

The words are both ominous and strangely comforting. I can't decide if I want to run in the opposite direction or throw myself into whatever it is he's suggesting. Either way, I know I can't keep running forever.

"I'm not afraid of fire," I say, a little more boldly than I feel. "I'm afraid of burning everything down in the process."

Luca's eyes flicker with something—approval? Amusement? It's hard to tell. He steps closer, his presence overwhelming in a way I can't quite explain. The park, the city, everything around us seems to blur until it's just the two of us standing here, suspended in some tense moment where everything is possible and nothing is certain.

"You think you're alone in this," Luca says, his voice quieter now, but there's an edge to it that I can't ignore. "But you're not. You're never really alone, even when it feels that way."

I'm not sure if he means it in the way I want him to, or if he's just trying to get me to trust him, but either way, the connection between us tightens, and for the first time in days, I feel something other than fear. It's not relief, exactly, but it's close enough that I cling to it like a lifeline.

I take a step forward, feeling the tension between us snap tight, but the moment passes too quickly, leaving me standing alone again, the weight of my decision looming over me. "Then show me," I whisper. "Show me how to escape."

The silence between Luca and me stretches, taut like a wire pulled to its breaking point. His eyes linger on mine, calculating, as if he's assessing how much of me he can see, how much I'm willing to reveal. There's something dangerously compelling in the way he holds himself—self-assured, poised, as if he's seen it all and then some, and none of it has phased him. It's impossible to ignore the tension, that tight, electric current crackling between us, making my breath catch in my throat. I don't trust him. Not fully, not yet. But I'm too desperate to care.

"Show me how to escape," I repeat, the words hanging in the air like an unspoken promise. But something in my voice betrays me, cracks the illusion of certainty I'm trying to build. I'm not sure if I'm asking for help or for something more, something that threatens to blur the lines between what's necessary and what's... forbidden.

Luca doesn't answer right away. His lips twist into something that could be a smile or the beginning of a smirk—it's hard to tell with him. There's something unreadable about the man. Even in the small moments when he lets his guard down, there's a distance, a barrier between him and the rest of the world.

"You're asking for a lot," he finally says, his voice low, but with an edge that makes the words feel heavier than they are. "And you should be careful what you wish for, because I don't do things halfway."

The way he says it makes the air between us thick with anticipation. I want to ask him what he means, but the thought of pushing too far, of unraveling whatever thread of control I have left, keeps me quiet.

Instead, I turn my attention to the park around us, the soft rustle of leaves above us the only sound filling the space. I could stay here forever, wrapped in the comfortable quiet of this little oasis in the heart of the city. But I know it's an illusion. There's no such thing as peace when you're caught in a game you didn't sign up for, a game where the stakes are higher than you could ever imagine.

"Tell me what it takes," I finally say, my voice firmer than I feel. "I'll do whatever it takes to get out of this."

Luca's gaze narrows, his eyes darkening as if he's studying something beneath my skin. I can't help but shiver, a strange feeling creeping over me. There's a flicker of something in his expression—something that could be pity, or perhaps... admiration. I can't tell, and I don't want to.

"You'll regret it," he murmurs. "But if you're set on this, there's only one way out."

I hold my breath, waiting for him to finish, to tell me what I need to hear, to give me a way out, but he just looks at me for a long moment, as though weighing the consequences of his next words. The moment stretches, and I feel myself slipping, edging closer to the edge of a precipice I can't see, but somehow feel all around me.

"What's the catch?" I ask, my voice barely above a whisper, and there's a part of me—just a tiny, rational part—that is trying to protect me, to keep me from going too far, from making a mistake I won't be able to undo.

Luca's lips curl into that faint, dangerous smile again. "There's always a catch," he says. "You'll have to work with me. Not just for the short term. For the long haul."

I nod slowly, trying to digest what he's implying. "And after that? When I'm free?"

"You'll owe me," he says simply. "And I don't forget debts."

The words hang between us, heavy and charged with an implication I'm not quite ready to unpack. Owe him? For what? And what would the cost be? My stomach twists, the weight of what I'm agreeing to settling in my chest like a stone.

But there's no turning back. Not now. I've already stepped off the edge, and there's no solid ground left to hold me up.

I take a deep breath, the cool air of the park swirling around me as I look at him, my mind racing, heart pounding in my ears.

"I'm in," I say, the words feeling final, irreversible.

Luca doesn't respond immediately, but there's a flicker of something in his eyes. It's brief, a flash of something I can't quite name. But before I can even think to ask, he turns on his heel, his jacket fluttering behind him as he starts to walk away.

"You're going to need to trust me," he calls over his shoulder without looking back. "And don't ever forget—nothing comes without a price."

I stand there, the weight of his words settling over me like a shadow. For a brief moment, I wonder if I've made a terrible mistake. But the feeling is fleeting, replaced by something else—something darker and far more thrilling.

The decision has been made. And now, the consequences are mine to bear.

As I head back to my apartment, my mind spins with the unknowns of what's to come. I can't stop thinking about Luca, his inscrutable expression, the way his words wrap around me like chains. I try to convince myself that this is the only way. The only way out. But doubt gnaws at me, whispering that perhaps I've just stepped into something much worse than the marriage my uncle had planned for me.

The elevator ride up to my floor feels endless. The clattering of its cables and the soft hum of the motor are the only sounds, a stark contrast to the storm in my mind. When the doors open, I step into the hallway, only to freeze in my tracks.

There, leaning casually against my door, is someone I never thought I'd see again.

My fiancée.

Chapter 7: Beneath the Mask

The ballroom swelled with laughter and the rustle of silk as the chandeliers overhead flickered like stars suspended in the twilight. The air was thick with the scent of roses and vanilla, mingling with the sharp bite of expensive cologne. I stood at the edge of the crowd, trying not to blend into the backdrop. The mask that adorned my face felt more like a shackle than a statement of allure. It was delicate, gold-edged, its intricate design leaving little to the imagination. Beneath it, I could already feel the heat of my own skin betraying the mask I wore—not the one of feathers and sequins, but the one I'd learned to hide behind long ago.

My mother had always loved the masquerade. She'd say it was a perfect reflection of the world itself—everyone putting on their best smiles, their finest costumes, while underneath, secrets festered and lies twisted like the vines on the manor's garden trellis. I, on the other hand, had never seen the appeal of it. A party where every invitation came with an unspoken rule that the person you were in the daylight had to be put away like a prized porcelain doll. But here I was, trapped by my own sense of duty, swaying with the music, pretending that all the sparkling gold and diamond-encrusted masks somehow made the night more magical.

I took a sip from the crystal glass in my hand, watching the dancers spin on the polished floors. The laughter, the soft murmur of conversation—it was all so very much like a dream you had when you didn't want to wake up.

"Careful with that," a low voice murmured next to me, startling me from my thoughts.

I turned sharply, instinctively pulling away from the figure now beside me. A tall silhouette, his mask a dark, angular work of art that left little of his identity revealed except for the hint of sharp cheekbones and a jawline too perfect to be anyone else. Luca.

Of course, it had to be Luca. The only person I knew who could make a dark corner feel like a dangerous place. He stood there, his presence imposing despite the sea of people around us. There was a strange tension in the air as his eyes met mine, flicking down to the glass in my hand before he raised an eyebrow.

"Do you have a death wish?" he added with a hint of a smirk.

I felt my chest tighten, and for the briefest moment, I almost thought he might be mocking me. I looked down at the glass again, the dark liquid swirling beneath the surface, almost as if it too could sense the shift in the air. It was just champagne, I told myself. But with Luca, even the simplest things could feel like a trap.

"Are you always this dramatic?" I shot back, holding the glass just out of reach, though I knew it was too late for subtlety.

His lips curved into a smile that didn't quite reach his eyes. "Maybe. But you'd know, wouldn't you? Being surrounded by all this," he gestured loosely at the guests swirling around us. "Pretending that everything's fine, when underneath, it's all a house of cards."

I knew what he meant. The carefully curated smiles, the forced laughter—every one of these people, myself included, were just playing parts in a story that had long since lost its meaning. A story that had been written for us long ago. But the way Luca said it, with that cold edge to his voice, made it sound like he could see right through me. And I hated him for it, but I also admired it.

"I'm surprised to see you here," I said, my voice sharper than I meant it to be. "I thought you didn't play by the rules."

He chuckled, low and knowing, and for a moment, I wondered if he was just as trapped as I was. "I don't," he said. "But sometimes, the rules are the only way to get what you want."

That was the thing about Luca. He always spoke in riddles, his words wrapped in layers that I could never quite peel back. And yet, he had this way of getting under my skin, as if he knew exactly how to provoke me without saying a single thing that was truly real.

The music shifted, the strings of the orchestra pulling a slower, more sensual melody into the air. A signal, I realized, as he extended his hand toward me, the tips of his fingers just brushing the back of my wrist.

"Shall we?" he asked, his voice as smooth as velvet.

I stared at his hand for a heartbeat too long. He was still hidden behind his mask, and yet, I could see him—see the cocky arrogance, the sharp intelligence, the unspoken challenge. And for reasons I could neither understand nor explain, I found myself nodding.

I placed my hand in his, and the world shifted. His fingers closed around mine with a surprising gentleness, guiding me onto the dance floor. We moved together, our steps aligning as if we had practiced this choreography in some forgotten life. There was no space between us, but it wasn't the proximity that caught me off guard—it was the way he made me feel.

"I didn't think you knew how to dance," I muttered, trying to keep my voice steady.

"You don't think I'm capable of anything?" His tone was playful, but there was a bite to it, something dangerous lurking beneath the surface.

"I think you're capable of plenty of things," I said before I could stop myself. "But none of them are good."

His laugh was low, just for me, a sound that vibrated between us. "I'm hurt."

And that was it. The mask I had worn for years—the one of indifference, of dismissing him and everything he stood for—cracked, just for a second. But that second was enough.

The floor beneath us seemed to hum with the music, every note tugging at the strings of my nerves. I should have pulled away, should have slipped my hand from his grasp and walked off the dance floor with all the dignity I could muster. But instead, I found myself leaning into his touch, his fingers light but insistent against the small of my back as we glided through the throng of masked faces. The room had transformed—what had once felt like a gilded cage now seemed like an open expanse, and for the first time that evening, I felt exposed. Not because of the mask I wore, but because of the quiet tension that rippled between Luca and me, building with every step we took in unison.

"Do you always dance this well?" I asked, the sarcasm slipping out of me like water through cracks in a dam. His effortless movements were a testament to years of practice, a quiet grace that belied the sharpness of his words.

His lips twitched, the corners curling just enough to make me wonder if he was amused or genuinely pleased. "I tend to do things properly when I'm not distracted."

I wanted to snap at him, to remind him that I wasn't some distraction, but I stopped myself. Instead, I focused on the way his hand seemed to burn through the fabric of my dress, how the subtle shift in his gaze made everything feel more intimate than I was prepared for. In the confines of the masquerade, where everyone hid behind ornate masks, Luca's presence felt like a sharp, singular truth.

I tilted my head, studying him beneath the layers of mystery. The dark mask he wore only added to his allure, making him appear even more enigmatic, as though he belonged to a world far removed from my own. The way the light bounced off the edges of his mask created a soft glow against his sharp features, casting him in a near ethereal light, though I knew better than to mistake him for anything other than what he was—an unpredictable force of nature. A challenge. A complication I didn't need.

"Why don't you stop pretending, Luca?" I asked, the words slipping from my lips before I could fully think them through. There was something about the weight of the moment, about the way we moved together in perfect synchrony, that made the question seem inevitable. "We both know you're just as trapped as the rest of us."

His gaze flickered down at me, but there was no pity in it, no hint of sympathy. Instead, his eyes burned with something much darker, much more dangerous. "I'm not pretending, Amelia," he said, his voice low, the words more like a challenge than an admission. "You're the one who keeps hiding behind walls. Always running, always retreating into that... world of yours."

My breath caught at his words, and for a moment, I wondered if he could hear my heartbeat, or if it was only the music that drowned it out. He was right. I had spent my whole life hiding—hiding behind the façade of wealth and privilege, behind the expectation that I could play the part of the perfect daughter, the dutiful heiress. But I hadn't counted on him. On Luca.

I opened my mouth to respond, to deflect his pointed words with some biting remark, but before I could form the retort, the music shifted again. The slow, sweeping waltz that had seemed so elegant moments before now felt like a trap. The tempo quickened, and the room around us blurred into a dizzying whirl of color and laughter. My pulse quickened with it, my senses heightened by the movement, the heat, and the proximity between Luca and me. I could feel his breath against my skin, warm and steady, and the moment stretched taut like a bowstring ready to snap.

Luca's fingers tightened slightly on my waist, drawing me closer. It was a simple gesture, but it sent an unexpected jolt of heat through my veins. I tried to breathe evenly, tried to remind myself that this was just a dance, just another part of the evening's charade. But his presence, the way he held me as though I belonged to him, was enough to make me question every single assumption I'd ever had about control.

"What do you want from me?" The question came out sharp, too sharp for the soft ambiance of the ballroom, but there was no taking it back now. I wanted to know, needed to know. Why he always seemed to be everywhere I turned, like a shadow that refused to leave.

His eyes flickered, unreadable for a moment, and then a flicker of something—amusement, perhaps—danced in their depths. "Want from you?" He leaned in closer, his breath sending a shiver down my spine. "You overestimate your importance."

The words were light, but the undertone was not. His lips hovered near my ear, his voice soft but deliberate. "I don't need anything from you, Amelia. But you? You need something from me."

I froze. There was no answer I could give that wouldn't unravel me, no witty quip to cover the truth buried beneath his words. I had spent my life keeping everyone at arm's length, never letting anyone get close enough to see the cracks. But Luca had a way of seeing straight through the armor I'd built, and with every word he spoke, every touch he gave, he stripped away another layer of protection.

"Maybe I do," I said, my voice barely a whisper, but it was enough to send a flicker of something dangerous flashing in his eyes.

Before either of us could say more, the waltz ended, and the music shifted again. The dancers scattered, the elegant stillness replaced by laughter and the clinking of glasses. I stepped back, trying to regain my footing, my composure, but Luca wasn't about to let me slip away that easily. He held my gaze for a moment, his fingers lingering on my wrist as though marking his territory—though it was hard to tell if the claim was for my body or my soul. And then, as the crowd began to part, he smiled, his lips curling into something both charming and ominous.

"You're right about one thing, Amelia," he said, his voice soft but carrying an undeniable weight. "You are trapped. But I'm the one who holds the key."

And with that, he turned, leaving me standing in the middle of the ballroom, surrounded by masks and lies, my pulse still racing, and the truth just beyond my reach.

I tried to shake the feeling that had settled deep within me—like a smoldering ember just waiting for a spark to ignite. Luca's words lingered in the air between us, wrapping themselves around my thoughts like a velvet ribbon I couldn't untangle. The dance floor felt both too small and too vast at the same time, a paradox that pressed in on me as I struggled to breathe.

The lights overhead glinted off the intricate details of our costumes, casting shadows that danced with the music. My skin felt impossibly warm, a flush that had nothing to do with the heat of the room or the champagne swirling lazily in my glass. Luca had this effect on me, this ability to make the world seem like it was spinning a little faster, a little harder, just with a single glance. And worse still, I was beginning to realize how much I hated that he was right. I had spent years hiding behind my privilege, behind this gilded cage of an existence, and Luca knew it. He could see it all—the carefully constructed façade, the brittle walls I'd built to keep everyone out.

He was too perceptive. It was maddening.

I caught sight of his face again, the mask he wore barely concealing the devilish amusement dancing in his eyes. There was something about the way he stood, that slight tilt of his head, as though he had all the answers to questions I hadn't even thought to ask yet. It infuriated me, how calm and collected he was, while I felt like I was teetering on the edge of something I couldn't control.

"You know," I said, the words tumbling out before I could stop them, "it's exhausting, always pretending. To be perfect. To be everything they want me to be." I wasn't sure if I meant it for him or for myself. Probably both. But the truth felt strange and freeing as it escaped my lips, as if it had been buried in the pit of my stomach for far too long.

Luca's gaze softened, just for a second. The change was subtle, but it was there, like the flicker of light on a darkened horizon. He didn't say anything at first, and I wasn't sure if he had heard me or if he was simply weighing the meaning behind my words. But then, as the orchestra shifted to a lighter, more playful tune, he gave me a half-smile—a smile that didn't reach his eyes.

"You're not the only one trapped, Amelia," he said, his voice dropping to a whisper, almost as if the words were meant for me alone, in this space that had suddenly grown too intimate. "But the worst prison isn't the one you're born into. It's the one you build for yourself."

The words hit me harder than I expected, and for a moment, I forgot how to breathe. He wasn't wrong. I had built myself a prison out of expectations—others' expectations, my own—and now I couldn't remember what it would feel like to break free.

I opened my mouth to say something, to refute him, but nothing came out. There was a quiet understanding between us, an unspoken truth that neither of us was ready to confront.

Luca stepped back, pulling me out of my thoughts, and for a moment, the world seemed to snap back into focus. The music had shifted again, faster now, the tempo urging us to pick up the pace. He twirled me, his hands firm but not rough, and my body responded without thinking—without asking for permission. The space between us felt charged, alive with something I couldn't place.

"Careful," he said with a mock-seriousness, his eyes catching mine as he spun me. "You might end up enjoying yourself."

"Don't be ridiculous," I retorted, though the words felt hollow even as they left my mouth. The truth was, I didn't know how to stop this—how to stop the feeling that was building, slowly and steadily, like the rising tide of the ocean, pulling me deeper into this dance, into this game I never wanted to play.

Luca's smile widened, a sly, knowing expression that made my chest tighten. "You're not fooling anyone."

I wasn't sure what hurt more—the fact that he could see right through me, or the fact that I didn't know how to keep up this pretense any longer.

Just as the thought settled in my mind, there was a sudden shift in the crowd. A ripple passed through the dancers, the room suddenly growing louder with the buzz of voices, the clink of glasses, and the soft murmur of conversation. The feeling of being watched—of being on display—settled over me like a thick, oppressive fog. I could feel eyes on us, on the two of us dancing in the center of it all, and I realized, too late, that Luca had noticed it too.

He didn't look at the crowd, but I could see the change in his posture—the slight tension in his shoulders, the subtle way his hand tightened on mine. It wasn't a fear. It was something else. Something colder.

I glanced around, trying to catch a glimpse of what had caused the shift, but all I saw were masks—beautiful, intricate masks that concealed the faces of the people around us. I knew, then, that this masquerade wasn't just about hiding identities. It was about control. Control over what people saw, what they believed, and what they could never know.

"Look at them," Luca said, his voice a low murmur against my ear. "They're all pretending. They always are."

I stiffened, the weight of his words settling heavily in the space between us. I knew what he meant. The people at this party, at this estate, they wore their masks just as I did. The only difference was that theirs were more obvious, more blatant in their deception. And that knowledge made me sick to my stomach.

But as I turned to face him again, the crowd suddenly parted, and there, standing in the doorway, was someone I had not expected to see. My heart dropped in my chest as I recognized the figure. The last person I thought would walk through those doors.

And as he made his way toward us, a chill ran down my spine, because I knew—deep down, I knew—this would change everything.

Chapter 8: The Price of Loyalty

The stench of gunpowder still hung thick in the air as I crouched over Luca, the harsh fluorescent lights of the warehouse above flickering erratically. The sound of distant sirens filtered in from the street, but here, inside this concrete tomb, everything was eerily still. I could hear the rough scrape of his breath as it rattled in his chest, the blood trickling steadily from the gash across his side.

"Don't," he rasped, his hand weakly gripping mine as I reached for the torn edge of his shirt, trying to press it against the wound. "I'm fine."

I scoffed, looking down at him with a mixture of disbelief and irritation. "You're not fine, Luca. You're bleeding all over the floor. If that's your idea of fine, I'd hate to see you when things go south."

His lips twitched into that familiar half-smirk, though it quickly faded into a grimace. "What are you, some kind of nurse now?"

I couldn't help but roll my eyes. "I'm not. But I'm also not a complete idiot." I pressed harder against the gash, trying to staunch the flow of blood. His skin was hot under my touch, and I had to resist the urge to flinch when his body jerked in response to the pressure. "Stop making jokes, Luca. It's not cute anymore."

His eyes flickered toward me, but there was something different in them now—something I couldn't quite place. Maybe it was the way his features softened, or the way the weight of his usual bravado seemed to have slipped, leaving him vulnerable in a way I hadn't expected.

"Wouldn't want you to get bored," he muttered. But there was no teasing in his voice this time. Just a quiet acceptance, like he was surrendering to whatever was coming next. Whatever that was.

I bit my lip, focusing on the task at hand. It was stupid, really, how much I found myself caring about the guy. I'd sworn years ago that I wouldn't get tangled up with anyone like him—someone too dangerous, too unpredictable—but here I was, crouched at his side in a warehouse full of spilled product and shattered glass.

"You're a mess," I said, trying to keep my voice steady as I applied pressure to the wound. "What the hell happened, Luca?"

His eyes flickered up to meet mine, the sharp edges of his usual confidence dulled by pain. "I didn't see it coming. Thought the shipment was clear. Guess I was wrong."

Of course he was wrong. Nothing with Luca was ever simple, never straightforward. His whole life was a constant game of high stakes and constant shifting alliances, none of which seemed to favor the people closest to him.

"You should've been more careful," I muttered, not expecting an answer. I was stalling, giving myself a moment to think, to figure out what I was supposed to do next. "Where's the rest of your crew?"

"They didn't make it," he said, and the words were a punch to the gut. There was no sadness in his voice, just a flatness that unsettled me more than anything else. "Not that I expected them to."

I swallowed hard. "Luca—"

"Don't," he interrupted, his voice hoarse. "I don't need your sympathy."

I clenched my jaw, the anger rising in me like a tide. Sympathy? That was the last thing I had for him. But damn it, I could feel the panic creeping up my throat, the irrational urge to do whatever I could to make sure he didn't slip away on me.

"You're an idiot," I said finally, my voice thick with something unspoken.

The silence stretched between us, thick and oppressive. Luca was still breathing heavily, his chest rising and falling with the effort, but he was no longer trying to push me away. His fingers tightened weakly around my wrist, his gaze never leaving my face.

I focused on the blood, trying to ignore the tension crawling between us, the unspoken weight of something that was slowly shifting, and I hated myself for it.

It was strange—how, in that quiet moment, I realized just how much I didn't want him to die here. In a place like this, in a life like his.

Luca had built his empire on lies and deception, on taking what he wanted and leaving destruction in his wake. He was dangerous, calculating, and I hated him for it. But now? Now I couldn't ignore the fact that, beneath all the bravado, all the sharp edges, he was still human. And I wasn't sure if that made him more dangerous, or more...real.

"You don't get to die on me, Luca," I said, my voice breaking a little more than I intended. I wanted to sound tough, but the truth was I wasn't sure how to deal with the fact that he was right here, dying in front of me.

He shifted, groaning in pain as his eyes met mine. "I never asked you to save me."

"I know," I said, gritting my teeth. "But I'm doing it anyway."

There was something in his eyes, a flicker of something like gratitude—or maybe it was just the delirium of blood loss. Either way, I didn't care. I wasn't going to let him die in some filthy warehouse. Not like this. Not when, for the first time in years, there was something between us that felt almost like a connection.

It was a horrible idea, I knew. Letting myself care. Letting myself get involved with someone like him. But in that moment, it didn't matter.

The steady hiss of the air conditioning was the only sound, a sharp contrast to the chaos that had unfolded in this very room just hours before. Luca was sprawled across the couch in my cramped, almost-too-small apartment, looking like he belonged anywhere but here. His thick, dark hair was matted against his forehead, and his usual crisp suit was stained and torn, a far cry from the polished look he normally projected to the world. If anyone had told me that I'd be playing nurse to a man like him, I would've laughed, then probably thrown them out the door. But here I was, rummaging through the first aid kit for bandages as he lay there, looking ridiculously vulnerable.

"You're awfully quiet," he said, breaking the silence, his voice hoarse. It didn't help that his words were laced with that infuriating drawl of his—like he knew something I didn't, always a step ahead. It was one of the many things that had always grated on my nerves about him.

I didn't look up, focused on wrapping a fresh gauze around his side. "You're lucky I'm not charging you for my services. I'm not in the business of tending to wounded criminals."

He chuckled softly, the sound full of sharp edges, and I couldn't help but feel a stir of something—whether it was sympathy or irritation, I couldn't quite tell.

"Lucky for me," he replied, "I'm not in the business of making things easy for you."

I finished tying the bandage, my fingers brushing against his skin, and for a moment, I let the silence stretch between us. The kind of silence that felt like a thin thread, pulled taut, but still hanging by a thread of its own. I glanced up, meeting his eyes, and was momentarily taken aback. They were darker than usual, deeper, like he'd let a little more of himself slip through the cracks.

"You're still a pain in the ass," I said, just to fill the space between us. But my words didn't come with the same bite they usually did. It was strange, how much I was starting to soften, just a little. Just enough that it made my chest ache.

Luca's smile, though strained, softened too. "I've been told worse," he muttered. He shifted slightly, adjusting himself on the couch, and winced. "But you're right. I'm not exactly making this easy for either of us."

The honesty in his voice caught me off guard. I didn't know how to respond to that. Not when everything about him screamed that he had a heart made of stone, carefully crafted and guarded. But here he was, bleeding out on my couch, looking at me like he might just crack under the weight of whatever he was hiding. It unsettled me more than I wanted to admit.

"Stop looking at me like that," I said, my tone sharper than I intended. "You'll survive. You always do."

Luca laughed, but it was a dry, humorless sound. "I don't know about that," he said, his voice barely above a whisper. "Some days, I'm not so sure."

I froze, the words hanging in the air like a grenade waiting to go off. It wasn't like him to let that much slip, to show that kind of vulnerability. He'd always been the one to keep everything locked down tight. The fact that he was willing to let me see this, in the quiet aftermath of our chaotic encounter, was a dangerous thing. And part of me wondered if it wasn't just the blood loss talking.

"Don't start with me," I said, more to cover up the fact that I didn't know how to handle this sudden shift in dynamics. "I'm not here to listen to you whine."

But even as I said it, I realized I didn't mean it. I wasn't here to dismiss him. I wasn't here to treat him like the villain he often played. The truth was, I didn't know why I was here at all. Maybe it was the fact that, in the chaos of the night, I'd seen a side of him that I hadn't expected—something real, something human, even if he refused to acknowledge it.

Luca raised an eyebrow, that cocky glint returning to his eyes despite the pain. "You know, you're pretty good at pretending you don't care."

I leaned against the wall, trying to avoid the heat in my cheeks. "I'm not pretending. I just don't—"

"Don't what? Don't care?" he interrupted, his voice sharp, but there was something else behind it—an edge of something like hope, but he buried it quickly.

"I don't know why I'm even bothering with you," I muttered, crossing my arms. "I should've left you to bleed out in that damn warehouse."

There it was again—his laugh, rough and strained, but genuine. "You can't help it, can you?"

"What?" I shot back, exasperated. "Help what?"

"Help yourself," he said, his eyes dark with something I couldn't name. "You can't help but fix people. Can't help but fix me. You're like a walking charity case."

I opened my mouth to protest, to say something sharp, but the words died on my tongue. Because he was right, wasn't he? Damn it. I was starting to care—more than I should, more than I wanted. And I hated that about myself. I hated that I'd let him weasel his way into my life, into my space, so easily.

But there was nothing I could do now.

"I'm not fixing anyone," I said, my voice softer than I intended. "I'm just trying to get you out of here in one piece."

"Yeah," Luca murmured, "one piece."

For a long moment, neither of us spoke. He closed his eyes, the weight of the situation sinking in, and I let myself sink into the quiet, letting the strange tension between us twist tighter with each passing second.

The stillness of the night was almost oppressive, the low hum of the refrigerator in the corner the only sound that filled the room.

Luca, still sprawled on the couch, had drifted into an uneasy sleep, though it was clear he wasn't fully out of the woods yet. His breaths were shallow, the pain from his injuries still clearly taking its toll. I wasn't sure if I should feel more concerned or annoyed, because damn it, I wasn't supposed to care about him. This was supposed to be temporary—a quick fix before he disappeared back into his underworld of shady deals and blood money.

I stared at him, watching the rise and fall of his chest, each movement stirring a wave of conflicting thoughts. There was something about him that made it hard to let go of the anger I had been carrying for so long. His whole life was built on deception, on cutting corners and stepping over people, and yet, here he was, vulnerable in a way that I couldn't ignore. The man who ran this city like he owned it was suddenly lying in my apartment, relying on me to patch him up. It was a stark reminder of just how unpredictable this game was, and how quickly the tables could turn.

I walked over to the small kitchenette, pouring myself a drink—a shot of bourbon, neat, the burn of the liquid a temporary distraction from the knots of tension coiling inside me. I didn't need this. Didn't need him, not like this. But there was no denying the pull, the subtle shift in the way I saw him now, stripped of all his usual armor. It was impossible to ignore the fact that, despite everything, I felt responsible.

"You always drink alone?" The voice came from behind me, rough but undeniably clear. I didn't even have to turn around to know Luca was awake.

I didn't answer right away, swirling the amber liquid in my glass, then tossing it back in one smooth motion. "It's quieter that way."

I finally turned, facing him, and watched as he shifted on the couch, one hand resting on his side. The bloodstained bandage was still there, but I'd done my best to clean him up. I wasn't about to let him bleed out just because he had a terrible attitude.

"You always act like you don't care," he said, his voice quiet but heavy with something else, something unspoken. "But you do, don't you?"

I clenched my jaw, the words lodged in my throat. "I don't have time for this," I muttered, walking back to the small table by the window and staring out at the city below. It was just past midnight, the streets of Chicago alive with the kind of energy that never seemed to stop, even when the rest of the world slept. The lights from the city stretched out before me, a sprawling grid of life and chaos, just like the life I'd chosen.

"I think you do," Luca's voice cut through the silence again, insistent, almost teasing. He was no longer the hard-edged figure who had barged into my life with his cold arrogance. There was something different about him now, something that felt like it reached beyond the walls of our history. I could feel it in the way he spoke, the subtle vulnerability that slipped through despite his best efforts.

I turned slowly, meeting his gaze. "What exactly are you trying to say, Luca?"

He studied me for a moment, as if weighing his next words. "I don't know. But I think you're lying to yourself."

I narrowed my eyes, the sharp edge of annoyance cutting through the strange mix of emotions twisting inside me. "Don't do this. You don't know anything about me."

"Maybe I don't," he said, his voice quiet but certain. "But I know a thing or two about pretending."

I took a step toward him, ready to throw a sharp retort his way, but something in the intensity of his gaze stopped me. There was a depth to him now that I couldn't quite place, a softening that, if I were honest with myself, unsettled me. How had we gone from enemies to this? From his usual biting remarks and my eye-rolls to this strange, uncomfortable... connection?

"Why are you still here?" I asked, the question coming out more desperate than I intended. "Why haven't you just walked away?"

Luca's expression shifted, his lips tugging into something between a smile and a grimace. "Maybe because you haven't made me leave yet."

I swallowed hard, the words hanging between us like a taut wire. This was dangerous. I knew it. He was dangerous, the kind of person who left a wake of destruction behind him. And yet, I couldn't shake the feeling that somehow, in some twisted way, we were both standing on the same shaky ground.

"I'm not your damn charity case, Luca," I said, trying to steady my voice, though it cracked just slightly.

He laughed then, though it was strained. "If I wanted charity, I'd have gone to my mother."

I scoffed, unable to hold back a small, sarcastic laugh of my own. "I don't think anyone's going to mistake you for a saint."

"No," he agreed, his gaze never leaving mine. "But I'm not the devil either."

I was about to respond, to throw another barb his way, when the door to the apartment rattled unexpectedly. The sound was sharp and unexpected, like a thunderclap in the quiet of the room. Both of us froze, tension instantaneously rising. Someone was at the door. My heart skipped a beat, a sick feeling creeping up my spine.

"Did you invite someone over?" Luca's voice was low, his earlier banter gone, replaced with a cold edge.

"No," I whispered, stepping toward the door, my fingers brushing the handle. The hairs on the back of my neck stood up, and I realized—too late—that I had no idea who was on the other side.

The knock came again, louder this time. And then a voice, muffled through the door.

"You better open up, sweetheart. We need to talk."

Chapter 9: Crossing the Line

The wind was sharp, biting at my face as I stepped out of the apartment. The city hummed beneath me, alive with its usual late-night thrum—the distant clatter of a train, the low murmur of a group of people lingering outside a bar, the occasional honking of cars that should have already learned patience by now. But none of that mattered. Not when the weight of the conversation from earlier still pressed against my chest, each breath coming shallow as I tried to shake it off.

Luca's words echoed in my mind, repeating like a cruel loop. You don't know what it's like to fight for survival. A part of me wanted to laugh bitterly. I could feel the jagged edges of my frustration cutting through the slick calm I had worked so hard to maintain. But I didn't laugh. Not now. Not when the night had settled into the kind of quiet that only made you feel more alone.

The streetlights flickered overhead as I walked, my boots tapping rhythmically against the cracked pavement. A strange, unease curled in my stomach. No matter how many times I had walked these streets, no matter how much I had promised myself I was done with the life I had been born into, I never really felt like I had stepped out of its shadow. It followed me everywhere, like a second skin I couldn't shed.

"I'm not saying you don't fight for survival," I had told Luca, my words sharp, desperate to make him understand. "But surviving isn't the same as living. I want to live. I want to breathe and—" I stopped myself before the words could spill too freely. We both knew that life wasn't just about dreams and hopes. It was about choices, and I had already made mine.

His response had been the same as it always was when the conversation drifted into dangerous territory. A thinly veiled judgment, his eyes narrowing as if he could pierce through my soul.

You think you can just walk away? His voice had been steady, but there was a darkness in the undertones I could feel in my bones.

The argument had come too quickly—too sharply—and I had walked away before things could devolve into something worse. But now, out here in the cool night, with only the streetlights for company, I realized that I couldn't outrun it. I couldn't outrun him.

I pulled my jacket tighter around me, feeling the fabric cling to my skin like it was trying to hold me in place. Maybe that was what Luca had always been for me: a tether to the past I had spent so long trying to escape. But even as I walked farther from him, I knew it wasn't just his presence I was trying to outrun. It was the fear that I might be making a mistake—again. That maybe I didn't know what I was doing. That I wasn't strong enough to walk away from everything I had known.

The city's skyline loomed in front of me, its lights glimmering like a promise. In a place like this, everything was always shifting—always changing. But change was hard, especially when the person you loved couldn't see the world the same way you did. I had been taught to fight for every inch I gained, to protect what was mine, and to take nothing for granted. But what if there was more to life than just holding on?

As I turned the corner, a familiar figure appeared in my peripheral vision, standing under the dim light of a convenience store. It was Danny, his hands shoved into the pockets of his jacket, his stance relaxed in a way that made him look out of place. I paused for a second, trying to decide whether to keep walking or approach him.

He caught my eye before I could make up my mind.

"Hey, you look like you're running away from something," he said, his voice teasing, but there was a softness in his gaze that made me pause.

I frowned, crossing my arms over my chest. "Maybe I am."

Danny stepped closer, the light catching the mess of dark curls on his head, making him look more like a shadow than a person. He grinned, a crooked smile that always seemed to land somewhere between genuine and mischievous.

"Careful. Running away doesn't always get you far."

"Maybe," I said, my voice barely above a whisper. "But sometimes, it's the only choice you have."

He regarded me for a long moment, as if he could see the war raging inside me, the uncertainty I had carefully buried. "I get it," he finally said. "You don't have to explain. Just... don't run so fast you forget to look back at what you're leaving behind."

I didn't know how to respond to that. The words hung in the air, heavy and unresolved, like a truth I wasn't ready to face. But before I could speak, Danny turned, his gaze still fixed on me. "I'll catch you later," he said, and then, with a nod, he disappeared into the night, leaving me with more questions than answers.

I stood there for a long time, letting his words settle over me. The night had grown colder, the breeze biting at my cheeks, but the city felt strangely silent now, as though it, too, was holding its breath, waiting for me to make a decision.

And as I stood there, I realized something. The fight for survival wasn't just about pushing forward or holding on. It was about deciding, over and over, which pieces of yourself you were willing to lose—and which ones you would fight to keep.

I didn't go home that night. I couldn't, not with Luca's words still haunting me like a fog I couldn't escape. I walked aimlessly, letting my feet carry me wherever they wanted, while my mind tried and failed to settle into anything resembling peace. The city at night had always been a refuge for me, but tonight, it felt as cold as the glass of whiskey I'd abandoned on the bar counter earlier.

I ended up at a small diner near the edge of the East Village, one of those places that never closed, where the neon sign buzzed as it flickered, casting an eerie glow over the cracked sidewalk. Inside, the smell of burnt coffee and sizzling bacon hung thick in the air. The diner was empty save for an old man hunched over a cup of coffee in the far corner and the waitress, a young woman with a tattoo sleeve on one arm, scrolling through her phone behind the counter.

I slid into a booth, not bothering to ask for the menu. I had no appetite, but the routine of it—the sticky vinyl seats, the buzz of the fluorescent lights overhead—was soothing. The waitress glanced at me briefly before continuing her scrolling, a quiet acknowledgment of my presence but nothing more. She didn't seem to care. That suited me fine.

I turned my attention to the window, watching the city shift in the dark. The sounds of late-night traffic filtered in, muffled by the glass, but the stillness in my chest was louder than anything outside. The question hung there—could I ever truly escape? The pull of the family business was strong, tangled deep inside my veins like a poison I could never fully purge. But what else was there for me? What else could I do with my life except live in the shadows of the decisions others had made for me?

"Hey." The voice broke through my thoughts, and I turned to see the waitress standing at my table. She didn't ask if I wanted anything, just slid a cup of coffee in front of me with the kind of indifferent carelessness that made her seem both utterly bored and strangely competent at the same time.

I met her gaze briefly before reaching for the cup. "Thanks."

"No problem," she muttered, and without another word, she was gone, disappearing back into the haze of low light and quiet clinks of silverware.

The coffee tasted like nothing special—burnt, weak, the kind of thing you'd drink out of necessity rather than desire. It wasn't enough to make me feel any better, but it was enough to keep the weight of everything pressing on my chest at bay. I didn't need comfort right now. I needed clarity. Or maybe I needed to stop thinking so damn much.

The door opened again, and the familiar chime made me glance up just in time to see Luca step inside. His silhouette caught in the neon glow of the diner sign, looking out of place, like he'd walked straight out of a dream I didn't want to have.

I froze, my fingers stilling on the edge of my cup. For a moment, I debated pretending I hadn't seen him, maybe slipping out the back door, letting the world sort itself out without me. But he was already moving toward me, those dark eyes locked on mine with an intensity that made me wonder if I would ever be able to hide from him again.

He slid into the booth across from me without waiting for an invitation, his coat brushing against the worn leather of the seat, a small but noticeable crease forming on his brow. He didn't speak at first. He just sat there, the silence between us thick and heavy, the kind of silence that existed after words were exchanged that couldn't be taken back.

"Did you come to argue?" I finally asked, my voice coming out sharper than I intended.

Luca leaned back, looking around the diner with the same detachment he always carried when he walked into a place like this. "No. I came because you're here, and because you've got a way of running away from things." He reached across the table, his fingers just brushing the edge of my coffee cup. "I wanted to see if you were going to run again."

I narrowed my eyes, staring at him. "I'm not running."

"Are you sure?" His voice was low now, almost gentle, the edge gone from it, replaced by something I couldn't quite decipher. "Because that's what it feels like. You're running from me, from this... from everything."

The words stung more than I expected. "Maybe I'm running toward something," I said, my voice catching on the final syllable. I was already off balance, and I knew it. "Maybe I'm running toward a life that doesn't come with chains wrapped around my wrists."

Luca was silent for a long moment, and for the first time in a long time, I wondered if he might actually understand. But then he spoke, his voice rough around the edges, like he was still fighting a battle he'd been fighting for years. "You think I don't want that too? You think I don't want something more than what I've been given? You're wrong." He looked at me with that same intensity, his eyes almost pleading. "But this thing we're tangled in, the family, it's not something you can just turn your back on. You can't walk away like it doesn't matter."

I wanted to scream. I wanted to tell him that it did matter—that it mattered more than anything in the world, and that's exactly why I had to leave. But the words tangled in my throat, caught between everything I knew to be true and everything I desperately wanted to believe.

I wasn't ready to say it—not to him, not to anyone. But as I looked into his eyes, I realized something else. Maybe Luca wasn't the one I needed to escape. Maybe the only person I needed to run from was myself.

The diner had started to feel like the last place I should be, a quiet observer to a conversation that was quickly slipping from my control. The air between Luca and me crackled, the intensity of our words hanging in the heavy silence like an unwelcome guest. He hadn't moved, hadn't broken eye contact, and that unflinching gaze of his felt more like an accusation than a conversation.

"I don't want to leave you," I said, the words tumbling out before I could stop them. It was the truth, but it wasn't the whole truth. Because it wasn't just Luca I wanted to leave behind. It was the entire world we'd created together. It was the weight of the life we had built with too many secrets, too many compromises.

He stiffened, as if my admission hit him harder than he was ready for. "I don't need you to want to leave me," he said quietly. "I just need you to understand why I can't let you go."

A flicker of panic rose in my chest, quickly swallowed by a sharp breath. I leaned forward, gripping the edge of the chipped table as if it would keep me grounded in the face of his unyielding determination. "You're not listening," I said, the words thin and strained. "I'm not asking for permission. I'm telling you that I need something more. Something that isn't tied to you, to us, to this place."

Luca's mouth tightened, the vein at his temple pulsing with the effort of holding himself back. "I don't care about the money or the power or any of that," he shot back, his voice rising now. "It's not about that. It's about survival, about not losing everything we've fought for. What would you do if you just walked away, huh? What would be left?"

My eyes blurred as I stared at him, and the truth of his question cut through the haze of my frustration. I didn't know what would be left. Not yet. Not without him, not without the life that had defined me since I could remember. I could feel the pull of the past, a chain tugging at my chest, trying to reel me back in. And the worst part was—Luca wasn't wrong. I wasn't sure who I was without it.

"You want me to stay and be miserable, then," I said softly, bitterness curling around the words like smoke. "To stay and fight battles that aren't even mine anymore, because that's what you want. But I'm telling you, Luca, I'm done. I'm tired."

He leaned back in his seat, running a hand over his face, the silence between us stretching longer than I could bear. "So, what now?" His voice was almost unreadable, the hardness gone, leaving behind something raw and uncertain.

"I go," I said, my voice trembling for the first time. "I leave. I don't know where yet. I don't know how. But I have to." I shook my head, as if to shake away the lingering doubts that had been eating at me since this conversation began. "I can't keep living like this, Luca."

His expression softened, and for a brief moment, I saw a flicker of vulnerability in his eyes that almost made me want to reach across the table and pull him back from whatever dark place he was retreating to. But then the door of the diner opened with a gust of wind, and the moment between us snapped like a rubber band pulled too tight.

I turned instinctively toward the noise, my heart skipping in my chest. But it wasn't who I expected.

"Got a minute?" The voice was low, almost menacing, and it made the air around me freeze.

The figure in the doorway was tall, broad-shouldered, wearing a coat too heavy for the warm spring night. His face was partially obscured by the shadows, but his eyes were clear—sharp, calculating. And it only took me a second to recognize him.

Julian.

I had hoped I wouldn't see him again. I had hoped the world had forgotten about him, that whatever dark business he'd been involved in would stay buried. But no such luck. The ghost of my past had come to collect, and there was no escaping this time.

Luca's body tensed immediately, the muscles in his shoulders stiffening as his gaze fixed on Julian with an intensity that almost made me flinch. There was no love lost between those two, and it was clear from the way they sized each other up that old grudges had never quite been put to rest.

"You're not welcome here," Luca growled, his hands tightening into fists on the table.

Julian didn't seem fazed. His gaze flicked to me briefly, a quick, calculating glance, before settling back on Luca. "You always were a little too protective, weren't you?" he said with a smirk, his voice dripping with sarcasm. "This isn't about you, Luca. It's about her."

I felt the words settle over me like ice water, and before I could react, Julian was already stepping into the booth, sliding into the empty space next to me without invitation. His presence was suffocating, like a weight I couldn't shake off.

"You've got yourself in too deep, sweetheart," Julian said, his breath warm against my ear. "You think you can just walk away from all this? From me? From what we've built together?"

I recoiled instinctively, but he didn't let up. His hand landed on the back of my chair, an unspoken threat hanging in the air.

"I'm done," I whispered, barely hearing my own voice over the pounding of my heart in my ears.

Julian leaned in closer, his face just inches from mine. "You think you can walk away from me?" he repeated, his words slower now, more menacing. "You think you can just disappear without consequence?"

The air between us turned cold. I felt Luca's body shift beside me, his muscles coiling, ready to spring. But before I could say anything, Julian's voice dropped lower, almost a growl now.

"Not this time. You're not getting out. Not unless you make a choice."

A shiver ran down my spine. I didn't know what he meant. I didn't know how far he would go to make me stay.

But whatever this was, whatever game Julian was playing, I wasn't sure I could win.

Chapter 10: Secrets in the Smoke

I had never seen the docks like this before—not in all the years I'd spent watching them from my small, cluttered office window at McGregor & Sons. The city, usually a well-oiled machine of clanking steel and honking horns, was silent now, save for the relentless lapping of water against the piers and the occasional distant wail of a siren. It was the kind of silence that pressed in on you, suffocating, like the world was holding its breath, waiting for something to happen.

The fire was still smoldering, its blackened remnants curling in on themselves like a secret that didn't want to be known. A thick fog of smoke clung to the air, coating everything in a fine layer of ash, but the real damage wasn't in the charred remains of the docks. The real damage was in the cargo that was gone—gone up in smoke, just like my carefully constructed life. The shipment that had been lost was far too valuable to simply shrug off. It wasn't just merchandise; it was the kind of freight that could shift entire fortunes if it fell into the wrong hands. And now, I was in the thick of it.

It wasn't just a fire, not anymore. It was a statement. And in a city like this, where loyalties were as fragile as glass, a statement could unravel everything.

"You think I'm a traitor?" I asked, my voice sharper than I intended. I hadn't meant to confront him like this, hadn't meant to drag the truth out, but here I was, standing next to Luca underneath the sickly yellow glow of the streetlights, feeling the weight of his gaze more than the weight of the burning docks.

Luca—his name always felt foreign on my tongue, like something too heavy for me to handle—glanced at me, his eyes hard, unwavering. The kind of eyes that had seen too much to ever soften.

"I think you're trouble," he said, the words cutting through the air between us like a blade. But there was something else in his tone, a hint of uncertainty, something unspoken, buried beneath the sharpness of his accusation.

I wanted to call him out on it. I wanted to yell, to demand that he take back that look, that accusation, that suggestion that I might be part of something I had no business being involved in. But the words never came. Instead, I stood there, gripping the straps of my leather bag tighter, trying to shake the sudden sense of nausea creeping up on me.

I wasn't a liar. I never had been. But something was wrong here—something that didn't add up—and the more I thought about it, the more I realized that the threads of this whole mess had started to tie themselves to me, whether I wanted them to or not.

The air smelled of saltwater, burning wood, and the faint hint of something sweeter, like the kind of smoke you only got from a fire that wasn't supposed to burn in the first place. It was the smell of secrets, if secrets could burn.

"You really don't trust me, do you?" The words slipped out before I could stop them.

Luca didn't answer immediately, his gaze fixed on the remnants of the docks as if they were the most important thing in the world. There was a tension in his jaw, a flicker of something I couldn't quite read. For a moment, I thought he might walk away, as he often did when things started to get too complicated. But he didn't. Instead, he leaned in, just slightly, enough that I could feel the heat of his presence even in the cool night air.

"I don't trust anyone," he said, and there it was—the truth, as blunt and unrelenting as ever.

I wasn't sure if I should feel relieved or insulted. Was this what passed for honesty between us? Was this how he dealt with the people in his life—by pushing them away, even as they reached for him? Maybe that was what had made him so good at his job. Maybe that was why, even now, he was here, standing in front of me, investigating the very thing that could ruin me.

"Well, I'm not anyone," I shot back, the words laced with more venom than I intended. The moment they left my mouth, I regretted it, but there was no taking them back.

Luca's lips twitched, the barest hint of a smile playing at the corners. It was gone before I could make sense of it, but it lingered in the air like a promise.

"You're not anyone," he echoed, his tone softening just slightly, enough to make me wonder if he was second-guessing himself. "But you are trouble. The kind I can't walk away from."

There it was again, that feeling—the one that always lingered just beneath the surface, like a bruise that refused to heal. It wasn't just the fire. It was him. It was the way he looked at me, the way he didn't look at me, the way his presence seemed to fill the space between us no matter how much I tried to push it away.

I wanted to ask him why he had to be the one to investigate this, why it had to be him looking for answers when all I wanted was to forget about the whole damn thing. But I didn't. I couldn't. Not when I had a sinking feeling in my gut that told me this wasn't just about the docks. This was about something bigger, something darker, something neither of us was ready to face.

The fire, the investigation, the suspicion—all of it was building, like the storm clouds that gathered on the horizon before a summer thunderstorm. And we were both caught in the middle, whether we liked it or not.

The sound of Luca's footsteps against the pavement echoed in my ears as we made our way away from the docks. The remnants of the fire still clung to the air, each breath tasting like smoke and saltwater, as if the entire world was trying to claw its way back from the edge of something it had barely survived. His silence was deafening, each step a reminder that we were not friends. Not anymore.

I had tried to avoid this—to avoid him—but the city had a way of forcing connections when you least wanted them. We hadn't spoken about it directly, but the unspoken tension hung in the air, thick and palpable, like we were both avoiding something we couldn't face.

"You're not going to leave me alone, are you?" I muttered, pulling my coat tighter around my shoulders as a gust of wind whipped past us.

Luca didn't respond immediately. For a moment, I thought he hadn't heard me, but then he spoke, his voice low and steady, like a current running underneath a calm surface. "Would you want me to?"

I wanted to tell him no. I wanted to tell him that I could handle things on my own, that the last thing I needed was his watchful eyes and constant scrutiny. But the truth was, I couldn't. Not anymore. Not with the fire still burning in my peripheral vision, not with the weight of the lost shipment pressing down on me, and not with the gnawing feeling that something was far more dangerous than it appeared.

"I didn't ask for your help," I said, my voice sharper than I intended.

His eyes flicked to mine for just a moment, too brief to read, but I could feel the shift, the slight loosening of the tension between us. "I didn't think you did." His words were as dry as the dust settling on the pavement, but there was something else beneath them, something that suggested he might just be holding back.

We walked in silence, the kind of silence that wasn't comfortable, the kind that made you want to fill the space with something—anything—but couldn't. The city buzzed around us, oblivious to our quiet struggle, the neon lights from bars and street signs flickering in the distance like beacons of normalcy in a world that no longer felt normal.

We reached the corner of Seventh and Franklin, where the city's heart still beat with the steady rhythm of midnight. A food truck sat near the sidewalk, its lights casting a soft glow on the crowd of people milling around it. The smell of tacos and hot dogs wafted in the air, a strange contrast to the heavy, acrid scent of smoke that still lingered in my nose.

Luca stopped at the corner, his gaze sweeping over the crowd with that familiar wariness I had come to expect. "You need something to eat?"

I looked at him, surprised by the offer. He wasn't the type to extend kindness without a reason, and this—this felt like the beginning of something he wasn't quite willing to name. "I'm not hungry," I replied, though my stomach betrayed me with a low growl.

"Suit yourself," he said, pulling his coat tighter around his shoulders. His eyes lingered on the food truck, but there was no real interest there. It was just one more distraction in a city full of them.

I wanted to ask him what he was thinking. What he was really thinking. The Luca I knew didn't do things without a purpose, didn't engage in unnecessary small talk or polite gestures. This wasn't about food. It was about something else entirely, something far more complicated than a simple meal.

The air shifted again, heavier now, like the pressure of an oncoming storm. Luca turned toward me, his eyes narrowed, his expression unreadable. "I'm not here to make friends, you know."

"I hadn't noticed," I said, my voice laced with sarcasm.

He didn't laugh. Didn't even smirk. Instead, he stepped closer, close enough that I could feel the heat of his body, the subtle, almost imperceptible tension in the air between us. "I'm here because you're in over your head. And whether you like it or not, you're going to need me."

The words hung in the air, thick and loaded, like a promise I wasn't ready to hear. I opened my mouth to retort, but nothing came out. He was right, I knew that. But there was something about hearing him say it out loud, hearing the certainty in his voice, that made me feel both exposed and vulnerable.

"You don't know what you're dealing with," I said, finally finding my voice. "This isn't some petty business deal gone wrong. This is bigger than you think."

He studied me for a long moment, his eyes sharp and calculating. I couldn't read him, not completely. It was like he had built walls around himself that I wasn't allowed to cross. But that didn't stop me from trying.

"I know more than you think," he replied, his voice so steady it was almost unsettling.

The confidence in his tone made my stomach flip. I wasn't sure if I hated it or admired it, but I knew one thing for certain: I didn't want him to be right. Not this time.

"Then why don't you figure it out without me?" I snapped, feeling the familiar anger welling up inside me. "You've got all the answers, don't you?"

Luca didn't flinch. "You're not the first person to think that," he said, his gaze lingering on me for just a beat longer than necessary. "But I'm not doing this for you. I'm doing it for what's left of this city."

For a second, the walls between us cracked. I saw something—something human—flicker in his eyes. It was brief, gone in the blink of an eye, but it was enough to make me wonder if there was more to this whole mess than either of us realized.

I didn't know how long we stood there, in the cold night, in the middle of a city that had forgotten how to be anything other than a battlefield. But eventually, Luca turned and walked away, leaving me with the taste of smoke in my mouth and a question I didn't want to ask: what was he really hiding?

The streets of the city had never felt so alien to me. It wasn't just the chaos of the fire still lingering in my mind, nor the suspicion that clung to my skin like the ash coating the backs of my hands. It was Luca—his presence, as unwanted as it was undeniable. I couldn't shake the feeling that we were both playing a game where the rules kept changing, and neither of us had the right to question the moves we were making.

I hadn't expected him to follow me, let alone stick around long enough for us to have this strange, uncomfortable dance. When we parted earlier, I thought I'd heard the last of him. But there he was, waiting by my door, his broad shoulders outlined by the dim streetlights.

For a moment, I almost walked right past him. Maybe I could just pretend I hadn't seen him. Maybe if I ignored him long enough, he'd disappear. But Luca wasn't the kind of man who could be ignored. Not unless you wanted to end up with something far worse on your conscience than a little conversation.

"Back again?" I said, leaning against the brick wall of the apartment building, arms crossed, trying to look casual.

"I could say the same to you," Luca replied, the corner of his mouth quirking up slightly, but it was a smile that didn't reach his eyes. "I'm starting to think you enjoy these late-night strolls."

"Not with you," I shot back, my tone sharp, but it wasn't just the edge in my voice that surprised me—it was the way his words seemed to sink in deeper than they should. Was I starting to let him under my skin? The very idea made my pulse quicken, but I wasn't ready to admit it. Not yet.

Luca didn't say anything for a long moment, his gaze fixed on the street ahead, as if there was something far more important than my irritation taking his attention. The stillness between us was heavy, like two people who had a thousand words to say but not the courage to speak them.

"You don't get it, do you?" I asked, the words slipping out before I could stop them. "You're not helping. You're just making this worse."

His gaze flicked to me, just briefly, and for the first time, I saw something akin to empathy flash in his eyes. But it vanished as quickly as it had come. "I'm not here to make it better for you. I'm here to make it better for the rest of the city."

I blinked, thrown by the shift in his tone. "What does that even mean? You're just a detective."

"And you're just a businesswoman," he shot back, his voice low, but with that unmistakable bite to it. "But we both know this is bigger than that. The fire wasn't a random accident. Someone made sure it happened. And I need to figure out who."

"You're wasting your time." I took a step back, suddenly feeling like I needed space, even if that meant walking away. But Luca didn't move. Didn't flinch. He just stood there, his silhouette outlined by the harsh glow of the streetlamp, watching me with those eyes that knew far too much.

"That's where you're wrong," he said quietly. "I'm not wasting my time. And neither are you."

I shook my head, frustrated with his cryptic tone. "You think I did it, don't you? That I somehow orchestrated this disaster to cover my tracks."

"I don't know what you did." His voice was colder now, the challenge in it unmistakable. "But I know you're hiding something. And I'm not going to stop until I find out what."

My heart skipped a beat, a cold chill creeping down my spine. I wanted to argue, to tell him he was wrong. But the truth was, I had no idea what had really happened at the docks, no clue how far the web of lies stretched. There were too many people involved, too many shadows moving behind the scenes. And one of those shadows—just one—was bound to be mine.

"I'm not your enemy, Luca," I said, my voice softer this time. I meant it, but that didn't make it any less complicated.

"I never said you were." He finally turned, his gaze lingering on me for just a moment longer before he walked away, disappearing into the shadows of the alley.

But the words lingered. I'm not your enemy.

The wind picked up, cutting through the night like a blade. I wrapped my arms around myself, the chill seeping into my bones. This wasn't how I'd expected my life to turn out. This city—this mess—was supposed to be mine. I'd worked hard to carve out my place in it, to make sure no one could pull me under. But now it felt like I was sinking, and every step I took only pulled me deeper.

My phone buzzed in my pocket, jolting me out of my thoughts. I pulled it out, expecting a message from my assistant, maybe an update on the shipment or a new threat from one of the competing businesses that had started sniffing around. But what I saw made my stomach drop.

A picture. A blurry image of the docks, the fire still raging in the background, with a single, chilling message: You're next.

I felt the blood drain from my face as I stared at the screen. For a moment, everything around me felt like it was slipping out of focus. My pulse thudded in my ears as my hand trembled, the phone slipping from my fingers and landing on the pavement with a dull thud.

I was no longer just in danger.

I was a target.

And someone knew exactly where to find me.

Just as I reached for my phone, I heard it—footsteps. Someone was coming toward me, quick, determined. A figure emerged from the darkness, and my heart stopped as I recognized the outline of a familiar face. But it wasn't Luca. It wasn't anyone I expected.

And the gun in their hand—pointed directly at me—left no room for doubt.

Chapter 11: The Cost of Betrayal

The rain was relentless, slapping against the windows of my apartment with the kind of fury that could make a person think the sky was trying to tell us something. I stood in front of the mirror, staring at the woman I barely recognized. My reflection was blurred by the tension that had settled over me like a storm cloud—heavy, suffocating, full of unspoken words. My clothes, once crisply ironed, now hung loosely on my frame, the creases in my blouse a testament to the sleepless nights. The makeup I'd put on was a faint memory, the dark smudges under my eyes a permanent feature.

The city outside was a blur of neon lights, the glow from the streetlamps casting shadows that flickered with the rain. There was no comfort to be found in the view, no solace in the cold blue of the night sky. I'd been avoiding the truth for days, but it was catching up with me now, one breath, one glance at the phone screen, at the whispers behind my back, at the dead eyes of people who had once been allies.

Luca had been watching me, I could feel it. Ever since the accusations against my uncle had surfaced, ever since that damned photograph had landed on my doorstep, he'd been like a shadow, his presence both a comfort and a threat. His loyalty was a double-edged sword, and he wasn't the kind of man you could trust easily—especially not when you had your own secrets. The problem was, I didn't know if he was watching me because he believed I was guilty, or if he was still waiting for me to prove my innocence. I had a feeling it was the latter, but the truth? That was harder to find.

I ran a hand through my hair, tugging at the strands as I took a deep breath. The betrayal wasn't just a feeling anymore—it was evidence. Physical evidence. The picture of my uncle, alone in the darkened alley, handing over a briefcase to someone whose face was hidden in shadow. My stomach churned every time I thought about it. I couldn't be sure who had taken it, but I knew one thing for certain: someone I loved was involved, and it hurt more than I wanted to admit.

I wasn't a detective. I wasn't even close. I had never needed to think that way, never had reason to. I'd lived my life in the comfort of knowing what was mine and what wasn't—until this moment, when the lines blurred, and I found myself staring down the very real possibility that the people I trusted most were the ones who had pushed me into this corner.

And then there was Luca.

I hadn't expected to find any shred of empathy in him, but there it was, lurking just beneath the surface. I had told him I didn't trust him, and he'd nodded, almost approvingly, like the words were something he had been waiting to hear. There was no argument, no protest, and that unsettled me more than I cared to admit. He wasn't trying to convince me of anything, wasn't making excuses. He simply accepted my doubt, as if he had already been preparing for it.

But then, there was that moment, just a few days ago, when I had caught him watching me—really watching me—with those dark, guarded eyes that seemed to see more than they should. I'd asked him about the photograph, about the possible betrayal. His response had been cold, deliberate, and yet, for a second, there had been something in his gaze that suggested he knew more than he was willing to share.

It was that moment that made me question everything.

"Don't you want to know the truth?" I'd asked him, my voice trembling more than I intended.

His lips had curled into something too close to a smile for my liking. "Truth's a funny thing. Everyone's got their own version of it. But yours?" He'd leaned in just a little, his breath warm against my skin. "I'm not sure I want to know yours just yet."

I hadn't responded, not because I couldn't, but because I didn't know what the right answer was. What could I possibly say when I wasn't sure of the truth myself?

Luca's words echoed in my mind now as I walked to the window, pressing my palms against the cold glass. The city lights flickered in the distance, their glow hazy in the rain-soaked night. Somewhere out there, my uncle was either guilty or innocent, but the evidence didn't lie. It pointed to him. Or did it?

There was a rustle of paper behind me, and I turned, startled. Luca stood at the door, his silhouette sharp against the dim light, a folder in his hand.

"I'm not here to talk about trust," he said, his voice low, controlled. "I'm here because I think you're being played. And I'm not sure by who."

I raised an eyebrow, skepticism mingling with curiosity. "Played? By who, Luca?"

He stepped forward, and I instinctively took a step back. "By someone close to you," he said. "Someone who's been hiding in plain sight."

My pulse quickened. "What does that mean? You think I'm being framed?"

Luca set the folder down on the table between us, the contents spilling out like a confession. My heart stopped as I saw what lay there: another photograph. The same alley. But this time, the figure in the shadows was unmistakable. My uncle, sure, but the person standing next to him was... me.

"Who else has seen this?" I whispered, my throat dry.

Luca met my gaze, his expression unreadable. "I don't know. But I'm guessing you're not the only one who's wondering if you're the one being set up."

The air between us thickened, heavy with the unsaid. I had to choose. Protect the ones I loved, or prove my own innocence. Either way, betrayal had a price.

The room felt smaller now, as though it was closing in on me with each passing second. Luca's gaze never wavered, the intensity of it pressing against me like a weight I couldn't escape. His words hung in the air, stark and blunt, like the cold steel of a knife sliding through the silence between us. "Good," he'd said. "You shouldn't." As if the trust I was offering—however tentative—was something to be discarded, a burden too heavy to carry.

I shifted uneasily, crossing my arms, a defensive reflex. "Is that how you always operate? No pretenses, no niceties?"

He didn't answer right away, instead letting the question settle between us like a lingering smoke. Finally, with a small, almost imperceptible shrug, he spoke. "Pretenses don't do much for me. And niceties?" He raised a brow. "They usually complicate things."

I snorted, unable to suppress the sound. "And you think that's charming?"

Luca's lips quirked up, the faintest of smiles tugging at the corners of his mouth. "You're an easy person to annoy, aren't you?"

I didn't have a comeback for that. Truth was, I was easily annoyed, especially when the world felt like it was unraveling around me. And right now, everything—every familiar thing I thought I knew—was coming apart at the seams.

I glanced down at the folder on the table, the photograph of me with my uncle glaring up at me from the stack of papers. My mind raced, trying to piece together the puzzle, trying to see the full picture through the chaos of it all. I wasn't sure what part of this twisted mess hurt the most—the betrayal of someone close to me, or the fact that my own image had been caught in the middle of it.

Luca's voice cut through the tension, smooth and level, as though this wasn't the most uncomfortable situation he could have put me in. "You don't have to protect anyone, you know. Not even him."

I swallowed hard, the words feeling thick in my throat. "What do you know about loyalty, Luca? You think it's easy to just—just walk away from people you've spent your life protecting? You think I could just... let this go?"

His eyes narrowed slightly, a flicker of something almost like curiosity passing over his features. "Is that what you're doing? Protecting someone? Or are you just trying to hide your own guilt?"

I sucked in a sharp breath, the accusation landing with a sting I wasn't prepared for. "I'm not guilty of anything."

"But you're not innocent either, are you?" He let the question hang, a deliberate pause that seemed to stretch longer than it should have.

I clenched my fists at my sides, willing myself not to react. But damn, there was no denying it—he was right. In the grand scheme of things, I was as guilty as anyone. I had been complicit in the lies, in the shadows, in the half-truths that had built my world. But none of that made me a criminal. None of that made me responsible for whatever my uncle had done.

"I don't know what you think you know, but I haven't done anything wrong," I said, my voice taut with frustration. "I'm not the one who's been hiding in the dark, making deals I don't understand."

His gaze softened, but only just. "No, but you're the one caught in the middle."

I stood there, silent for a moment, unsure of how to respond. The weight of his words settled over me like a storm cloud, dark and heavy, making it hard to breathe. He was right, and worse—he had a point. But the truth was, I didn't know what was worse: the fact that I was caught up in this mess, or the fact that I had no idea how to get out of it.

I turned away, pacing in tight circles, desperate to shake off the suffocating feeling creeping up on me. "I didn't ask for any of this. I didn't ask to be the one everyone looks at like I have some big secret hanging over my head."

Luca's voice stopped me in my tracks. "You can't control what happens to you, but you can control how you deal with it."

"Is that supposed to be comforting?"

"Depends on how you look at it," he said, his tone wry, almost teasing.

I couldn't help but laugh, bitter and sharp, escaping before I could stop it. "Right. Just keep it all together and pretend like everything's fine. The perfect little soldier. Maybe that's what you're used to."

His expression faltered for a brief moment, just long enough for me to see the cracks. But then, just as quickly, his mask was back in place. "You're wrong. I'm not the perfect soldier. But you've got a choice to make, and no one can do it for you."

The silence stretched between us again, only this time, it wasn't as suffocating. It was loaded with something else. Something... complicated. I wasn't sure whether to hate him or thank him for laying it out so bluntly. I had no illusions about the kind of man Luca was. He was dangerous in ways I didn't yet understand, but there was something about him—something in the way he spoke, in the way he looked at me—that made me feel like maybe, just maybe, he wasn't as cold and calculating as he liked to pretend.

I turned back to the table, reaching for the photograph. The man in the shadows, the one I'd spent so many years of my life admiring, was staring back at me. And there I was, standing beside him, a part of something I didn't understand. The room felt too small again, the air too thick, and I was suddenly tired. Tired of pretending, tired of trying to put the pieces together when it felt like they didn't belong.

Luca was watching me, but I couldn't look at him. Not yet. Not until I figured out if I could trust myself again.

I had a million thoughts swirling through my head, each one louder than the last, until I couldn't focus on any of them for more than a few seconds. The room was suddenly stifling, the walls pressing in as if the universe itself were closing its grip around me. I needed space, I needed clarity—but more than anything, I needed to figure out who I could trust. And right now, I wasn't sure I trusted anyone. Least of all Luca.

He was still standing there, silent and unnervingly calm, watching me like a puzzle he was trying to solve. For a split second, I wondered if he was genuinely concerned or just waiting for me to crack. The way he'd been looking at me—intense, almost clinical—made it hard to tell.

"You're a real piece of work, you know that?" I said, the words tumbling out before I could stop them. "You've got this all figured out, don't you? Like you've seen it a thousand times before."

Luca leaned against the doorframe, his posture casual but his eyes never leaving mine. "No," he said slowly, "I've seen people like you. People who think they have control. But they don't. They're just playing catch-up."

I bristled. "And you think you're better at this than me?"

"I think I'm better at seeing through the smoke," he replied. "You're distracted by all the wrong things."

I stared at him, not knowing if I wanted to scream or laugh. "You don't know what you're talking about. You think you have all the answers, but you're just like everyone else. You've got your own agenda. I can see it."

He stepped closer, his eyes narrowing. "Is that so? And what do you think my agenda is?"

"Maybe you want me to fail," I said, the words harsh and bitter. "Maybe you want me to lose. So you can win. Or is it just that you've got nothing better to do than watch people like me stumble around?"

Luca's lips twitched. For a moment, I thought he might actually smile, but it never fully formed. "You've got a way of thinking you know people. But you're wrong about me. I'm not the one you need to be worried about."

I exhaled sharply, irritated by the cryptic way he spoke. "Then who should I be worried about, huh? Because right now, I'm starting to think you're the last person I want to be around."

The words left my mouth before I could rein them in. The tension between us shifted, like the sudden crack of thunder in the distance that hinted at a storm about to break. Luca didn't flinch. He didn't even seem surprised by my anger. Instead, he studied me—carefully, with the precision of someone who was always two steps ahead.

"Maybe you should be worried about the people you've been trusting," he said softly. "The ones closest to you. Because right now, you're playing a dangerous game, and you've got no idea who the real players are."

I froze, his words sinking into the pit of my stomach. I couldn't speak for a moment. The air around me felt thick, like I was suffocating in it. My head spun with the possibilities—who could it be? My uncle? Someone else? My thoughts trailed off as I considered all the ways this could go wrong.

"Don't look at me like that," Luca said, his voice lower now, almost like a warning. "I'm not your enemy. But if you keep ignoring the facts, you won't know who your real enemies are until it's too late."

I wanted to scream at him, tell him to stop talking in riddles. But the look in his eyes—the way his words seemed to slice through everything I was trying to deny—made it hard to argue. I'd spent so much time focusing on my uncle, on protecting him, that I hadn't even stopped to think about the bigger picture. About who else might be pulling the strings.

I took a step back, suddenly feeling smaller than I had in days. "You're telling me I've been blind this whole time. That I've been trusting the wrong people?"

Luca didn't answer right away. Instead, he walked over to the window, standing at the edge like he could see the whole city stretched out before him. It was strange how he was always calm, always distant, like he had already accepted whatever this mess was. Meanwhile, I felt like I was drowning in the uncertainty of it all.

"I'm telling you," he said finally, "that you've been focusing on the wrong things. The wrong people."

I wanted to ask him what he meant. Who he was talking about. But before I could, there was a knock at the door. It was quick and sharp, the kind of knock that sent a rush of adrenaline through my veins. I turned toward it, my heart suddenly racing, my mind racing through all the possible scenarios. Who could be here now?

Luca stiffened, his eyes flicking to the door. "Stay quiet," he said quickly, his voice tight.

I didn't argue. I didn't have time. The knock came again, louder this time, followed by a muffled voice on the other side.

"Open up. We know you're in there."

My blood ran cold. I recognized the voice—Agent Lawson. The very same agent who had been sniffing around my uncle's business for weeks. The very same agent who had a knack for showing up at the most inconvenient times. And now, it seemed, I was the one on the other end of his attention.

Luca's hand shot out to stop me as I made a move for the door, his grip firm. "Don't. Let me handle this."

I stared at him, eyes wide with panic. "Handle what, Luca? They know we're in here. They know I'm involved. This—this could be it."

Luca's gaze was calm, but there was something in the way he was holding himself, some faint tension in his jaw, that told me he knew exactly how dangerous this moment was. "Just let me talk to them," he said quietly.

But as I watched him, I had this sinking feeling deep in my chest. Whatever was about to happen next, it was going to change everything.

Chapter 12: The Dance of Danger

The air in the room is thick with tension, almost as heavy as the velvet curtains that hang along the walls, casting everything in a dusky, intimate light. The city outside—the low hum of traffic, the occasional clink of a distant bottle clashing with another at a bar—fades to a background murmur, leaving only the thrum of my pulse to fill the silence. Luca's breath on my skin is warm, lingering like the aftertaste of whiskey. He's so close, I can feel the heat radiating from him, the rigid line of his body pressed against mine, an accidental brush of fingers against the bare skin of my wrist. I don't pull away.

It was supposed to be simple. The meeting, the charade, the act. But the longer I stay in this game, the more I start to wonder if I'm playing the part of the damsel or the villain.

Luca watches me with a gaze that's equal parts irritation and amusement, like he knows exactly what I'm thinking, like he has the power to unravel me with one word. But the truth is, this is the last thing I wanted to do. Team up with him. Stand by his side like we're some power couple from a tabloid headline. And yet, here we are, trading glances and pretending we belong together.

The deal we're about to close could make or break me. It's worth more than the piddling amounts of money I've spent on overpriced coffee, more than the rent I pay for my apartment with walls so thin I can hear my neighbors argue over whose turn it is to buy the next pack of toilet paper. This isn't about survival; this is about dominance. About proving that I've worked my way to the top, that I can navigate this world of corporate sharks without drowning. And this? This meeting, with its finely tailored suits and delicate glasses of vintage champagne—it's my chance to show that I can play with the big leagues.

Except for Luca.

"Don't look at me like that," he murmurs, his voice low and rough like gravel sliding against pavement. "I'm not here to hold your hand, okay?"

I glance up at him, trying not to be distracted by the arrogant tilt of his lips, the dangerous gleam in his eyes. "Good thing," I snap, flicking a lock of hair from my face, "because I don't need a hand-holder. I'm not the damsel in distress, Luca."

He chuckles darkly, a sound that vibrates through the air between us. "Well, you sure don't act like a distressed damsel. You act like someone who's about two seconds from either throwing a drink in my face or using that knife you're hiding in your heel."

I raise an eyebrow, a smirk tugging at the corner of my lips. "Maybe I am."

We've danced this dance before, in different places, at different times. But never like this. Never in this gilded cage, surrounded by polished faces that don't look at you, but through you. The kind of people who smile with their mouths, but never with their eyes. They're here for one thing, and one thing only—control. They don't care if you're bleeding on the inside. They care only about who gets the last word, who signs on the dotted line, who walks away as the victor.

"Remember," Luca says, his voice suddenly serious, "we're supposed to look like we belong here. Like we're... a couple." The word tastes strange on his lips, like it's foreign and out of place.

I give him a look that could melt steel. "A couple? Really? You think anyone's going to believe that? We can barely stand each other."

He shifts, the faintest twitch of a smile dancing on his lips. "That's the point. It's more believable that way."

Before I can respond, the door swings open, and a group of sharply dressed executives saunter in like they own the room. The buzz of conversation drops as they settle into their seats, all eyes on us. I feel the weight of their gaze, the scrutinizing eyes that peel me open like a book. The one who speaks first has a voice like a dull knife—too smooth, too deliberate. "Shall we get started?"

Luca doesn't take his eyes off me as he steps closer, his hand finding the small of my back. It's not romantic. It's strategic. But it still sends a shock through me. His touch, cold and sure, is like a reminder that we're not playing a game. We're playing for keeps.

I force my shoulders back, lifting my chin. "Of course," I say, my voice smooth, practiced. The words come easy, but my heart is thundering beneath the surface, a constant reminder of the danger that's always lurking. I nod to the table. "Shall we?"

Luca's hand slips from my back to my hand, and I resist the urge to yank it away. Instead, I tighten my grip slightly, letting him think I'm playing along. The contract is set out before us, the ink of the deal looking like a challenge—a dare—and I know, deep down, that if I blink, I'll lose.

The negotiations unfold with all the grace of a slow-moving train wreck. Smiles are exchanged, but they don't reach eyes. Words are sharpened, but no one seems to care who gets cut. Through it all, I can feel Luca beside me, his presence solid and unnervingly steady, like a rock in a river that keeps flowing no matter how fast or how hard the current pulls.

But as the hours stretch on, something strange happens.

I start to wonder if I might be the one swept away. If, after all this time pretending, the line between real and fake starts to blur just a little too much.

The negotiations drag on, every word a slow dance of power and calculation. The room hums with a muted tension, the subtle click of glasses on the table punctuating the silence as we take turns speaking, feigning camaraderie. But all I can feel is the pull of Luca beside me—close enough to be a ghost, but far enough to remind me that he's not part of the show. Not really.

His hand is still resting casually on mine, a gesture that should be comforting, but is anything but. It's like a damning reminder of the web we've both gotten tangled in, the lie we've woven too intricately to escape. We're not a couple. I can't stand him. He's ruthless, calculating, and worse—he knows exactly how to get under my skin. And yet, this façade we've built has become so seamless that when he looks at me, I almost start to wonder if I do belong here, in this high-rise of glass and marble, playing the part of someone I'm not.

I glance up at him, and he's watching me intently, his eyes heavy with some unreadable emotion. I almost feel like I'm drowning, but I don't look away. Not yet. His lips twitch into that infuriating half-smile, the one that always seems to hint at a secret joke only he's privy to.

"Relax," he murmurs under his breath, barely moving his lips. "They don't bite."

His words come too easily, too smoothly, and I can't help but roll my eyes. "You mean they haven't decided which one of us they'll chew up first, right?"

He chuckles quietly, a sound that's half-mocking, half-enticing. "Something like that."

I bite my tongue to stop the sarcastic remark that's poised on the tip of my lips. For a moment, I forget the ruse, forget the contract, and forget the polished executives around the table. It's just Luca and me, and in that quiet space between us, I wonder how much of this—this act—he truly believes. He's a man who thrives on control, on the delicate balance of power, and right now, the power is in his hands. I'm just the bait.

The meeting continues, but the conversation becomes a blur. The words they speak bounce off me like static, too distant to hold my attention. All I can focus on is Luca, his subtle gestures and the way his breath hitches just slightly when I shift my weight, as if he's aware of every movement I make. And I don't know if I should be flattered or terrified.

Finally, after what feels like hours, the meeting winds down, the deal finalized with a handshake that feels more like a threat than a gesture of goodwill. The silence in the room is thick with unspoken things, things I can't quite put into words but that tangle in my chest like a knot.

As the others rise, offering me polite but distant smiles, I can't help but notice how they look at Luca—not as a business partner, but as a force to be reckoned with. It's like they see something in him that I don't, something beneath the surface that I can't quite comprehend.

When we're finally alone, the air feels suffocating, the weight of the evening pressing down on me like a heavy blanket. I take a deep breath, desperate for a moment of clarity.

"Well," I say, trying to shake off the lingering tension, "that wasn't so bad."

Luca turns toward me, his gaze cool and unreadable. "You were the perfect picture of charm," he says, his voice dripping with sarcasm. "I almost believed it myself."

I scoff, crossing my arms. "Oh, please. You were hardly a convincing lover yourself. Half the time, I thought you were trying to make a point by glaring at everyone."

His lips curl into a wicked grin. "Maybe I was."

I narrow my eyes at him. "You're insufferable."

He steps closer, his presence filling the room in a way that leaves me breathless, unnerved. "And yet, you're still here. Still playing the part."

I open my mouth to retort, but he's not finished. His voice softens, just slightly, like a shift in the wind before a storm.

"Tell me, Julia," he says, his tone low and dangerous, "when does the act stop? When does the real you show up?"

I freeze, my heart pounding in my chest. For a split second, I wonder if I've crossed a line, if he's figured me out. If this whole thing has been nothing more than a game to him from the start. But then, his eyes flicker, just a flash of something unreadable, and I'm not sure if I should trust it.

I swallow hard, forcing my voice to remain steady. "The real me? There's nothing to see. This—" I gesture around the room, "—this is just business."

He watches me for a moment, his gaze intense, like he's searching for some crack in the armor. "I don't think you're as immune as you pretend to be," he murmurs, almost to himself. "I think you might be more like me than you'd care to admit."

I stare at him, a cold shiver running down my spine. I don't know if it's the truth I hear in his voice or the challenge in his words, but something inside me shifts, just a fraction.

I take a deep breath and try to steady my racing thoughts. "If we're done here," I say, turning toward the door, "I'll be on my way. There's nothing more to discuss."

But Luca doesn't move, and I realize, with a jolt, that I'm not in control here. Not anymore. The lie, the charade—it's taken on a life of its own.

The words hang in the air between us, charged with an unspoken tension, the room spinning ever so slightly as if the whole world were holding its breath, waiting for a move. I've never been good at pretending, but tonight, for the first time, the act feels almost too natural. It's as though the line between fiction and reality is beginning to blur. I want to shake off the sensation, to laugh it away, but the heat of his breath against my skin doesn't allow for any of that.

He's right. I'm not a great actress, but right now, I'm more convincing than I ever expected. The entire evening has felt like a series of moments where I was supposed to be playing a role, each time looking at Luca, each time realizing I've somehow forgotten where the performance ends and where I begin.

I don't pull away. Instead, I stand there, looking at him through narrowed eyes. His smile hasn't changed, but there's something different about it now, something quieter, more knowing. He's waiting for a response, watching me with a sort of quiet amusement, like he's already figured me out. And yet, I'm not quite sure if I've figured him out.

"What if I told you I'm not pretending?" I say, my voice coming out rougher than I intended. "What if I told you I've gotten quite good at it?"

He arches an eyebrow, the movement slow, deliberate. He takes a step closer, and I swear the air thickens in his wake. "Then I'd say you're fooling yourself," he replies, his voice low, almost tender. But it's the kind of tenderness that makes your skin crawl, not soothe.

We're playing a game now. A dangerous one. The kind of game where the stakes are high enough that you can't walk away without losing a little piece of yourself, whether you realize it or not. And I'm not sure if I want to keep playing or if I'm already too far gone to stop.

Luca's gaze doesn't waver as the silence stretches between us, long and suffocating. The sound of the city outside—an occasional honk or the shuffle of footsteps on rain-slicked pavement—fades into the background. In this moment, all I can hear is the erratic beat of my own heart, louder than any noise outside these walls.

Finally, I break the silence. "I'm not one of your toys, Luca. I'm not some game for you to win."

He doesn't respond immediately, his lips curling into that half-smile again. His eyes—those dark, unreadable eyes—lock onto mine with an intensity that makes my stomach flutter despite myself.

"No, you're not," he says quietly. "But I wonder if that's what makes you so... interesting."

There it is again, that edge in his voice. The implication that I'm not just a pawn in this game; I'm the prize. And that's a dangerous thing to be in a game like this, because it means everything is a calculation. Even when it doesn't feel like it.

I take a deep breath, forcing myself to meet his gaze without flinching. The conversation we're having isn't about business anymore. It's about something much messier, something neither of us is willing to acknowledge—at least, not out loud. The moment stretches, and I know I need to break the connection, to find a way to step back before the lines blur completely.

But before I can say another word, the door swings open with a jarring creak, cutting through the tension like a knife. A familiar face steps inside—Raymond. The man who's been trying to buy my company for months, a shark in a tailored suit.

"Looks like the deal's done," he says, his tone far too chipper for my liking. His eyes flick from me to Luca and back again, a knowing smile tugging at the corners of his lips. "Didn't think I'd be interrupting anything... personal."

Luca doesn't even blink. He straightens, taking a step back and offering Raymond a look that's so practiced, so perfect, it's almost chilling. "Nothing personal, Ray," he says smoothly. "Just business."

I fight to keep my expression neutral, but it's harder now, with the remnants of that intimacy still hanging between Luca and me, like a whisper. I don't want to be here anymore. I don't want to pretend. I want to take a breath without feeling his presence pressing against me, wanting to consume me.

Raymond moves toward the table, tossing a glance in my direction. "So, Julia, what's next for you? I trust you're ready to finalize the next steps?"

I swallow, my throat dry. This is it—the moment I've been waiting for, the moment where I can take control and walk away.

But instead, Luca turns to me, his eyes flashing with a glimmer of something—something I can't quite decipher. He's not done. He doesn't want me to walk away. He doesn't want this to be over.

"Next steps?" I say, my voice much steadier than I feel. "I think we'll need to rethink the terms. There's a lot to discuss."

Raymond raises an eyebrow, clearly surprised. "I'm not sure I follow, Julia."

Before I can elaborate, Luca interrupts, his voice smooth, confident. "She's right. We'll need some adjustments. It's a deal-breaker if we don't have a few conditions changed."

I open my mouth to protest, to tell him to stop, but I catch the look in his eyes—something that almost looks like... triumph? Or is it challenge? Either way, he's not backing down.

And for the first time, I wonder if maybe, just maybe, I've walked into a trap I won't be able to escape.

Chapter 13: Blood and Promises

The air was thick with the smell of earth and rain, and a faint mist curled through the trees, painting everything in muted shades of gray and green. The countryside had once been picturesque, like something from an old postcard. But now, with every passing minute, it felt more like a wild, untamed stretch of land that seemed determined to swallow us whole.

I tightened the straps on my boots, the leather stiff and uncomfortable, but necessary. My fingers were numb from the cold, but it was better than facing the sharp sting of regret, which felt infinitely worse in moments like these. I could feel Luca's eyes on me, even though I wasn't looking at him. The tension between us had been simmering ever since we'd been forced to flee, and now, miles from civilization, it was like a storm waiting to break.

"You're not who I thought you were," I said, the words tasting bitter as they left my lips.

The quiet hum of the wind through the trees was the only sound for a moment. Luca didn't respond at first, his figure blending into the shadows of the dense forest. He moved with the same deliberate pace, as though everything had already been calculated and nothing, not even the threat of the unknown, could disturb his composure. That quiet confidence had irritated me from the very start.

When he did speak, his voice was low, almost too controlled. "Neither are you."

I stopped walking, the weight of his words pressing into me like a physical force. I turned to face him, eyes narrowing as I tried to read his expression, but he was impossible to decipher.

"What's that supposed to mean?" I demanded. The edge in my voice felt foreign, but it was there, sharp and defensive. He had a way of making me feel like I was walking on the edge of a cliff, unsure if I'd fall or fly.

Luca didn't flinch. He merely adjusted the pack on his shoulders and gave me that infuriating half-smirk, the one I had come to loathe. He took a step toward me, closing the space between us, and I resisted the urge to step back. His proximity was like a magnet pulling at my center, making it impossible to think straight.

"You didn't come here for the reasons you told me," he said, his voice now quieter, a thread of something almost personal in his tone. "You're not the innocent little lamb you make everyone believe."

I exhaled sharply, my breath coming out in a puff of mist. "And you're not the hero you act like you are," I shot back, the words slipping out before I could think better of them.

The tension between us crackled in the air, sharp and biting, like the first hint of a thunderstorm. It had always been there, beneath the surface. But now it felt unavoidable, suffocating, like we were both trapped in a game where the rules were made up as we went along. And maybe, just maybe, I didn't mind being trapped here with him.

Luca's eyes glinted with something dangerous as he took another step forward. His jaw was clenched, but there was something in his gaze that made my pulse quicken. He seemed to be studying me, looking for something, but what? I wasn't sure if I wanted to find out.

"Do you even know what you're doing?" I said, my voice low and challenging.

He tilted his head, the faintest hint of a smile playing at the corners of his mouth. "I know exactly what I'm doing. Do you?"

I opened my mouth to reply, but the words caught in my throat. The answer was no. I didn't know. Not anymore. I had come here hoping to find something—answers, maybe, or redemption, or maybe just an escape from the mess of my own life. But now, lost in this wilderness with him, I felt like I had left all my certainty behind.

A sudden rustle from the brush snapped us both to attention. I turned my head instinctively, every muscle in my body going taut. Whatever it was, it wasn't friendly.

Luca's hand was already on his gun, his movements fluid, precise. I stepped back, instinctively reaching for my own weapon, though I knew it was useless. There was no way I could ever be as quick or as skilled as Luca.

The rustling grew louder, and I felt the hairs on the back of my neck stand up. It wasn't just the threat that made my heart race; it was the realization that this—this chaotic, unpredictable world—was our reality now. There was no turning back.

"Stay close," Luca muttered, his voice all business now.

I nodded, but the knot in my stomach tightened. If anything, staying close to him was the last thing I wanted to do. The tension between us was unbearable, and yet, I found myself drawn to him like a moth to a flame. It was a dangerous attraction, the kind that could burn you alive if you weren't careful.

We crept through the trees, moving as quietly as we could. The underbrush was thick, the ground uneven beneath our feet. I tried not to stumble, though I could feel the weight of Luca's gaze on me, even through the darkness. His silence was maddening, but I didn't dare speak. There were no words left between us that didn't feel like raw, exposed nerves.

The rustling grew louder. Closer. And then, just as quickly as it had started, it stopped. A chill ran through me, and I instinctively reached for Luca's arm, my fingers brushing against the rough fabric of his jacket.

He turned to me, his eyes flashing with something like annoyance, but it quickly faded, replaced by a sharpness that only made my heart beat faster.

"Something's not right," he murmured.

I didn't have to say anything. We both knew that nothing was right. Not anymore.

We moved through the dense undergrowth like shadows, each step heavy with the weight of what we'd left behind and what we still had yet to face. The night was a cloak, thick and impenetrable, and despite the unsettling silence that had followed the rustling, I couldn't shake the feeling that something—someone—was watching us. It wasn't the kind of paranoia that comes with too many bad decisions; it was the kind of fear that lodges in your throat and tells you that the danger is already too close.

Luca's movements were fluid, instinctual, as if the wilderness was nothing more than another terrain he could navigate without a second thought. The flicker of moonlight that filtered through the trees caught the edge of his jawline, casting his face in harsh relief. His expression was unreadable, like it always was. There were times when I hated how little I knew about him, how much of him remained a mystery wrapped in stubborn silence. And then there were moments like this, when I resented the fact that it felt like he was the only person who might understand this twisted mess we were in.

I didn't know what had brought him here, why he'd stayed when the easy way out would've been to disappear, just like everyone else in my life. He wasn't a hero—if anything, he was just as flawed as the rest of us. But there was something in the way he moved, something purposeful, that made me wonder if he'd seen enough of the world to know exactly when to hold on and when to let go.

I couldn't afford to dwell on that now. The fog still hung thick in the air, curling around our feet like a sentient thing. I couldn't tell if it was the cold making my chest tight or something deeper, something heavier. It was the kind of night where you don't want to ask questions you already know the answer to, because it'll only make everything worse.

"Do you hear that?" I asked, my voice a whisper that seemed too loud for the stillness.

Luca didn't even flinch. He had already stopped walking, listening. His eyes flicked to the trees around us, scanning, sharp. I felt the tension in the air shift, like the entire world was holding its breath.

He held up a hand, signaling for silence. There it was again—the sound. Faint, but distinct. The unmistakable crack of twigs snapping underfoot.

"Someone's out there," I said, the words more statement than question.

Luca nodded once, but there was no time for further discussion. His hand was already on the strap of his pack, reaching for something—a weapon, I assumed. The world around us was heavy with anticipation, and my heart thudded in my chest, every beat feeling too loud in the quiet.

I didn't want to admit it, but I knew we were in trouble. We were alone out here, with no way to signal for help, no way to escape if things went south. All we had were each other. And right now, that didn't feel like a blessing.

Luca crouched low, his movements smooth, almost graceful. I followed suit, huddling close to the earth, though I couldn't ignore the sharp discomfort in my legs. I wasn't used to moving like this—silent, calculating, patient. My entire life had been about pushing forward, making things happen, staying one step ahead.

But now, out here in the dark, everything felt like it was slipping away.

The sound of footsteps grew louder, closer. I swallowed hard. Whoever it was, they were moving fast. Too fast.

"Do you think they're looking for us?" I asked, barely above a breath. The air felt thick, heavy in my lungs, like it had become another obstacle in our path.

Luca didn't answer at first. Instead, he shifted his weight, crouching even lower, his dark eyes scanning the perimeter, searching for anything out of place. The seconds stretched between us, taut and unforgiving.

Then, with a suddenness that made me flinch, he moved. Not fast, not a rush—but deliberate, like he knew exactly what was about to happen. My instincts kicked in, and I followed his lead, though the confusion in my mind was a poor match for the calm certainty in his.

We crept forward, moving along the edge of the tree line, staying hidden in the shadows. I couldn't remember the last time I'd been so aware of my surroundings—every rustle of leaves, every snap of a twig, every change in the breeze felt like it could mean the difference between life and death. And still, there was the constant presence of him beside me, that silent, brooding figure who made it all feel almost…manageable. Almost.

A movement caught my eye—a flash of something darting between the trees. My breath caught in my throat, and for a split second, I thought I saw something—or someone—glimpse in our direction.

"Stay low," Luca hissed, his voice barely audible.

I didn't need him to tell me twice. I dropped to the ground, my heart hammering in my chest, and watched as he disappeared into the darkness ahead. His figure melded with the night, a shadow among shadows. The only indication he was there was the faint rustle of his clothes and the steady rhythm of his breath.

It was impossible to predict what would happen next. Who was out there? Were they the same people who'd attacked us earlier, or was this something—someone—else? The possibilities churned in my mind, each one darker than the last. But I couldn't afford to get lost in my thoughts now. I had to stay alert. I had to survive.

I stayed crouched, waiting for the signal from Luca. My pulse was a drumbeat in my ears, but I managed to silence my thoughts long enough to listen.

And then, just as suddenly as it had started, the footsteps stopped.

It was eerily quiet.

"Luca?" I whispered, my voice barely a tremor in the wind.

There was no answer. The silence stretched on.

The silence that followed was stifling, oppressive even, like the air had thickened in a way that made it impossible to breathe. The cool night should've been a relief, but it only made everything feel sharper—more real, more dangerous. I could still feel the weight of Luca's words hanging between us, heavy and unspoken, like they had dug trenches where our relationship had once stood. But the moment was too fragile for reflection. Too dangerous.

The sound of footsteps had stopped, and all I could hear now was my own pulse racing in my ears. My senses were on high alert, every nerve trembling with the anticipation of what was coming next. I barely dared to move, barely dared to breathe, but I couldn't shake the feeling that something was coming for us. I glanced sideways, searching the dark perimeter for any movement, but all I saw was the oppressive blackness of the trees surrounding us.

Then, a sharp snap of a branch split the air like a gunshot. I instinctively flinched, heart slamming against my ribs. But Luca—Luca didn't flinch. His body was a taut wire, every muscle braced and ready, his eyes scanning the horizon like he could see through the dark. His focus was so absolute, so unnerving, that for a second, I forgot to breathe.

Without a word, he signaled for me to follow, and we moved, slipping through the trees like shadows ourselves. I barely made a sound as I moved in his wake, but every part of me was alive, thrumming with an energy I didn't want to admit I was scared of. The further we went, the more tangled the underbrush became. The leaves underfoot were thick and wet, clinging to my boots with every step, and I cursed under my breath. We were no longer just trying to survive—we were running.

My mind kept racing. Had they found us already? Was this another ambush? My stomach churned at the thought. But something about the quiet—the strange, creeping quiet—made my skin prickle. Whoever was out there wasn't following. No, it wasn't even that. They were waiting.

I felt the shift before I saw it. There was something off about the trees ahead, the way they parted just slightly too neatly. It was a trap. It was too perfect. I didn't need Luca to confirm it; I could see the outline of something dark, something heavy, looming just ahead.

"Luca," I whispered sharply, but he was already ahead of me, moving with the predator's grace I had learned to fear.

He was too fast for me to catch up, his figure blurring into the shadows. The tension between us felt like a wire stretched tight—too tight, like it was bound to snap. I hesitated for just a second, just long enough for doubt to creep in. Was I making the right choice by following him? By trusting him?

But then I heard it—something heavy moving through the trees, the unmistakable rustle of a body shifting just behind me. I froze, my throat tight, unable to move, and the weight of the air seemed to press down on me, suffocating. It was a low growl that did it—low and guttural, like something inhuman.

I spun around, instinctively reaching for my gun.

Nothing.

The clearing I had thought I heard it in was empty. But the feeling, the suffocating sense that we weren't alone, didn't leave.

Luca was already crouched, crouching in the darkness, and for a second, I wondered if he'd heard it too. Or if he already knew what was coming.

"Stay close," he said, his voice low but steady. He was still so composed, so utterly calm, but I could feel the tension in him, a kind of quiet fury that made my skin prickle. "And don't make a sound."

I wanted to ask him what was going on. I wanted to demand answers, to scream and make him tell me exactly what he was thinking, but I knew that would get us both killed. I nodded instead, silently cursing the fact that I was so damn out of my element.

We crept forward, inch by agonizing inch, the world around us darker than it had been a moment ago. The shadows seemed deeper now, like they were closing in, pulling us into something we couldn't escape. And then, in the distance, I saw them. A pair of glowing eyes. Cold, unblinking, and unwavering.

My breath caught in my throat, and for a moment, I thought I was seeing things. But no. They were real. They were there.

A chill ran down my spine. I wasn't sure if it was fear or adrenaline, but it didn't matter. My body knew what to do even if my mind couldn't keep up. I sank back into the shadows beside Luca, my heart thudding as I tried to steady my breathing.

The eyes didn't blink. They didn't move. They just watched, unblinking, unmoving.

And then the rustling started again. Closer. And this time, it wasn't just one set of eyes. It was several. More shapes, more forms, slowly materializing from the darkness like ghosts, like things that shouldn't be real. They were moving toward us, but they didn't make a sound.

The stillness was unnatural. No wind, no crickets, no animals. Just that silence. That dead, unsettling silence.

I could hear Luca's breath beside me, controlled, steady, but I could feel the muscles in his body tightening, preparing for something. He didn't need to say anything—I knew it was coming. Whatever this was, it wasn't going to be quiet anymore.

The first figure emerged from the darkness, tall and thin, its face shadowed, its eyes still glowing with that eerie light. It stepped forward, and the ground beneath it seemed to shift, as though the earth itself recoiled from the presence of whatever this thing was.

And then, like a wave crashing against the shore, the others came forward, a ragged group that moved as one, their eyes glowing like lanterns in the dark. My heart stopped.

I didn't know what they were. But I knew we couldn't outrun them.

And when Luca turned to look at me, his eyes filled with something—something far more dangerous than fear—I knew it was too late to run.

Chapter 14: Threads Unraveling

The streets of Chicago felt different after everything that had happened. The sharp edge of winter still clung to the air, a faint reminder that the city hadn't quite let go of its cold grip. But for me, it wasn't the temperature that made my skin prickle—it was the suspicion that lingered just beneath the surface. Things weren't adding up. They never had, really, but now? Now I couldn't ignore it.

I walked along the snow-crusted sidewalks, my boots crunching with each step, the sound a steady rhythm beneath the hum of the city. Everything seemed normal enough—the bustling pedestrians, the scent of coffee wafting from every corner café, the sharp honk of horns cutting through the air. But underneath it all, there was a current. A tension I hadn't felt before.

Luca had been distant since the attack, his phone never far from his hand, his eyes constantly scanning the shadows. When he looked at me, there was a certain coldness, a layer of distance he'd never allowed before. It should've been a relief, in some strange way—no more secrets, no more questions. But instead, it gnawed at me. The air between us had thickened, and every glance, every word, felt heavier than it ever had before.

"I'll be home late tonight," he said last night as we sat at the kitchen table. His voice, deep and methodical, didn't match the quick flicker of unease in his eyes. He didn't meet my gaze as he spoke. "I have to take care of some things." His usual confidence was wrapped in a veneer of something darker, something that felt too much like guilt. I wanted to push him, to ask him what "things" he had to take care of, but instead, I nodded, pretending I didn't already know it was all a lie.

The moment he left, I couldn't shake the feeling that I was standing on the edge of a cliff, and any wrong step would send me tumbling into an abyss of truths I wasn't sure I was ready to face. But that feeling—it wasn't just about Luca. No, there was something far deeper at play here, something about the Vellano empire, the tangled web of power and corruption, that I hadn't quite pieced together.

I turned the corner, my eyes scanning the familiar storefronts—Café au Lait on the left, the small bookstore I loved on the right, the old brownstone building where I rented my apartment looming ahead. Everything seemed unchanged, ordinary, but nothing ever was. Not anymore.

I felt the flutter of my phone in my pocket, a familiar buzz that sent a little jolt through me. With a quick glance, I saw it was a message from Luca.

"We need to talk."

I felt my stomach tighten. He'd never said that before. Not to me. It wasn't just a message; it was a warning, a subtle shift in the dynamic that I couldn't ignore. But what could he possibly need to talk about now? Hadn't we said everything that needed to be said? Or maybe, there were things I still didn't know.

I pushed open the door to my building and walked up the creaky stairs to my apartment. The place smelled faintly of old wood and the lingering scent of my lavender candles. I kicked off my boots, the soft thud of my feet against the hardwood floors grounding me.

But as I set my keys down on the counter, the stillness in the room felt all wrong. It was too quiet. My pulse quickened. I moved toward the window, peeking through the curtains, half-expecting to see someone—or something—waiting for me in the shadows. But the street outside was empty, the city just as it always was.

I glanced back at my phone. Another message from Luca.

"It's about the Vellanos."

My breath caught in my throat. The Vellanos. I'd always known that the family's influence ran deep, but lately, the pieces I'd been trying to fit together weren't just difficult—they were dangerous. There were things about Luca, about the Vellanos, that I hadn't asked. Things I hadn't wanted to know. But if Luca was offering me an in, a peek behind the curtain, I wasn't going to waste it.

I took a deep breath and hit the call button, the phone buzzing in my hand. It only took a few seconds before his deep, familiar voice answered.

"Luca." My tone was steady, even though my heart was pounding. "What's going on?"

There was a long pause on the other end. And then, his voice came through, quieter than usual, almost strained. "Meet me at the usual place. I'll explain everything."

That was it. No elaboration, no comfort, just that. My instincts told me to ignore him. To turn away, to shut myself off from whatever mess he was tangled in. But I couldn't. I knew that. Deep down, I knew that I had already crossed a line that couldn't be uncrossed.

I grabbed my coat and headed out the door. The cold hit me like a slap in the face, the chill nipping at my skin as I walked down the stairs and onto the streets. I made my way through the city, each step heavier than the last, the weight of uncertainty pressing against my chest.

And yet, even as I walked toward him, the thought of Luca, of what he might reveal tonight, I couldn't shake the feeling that everything—everything I thought I knew—was about to unravel.

The city felt different tonight, the usual buzz of cars and chatter strangely muted as if even Chicago knew something was about to shift. The usual hum of life around me—the echo of heels on pavement, the low murmur of conversations in passing—seemed to fade into the background as I walked toward the familiar alleyway.

It had been a while since I'd come this way, but the memories of our last meeting, the tension that had gnawed at us both, still hung thick in the air.

I reached the dimly lit corner of a side street, where the shadows cast by the overhanging awnings created a sense of secrecy, of things half-hidden. A small diner at the corner blinked its neon lights, its cozy glow providing the only warmth on this otherwise cold night. Luca stood there, leaning against the brick, his figure silhouetted in the faint light. His usual confident stance seemed somehow more guarded tonight, like a lion in a cage, pacing at the edge but too wary to strike.

"You look...," I began, but my voice faltered. I didn't know what to say. Not tonight. Not when everything felt different.

"Different?" His lips twitched, and for a moment, there was the flicker of that boyish grin I was used to, but it didn't last long. He shoved his hands in his pockets, the way he always did when he was uncomfortable. "I guess I've had a lot on my mind. How about you?"

I stepped closer, the chill of the air prickling my skin. "A lot. More than I think I'm ready for."

His eyes softened for the briefest moment, but the mask quickly returned. "I'm sorry, Emily. I never wanted to drag you into this mess. Into my mess."

"You're being cryptic again," I said, my words slipping out sharper than I intended. I wasn't sure if I was angry at him or frustrated with myself. Or both. "Just tell me what's going on. What's happening with the Vellanos? Why are they—why are you—acting like this?"

His jaw tightened, and I could see the muscles in his neck flex. He wasn't going to make it easy. I could tell that much. But the distance between us was no longer just physical; it was everything.

Something had changed between us, something I wasn't sure I could fix, even if I tried.

"The Vellanos..." He trailed off, his gaze flicking nervously toward the street. A few people passed by, heads down, minds focused elsewhere, but the air around us thickened with unspoken things. "There's a lot you don't know. A lot I've kept from you."

"And why is that?" I asked, taking another step closer. His eyes locked onto mine, and for a moment, I thought I saw something flicker in the depths of his gaze—something raw and untold. But then, just as quickly, it was gone.

"Because I thought I could keep you out of it. Keep you safe," he said, his voice rougher than usual. "But now it's all coming down. All of it."

I crossed my arms over my chest, fighting to keep my composure. "Luca, you're not making sense. You're never making sense. You act like you're trying to protect me, but all you're doing is pushing me further away. I need the truth. I need you to stop lying to me."

He flinched, the smallest movement, but I saw it. His mask slipped for just a second, and the man I thought I knew—the one who was always so sure, so invincible—was gone. In his place was someone unrecognizable, someone carrying a burden too heavy to bear alone.

"This is bigger than you think," he murmured, his eyes darkening. "Bigger than anything I ever wanted to drag you into. The Vellanos don't just run the city. They run everything—business, politics, even the police. You've got no idea what it's like to be in the center of it all."

I swallowed hard, my throat tightening. "I'm in the center now. You've brought me here."

Luca took a step forward, his presence looming over me, and for a moment, I was acutely aware of the space between us. "I didn't mean to. I didn't want you involved. But it's too late now. You're too deep, and so am I."

"You're not making sense, Luca. What happened? What aren't you telling me?" My voice cracked slightly, betraying the fear I'd been fighting to keep buried.

He looked away, his eyes flicking to the street once more, as if seeking an escape. I could see the struggle on his face. I could feel the tension coiling between us, thick and suffocating. The Vellano empire wasn't just a family business—it was a shadow, a beast with many heads, and I was standing in the middle of its jaws.

"I told you," he said, his voice low, "it's bigger than both of us. There are things... dangerous things, things I can't undo."

"What things?" I demanded. My heart was hammering in my chest, each word slicing deeper.

He sighed, exhaling sharply as he scrubbed a hand over his face. "There's a deal. A trade. A partnership I made before I even met you. I thought I could control it. Thought I could—"

"What did you do, Luca?" The words slipped out before I could stop them, fear and frustration blending into something too heavy for me to ignore.

His eyes locked with mine, the weight of the moment pressing down on both of us. And then, just as quickly, the walls came back up. He was Luca again, the man I thought I knew—the one who always had an answer, a plan, a way out.

"I'll fix it. I'll fix everything. You just need to trust me."

I shook my head, backing away slightly. "Trust you? You've been lying to me since day one. What makes you think I can trust you now?"

His face fell, but only for a second. Then he was back to his usual self—distant, guarded. "I never wanted you to be a part of this, Emily. But you are now. And I'll do whatever it takes to keep you safe."

But his words, the ones that should have reassured me, only deepened the doubt that was already growing. The more he said, the more I realized: the more I trusted him, the more I was likely to lose.

I stood there, the icy wind biting at my skin, the weight of Luca's words hanging heavy in the space between us. His eyes, once so full of certainty, were now shrouded in something darker, something that pulled at the edges of my trust like a slow, deliberate unraveling. I wanted to walk away, wanted to storm off and never look back, but something—some primal urge to understand, to know the truth—kept me rooted to the spot.

"I told you," Luca said again, his voice low but strained, like it was taking every ounce of effort to keep the walls up. "You don't understand what I've been trying to protect you from. You don't get the danger."

"The danger?" I echoed, my voice a little sharper than I meant it to be. "I think you don't understand what I'm capable of, Luca. I'm not some fragile thing you can lock away and protect. I'm in this now, whether you like it or not."

He stiffened at my words, a brief flicker of something—I wasn't sure if it was anger or fear—passing across his face. He pushed off the wall and took a step toward me, his boots scraping against the wet pavement, the sound almost too loud in the quiet of the alley.

"You think you know what you're dealing with? You have no idea," he said, his words rough with frustration. "I've been in this world long enough to know that you never get out unscathed. You think you can just waltz in and make it right?"

I stared at him, heart pounding in my chest. "I don't need you to tell me what I'm capable of. I've been in enough messes to know how to handle myself."

He took another step closer, the space between us shrinking, and for a moment, it felt like everything was closing in. Like the walls of the city were tightening, pressing in on us both, suffocating the air around us. "This isn't just a mess, Emily. This is a war."

The words hit harder than I expected. War? How could I have been so blind? I had been chasing the wrong answers, asking the wrong questions. I had thought that it was just about the Vellano family, just about the empire they'd built. But no—there was something much bigger at play here, something deeper. Something that had been waiting to destroy everything.

"And you didn't think to warn me about this?" I whispered, the words coming out like acid. "About the war, the danger—everything that's been right in front of me?"

Luca looked away, guilt flashing across his face. "I never wanted you to be involved, Emily. But now... now I don't know how to get you out of it."

My mind raced, and for the first time, the pieces seemed to fit together—not in a way that made sense, but in a way that made my heart race with dread. I had been thinking small, thinking about the immediate, the here and now. But Luca was right. This was bigger than anything I'd imagined. This wasn't about a family feud or a betrayal. This was about survival—on a scale I couldn't begin to comprehend.

Before I could form another word, a noise interrupted us, a distant echo of a car door slamming shut. Luca's eyes snapped to the source of the sound, his whole body tensing, alert. "They're here," he muttered, more to himself than to me.

My pulse quickened. "Who? Who's here?"

He didn't answer, didn't have to. His actions spoke louder than words as he reached for my arm and pulled me toward the alley's narrow entrance, dragging me into the darkness with him. My heart hammered against my ribcage, the adrenaline coursing through me as I tried to make sense of everything.

We ducked into the shadows, just as the sound of footsteps—urgent, purposeful—grew louder. I could hear muffled voices now, low and indistinct, but there was something about the tone that made my blood run cold. This wasn't just an ordinary late-night stroll through the city; these were men on a mission. Men who didn't care about anything other than what they'd come to take.

Luca's grip on my wrist tightened, his fingers digging into my skin as he pulled me further into the darkness. "Stay quiet," he hissed. "Don't make a sound."

I nodded, though every part of me wanted to shout, wanted to ask him why—why hadn't he told me everything? Why had he kept me in the dark, playing this dangerous game with my life? But now wasn't the time for questions. Now was the time to survive.

We crouched against the cool brick wall of a nearby building, my heart thudding painfully in my chest as the footsteps grew closer. I held my breath, trying not to make a sound, trying to stay as still as possible, but I could feel the weight of the situation pressing on me, suffocating me in its intensity.

Luca's breath was shallow beside me, his body rigid with tension. I could feel the faint tremor in his hand where it still gripped my wrist, and I realized just how much of this had never been in his control. How much of it—all of it—had been spiraling out of his reach from the very beginning.

The footsteps stopped, and I barely dared to breathe, afraid that even the slightest sound would give us away. My eyes darted around the dark alley, looking for any escape, but the street was a labyrinth of shadows, each corner hiding something I couldn't quite see.

Suddenly, a voice broke the silence, harsh and sharp. "Where are they?"

It was the kind of voice that made the hairs on the back of my neck stand up. The kind that promised danger. And it wasn't just directed at Luca.

It was directed at me.

I swallowed hard, my mind racing. "Luca," I whispered, barely able to form the words. "What is happening?"

He didn't answer. Instead, his eyes met mine—wide, frantic—and for the first time, I saw fear in his expression. Real fear. Fear for me. Fear for both of us.

And then, just as quickly as it had come, the light of the alley flickered. The men were moving again, their voices growing louder.

This wasn't a game anymore. This was war. And now, I was in it, whether I liked it or not.

Chapter 15: The Truth Beneath the Surface

The sun hung low over the skyline of Chicago, casting long shadows across the quiet streets, where the scent of fresh rain lingered in the air, mingling with the faint aroma of exhaust and old coffee. It was a city that pulsed with secrets, a place where the truth was always a little bit out of reach. But tonight, I was determined to find it, even if it meant digging up things I wasn't sure I was ready to uncover.

I stood in front of a dilapidated brownstone on a street that had seen better days. The peeling paint on the building matched the state of my nerves, each layer cracking and crumbling as I stepped closer to the door. It wasn't the sort of place you came to unless you had no other choice, and for once, I was that desperate.

I could feel the weight of Luca's betrayal pressing down on me, each breath coming harder than the last. It had been days since I'd first started to notice the cracks in the story he'd been feeding me. Small things at first—a missed phone call, a late-night text he wouldn't show me, a slip of his hand as it brushed against mine. Nothing that could have tipped me off if I hadn't been looking for it. But I had been, and now I couldn't unsee it.

The door creaked open before I could knock. His face, usually so confident, so impenetrable, was now lined with something I couldn't quite place. Fear, maybe. Or guilt. But there was no mistaking the flicker of recognition in his eyes as he stepped back, motioning for me to enter.

I didn't need an invitation.

The air inside was thick with the smell of cigarette smoke and something more metallic, like the scent of regret clinging to the walls. Luca didn't speak as he led me down the narrow hallway, his footsteps echoing in the silence. It was as if he was trying to avoid saying anything that might tip me off, as if the truth could slip through his lips at any moment if we weren't careful enough.

The dim light from the cracked bulbs above cast a yellow hue over everything, making the place feel even more like a forgotten relic of a time no one cared to remember. It was a far cry from the sleek, polished world Luca usually moved in, a world I had been so eager to be a part of. But tonight, all of that seemed irrelevant. What mattered was the truth. Or, more precisely, what he had been hiding from me.

I stopped in the middle of the room, turning to face him, and couldn't help but notice the way his jaw clenched, the way his hands fidgeted at his sides. He wasn't the calm, collected man I had come to rely on. He was a stranger. And that realization hit me harder than I expected.

"Luca, what's going on?" I asked, my voice softer this time, almost pleading.

He met my gaze, but there was nothing reassuring in his eyes. Only a deep, unspoken sorrow. "It's not what you think," he muttered, his voice low, almost a whisper.

I shook my head, frustration bubbling to the surface. "Stop. Don't feed me that anymore. I need the truth. The real truth."

He took a deep breath and let it out slowly, like he was gathering the courage to say something that would change everything. I could see the internal struggle written across his face, the tension in his shoulders, the way he kept looking away, as if he were afraid to face me fully.

"What are you hiding?" I demanded, my voice trembling.

For a moment, he was silent, and I thought he might not answer at all. But then, finally, he spoke, his words hanging in the air between us like a heavy fog.

"Something you're not ready to hear," he replied, his expression haunted, distant. "Something that might break us."

I swallowed hard, the words cutting through me like shards of glass. I didn't want to hear that. I didn't want to believe that what had once seemed so simple could suddenly spiral into something unrecognizable.

"I don't care what it is," I said, my voice steady now, a resolve I hadn't known I possessed seeping through. "I need to know, Luca. I deserve to know."

He stared at me for a long, agonizing moment, as if weighing the cost of telling me. Then, with a quiet curse, he finally spoke.

"There's more to my past than you think. More than I've ever let you see," he said, his words slow and deliberate, like they were dragging a part of him out into the light that he'd rather keep buried.

I felt the air leave my lungs, a cold rush of disbelief and confusion washing over me. "What are you talking about?" I asked, my voice barely above a whisper.

"I've been involved in things—things I promised I'd leave behind," Luca confessed, his voice cracking under the weight of the admission. "But they don't just go away. Not when you've made the kind of deals I've made."

The pieces began to click into place, but I couldn't quite put them all together. The late nights, the strange phone calls, the tension that hung between us like an unspoken truth. It wasn't just about business. It was about something darker. Something far more dangerous than I had ever imagined.

"What kind of deals?" I asked, my heart pounding in my chest, each word feeling like a step closer to something I couldn't undo.

He didn't answer right away. Instead, he took a step back, his eyes darting to the door as if he were considering whether to run, to leave it all behind. But then he looked at me again, and there was a flicker of something in his gaze—regret, maybe, or sorrow—but also a hint of resignation.

"I can't protect you from it anymore," he said quietly, his voice thick with emotion. "And I don't know how to make things right."

The air between us thickened, the unspoken truth hanging in the space like a guillotine waiting to fall.

The words he spoke hung in the air like a cloud, thick and oppressive. I could almost feel the weight of them pressing down on my chest, tightening my breath until I thought I might suffocate. His gaze never wavered, but there was a coldness in it that I hadn't seen before, a quiet defeat that settled between us, making the air feel even heavier than it had moments before.

I wanted to scream at him. I wanted to demand that he tell me everything, right there, but I couldn't bring myself to. Instead, I stood there, rooted to the spot, feeling the floor beneath me tilt slightly as if the whole room was beginning to crumble. The overwhelming silence stretched between us, louder than any words we could have spoken.

Luca shifted his weight from one foot to the other, his hands still hanging by his sides. His fingers twitched once, almost imperceptibly, and for a moment, I thought I saw something flicker in his eyes—a flash of guilt, perhaps, or fear—but it was gone before I could place it. The man I had spent so many months with, the one who had looked at me with such certainty, was now nothing but a stranger, his secrets echoing off the walls like a warning I hadn't heard until it was too late.

"You can't keep doing this," I said, the words tumbling out, trembling with the hurt I couldn't hold back. "You've been keeping things from me. Big things. How long were you going to wait until you told me, huh? Until I found out the hard way?"

His lips pressed together, a thin line that said more than any words ever could. I was sure he was about to say something,

something to reassure me, to calm the storm he had clearly seen brewing in my eyes, but instead, he let out a breath, ragged and low.

"Some things... they don't go away, not just because you want them to," Luca finally said, his voice hollow. It didn't sound like him—didn't sound like the man who had laughed at my stupid jokes, or kissed me in the rain on the rooftop, or held me close when the world felt too big and too loud. This man, standing in front of me now, was nothing like the one I thought I knew.

I took a step toward him, the air between us crackling with tension. "You're not making any sense," I whispered, hoping that somehow, my desperation would make him see reason. "What do you mean, Luca? What do you think will happen if you just tell me the truth?"

He winced, a muscle twitching in his jaw. For a moment, I thought he might crack, might crumble under the weight of my words, but then he straightened himself up, his posture stiffening, the walls he'd built around himself rising again.

"You really don't want to know," he muttered, shaking his head, but I could see the glint of something darker in his eyes. "If I tell you, it changes everything. You won't look at me the same way again."

The words hit me like a slap, my breath catching in my throat. "How could you say that? How could you think I'd—"

"I'm not who you think I am, Ivy," Luca cut in sharply, his voice suddenly so raw it startled me. "I've never been who you think I am. And I've spent every goddamn second of the past year trying to keep you from knowing just how far I've fallen."

I froze, his words sinking in like stones into still water, sending ripples through every part of me I had been trying so desperately to keep whole. My mind raced, pieces of the puzzle I'd been trying to put together suddenly shifting into place. His secrecy, his sudden absences, the way he'd never let me get too close to his past. It wasn't just a matter of privacy; it was something far worse.

"You're involved in something illegal, aren't you?" The realization slipped from my lips before I could stop it, the words tasting sour in my mouth.

Luca's face hardened, and for the first time since we'd met, I saw fear—not for himself, but for me. His eyes darted around the room, as if he were looking for a way out, a way to make this all go away. But there was no escape. Not anymore.

"I didn't want you to know," he said, his voice tight, regret lining every syllable. "I never wanted you to get caught up in this mess. But now—" He stopped, swallowing hard. "Now it's too late."

I wanted to say something, anything that would make him see how wrong this was, how utterly ridiculous it was for him to think that keeping this from me was a form of protection. But the words stuck in my throat. How could I even begin to process what I was hearing?

"You don't get to decide what I know, Luca," I said, my voice low but unwavering. "I deserve the truth, all of it, no matter how ugly it is. You owe me that much."

He winced at my words, but I could see the truth of them reflected in his eyes, that familiar flicker of vulnerability that had always been hidden beneath the surface, just out of reach. But now it was exposed, raw and unguarded.

"I didn't want you to see it like this," he whispered, more to himself than to me. "I didn't want to drag you into my world. But I can't hide from it anymore, and neither can you."

The weight of his confession hung between us, but I wasn't ready to let him off the hook—not when everything I'd believed about him was suddenly in question. "You've been lying to me, Luca. And I don't know how to fix that. I don't know if I even want to."

He opened his mouth as if to say something, but then stopped, closing his eyes briefly, as though bracing himself for the fallout. When he spoke again, his voice was a strained whisper, the words heavy with a truth I wasn't sure I was prepared to bear.

"Then maybe it's already too late to fix it, Ivy."

The air between us crackled with the unsaid, thick as the summer humidity that lingered in the city's bones, even as the evening drew near. I could feel the weight of his words still hanging around us, like smoke, refusing to dissipate. Luca stood there, so close, but it felt like miles stretched between us. The man I had loved, trusted, held close, was no longer the same person, not in this moment. Not in the silence that pulsed with unspoken truths.

"You've already said more than you should," I finally managed, the words more an accusation than a question. My heart felt like it had lodged itself in my throat, each beat an attempt to break free. "What does that even mean, Luca? You're trying to keep me in the dark, but I can see it now. You've been lying to me for months. Maybe longer."

His lips twitched, almost a smile, but there was no humor in it. No warmth. "Lying's a strong word."

I laughed—a harsh, bitter sound that filled the room. "Oh, I think it's the right one. You've been lying by omission, you know that, right? Keeping secrets like they're some kind of shield. But the thing is, you can only hide things for so long. And now, here we are."

He didn't look at me, his gaze fixed on a spot somewhere over my shoulder, somewhere past me, like he was seeing something I couldn't. Something that wasn't meant for me. His body seemed smaller in the dim light, his usual confidence deflated, but still, he refused to let me in.

"I never wanted you to see me like this," Luca muttered, almost to himself. "You wouldn't look at me the same if you knew everything. If you understood the things I've done... the things I've had to do."

"You're right," I said, each word a stab in the quiet. "I wouldn't look at you the same. But I'll be damned if you think I can walk away from this, just pretend none of it happened. If you think I can pretend I didn't notice, that I didn't care enough to dig, you're wrong. I have to know, Luca. I have to understand why."

He took a long breath, finally meeting my eyes. There was a flicker of something—regret, maybe? Or was it fear? His brow furrowed, and I could feel his internal struggle like a tug of war inside of him. The silence that stretched between us seemed endless, filled with years of untold stories and unspoken apologies.

"You think you're ready to hear it?" Luca asked, his voice sharp, like a man edging closer to the edge of a cliff. "Because once you know, there's no going back. I'm not the guy you've been holding on to, Ivy. I never was."

I took a deep breath, shaking my head. "I'm already in this. I'm already invested in you. You don't get to drop some cryptic line and think that'll make me walk away. That's not how this works."

For a moment, there was nothing but the sound of our breaths and the hum of the refrigerator in the corner. The seconds dragged on, ticking away in the stale air as I waited for him to speak again, to finally reveal the truth that had been simmering between us for so long.

Finally, Luca moved, his hand reaching into his jacket pocket. He pulled out a small, weathered envelope and tossed it onto the coffee table between us, his eyes not meeting mine as he spoke.

"I didn't want you involved, Ivy," he said, his voice thick with something unspoken. "But it's too late now. You're already deeper in than you realize."

I glanced at the envelope, the thin paper so unassuming, so simple in its plainness, yet it felt like it carried the weight of everything between us. I hesitated, unsure whether I should touch it, but I knew the answer before I even made the move.

With trembling hands, I reached forward and unfolded the paper. Inside was a single photograph, yellowed at the edges, a snapshot of a place I recognized immediately: the docks along the riverfront, the old warehouses that had long since been abandoned. But it wasn't the buildings that struck me. It was the people in the photo—three men, Luca among them, standing side by side with grim faces, their hands tucked into their pockets. They were standing by the water, the darkened sky above them reflecting in the glassy surface of the river.

Luca had never mentioned the docks before. He'd always been so careful about the parts of his life that existed outside of the time I'd known him. But this? This was something different. Something I couldn't ignore. The men in the photograph weren't just innocuous figures—there was a heaviness to their stance, a tension in the way they held themselves, that made my stomach turn.

"What is this?" I asked, my voice barely above a whisper as I lifted my eyes to meet his. "Who are these people? What am I looking at?"

Luca didn't answer immediately. Instead, he ran a hand through his hair, pushing it back from his forehead with frustration. His eyes flickered to the photo before shifting away again.

"It's a part of my life you weren't meant to see," he said, the words clipped, cold. "And it's the part that's going to ruin everything if you keep digging. The people in that photo... they're not just anybody. They're connected to things I promised myself I'd leave behind."

I wanted to ask him everything. I wanted to scream, to demand that he explain himself, but the look on his face—the raw pain and the depth of what he wasn't saying—stopped me cold.

"And if I keep digging?" I asked, the words coming out before I could stop them. "What happens then, Luca?"

For the first time since we'd met, Luca's gaze faltered, his shoulders sagging with a burden I couldn't yet understand.

"If you keep digging, Ivy, you might just find that you're not the one who's in danger anymore." His voice was barely audible now, like a confession he couldn't take back. "And when you do find out what's really going on, it might already be too late to save yourself."

I felt the blood drain from my face. The room seemed to spin, the walls closing in around me as the weight of his words crashed over me like a tidal wave. And then, as if on cue, the sound of a door slamming in the distance echoed through the building—footsteps, too heavy to ignore, drawing closer.

I had no time to process, no time to think. But one thing was certain: I was no longer just a bystander in Luca's life. And whatever he was mixed up in, it was coming for me now, too.

Chapter 16: Beneath the Iron Mask

The silence thickens around us, suffocating in its weight. Luca's gaze doesn't waver from mine, his dark eyes gleaming with an intensity that's unsettling, yet impossible to look away from. The faint scent of cologne lingers in the air—rich and smoky, a reminder that he's still here, standing in my kitchen, his presence filling the space in ways I can't ignore.

My fingers curl against the countertop, the smooth marble cold beneath my skin. I could scream, I could run, I could pretend none of this is happening, but that would mean admitting something I'm not ready to face.

"I didn't ask for your confession, Luca," I say, my voice trembling just enough to betray the control I'm trying so desperately to hold onto. "You should've stayed in your cage, like everyone else. Silent. Invisible."

He doesn't flinch. Instead, he steps closer, one slow, deliberate movement after another, until I can feel the heat from his body, the crackling electricity between us. It's as if he's trying to close the distance not just physically, but emotionally, too, as though he believes his proximity will somehow make the impossible more tangible.

"You think I have a choice?" His voice is quiet but piercing, and my breath hitches in my throat. "I didn't ask for this debt either, Amelia. I didn't ask to be entangled in this mess, but here I am. And you... you think I can just walk away? You think that would make anything better?"

His words sink in, dragging me deeper into a web I've spent so many years trying to avoid. The betrayal, the unspoken truth hanging between us—his past, my uncle, the weight of their shared history—it's all unraveling like a ball of yarn in my mind, twisting and tangling around the pieces I'd carefully kept in place.

I turn my back to him, but I can still feel his presence like a force pushing against my spine. I grip the edge of the sink, needing something to steady myself. I have no clue how to react to any of this. Anger? Disbelief? Hurt? They all vie for attention, but none of them seem adequate. What do you do when the person you've trusted, the person who's become an anchor in the storm, reveals they've been a part of the very chaos you've tried to escape?

"You're lying to me," I whisper, my voice barely a breath. "You're hiding something. If this was truly a matter of debts and loyalty, why not come clean sooner? Why wait until now?"

The question is out before I can stop it, and I feel foolish for asking it. It's as if I'm begging for him to give me a reason to hate him, to push him away, to make the decision easier. But Luca doesn't flinch. He simply stands there, looking at me, his expression unreadable.

"I didn't lie," he says, his words measured, careful, as though he's trying to pull together pieces of a puzzle that have long been scattered. "But there are things you don't understand. There are things I can't explain, not yet."

"You think I'm some innocent little girl, don't you?" I spin to face him, finally unable to keep the bitterness at bay. "You think I don't know what happens in this world? What people like you are capable of?"

His lips twitch slightly, the hint of a smirk playing at the edges of his mouth, but it's gone before I can truly catch it. "I think you've seen more than you want to. You've grown up surrounded by lies, Amelia. You've learned to bury the truth deep enough that it doesn't even bother you. But there's a cost to that. A price you haven't even started to pay yet."

The words stoke a flame in me, igniting the fury I've kept so carefully under wraps. But before I can snap back, I feel it—a shift in the air, a tension so thick I can taste it. It's something heavier than the secrets we're both carrying, something deeper. There's a hunger in his gaze now, a hunger that makes my stomach tighten, my skin prickle, and every instinct in me scream to flee.

But I don't.

I stand my ground, even as the distance between us closes, until his breath is on my cheek, hot and heavy, like it's meant to scorch me. The suddenness of it catches me off guard, and I stagger back, bumping into the counter, but Luca doesn't give me a chance to regain my footing. His hand shoots out, steadying me, a touch that should feel like comfort but instead ignites something entirely different.

"You think you're the only one who's trapped in all of this?" he says, his voice now a soft rasp against my ear, and I shiver, whether from the chill in his tone or the heat in his proximity, I can't tell. "You think I don't feel it? Every damn day?"

I pull away from him, shaking my head, but the sudden movement only brings me closer to him. I'm drowning in this space, in his words, in the need I've been too stubborn to acknowledge. I'm suffocating, yet I can't breathe without him. And it scares me more than I care to admit.

"I don't need your pity, Luca," I whisper, the words slipping out before I can stop them, my voice cracking with something raw and real.

He doesn't answer. Instead, his gaze holds mine with such intensity that I wonder if he can see straight through the walls I've built. If he knows all the places I've hidden myself in, all the ways I've kept the truth buried deep enough that even I can't quite find it.

"I'm not giving you pity, Amelia," he says, the words laced with something darker, something that doesn't fit the man I thought I knew. "I'm giving you a warning. A chance. You're not as safe as you think."

I want to scream at him, demand to know why he waited until now to drop this bombshell on me, why he had to wait until I'd already tangled my life so thoroughly in his. But the words don't come. They get stuck somewhere between my heart and my throat, caught in the web of confusion and betrayal and—if I'm being honest—something darker, more dangerous, that I don't want to admit to myself.

His eyes flicker, just for a second, to the door behind me. And in that split moment, I know that if I move—if I take one step in the direction of that exit—I'll leave him standing here, locked in whatever trap he's wrapped himself in. Whatever ties bind him to my uncle. Whatever debt he thinks he owes.

But the words slip through before I can stop them. "What exactly are you asking me to do here, Luca? Do you want me to save you? Or is this just your twisted way of trying to make me feel sorry for you?"

I take a step forward, closer to him now, and I don't know if it's a show of strength or just my body acting out some impulse I can't explain. He's too close, too magnetic, and I can almost feel the weight of the things he's not saying. They hang between us like an unspoken dare.

"You're not the one who needs saving," he says, his voice almost a growl, low and resonant. "You're the one I've been trying to protect."

I laugh—a sharp, bitter sound that echoes off the kitchen walls, and it tastes wrong coming from me. "Protect? From what, exactly?"

His gaze never leaves mine, and in that moment, I know he's trying to figure out if he should explain, if it's worth it. "I've made too many mistakes to count," he says quietly. "But you don't get to be angry at me for the choices I've made. Not yet."

I snort, the bitterness and resentment swirling like venom in my veins. "Not yet? Not yet, Luca?" The room feels impossibly small now, the walls pressing in, and I feel like I'm suffocating. "I've been stuck in this nightmare of your making for months, trying to figure out what your game is, what you want from me, and now you're telling me you're just trying to protect me? You should've told me this, Luca. A long time ago. Not after you've had me tangled in all of this. Not when I've already started to—" I stop myself, unwilling to finish that thought. There's no way to say it without it sounding like I'm already in too deep.

His expression softens, just a little, his brow furrowing like he's not entirely sure what to say. "I didn't want you to be involved in this. I didn't want you anywhere near my mess."

I look away, focusing on the small, familiar details around me—the chipped edge of the kitchen counter, the faintest trace of dust on the window sill—anything to avoid the overwhelming intensity of his gaze.

"But here we are." His voice has dropped an octave, and when I glance back at him, his face is set with a stubborn resolve that almost makes my pulse quicken. "And I'll make sure you walk away from it, Amelia. You just need to trust me."

I shake my head, the frustration in me boiling over now. "Trust you?" The word tastes bitter, like sour wine. "You've lied to me from the start. You've built this web of lies around me, and now you want me to trust you? After everything? After everything you've kept hidden? How can I possibly—"

I cut myself off, realizing the words aren't just coming from anger, but from fear. Fear that what I thought I knew about Luca, what I believed about him, was never real. Fear that he could destroy me with one word, one secret, one twist of the knife.

He steps closer, too close, and my pulse jumps. "I'm not asking for your trust, Amelia. Not yet." His hand reaches for mine, a tentative gesture, like he's not sure if I'll pull away. "I'm asking for a chance to prove that I can fix this. That I can fix what's broken between us."

There it is again. The pull, the magnetic force between us that feels like an insatiable need. It's like standing too close to an open flame, knowing that the longer I stay, the more I'll burn, but too mesmerized by the heat to step back.

My chest tightens, but I won't let him see the effect he has on me. "What's broken between us?" The words feel raw, the bitterness thickening my throat. "You think you can fix this? You think that after everything you've done, everything you've kept hidden, that you can just waltz in and make it all go away?"

I hear myself and know it's irrational. I know the heat of my emotions is clouding my judgment. But it doesn't matter. The distance between us feels like an ocean, a chasm of broken trust and jagged edges, and I'm not sure I can cross it. Not without sinking.

"I'm not asking for forgiveness, Amelia," Luca says quietly, his hand still hovering just inches from mine. "I'm asking for you to look at me—really look at me—and understand that I didn't do this to hurt you."

But that's the thing, isn't it? Because I already know he never meant to hurt me. But what about the hurt I've felt because of him? The way he's woven himself so deeply into the fabric of my life that now, letting go would feel like cutting off a part of myself. Even if I wanted to escape, there's no way I could sever this tie. I know too much now. I'm in too deep.

I pull away, taking a step back, my breath uneven. I can't—no, I won't—let myself be caught in the web of his intentions. Not until I know the truth. Not until I can see beneath the mask he wears.

"We'll see, won't we?" I say softly, though the words feel like shards of glass in my mouth. "We'll see if you can fix it."

I can feel the air between us crackling, charged with something too complicated to be defined by a simple glance or an easy word. Luca stands there, close enough that I can feel the heat of his body, but still far enough away that it feels like he's placed a gulf between us—one I don't know how to cross. His confession—his sudden vulnerability—sits like a bruise, dark and bruising, beneath the surface of everything I thought I knew.

I should be angry. Furious, even. The lies, the manipulation, the fact that he's been keeping secrets like a dog hoarding bones—these should be the things that drown out everything else. But there's a quiet voice, deep in the back of my mind, whispering that there's more to this. That there's something beneath the iron mask Luca wears—something that even now, as he stands before me, raw and exposed in ways I've never seen, is still too dangerous to ignore.

"Don't play the martyr with me," I say, my words sharper than I mean them to be. "You don't owe me anything. You never did."

He doesn't flinch at my words. He's used to this—used to the walls I put up, the armor I wear like a second skin. But I can feel him still, beneath that calm exterior. He's testing me, pushing me to react, waiting to see if I'll break the way I always do.

"I know," he replies, his voice tight, but there's a flicker of something in his gaze—something that says he understands, even if he doesn't want to. "But I owe your uncle more than you could possibly know. And until that debt is repaid, I'll do whatever I can to keep you safe."

I laugh again, bitter and hollow, unable to stop it. "Safe?" The word tastes like a joke on my tongue. "Safe from what? From you? From him?" I gesture vaguely to the whole situation, the tangled mess we've found ourselves in.

He steps forward, his shadow falling over me like a storm cloud. The distance between us has closed, but instead of feeling comforted, I feel cornered. "Not from me, Amelia. From what's coming."

I don't have the strength to fight anymore, not really. The confusion, the betrayal, the anger—it's all muddled now, a strange cocktail that leaves me feeling dizzy and unsure. I know he's right about one thing. Something's coming. I can feel it, like the low hum of a storm on the horizon.

"Don't give me that," I murmur, running a hand through my hair, trying to find some kind of control in the chaos. "You've been dodging me, hiding from me for months. What's so damn urgent now? Why should I believe a word you say?"

His eyes darken, and for the first time, I see something close to desperation in his expression. "Because if you don't, Amelia, you're going to end up in the middle of something you can't walk away from. Something I never wanted you involved in, but now? You've got no choice."

He moves again, his hand brushing against mine, and for a brief second, I feel the shock of it—electric and foreign, like a live wire that snaps me back into focus. His fingers hesitate, just long enough for me to pull away, but I can see the struggle in his face. The battle between keeping me at arm's length and pulling me into something far deeper.

I can't breathe in the space between us. It's like we're both drowning, only neither of us knows how to swim.

"What are you asking me to do, Luca?" My voice cracks, though I wish it didn't. I can't show him how much this is affecting me, can't let him see that I'm just as lost as he is in this.

His lips part as if he's about to speak, but nothing comes out at first. His brow furrows as though he's weighing something heavy, something buried under all the lies and secrets. Finally, his voice breaks through the silence. "I'm asking you to trust me."

The words land between us, heavy and impossible. The simple plea, the simplicity of it, makes my pulse stutter. I don't want to. I don't want to trust him. He's lied. He's kept me in the dark. But the desperate edge in his tone—something in the way he's watching me, like he's begging me to see the truth—makes me hesitate.

"I can't," I whisper, the words feeling too fragile for the weight of the room. I turn away from him, my hand pressing against my mouth to still the tremble that threatens to betray me. "I can't trust you, Luca. I can't even trust myself right now."

He doesn't reply, but I feel him there—just behind me, his presence pressing against the air like an electric current. It's almost too much to bear, the weight of everything left unsaid, the space between us pulling tighter with each passing second.

And then, as if the universe is reminding me just how far gone we both are, my phone rings, slicing through the tension in the room like a blade. I jump at the sound, the unexpected intrusion breaking the moment. I look down at the screen, the name flashing across it like a warning sign.

It's my uncle.

Luca's eyes flick to my phone, his expression unreadable. His jaw tightens, and for the first time, I see the barest hint of something like fear—real fear—cross his face.

"Don't," he says, his voice low, but there's a distinct note of urgency in it now. "Don't pick up."

But it's too late. I answer the call before I can even think about it.

"Amelia," my uncle's voice crackles through the line, sharp and brittle. "Get out of there. Now."

The command is clear, but it's the fear in his tone that makes my blood run cold.

"What's going on?" I ask, panic threading through my voice, though I try to keep it steady. "What's happening?"

"You don't have time for this. You need to leave now, Amelia."

Before I can reply, the call abruptly ends, leaving nothing but the eerie silence between me and Luca.

I look at him, my heart hammering in my chest, as a chill crawls up my spine.

"Now what?" I whisper.

Luca's eyes darken, his hand suddenly gripping my arm with surprising force. "Now, you get in the car. And you don't ask questions. Not yet."

Chapter 17: The Web Tightens

I could feel the tension curling through the heavy air of the estate, thick like the steam rising from the freshly poured coffee in front of me. The grand dining room had always been the sort of place where secrets whispered behind velvet curtains, yet never in all my years had it seemed more suffocating. My fingers brushed the rim of my cup, its warmth a fleeting comfort in the sea of discomfort that settled within me.

Uncle Victor's voice, smooth and polished, floated from the other side of the room, where he was speaking to Emiliano DeLuca. It was a tone I knew well—a public voice, layered with charm and politeness, designed to disarm. And yet, there was something colder, sharper about it this time, something that made the hairs on the back of my neck stand on end.

Emiliano DeLuca. The name alone sent a ripple of unease through my stomach. The DeLucas weren't known for their generosity of spirit. The family had built their empire on a foundation of shadows and alliances forged in darker places, their influence stretching across the city in ways most didn't dare to imagine. And now, here he was, in our house, under the guise of diplomacy, looking every bit the part of a man who was accustomed to both power and manipulation.

I couldn't help but watch him from the corner of my eye, his dark eyes taking in everything with an intensity that bordered on unsettling. His raven-black hair, perfectly styled, contrasted sharply against his sharply tailored suit. His smile was a weapon—too smooth, too practiced. Every inch of him screamed control, and it was hard to tell if he was genuinely interested in Uncle Victor's words or if he was simply toying with us, waiting for the right moment to strike.

And then, his gaze shifted to me. For a moment, our eyes locked, and I felt it—a strange, almost electric pull between us, as though his eyes were searching, probing, weighing the value of my very soul. I quickly averted my gaze, focusing on the untouched coffee in front of me, my hands gripping the delicate porcelain cup a little too tightly. My heart was pounding now, not just from the unsettling weight of his gaze but from something deeper, something I couldn't yet name.

"Perhaps, Miss Montgomery," Emiliano's voice cut through the charged silence like a blade, smooth and cold, "you'd care to join us? I hear your uncle speaks of your keen sense for strategy. It would be a pleasure to hear your thoughts."

I stiffened at the suggestion. Uncle Victor's world, his plans, were not ones I had any interest in participating in. I had enough on my plate as it was—managing the family's art gallery, keeping up appearances, maintaining the delicate balance between the public and private lives. Politics, especially the kind that smelled of old blood and unspoken deals, wasn't a place I intended to tread.

"Thank you, but no," I replied, my voice betraying none of the discomfort that twisted inside me. "I'm afraid I leave the more... calculating conversations to my uncle."

Emiliano's smile didn't falter, but there was a flicker of amusement in his eyes. "A wise woman," he said, as though the words were both a compliment and a subtle challenge.

I wanted to ignore him. I wanted to disappear into the background, to become nothing more than a passing presence in this room. But I couldn't. Not when every part of this interaction felt like it was unraveling a thread I wasn't ready to pull.

The conversation between my uncle and Emiliano continued, their voices blending into the background hum of the estate. I could feel the weight of their words, even without hearing the specifics. Every now and then, Uncle Victor's laugh would ring out, low and humorless, a reminder of the man I had known all my life—the man who had raised me, for better or worse.

But there was something off today. A subtle shift in the way he spoke. I could see it in the way he gestured toward Emiliano, the careful way he chose his words, the way he leaned in just a little too close when their conversation deepened. And the closer I looked, the more I realized—I was no longer a passive observer in this world. I had never been.

Hours passed, and dinner was served, the soft clink of silverware against fine china creating a rhythm that somehow felt too precise, too choreographed. Emiliano had become more than just a guest; he was a predator, circling, waiting.

I excused myself from the table, desperate to escape the suffocating atmosphere, but as I moved to leave the dining room, I overheard their voices once more, drifting toward me like the scent of old leather.

"Victor," Emiliano's voice was a murmur, low and dangerously calm. "You understand the consequences of this alliance, don't you? If we're going to move forward, we both know what needs to be done. You don't just tie the families together in business—this is a full merger. A new generation, if you will."

A chill crawled up my spine as I stopped just beyond the threshold of the door, hidden from view but not from hearing. My uncle's voice followed, smooth and patient. "Of course, Emiliano. But I trust you understand that my niece is no mere pawn in this game. She will serve her purpose. In time, you will see."

The words hung in the air like a poisoned gift, too sharp to be ignored. I wasn't just the niece anymore. I wasn't just some unassuming heir to an estate. No, I was something else—a piece in a much larger puzzle. And if I wasn't careful, I might be the one who was sacrificed for the sake of a game I never even knew I was playing.

I pulled away, my heart thundering in my chest, the taste of betrayal bitter on my tongue. What had Uncle Victor planned for me? What was I to become in this dangerous dance between two powerful families?

The weight of the night pressed down on me like a thousand invisible hands, each one pulling me deeper into the web they were weaving—until there was no way out but to play along. But I had to be careful. This game wasn't over. Not yet.

I wandered the halls of the estate, aimlessly at first, but my mind kept circling back to the conversation I'd overheard. Uncle Victor's words, coated in calculated calm, gnawed at the edges of my thoughts like a persistent itch I couldn't quite scratch. *In time, you will see.* What was that supposed to mean? He always had a way of speaking in riddles, but this felt different—more ominous. More like a warning wrapped in the promise of something grand, but sinister.

I wasn't even sure where I was headed, but the stillness of the manor was suddenly too much. It was too quiet, too perfect—an uneasy silence that pressed in from all sides. The estate, with its sprawling grounds and endless rooms, had always felt like a safe haven, a place where I could hide in plain sight. But now, it was like a labyrinth, every corner holding a new secret I wasn't sure I wanted to find.

I turned a corner and nearly collided with Luca, who stood in the doorway, looking as if he had been waiting for me. His steady presence was like a lifeline, a reassurance that I wasn't entirely alone in this twisted world my family inhabited.

"You're tense," he remarked, his voice soft but laced with a quiet authority that always seemed to wrap itself around me, grounding me when everything else felt like it might slip away.

I didn't answer at first, my gaze slipping to the grand staircase at the end of the hall. Something about the way the ornate banister curved up toward the upper floors—distant and unreachable—made my chest tighten.

"I'm fine," I said at last, turning my gaze back to Luca. "I just... don't like this. Don't like him."

Luca's expression didn't shift, but I saw the brief flicker of understanding in his eyes. "No one does," he said with a slight tilt of his head. "But you don't need to worry about him."

I raised an eyebrow, crossing my arms. "That's easy for you to say. You're not the one he's watching like a hawk."

Luca's lips curled into a faint smile, but there was no humor in it. "No, I'm not. But I'm also not the one he wants. You are."

I froze, my breath catching in my throat. He didn't need to elaborate; his meaning was clear. I'd known, on some level, that Emiliano's attention wasn't entirely innocent. The way he looked at me—it wasn't just curiosity or polite interest. It was something deeper, something more dangerous. And Uncle Victor had let it happen, had encouraged it.

Luca took a step closer, his voice low, almost conspiratorial. "Look, I don't trust DeLuca either. And I've got your back. Always have, always will." His eyes locked with mine, and for the first time that night, I felt like I was seeing a side of him I hadn't quite understood before—a side that wasn't just the loyal friend, but something more. Someone who was ready to fight if needed.

I swallowed, my throat dry. "And what do you think he wants from me?"

Luca didn't answer right away. Instead, he glanced over his shoulder, as if checking for eavesdroppers. "What I think doesn't matter," he said finally, his voice barely above a whisper. "What matters is what you do next."

I felt my stomach knot. The weight of it all—of what Uncle Victor had planned, of what Emiliano wanted, of what I was becoming in their eyes—pressed down on me like a vise. For the first time in my life, I wasn't sure who I could trust.

But I had no choice but to play the game.

"I don't know what to do," I confessed, the words slipping out before I could stop them. "I don't want to be anyone's pawn, Luca. But Uncle Victor—he's not giving me a choice."

Luca was quiet for a moment, his gaze distant, as if he were considering something far beyond the confines of the estate. Then he stepped forward, his hand briefly brushing mine. "You've always had a choice. The question is whether you're ready to take it."

The weight of his words lingered as I nodded, my mind swirling with possibilities, none of them particularly comforting. I wasn't naïve. I knew the game that was being played. But how did I fit into it?

The silence between us stretched, uncomfortable but filled with something unspoken. I wanted to believe him. I wanted to believe that I could somehow control my own fate, even in the face of everything my family was thrusting me into. But nothing felt certain anymore.

Just then, I heard the sound of voices drifting down from the dining room. Emiliano's smooth, polished tone was unmistakable, and though I couldn't make out his words, there was an unmistakable coldness to it. It wasn't the kind of voice that belonged in a room of allies. It was the voice of someone who expected something in return—someone who saw power in places others overlooked.

Luca must have sensed my shift in focus, for he gave my hand a gentle squeeze before stepping back. "We need to move quickly," he said, his eyes scanning the hallway, as if he, too, could feel the tightening noose around us. "DeLuca is a man who doesn't wait for permission. And your uncle—" he paused, his jaw tightening. "He's not exactly known for being patient."

I nodded, my heart racing as I glanced toward the dining room. Emiliano's words were getting louder, more insistent. And something in me shifted again, a flicker of understanding dawning. This wasn't about just keeping the peace anymore. It was about survival.

I turned to Luca, my resolve hardening. "Then it's time I stop playing along."

The estate was unnervingly quiet after Luca left me standing in the hallway. The shadows cast by the dim chandelier stretched long, warping along the walls like silent sentinels. I could still hear the faint hum of voices drifting from the dining room, punctuated by the occasional clink of glass. Emiliano's low, smooth tone sent an involuntary shiver down my spine. The air was thick with something unspoken, the taste of it metallic and sour.

I didn't know what Luca meant when he said, It's time I stop playing along, but I could guess. If we were going to survive whatever twisted web my uncle and Emiliano were weaving, I couldn't afford to keep pretending I didn't see the strings. The idea of playing by their rules—of being a pawn in a game I didn't even understand—felt suffocating. And yet, what else was there? I was trapped. My every move was watched. My future wasn't my own, and every choice I made would set off a chain of reactions that could either burn bridges or destroy everything I held dear.

I turned back toward the grand dining room, my heels clicking sharply on the polished wood floors, the sound strangely loud in the hushed atmosphere of the house. I had to face them. I had to confront the truth—no matter how jagged it felt in my chest.

As I reached the doorway, I hesitated for only a second before stepping inside. The room seemed impossibly grander than it had just hours ago, its high ceilings and gleaming chandeliers now oppressive, the space too vast for what it held. Emiliano sat at the head of the long dining table, the silver candelabra casting a soft glow on his dark features, making him appear even more dangerous, like a predator in a velvet-lined cage.

Uncle Victor, ever the picture of control, sat across from him, his face unreadable but his posture stiff, as if every movement were carefully orchestrated. Both men were consumed by their conversation, but I couldn't shake the feeling that the moment I entered the room, their focus would shift, their game revealed for what it was.

Emiliano's eyes flicked to me as I entered, a predatory gleam lighting them up for just a second, before he masked it with a smile so practiced it almost seemed rehearsed.

"Ah, Miss Montgomery," he said smoothly, his voice low and velvety. "We were just talking about you." The words, laced with a cold undertone, hung in the air like a dare. His gaze traced my figure slowly, deliberately. "I do hope you're not being neglected while we talk business."

I swallowed hard, forcing myself not to flinch under the weight of his stare. "I wouldn't dream of interrupting," I replied, my voice steady despite the pounding of my heart. "You two must have much to discuss."

Emiliano chuckled, his eyes narrowing ever so slightly. "Oh, we do. But what's business without a little bit of personal involvement? After all, family matters tend to be so... intricate, don't they?"

My pulse quickened, the quiet menace in his words sinking deep into my bones. I kept my expression neutral, though my mind raced. What exactly had my uncle promised him? And how was I supposed to play this game without losing everything?

Uncle Victor cleared his throat, a subtle but deliberate reminder that I was not yet dismissed. "I'm sure you're eager to hear what we've discussed, my dear," he said, his voice all smooth charm. But there was a flicker of something behind his eyes, something I couldn't place. "Perhaps Emiliano would like to share his thoughts on how we can move forward. We've always been a family of action."

I stiffened, my hand gripping the back of the chair just a little too hard, the carved wood cool against my palm. What was he doing? Was he really throwing me into this?

Emiliano leaned back in his chair, stretching his long legs under the table as if he had all the time in the world. "I think it's quite simple," he said with a smile that didn't reach his eyes. "Your uncle and I have an understanding, but you, Miss Montgomery, are the final piece of the puzzle." His words were deceptively casual, but the weight of them hit me like a sledgehammer.

I took a breath, forcing my voice to remain steady. "I'm not a piece in anyone's puzzle," I said firmly. "I have a life of my own."

Emiliano's smile widened, but it wasn't kind. "Oh, but you do, darling. Your life has already been written for you. You just haven't realized it yet."

The words hung in the air, thick and suffocating. I couldn't breathe. I didn't know if I wanted to slap him or scream, but the worst part was the truth behind his words—the reality of what my uncle had planned for me, what I had unwittingly walked into. He was right. I was already part of this game. I had been for years, but now the stakes were higher, and I had no idea how to navigate the world my family had created.

I glanced at Uncle Victor, my heart a chaotic storm inside my chest. His face was as impassive as ever, but there was something almost smug about the way he watched me now, as if he were waiting for me to bend to the pressure. Waiting for me to fall in line.

The realization was like ice water being poured over me, numbing me from the inside out. This wasn't about an alliance. This wasn't about family. This was a trap, and I was the bait. Emiliano DeLuca was no guest in this house. He was the enemy, and my uncle was playing both sides. And I? I was caught somewhere in the middle, stuck in a game I didn't know the rules for.

Before I could respond, before I could even process what was happening, the door to the dining room swung open, and in the frame stood Luca. His posture was stiff, his eyes sharp as they moved between us. He said nothing, but his presence alone felt like a shot fired into the thick tension in the room.

For a long moment, no one moved. Emiliano's gaze flicked to Luca, calculating. Then, his smile returned—this time, colder, more knowing.

"So, it seems we have more players on the field than I anticipated," he murmured.

Chapter 18: A Fractured Alliance

The apartment smells like old wood and fading lavender, a fragrance that once felt comforting but now clings to the walls like an apology I didn't ask for. I'm perched on the edge of the worn-out sofa, trying to ignore the creaking noise it makes as I shift my weight. My fingers hover over the bandages, the edges of the cloth crisp against my skin as I trace the rough outlines of Luca's knuckles. His hand, with its weathered skin and calloused fingers, shakes ever so slightly under mine, but not in the way I thought it would. It's the tremble of restraint, like a tightly wound coil about to snap.

He doesn't speak at first, and I can't blame him. Silence has become the default setting between us in the last few days, ever since that disastrous meeting with Emiliano. The man's name feels like a sour taste in my mouth now, as if I've been chewing on something bitter for far too long and I can't find the way to spit it out. Emiliano has a way of making everything feel like it's under a magnifying glass, his sharp eyes and arrogant posture always calculating, always reading a script that's never been written for anyone but him. His demands have a finality to them, an edge that slices through the air and leaves nothing untouched.

I pull the bandage tighter, and Luca flinches slightly, though his face remains stoic. I've grown accustomed to his quiet moments, the ones where he says nothing, but his presence fills the room with an intensity that's almost too much to bear. There's a part of me that wants to ask him about the things we never talk about—his past, his loyalties, the ones that bind him to people like Emiliano. But I don't. Instead, I settle on a question that feels safer, like I can keep my distance this way, even though the space between us has never felt so narrow.

"Do you ever get tired of being his weapon?" The words slip out sharper than I intend, like I'm trying to wound him without actually touching him.

He meets my gaze, his dark eyes flashing briefly with something I can't place. It's not anger, not exactly, but it's a tightness in the corners of his mouth that tells me he's heard the question a thousand times before, from a thousand different people. But I'm different. I have to be. Or at least, I like to think I am.

"It's better than being his pawn," he says, his voice low and steady, though the weight of it presses into my chest. His words are more than just a response; they're a quiet admission of something I've been dancing around for too long. And despite myself, I find my breath hitching in my throat, the way it always does when I'm forced to confront the truth. The truth that Luca's life, his choices, have always been dictated by someone else. And the fact that I'm still here, still trying to make sense of it, feels like an unforgivable mistake.

But I can't walk away. Not yet. Not when everything between us still feels unresolved, like two halves of a puzzle that might fit together if we just keep trying.

"You don't have to do this, Luca," I whisper, the words falling from my lips before I can stop them. I feel like I'm pleading, but it's a kind of pleading I'm not even sure he'll hear. "You don't owe him anything."

The silence that follows is heavier than I expect, stretching between us like a taut wire, ready to snap. He doesn't answer immediately, which only makes the tension in the room rise, suffocating me in its intensity. His gaze shifts, drifting to the window where the last remnants of daylight spill across the floor, the soft orange glow fading quickly into twilight. It's like he's seeing something far beyond this room, far beyond us, and for a moment,

I wonder if he's already made his peace with whatever future lies ahead.

"I don't know what else to do," he finally says, his voice softer than it was before, the weight of his words settling in like a stone in my stomach. His hand twitches beneath mine, as if he's about to pull away, but he doesn't. He doesn't pull away, and I realize with a jolt that maybe he's waiting for me to do it instead.

It's the first time he's ever sounded uncertain, and it sends a ripple of something unfamiliar through me. Something like hope, or maybe just the fear that he's about to make a decision that will change everything. His voice, raw and unguarded, breaks through the walls I've been carefully constructing between us.

"You don't have to make excuses for him, Luca," I murmur, my fingers lingering on his, the space between us suddenly feeling far too small. "There's always another way."

I catch the briefest flash of something in his eyes, like a memory or a dream he can't quite grasp, and then it's gone. He pulls his hand away, but it's not out of anger, not entirely. It's more like he's trying to keep his distance, and I'm not sure whether it's from me or from the mess that Emiliano has forced him into.

"I'm not sure what that 'other way' is anymore," he admits, his voice so quiet I almost don't catch it. "I don't know if there's anything left to fight for."

The words sting more than I expect, like he's telling me that whatever I thought we had, whatever I thought I meant to him, was never enough. That it's always been about survival, and maybe it still is. The thought of it sits heavily in my chest, pressing against my ribs, and for a moment, I don't know how to breathe through it.

"So, what now?" I ask, my voice sharp even though I don't mean for it to be. "Do we just wait for Emiliano to burn everything down around us?"

He doesn't answer at first. Instead, he leans back, his eyes fixed on the floor. His jaw clenches, the muscles working beneath his skin, and for a moment, it seems like the entire world is holding its breath.

"I don't know," he finally says. His words hang in the air, heavier than the silence that follows. And for the first time in a long time, I wonder if we've already crossed the point of no return.

The silence stretches long between us, thick and almost tangible, as if the room itself is holding its breath. I could almost reach out and touch it, like an invisible wall keeping me on one side and Luca on the other. My fingers twitch, aching to finish the task I started, but something holds me back. There's a hesitation in his posture that's not quite defeat but certainly not hope either. I pull the bandage tight around his hand, the slight pressure grounding me, anchoring me to the moment.

"What if you don't have to choose anymore?" I murmur, my voice tentative, the words heavier than I expect them to be. There's something in them, a question I haven't asked aloud yet, but the answer hovers just beneath the surface. What if he walked away from it all? From Emiliano, from the constant tug of loyalty, from the endless line of decisions that always seem to close in on him. What if there was a way out?

His eyes flicker, sharp as glass, like he's heard me but doesn't want to believe it. "You think that's possible?" he asks, and there's something so raw in his tone that it stings. He doesn't sound like a man caught in the middle anymore. He sounds like someone who's been pulled too far in one direction and has nothing left to pull back.

I don't answer immediately, instead focusing on the motion of my hands as I finish tying the bandage, feeling the steady rhythm of my own heartbeat in the quiet of the room. It's a question I've asked myself more times than I'd like to admit. Could he really walk away from Emiliano's world, from this endless game of power and manipulation? Could he find a way to be free?

The thought of freedom sounds as impossible as it does desirable. I wish I could promise him that, but the truth is, I don't know what that looks like for someone like him. And maybe, deep down, I'm afraid of what would happen if he did leave. What would be left of him, or of us, when the dust settled?

"I think you're the only one who can decide that," I say, the words more for myself than for him. There's an honesty in them that I don't fully understand, but I say them anyway.

Luca shifts, his eyes flicking away from mine, back to the window. The evening sun is now gone, replaced by the oppressive quiet of twilight that seems to settle heavier the later it gets. The city outside is still buzzing with life, a sharp contrast to the stillness in this apartment. I know the noise is real, but somehow, in this moment, it feels distant, like we're in a separate world, one that's both ours and no one's at all.

He exhales slowly, the sound almost a sigh. "You always make things sound so simple." The way he says it is not cruel, but it's not soft either. It's the sort of remark someone makes when they've spent too long looking for simple answers to impossible questions.

"Simple?" I echo, my lips curling into a small, self-deprecating smile. "I wish. If I could simplify anything, it would probably be this godforsaken mess we're in."

I stand up, a sudden burst of energy hitting me. There's only so much I can do sitting here, trying to untangle threads that are already too knotted to be undone. I pace the room, the old floorboards creaking beneath my feet, the sound oddly reassuring in the midst of the tension. I'm doing this for myself, I realize. I need to move, to stop feeling like I'm trapped here with only my thoughts to occupy me.

"We can't keep waiting for Emiliano to make the next move," I continue, though I don't know if I'm trying to convince him or myself. "Every time he makes a play, it's like we lose a little more of what we had before. The longer we wait, the less power we have to change things."

Luca's eyes follow me as I walk, his gaze steady, almost measuring. "You think it's that simple? Just walk away from him? From all of this?"

I stop, mid-step, and turn to face him, my chest tight with the weight of his question. "I think we're both in this too deep," I say, the words coming out more raw than I intend. "But maybe there's a way to fight back without burning ourselves alive in the process."

The sharpness in his eyes dulls slightly, and for the briefest moment, I think I see a flicker of something—doubt, or maybe it's hope—something fragile but there, just beneath the surface. "And what if fighting back means losing everything? What if the cost of getting out is worse than staying in?"

The room feels even smaller now, like the walls are closing in around me, pushing me to the edge of something I don't understand. I wish I could give him an answer, a concrete plan, a way out that doesn't feel like jumping off a cliff. But I can't. No one can.

"I don't know," I whisper, the truth of it hitting me like a cold wave. I don't know what the right choice is. I don't know what the cost of either option will be. But I know I can't keep going in circles, waiting for Emiliano to decide our fate. Not when I'm sitting here with the only person I've ever trusted to stand beside me, and he's caught in the same trap I am.

I walk over to the small kitchen and start rummaging through the cabinets, needing the motion, needing something to do. I don't even know what I'm looking for, but I don't stop until my fingers close around a bottle of whiskey, its dark glass cool against my palm. I don't drink often, but tonight feels like the sort of night that calls for it.

I pour two glasses, the amber liquid catching the light from the streetlamp outside, and bring them back to the sofa. I hand one to Luca, and he takes it without a word, the weight of his unspoken thoughts hanging in the air like a storm about to break.

We drink in silence, the only sound the faint hum of the city outside, and the low, steady beat of our hearts, each of us wondering how much longer we can keep pretending we know what comes next.

The silence between us is thick enough to cut with a knife. I can feel the tension wrapping itself around my chest, squeezing with every breath I take. Luca doesn't say anything else, and I can't seem to find the right words either. The bandage on his hand feels like an inadequate gesture, a flimsy attempt to mend something that might be beyond repair. I drop my gaze, watching the way his fingers flex under the white cloth, as if testing the limits of the restraint I've just placed on him. There's a tightness in his jaw that wasn't there earlier, a sign of something that's building up inside of him. Something he's trying to keep contained, but only barely.

I take a step back, not wanting to crowd him, but my mind is racing, skipping over possibilities faster than I can catch up. What would it take to untangle the mess we're in? If we could just cut the ties to Emiliano, walk away from everything that's held us here... but I know better than to dream like that. I've seen too many people who've tried. People like my father, who believed he could outrun the consequences, only to end up trapped under them, buried so deep he couldn't breathe.

I want to believe Luca has more choices than that. I want to believe he's more than just a player in someone else's game.

But the reality is, we're both stuck in this, locked in a dance we didn't choose and can't seem to escape.

"I didn't ask for this," Luca finally says, his voice a low growl that vibrates with a frustration he's been holding onto for far too long. "I didn't ask to be part of any of it. But you can't just walk away from someone like Emiliano. You think he'll let you go that easily?"

I know he's right. I know the man has eyes everywhere, the kind of power that makes it impossible to just slip away unnoticed. There's no running from Emiliano without consequences, no matter how hard you try. I feel that in the pit of my stomach, that gnawing certainty that every move we make is being watched, calculated.

But that doesn't stop me from wanting to fight anyway.

"I'm not asking you to walk away," I say, the words coming out sharper than I intend. "I'm asking you to stop playing by his rules. Stop letting him dictate your every move."

Luca looks up at me then, his eyes cold, unreadable. For a moment, I wonder if I've gone too far, if I've overstepped the boundaries I've spent so long trying to maintain. But then he nods, just once, and I don't know whether to feel relief or dread. It's like he's acknowledging something—something that's been there all along, buried beneath the surface.

"We'll see," he mutters, his gaze dropping to the glass in his hand. "But it's not just Emiliano you have to worry about."

I watch him closely, the edges of his words curling into something I can't quite place. "Who else?" I ask, though I already feel the answer settling in the back of my mind, like a slow-burning fuse.

Luca doesn't answer, but there's a shift in the air, an undercurrent of danger that suddenly feels a lot closer than I'd like it to. The streetlights flicker outside the window, casting long shadows across the apartment as the night deepens. There's a soft hum of traffic below, the low buzz of the city that never quite shuts down. It's like the world is always in motion, but in here, in this room, it feels as though time has slowed to a crawl.

I set my glass down with a deliberate slowness, the clink of the glass against the table ringing out louder than I expect. Luca doesn't flinch, doesn't even look up. But there's something in his stillness, a tension so thick that it's almost suffocating.

"What are you trying to say?" I ask, the words coming out quieter now, as though I'm afraid to hear the answer.

He finally meets my gaze, and for the briefest of moments, I see a flicker of something in his eyes—something raw, something real. But it's gone before I can grasp it, replaced by that same guarded mask he always wears.

"There's more at play here than Emiliano. And it's not just about you and me anymore."

I swallow, the knot in my throat tight. "What are you talking about?"

Luca leans back in his chair, his eyes narrowing slightly as he studies me, his face unreadable. "You think Emiliano's the only one who wants to control you? That he's the only one who sees you as a means to an end?"

I feel the blood drain from my face, and for a moment, everything goes still. My heart skips a beat, and I realize I've been holding my breath, waiting for a truth I wasn't ready to hear. I take a step back, my mind spinning as I try to piece together what he's saying.

"You're not the only one with enemies, you know," he continues, his voice dropping to a low murmur, like he's letting me in on a secret too dangerous to speak too loudly. "You've made choices, too. Choices that have left a trail."

I blink, confusion thick in my chest. "What choices? What are you talking about?"

Luca looks at me with something that borders on pity, and I hate it. I hate the way he looks at me like he knows something I don't, like I've already missed something important.

"You think Emiliano's the only one keeping tabs on you?" he asks again, and this time, there's a hardness in his voice that sends a shiver down my spine.

I stand there, frozen, as the implications of his words hit me. The room seems to close in around me, the walls feeling smaller, the air harder to breathe. There's something bigger going on here, something far more dangerous than I could have ever anticipated.

"Who else?" The question slips out before I can stop it, barely a whisper.

Luca opens his mouth to answer, but before the words can escape, there's a sudden crash from the hallway—loud, unmistakable. I freeze. My heart slams against my ribs as I turn toward the door, dread pooling in the pit of my stomach.

Luca's expression hardens, his hand moving instinctively to the gun at his hip. I don't have to ask what's coming next. The question now is whether we'll be ready for it.

The door swings open with a violent bang, and everything in the room goes still.

Chapter 19: The Silent Threat

I didn't think I could feel more restless than I did last night, pacing through my tiny apartment with the curtains drawn tight as if I could hide from my thoughts. But tonight, I was wrong. The moment I step into the warmth of Luca's office, the weight of his words—heavy, deliberate—hangs in the air between us. The faint scent of cigar smoke clings to the room, but it's the tension that truly stings. He's always been an ocean of calm, no matter the storm brewing around him, but now... now, there's something jagged in the lines of his face, something that wasn't there yesterday.

"We can't afford mistakes anymore, Lena," he says, his eyes sharp as a hawk's, cutting straight through me. He's staring at the stack of papers on the desk like they're a puzzle that refuses to be solved, a betrayal he can't yet see but knows is waiting somewhere in the chaos.

I cross my arms over my chest, leaning against the doorframe with a casual ease I don't feel. The movement feels deliberate, like I'm holding up a mirror, reminding myself that I am not afraid. Not yet. "Mistakes are how we learn, Luca. If you think I'm walking into this with my eyes closed, you've got another thing coming."

The words are bitter in my mouth, sharp and bitter like coffee that's been left too long on the counter. He's silent for a long moment, not looking at me, but at the papers. His jaw tightens, then he exhales, a slow, deliberate release of air. And that's when I see it—the shift. The unspoken question he's holding back, the suspicion that's beginning to creep into his thoughts like smoke filling a room.

"Don't look at me like that," I say, the words sharper than I intended. "I know what's at stake, Luca. I didn't sign up for this to back out now."

He finally glances up at me, his eyes stormy. "It's not about backing out, Lena. It's about staying alive. It's about trusting the right people."

That hits me harder than it should. The hint of doubt in his voice is a cold slap across my skin. I can't help but clench my fists at my sides. This isn't the same Luca who'd pulled me out of the dark when I had nothing left. This isn't the same Luca I knew. This... this is something else, something I didn't expect. Something I don't understand.

"I'm not going anywhere," I say, my voice low, controlled. "And if you're questioning me, maybe it's time we stop pretending."

The words hang there for a moment, thick in the air. Luca doesn't answer. He doesn't need to. His gaze flickers briefly to the photograph on the wall—a family portrait, with all their smiles so bright it's almost painful. The Vescelli family, proud and untouchable. Until now.

"I need you to be honest with me, Lena," Luca says, his voice tight. "If there's something you're hiding, if you're involved in any way—"

"Don't you dare," I cut him off, my heart hammering in my chest. "I'm not your enemy, Luca. I never have been. And I won't be now."

The silence stretches between us, a gaping chasm that neither of us is willing to cross. My pulse races, but I refuse to back down. The man I thought I knew is slipping through my fingers like water, and I don't know how to stop it.

"You're not the enemy, Lena," Luca murmurs, but there's a weight to the words that doesn't reassure me. "But someone is. And whoever it is, they know us. They know everything about this family. They've been waiting for the right moment."

I nod slowly, my mind already racing ahead. A shipment sabotaged. A trusted ally dead. Rumors of betrayal buzzing like a swarm of angry bees. Someone has gotten too close to the heart of the Vescelli empire, and now, it's like the entire foundation is starting to crumble beneath us.

"We need to figure out who's pulling the strings," I say, the words coming out faster than I can think. "We can't wait. Every second counts."

Luca's eyes darken. "We've got to be careful who we trust, Lena. There's more at stake now than just the family business."

I don't know what to say to that. The weight of his words settles on my chest like a boulder, and for the first time since I got involved in this mess, I wonder if I've made a mistake. What if I'm too close to the center of all of this? What if the wrong choice, the wrong move, could destroy everything?

"What if the traitor is someone close?" I ask, almost to myself, but Luca hears me.

"Could be. Could be someone inside the family. Or worse—someone pretending to be a friend."

The room feels colder now. The shadows stretch across the floor like something reaching, crawling, waiting to consume me. My fingers twitch at my sides, and for a moment, I wonder if I could turn and leave, walk out of this office, and never look back. But I know I can't.

I'm in too deep.

The door creaks open, and we both turn toward the sound. A figure stands in the doorway, silhouetted by the dim hallway light. My heart skips a beat before I recognize the shape—Sal, Luca's second-in-command, the man with the unshakeable loyalty. Or so I thought.

"You're needed in the back office," Sal says, his voice flat, devoid of any warmth.

Luca nods, but he doesn't stand immediately. His gaze flickers back to me, a moment of silent understanding passing between us. Something's wrong. I can feel it in my bones.

"Don't let your guard down," Luca says quietly, as if the words are meant for both of us.

I nod, but inside, I wonder if I've already missed my chance to keep everything—myself, my position, and my future—intact.

Sal's shadow lingers at the threshold of Luca's office like an unwelcome visitor, his features unreadable in the dim light. His eyes flicker between us, as if weighing the space that's thick with words unspoken. I can feel the distance between me and Luca now, the tightrope I've been walking growing thinner with each passing second.

"Luca," Sal mutters, just enough to draw his attention. Luca straightens up from the chair, pushing a stray lock of dark hair from his forehead, though it quickly falls back into place. The tension in the room is palpable, as though the very air between us is charged with something unsaid.

"I'll be there in a minute," Luca says, his tone clipped, but he doesn't get up immediately. There's something in his posture, something stiff and tight, that wasn't there earlier when he was so focused on the papers. It's the way people hold themselves when they're waiting for a storm to hit, but they're not sure if it's already started or if they're still in the eye of it.

Sal doesn't move, doesn't speak, but the silence stretches long enough for me to sense his own awareness of what's happening. He knows. He knows what's brewing under the surface. I can tell from the faint tension in his neck, the way his hands remain at his sides like a soldier standing on alert.

"Sal, get out," Luca's voice has sharpened, and it's enough to make the man step back. Not with fear, but with respect—or maybe with a subtle knowing, the kind that suggests Sal's seen too much to question. Whatever is happening, he doesn't want to be caught in the middle.

"Got it," Sal says, the door clicking shut behind him, leaving us alone again.

I wait, standing there in the quiet, arms crossed, my mind racing. For a moment, I wonder if I've said something wrong, pushed too far. But then Luca looks at me, and it's like all the words I've been holding back rush to the surface, threatening to spill over. He's still Luca—still the man who promised we'd get through this together. But there's something colder in his eyes now, something guarded.

"Someone's been playing us," he says suddenly, his voice low, as though the walls themselves might be listening. "It's not just sabotage, Lena. It's more than that."

I step closer, my heels clicking sharply on the polished floor, but my eyes never leave his. "I've been saying that from the start. Whoever's doing this is close—closer than we think."

"Not just close." Luca's jaw tightens again, the muscle working beneath his skin. "They're inside."

The realization hits me like a slap, sharp and sudden. Inside. He's not just talking about someone from the outside trying to undermine us. He's talking about betrayal from within. Someone who knows the ins and outs of everything we've built. Someone who knows how we operate. Someone who can predict our next move with unsettling accuracy.

"Which means we've been trusting the wrong people," I say, my voice brittle with the weight of what it means. The very foundation of everything we've worked for is shaking, and there's no solid ground to stand on anymore. I feel the familiar pang of unease at the pit of my stomach—familiar because I've felt it every time something in this life has gone wrong.

Luca doesn't respond immediately, but I catch the flicker of doubt in his eyes. It's brief, but it's there. He's starting to second-guess everyone, even the ones he thought he could trust.

"I know what you're thinking," I add, my voice quieter now, "and I know what you're feeling. You're wondering if I'm the one who's been working against you."

Luca flinches as if I've struck him, and for a moment, I regret saying it. But the words are already out, hanging between us like a thread that can't be untangled.

"No," Luca says after a pause, his voice hoarse. "I'm not thinking that."

"You should." The words come out more forcefully than I intend, and I almost immediately regret them. "I don't expect you to trust me right now, Luca. I'm not the one in charge of this family, and I'm not the one who knows all the pieces of this game. But whoever is pulling the strings, whoever has been getting to us, they're too good. Too good to be ignored."

His eyes meet mine, dark and intense, as if he's searching for something—anything—to let him know he can still rely on me. But I don't know if I can give him that reassurance anymore. I can't promise him loyalty when everything in me is screaming that we're on the verge of unraveling. Not because of what's been happening, but because of what's been hidden from us all along.

"I've got no one left to trust," Luca murmurs, more to himself than to me, as if admitting it out loud is some kind of admission of failure.

The words hit me harder than I expect, like a punch to the gut. There's something bitter in them, something resigned. It's as though he's already given up on finding the one person who can help him fix this. His family, his people—his world—is beginning to crumble, and no one seems to have the answers.

"You have me," I say, without thinking. It's an automatic response, something that escapes before I can stop it. It's not meant to be a declaration, not really. It's just the truth—at least, it's the truth in my mind. But the way he looks at me, with those dark eyes that once seemed full of trust, now seems tinged with something else.

"You don't know what you're saying," he says softly. "You don't know what you're really a part of, Lena. This—this isn't something you walk away from."

It's a warning. I hear it, feel it in the air between us. But I'm too far gone now. There's no walking away. Not when everything I've built is teetering on the edge of destruction. Not when Luca's eyes, once so certain, now look haunted. And for the first time in a long while, I'm not sure I can save either of us.

Luca leans back in his chair, fingers pressing into the polished wood of his desk. The room feels smaller now, the walls pushing in with every passing second, as though the air itself is thinning. I can hear the faint hum of the city beyond the windows—Chicago, always awake, always moving, never pausing to let you breathe. Yet inside this office, it feels like we've both stopped, caught in some kind of endless loop where trust is a fragile thing, barely holding on.

"Do you want the truth, Lena?" Luca asks, his voice barely above a whisper. But I can hear it—the tension, the frustration, the flicker of something that could be regret or simply the quiet ache of too many sleepless nights.

I nod, my own throat tight. "I need it."

"I've been asking myself if I'm the one who's been blind to all of this. To what's really happening. To who's really behind it."

I swallow hard, trying to keep my composure. I'm not sure if I'm more afraid of the truth or the way his eyes—dark and intense—are studying me, as though they're searching for a crack in my armor. "We both know it's not about who's blind anymore. It's about who's been playing us all along."

Luca stands suddenly, as if his patience has worn thin, his gaze shifting to the window. His reflection in the glass mirrors the uncertainty I feel creeping up my spine. I could almost see the city lights flicker in his eyes, reflecting the same dissonance that's swirling in the pit of my stomach. But even as his back is to me, I know he's still listening. Waiting.

I walk closer, but I don't touch him. Not yet. There's too much space between us, too many questions unspoken, too much doubt hanging like a thick fog.

"We can't waste time," I say, my voice cutting through the silence. "Whoever's doing this is ahead of us, Luca. They've been watching us, planning... waiting."

His shoulders tense, and for a brief second, I catch the glimpse of his teeth gritted in frustration. "I know."

The words are simple, but it's the way they hang in the air that sends a shiver down my spine. He knows. He knows what's at stake. But is it enough?

He turns toward me then, his jaw set, eyes narrowed. "I need to know I can trust you," he says, his voice raw. "I need to know you're in this with me. All the way."

The weight of his words lands on me like a stone, heavy and cold. But there's a flicker of something in his expression, something vulnerable, almost pleading. It's the first time he's said it out loud, and I realize, with a sickening twist, that this might be more than a family betrayal he's worried about. It's the crumbling of something he thought was unbreakable.

"I'm not going anywhere," I reply, though I can feel the lie forming on the tip of my tongue. The truth is, I don't know if I can keep going. Not when it feels like every step I take is further into the dark. But for him? For us? Maybe I'll find the strength.

The silence is almost unbearable now, thick enough to choke on. Luca's gaze never leaves mine, and for a fleeting moment, I think I see a flicker of relief, but it's gone before I can be sure. He exhales slowly, his body tense, as if preparing for something he can't yet name.

Then, without warning, there's a sharp knock on the door. The sound cuts through the tension like a knife, jarring and sudden.

"Luca, we've got a problem," Sal's voice carries through the wood, tight with urgency.

Luca's eyes flash to the door, and for the briefest moment, I see a flicker of something cold, something hard, in the depths of his gaze. "Not now," he mutters, but Sal doesn't wait for an invitation.

The door creaks open, and Sal steps in, his face pale, his usual confidence shaken. "It's Carlos. He's dead."

I feel my breath catch in my throat. Carlos. A trusted member of Luca's inner circle. The man who'd been with us from the beginning, always loyal, always there. The man who, until this morning, had been untouchable.

"What happened?" Luca's voice is controlled, but I can see the sharp edge of panic in the lines of his face. It's the first time I've seen him unravel. The first crack in the fortress.

Sal swallows hard, shaking his head. "We don't know. He was found at his apartment, but... there's more, Luca. Someone left a message. Written on the wall, in blood."

Luca's eyes snap to mine, the weight of the moment settling over us like a cold fog. It's clear he's already making connections in his mind. He doesn't need to say it out loud. The message is clear: Carlos was silenced because he knew something.

"Get a team over there," Luca says, his voice sharp, commanding. "Now."

But Sal doesn't move. His eyes are locked on Luca, the concern written in the tight set of his jaw, the way his hands are clenched at his sides. "There's something else," he says slowly. "The message... it wasn't just a threat. It was a warning."

Luca's expression hardens, his fists clenching at his sides. "What kind of warning?"

Sal's gaze flickers to me for a second before he looks back at Luca. "It said, 'She's next.'"

I don't know if I'm prepared for the way the words hit me, the way they rattle through me like thunder shaking the very foundation of everything I thought was solid. My breath catches, and for a moment, it's as if the world around me has stilled.

"She?" I hear myself whisper, the word feeling foreign on my tongue, like a blade too sharp to touch.

Luca's eyes lock on mine, and in that instant, I realize the truth: this isn't just a fight for the family. This is personal.

Chapter 20: Stolen Moments

The barn smelled like hay and earth, a little musty but comfortably familiar, like a second skin I hadn't realized I'd missed. I stepped through the wooden doors, the soft creak of the hinges cutting through the night air. My footsteps, light on the dust-covered floor, barely made a sound as I ventured farther in, the faint glow of a lantern casting long shadows across the rows of stalls. It was quiet—except for the faint snorts and soft stomping of hooves that seemed to echo off the high beams.

And then I saw him.

Luca. He was kneeling next to the stall of a chestnut mare, one of his large hands gently tracing the horse's injured leg. His brow furrowed in concentration, a look of such unguarded tenderness that it nearly knocked the breath out of me. In all the time I'd known him, I'd never seen him like this. The man who stormed through rooms like a hurricane, who spoke in clipped, calculated words, was replaced by someone else entirely. Someone I hadn't even known could exist beneath the layers of arrogance and control.

I wasn't sure what drew me closer—perhaps it was the way the dim light reflected off his tousled hair, or maybe it was the way his shoulders relaxed in the stillness, the weight of his usual tensions forgotten for a brief moment.

"I didn't know you had this side to you," I said, my voice quieter than I'd intended.

Luca's head snapped up at the sound of my voice. For a moment, his eyes locked onto mine, as though trying to read something in me that I wasn't quite sure how to convey. There was no sharpness, no defensive edge in his gaze—just something raw, vulnerable even. And that scared me, because it meant I wasn't sure if I was ready for what it might unlock between us.

He stood up slowly, careful not to disturb the mare. She huffed gently and shifted on her feet, but it seemed to comfort Luca, rather than bother him. He didn't look at me at first, his focus still on the horse as he adjusted the bandage with slow, deliberate movements.

"There's a lot you don't know about me," he said, his voice softer than I'd ever heard it.

It was the most personal thing he'd said to me in weeks, maybe even months. His voice wasn't the usual authoritative tone he used when giving commands or explaining the fine details of some business deal or another. No, this was different. This was a confession, a crack in the armor that I'd been trying to pierce for so long. I wanted to push, to ask him about all the things I didn't know, but there was something about the way he looked at me then, as though unsure of how much to reveal, that held me back. It was as if the answer was more complicated than I could possibly understand.

"Tell me about the horse," I said instead, trying to steer the conversation into safer waters.

His lips quirked up in the faintest of smiles, but it didn't reach his eyes. "She's a fighter. Injured her leg during the last round of training. The vet says it's not too serious, but..." He paused, glancing at the horse. "She's too stubborn for her own good. Probably thinks she can keep going even if she's broken."

There was something in his voice then, a knowing bitterness that didn't sit right with me. Like he was talking about more than just the horse, like he was speaking about himself, or maybe even about us.

"You sound like you know a thing or two about stubbornness," I said, a teasing edge to my voice.

His gaze flickered back to me, sharp as ever, but the tension between us had softened somehow. The walls that had always been there, thick and impenetrable, seemed to have cracked open just a fraction.

"I suppose I do," he said, looking down at the mare, his voice turning quieter again. "Sometimes, being stubborn is the only thing that gets you through. Everything else can be... a distraction."

The words hung in the air like smoke, curling and dissipating before I could fully grasp them. I wasn't sure whether he was talking about me, or him, or some version of both of us that neither of us was brave enough to confront.

I took a step closer, feeling the distance between us shorten in a way that wasn't physical, but something deeper—something far more intimate. I could feel the weight of everything unsaid pressing in around us, the palpable charge in the air that neither of us was brave enough to acknowledge.

"You don't always have to do everything alone, you know," I said softly, my words carrying more weight than I intended.

Luca shifted, the muscles in his back tense under his shirt. "I don't need anyone's pity," he replied quickly, too quickly. His voice snapped back into the cold, detached tone he usually reserved for people he didn't want to deal with.

But this time, I wasn't backing down. Not when he'd shown me this side of himself. Not when I saw the vulnerability there, hidden beneath the surface, like a crack in stone that threatened to break wide open.

"Pity wasn't what I meant," I countered, my voice steady but warm. "I'm not offering it. I'm offering something else—understanding. That's different, Luca. And I think you might need it more than you realize."

His eyes narrowed, his jaw tightening as though he were about to say something sharp, something to shut me out again. But then he didn't. Instead, he looked at me—really looked at me—in a way that made my heart thump harder in my chest.

"You have no idea how much I've fought to keep everything under control," he muttered. His eyes flickered back to the horse, his voice softer now, almost... vulnerable. "But sometimes, it's like everything I do just gets harder and harder."

It was the first time I'd ever heard him admit to weakness. And despite the heavy, tangled mess of emotions swirling between us, I felt something shift. Not just in him, but in me, too. Something I didn't have a name for yet.

Before I could respond, Luca straightened up, wiping his hands on his jeans. The mare gave a soft snort of approval, nudging his shoulder gently, as though sensing his turmoil.

"Come on," he said, his voice a little steadier. "She needs some rest. I'll walk you out."

And as he led me back toward the barn door, I couldn't shake the feeling that something had changed, something I wasn't prepared for but knew I couldn't escape.

The cool night air brushed against my skin as Luca walked me back to the barn doors, his steps heavy with the weight of words unsaid. The mare behind us, her leg now bandaged and still, had settled into a quiet rhythm, her soft breathing barely audible in the silence between us. I felt the sharpness of the night close in, the stars overhead scattered like diamonds, indifferent to the quiet unraveling happening right in front of me.

I didn't know what to say. There was so much there, beneath the surface, so much in the air that could have shattered us if we weren't careful. I wasn't sure if I wanted to shatter anything. In fact, part of me wanted to preserve this fragile moment with Luca, this unexpected sliver of vulnerability that I hadn't known existed beneath all the layers he'd built around himself. But the other part—the part of me that had always been fiercely independent, the part that kept its distance from people like him—warned me to step away, to keep my emotions firmly in check.

Instead, I took a deep breath and found myself speaking before I could stop it.

"I don't understand you, Luca," I said, the words slipping out almost too easily. "How can someone so... guarded, be so good at this?" I motioned to the stables, to the mare, to the very air that felt alive with something unspoken.

He glanced down at the ground, his jaw tightening before he answered.

"People are good at different things. Some of us are just better at hiding what really matters," he muttered, his gaze flicking briefly to mine before returning to the dim lantern light that flickered near the barn.

There it was again. That feeling. That thread that seemed to pull at something deep inside me, making it harder to breathe. It wasn't just about the horse. It never had been. The words between us weren't just about what we were saying—they were about the things we couldn't say, the things we refused to admit even to ourselves.

I didn't want to push him. Not yet. But the silence stretched out too long, and the words I was holding back surged to the surface.

"Why don't you let anyone in, Luca?" I asked, the question raw and unrefined, even to me. The moment felt too fragile to cloak it in anything but honesty.

He froze, just for a second, and the faint flicker of hesitation was all I needed. There was something there, something I hadn't seen before, in the way his shoulders tensed. He looked like a man caught between two worlds—one that demanded he remain distant, and another that begged him to lean in. But his walls didn't crumble. Not fully. Not yet.

"You think you want to know everything about me," he said, his voice dropping to a tone that could've been mistaken for bitterness, but there was something deeper behind it. "But you don't. Trust me."

I wasn't sure if I believed him. I wasn't sure if I wanted to. My eyes narrowed as I studied him, trying to understand where this conversation was going, what had changed, what I was missing. But just when I thought I had a grasp on it, he turned away, brushing past me toward the horse's stall.

"I've spent a long time making sure people don't get too close," he continued, his voice quieter now, but with an edge I couldn't ignore. "It's not because I don't want them to. It's because if they do... they might see something they don't want to."

I took a step back, taken aback by the quiet intensity in his words. The air between us had shifted once again, but this time it felt more like a veil had dropped—something dark and heavy, like a secret that neither of us was quite ready to expose.

"Is that what you're afraid of?" I asked, more to myself than to him, but he heard it, and the slightest hint of a laugh escaped him, though it wasn't full of humor.

"No," he replied quickly, but there was a hardness to his tone that made my skin prickle. "I'm not afraid of anything."

The words didn't settle the way they should have. They hung in the air, unanswered, as if they didn't quite belong in the same sentence as the man who had just shown me a side of himself that wasn't stone-cold and impenetrable. He ran a hand through his hair, the movement quick and almost frantic.

"Then why..." I started, but the question stopped short when I saw it—his hand shaking, just the slightest tremor. It wasn't much, but it was enough to make me rethink everything.

"Just drop it," he said, the words clipped, though I could hear the weariness that laced them. "You don't get to ask questions about things that don't belong to you."

The stinging rejection in his voice should have pushed me away, but instead, it made me stand my ground, even though every instinct I had screamed at me to run. I wasn't sure why I felt this pull to him, this strange, almost magnetic force that seemed to settle into my bones whenever he was near. But I wasn't going to back down, not now.

"I'm not going anywhere, Luca," I said, my voice steady despite the wild tumble of thoughts racing through my head. "You're not going to push me away that easily."

For a long moment, we stood there, the space between us a taut line stretched thin, ready to snap. I didn't know if he'd fight me, if he'd make some excuse to walk away, or if he'd finally open up, let me in. But I wasn't ready to leave yet, not when there was something in his eyes—something that spoke of a man who had been carrying a weight for far too long.

Luca sighed, his shoulders slumping as though the act of holding himself together had drained every ounce of energy from him. He looked back at me, his expression unreadable, but beneath it, I could see the flicker of uncertainty.

"You're right," he said quietly. "You're not going anywhere."

And for the first time since I'd met him, I didn't feel the urge to run. Instead, I took a step closer, not because I was trying to make him talk, but because I was finally beginning to understand what it meant to truly stay.

The dim light of the barn hung between us like a thread, delicate yet unyielding. Luca's gaze lingered on me for a moment longer than I expected, his eyes darker now, caught between the shadows and the flickering lantern light. He stepped back from the mare, his hands still covered in a mixture of dirt and blood that wasn't his own. There was something almost reverential in the way he touched the horse's side, smoothing over her coat as though he understood the weight of the world that came with the responsibility of healing.

But this moment—this fragile piece of time we shared—was slipping away. I could feel it, the pull of everything unsaid, everything left unexamined. And yet, I couldn't help myself from stepping a little closer, the words coming faster than I could stop them.

"You don't have to keep up this façade with me," I said, my voice low but firm. "I'm not some... person to be guarded against."

Luca's shoulders stiffened, the muscles under his shirt tight with some hidden tension, but he didn't pull away. He didn't dismiss me either. Instead, his lips quirked in that half-smile of his—the one that said he'd been thinking of something else, something I wasn't quite privy to.

"And what would you do with me if I didn't keep up the façade?" he asked, his tone almost teasing, though there was an edge to it that didn't sit quite right.

I wasn't sure what I would do with him, to be honest. I didn't even know what I wanted. Or maybe I did, but the thought of saying it out loud—of admitting it—seemed like an invitation to expose parts of myself that I had buried deep. The parts that had no place in the polished, unflinching image I'd created for myself.

"I'd figure you out," I said softly, unable to help myself. The words slipped from my lips with the kind of honesty that felt dangerous. "And maybe... I'd let you figure me out too."

His gaze softened for just a moment, the harsh edge of his features momentarily giving way to something gentler. But it didn't last. His jaw clenched, the familiar wall descending back into place, and he straightened up, taking a step away from me, like the distance between us could protect him from whatever was starting to break free.

"I don't need you to figure me out," he said, his voice carrying that finality I'd come to recognize as his default. But there was something underneath it, something that felt like it might crack at any second.

I hesitated, unsure of what to say next, until my attention was caught by the mare. She shifted, restless, her eyes wide and dark as she searched the room with a focus that seemed to match the tension between us. Luca glanced over at her, his brow furrowing as he adjusted the bandage one last time.

"I think she's ready to go back inside," he murmured, but there was something about his tone—something fragile and fleeting—that told me he wasn't just talking about the horse.

I wasn't ready to let go of this moment, of the fragile connection we had shared, however brief it had been. I stepped forward, almost instinctively, not sure if it was a desire to help the horse or something deeper—something that had nothing to do with animals at all.

"I can help," I offered, before I could think better of it. "Let me."

Luca turned, catching my gaze with a look that was sharper than I expected. His lips parted, but before he could say anything, there was a sudden noise from the back of the barn—sharp and quick, a sound that sent the mare into a panic. Her hooves stamped against the hay-strewn ground, and she darted toward the far corner of her stall, her injured leg momentarily forgotten in the surge of fear.

"Damn it," Luca swore under his breath, his hands reaching for the reins that hung by the stall door.

I felt a strange knot tighten in my chest as I watched him move with a speed and grace that seemed out of place for someone so built, so... controlled. But there was something frantic in the way he approached the mare, his movements a blend of desperation and a calm that didn't quite match.

"Get back," he ordered, but there was an urgency in his voice now, something darker that made my heart race.

I didn't step back. I couldn't.

"Luca," I said, my voice barely above a whisper, but my feet stayed rooted to the ground. Something was wrong. I could feel it. Something was shifting between us, the air heavy with more than just the sound of the mare's restless movements. The space between us had grown too large, too tangled in the unspoken truths we were both afraid to confront.

He glanced at me, eyes narrowed. His gaze flicked down to the mare, and then back to me, like he was debating whether or not to say what was on his mind. But before he could, the door at the far end of the barn creaked open, and the sudden shift of the atmosphere made my heart skip a beat.

I barely had time to react before the figure stepped inside. It was a man—tall, with dark hair and a presence that seemed to fill the room even before his words reached us. His face was half-shadowed, but I could see the glint of something cold in his eyes.

"You've made a mess of things, Luca," the man said, his voice calm, too calm for my liking. "And now you're going to fix it."

The tension in the barn snapped instantly, the quiet moments we had shared disappearing in an instant, replaced by a new kind of uncertainty—one I wasn't sure I was ready to face. But as the man took another step forward, I felt a surge of something cold and sharp crawl up my spine.

Luca didn't say anything. His jaw clenched again, and I could see the muscles in his neck tighten, but there was something else in his eyes—something I hadn't expected to see in him.

Fear.

Chapter 21: A Dangerous Proposition

The city felt heavier today. The looming skyscrapers cast shadows so long they felt as though they were trying to smother the streets below. Each footstep echoed against the asphalt, the air thick with humidity that never fully lifted, as if the city itself was holding its breath. The clatter of traffic, the occasional shout of a pedestrian, and the distant hum of a train rattling overhead were the only sounds that punctuated the early afternoon. But all I could hear, all I could feel, was the weight of Emiliano's words hanging in the air like a cloud ready to burst.

He had come to me in the same smooth manner as before, that dangerous charisma threading its way through every word he spoke. It was the kind of charm that lured people into making choices they would later regret, a skill he wielded like a finely tuned instrument. The offer he extended had been simple, but the implications were anything but. A way out. A chance to leave it all behind—the tangled mess of family ties, obligations, and fear.

But at what cost?

It was a question I couldn't quite bring myself to answer, not yet anyway. Not until I could see the way his proposal danced in the light of Luca's reaction. And so, I found myself sitting in the worn leather chair by the window in Luca's apartment, the sun setting in shades of violet and gold outside. The apartment, though sparse, felt like a refuge—a place where the world could not follow. But even here, I was not safe from the storm that had been brewing.

Luca's eyes blazed with something akin to betrayal, a fire that simmered just beneath the surface of his usually calm demeanor. He crossed his arms, pacing with restless energy, as if he couldn't quite stand still long enough to let his thoughts settle. "You think he's offering you a way out?" His voice was low, edged with that familiar note of concern, but there was something else, something deeper. "You don't know him, not really. He's dangerous. More dangerous than you could ever imagine."

I swallowed hard, trying to ignore the tremble in my hands. "I don't know what you want me to say, Luca. I'm not asking you to like it. I'm just asking you to trust me."

"Trust you?" He stopped pacing, and his gaze turned to ice. "How can I trust you when you're considering his offer? After everything? Do you think this is some sort of fairy tale, that you'll just walk away from all of this and live happily ever after?"

I didn't flinch at his words, though they cut deeper than I cared to admit. Instead, I leaned back in the chair, forcing myself to meet his eyes. "I don't know what to think anymore. Every day, it feels like I'm trapped in a game I never agreed to play. I'm suffocating, Luca."

His expression softened, but the hardness didn't leave his voice. "I'm trying to protect you. You're not suffocating here. You're not suffocating with me."

I opened my mouth to respond, but the words caught in my throat. There was too much I wanted to say, but I couldn't find the right way to say it. I wanted to scream that I had no choice, that the family I was born into had already made all of my decisions for me, and no matter how hard I tried, there was no running from it. But the truth was, I wasn't sure I wanted to run anymore. Not from Emiliano, not from the life I had known.

His hand, warm and steady, rested on the back of the chair beside me, the closeness a quiet promise of protection. "You can't trust him. I'm telling you this because I know what he's capable of. You think he's offering you freedom, but it's a lie. There's always a price."

I couldn't argue with him. I had seen Emiliano's darkness, the coldness in his eyes when he spoke of the family, of the deals that had been made in the shadows. I had seen it in the way he handled business—slick, ruthless, always with a smile. And yet, there was something in me that still wanted to believe him. Maybe because I wanted to believe there was a way out, that I could escape this tangled web.

"I don't know what to do," I whispered, the weight of the decision pressing down on me like an anvil.

Luca's expression softened, and for a moment, I saw a flicker of the man I had once trusted completely. But then he stepped back, his face hardening again. "You're not the only one who has to make a choice here," he said, his voice flat, emotionless. "You're not the only one whose life is on the line."

I watched him turn away, his shoulders taut with unspoken tension. My heart twisted. He was right. I had no idea how deeply Emiliano's return had affected him, how many compromises Luca had made in the name of loyalty, how many lines he had crossed that I never could have imagined.

And yet, here I was, stuck between two worlds, neither of which felt like home.

The days dragged on in a strange haze, each one blurring into the next, the edges of time softened by my growing uncertainty. The weight of Emiliano's offer settled deep within me, a constant hum in the back of my mind, pushing and pulling with equal force. I had been raised to believe that loyalty was the only currency worth anything, but loyalty in this world was as fickle as the wind. It could turn on you in an instant, leaving you breathless and exposed, like a kite torn from its string.

Luca had been distant since our last conversation. I could tell he was angry, but there was something else behind the anger—a fear I hadn't expected to see in him. He was a man who had always carried himself with the unshakable confidence of someone who knew their place in the world. But now? Now he seemed unsure, as though the ground beneath his feet had shifted, and he was scrambling to find his balance again.

I found myself walking the streets more often in the days that followed. The city, bustling and alive, offered me no comfort. But there was something intoxicating about the anonymity of it all, the feeling that no one was watching, no one knew the weight of my choices. I'd slip into small cafes, order the same black coffee I'd always gotten, and just watch the world pass by. The sound of conversation, the clinking of cups, the laughter of strangers—all of it was a reminder that there was a world beyond this tangled mess I found myself in. A world that, for a moment, felt like it could be mine if only I could reach out and take it.

The rain came in the late afternoon, heavy and sudden, as if the sky had been holding its breath. I ducked under the awning of a bookstore, the scent of old paper and fresh rain mingling in the cool air. It was the kind of weather that made everything seem more intimate, more immediate. I watched as the streets emptied, pedestrians huddling under umbrellas, their steps quick and purposeful.

And then, through the shifting haze of water and city noise, I saw him. Emiliano. His figure cut through the mist, moving with that same predatory grace I had come to recognize so well. He was standing just a few yards away, looking out at the rain like it was the most interesting thing in the world.

I shouldn't have been surprised. He always seemed to find me when I least expected it.

I hesitated, torn between the instinct to turn and run and the curiosity that had already taken root. He must have sensed my indecision because he turned toward me, his lips curling into that knowing smile. The one that always seemed to promise something—something dangerous, something tempting.

"Fancy running into you here," he said, his voice smooth as velvet, cutting through the noise of the rain.

I frowned, crossing my arms over my chest, unsure of whether I was angry or just confused. "Should I be surprised? You always seem to find me, no matter how far I go."

Emiliano chuckled, the sound deep and rich, the kind of laugh that made you wonder if he knew more than he let on. "It's one of my talents," he said. "I know when people are running from something. And I know when they're ready to stop."

I raised an eyebrow, my skepticism not quite able to hide the curiosity that pricked at the edges of my mind. "And you think I'm ready to stop running?"

He took a step closer, his presence filling the space between us, and the air around him seemed to shift, becoming heavier, charged with the weight of unspoken promises. "I think you've been running for far too long. And I think you're finally starting to see that there's nowhere left to go."

The words struck me harder than I'd anticipated, and for a moment, I felt my heart skip, an unwelcome pang of uncertainty flickering to life in my chest. He was right, of course. I had spent so much time looking for an escape, for some way to untangle myself from the mess my life had become, but Emiliano was offering me the only way out that seemed real. A way to leave it all behind—the family, the lies, the debts that were slowly pulling me under.

But at what cost?

"You think you can just offer me an out and I'll take it?" I said, my voice shaky despite my attempts at defiance. "You think you have the power to fix everything with a smile and a deal?"

He didn't even flinch. "I don't need to fix everything. I'm just offering you a chance to choose something different. To take control for once, instead of letting everyone else dictate your life."

His words were sharp, calculated. He knew exactly what to say to get under my skin. I wanted to argue, to tell him that he was just using me, but a small voice in the back of my head whispered that maybe, just maybe, he was right. Maybe I had been letting others pull the strings for too long.

"You can't trust him," Luca's voice echoed in my mind, the warning clear and strong. But it was starting to feel more like a plea than a command. And the truth was, I wasn't sure I trusted Luca anymore, either. Not after everything he'd kept from me, after all the lies that had piled up between us like bricks in a wall.

"Do you want to know what it feels like," Emiliano continued, his voice low and intimate now, as if we were sharing some private secret, "to live without looking over your shoulder every damn minute of your life? To not be bound by someone else's rules, to have everything you want within your grasp?"

I swallowed hard, trying to push back the rising flood of temptation. His words were so close to everything I had ever dreamed of. Freedom. Choice. Power.

But the price, I knew, would be steep.

The rain had long since stopped, but the air remained heavy, thick with moisture and uncertainty. Emiliano's gaze still burned into me, his presence too close, too consuming, as though he were drawing me into a world where there was no escape. I felt it—his influence, seeping into my thoughts like ink spreading across paper. His offer, though wrapped in the promise of freedom, was nothing more than a gilded cage.

"You're good at this," I said, my voice quieter now, as if the words might betray me if I spoke them too loudly. "Making it sound like I'm the one in control, like I'm the one making the choice. But you've already decided for me, haven't you?"

A slow smile curled at the corner of his lips. It was a smile that spoke of secrets, of games played in shadows where no one could see the strings being pulled. "It's not about control," he said softly. "It's about possibility. The chance to take back what's yours."

I wanted to believe him. I wanted to believe in the illusion of control, in the fantasy that somehow, I could step away from the mess of my life without anyone noticing, without consequences. But beneath his words, I felt the sting of something darker. Something that said nothing came without a price, not in Emiliano's world.

I tore my eyes away from him, the weight of his gaze lingering like an invisible hand. The moment stretched, thick and uncomfortable, as if time itself was holding its breath, waiting for me to decide.

"And what about Luca?" I asked, my voice sharp despite the trembling in my chest. "What about him? You want me to walk away from everything, but what do you want in return?"

Emiliano's smile faded, replaced by a more contemplative expression. "Luca..." He paused, as though tasting the name on his tongue. "Luca is a complication. One I didn't expect. But even complications can be dealt with."

I felt a chill run down my spine at the casual way he spoke of Luca, as though he were a minor obstacle, something easily swept aside. The same man who had always been my protector, my anchor. The thought of Emiliano turning his cold, calculating eyes on him made my stomach twist.

"You're wrong," I said before I could stop myself, my voice raw with a mix of defiance and fear. "You don't know him like I do."

"Perhaps," he conceded with a shrug, his gaze sharpening. "But I know what I need. And I get what I need."

It was a warning, veiled beneath layers of charm and control. I had no doubt now that Emiliano wasn't offering me a way out; he was offering me a different kind of cage. One that glittered with promises of freedom, but which would hold me just as tightly as the life I was trying to escape.

"I don't want any part of this," I said, my voice steadier now, though my heart was pounding in my chest. "I'm not a pawn in your game."

His eyes narrowed slightly, and for the first time, I saw the flicker of something—annoyance, perhaps? Or was it something darker, something more dangerous? But whatever it was, it was enough to make the tension in the air shift, as if the world itself was holding its breath.

"You think you have a choice," Emiliano said, his voice low, almost a whisper. "But you don't. Not really. You've been playing the game since the moment you were born. The only question is whether you'll continue playing it by someone else's rules, or whether you'll make your own."

I took a step back, my pulse quickening. He was right, of course. In a way, I had been playing the game my whole life, trapped in a cycle of decisions made for me, of paths that had been laid out long before I ever understood what they meant. But now, as I stood here in the fading light, I realized something that had been gnawing at me for days. This wasn't just about Emiliano and his promises. It wasn't even about Luca, or the family, or the endless web of deceit that had wound its way through my life.

It was about me. For the first time in my life, I was standing at the crossroads, and I was the one who had to decide which way to turn. But the more I thought about it, the more the question lingered, heavy and unresolved. What would happen if I walked away from everything? What would happen if I chose to trust Emiliano?

"I need time," I said, the words slipping from my mouth before I could stop them. "Time to think."

His expression softened, but I could see the calculation behind it. He wasn't worried. He knew I would come around. In the end, we always did, didn't we? His people had a way of getting under your skin, convincing you that the world was nothing without them.

"I'll give you time," he said, his voice so smooth it could've been made of silk. "But not too much. Time has a way of running out when you're standing still."

I wanted to protest, to tell him I didn't need his games, but the words caught in my throat. The truth was, I didn't know what I needed anymore. Everything had become so tangled, so uncertain. There was no clean way out of this.

As Emiliano turned to leave, his footsteps echoing down the empty street, I felt a pang of something unfamiliar—doubt, perhaps. Or was it fear?

I didn't have the answer. And as I turned to head back into the warmth of the bookstore, I realized something that stopped me cold: the decision I had been so desperate to make wasn't just about my future—it was about Luca's as well.

I reached for my phone, my fingers shaking as I dialed his number, the weight of everything pressing down on me.

But when I heard the ringing on the other end, I didn't expect the voice that answered. Not Luca's voice. Not anyone I knew.

"Luca's gone," the voice said, cold and final.

And just like that, everything changed.

Chapter 22: The Depths of Betrayal

The kitchen was still warm from the afternoon sun, the golden light filtering through the sheer curtains like something stolen from a dream. I stood at the counter, hands half-frozen in midair, as I tried to gather the fragments of what had just happened. The sharp scent of rosemary from the bread I was baking mingled with the acrid tang of fear in the air—two scents that should never coexist, yet here they were. In that moment, the kitchen felt like a stage set for a tragedy, and I was the reluctant star.

The door behind me slammed open with the kind of violence that only family can manage. My uncle's presence filled the room like a sudden storm, the weight of his anger pressing against the walls, pushing out all the warmth that had so briefly existed. His eyes, usually soft and understanding, were hard now—stones set in a face that had long been accustomed to hiding the emotions of a lifetime.

"You think I don't know, don't you?" His voice was a low growl, the sort of sound you hear just before a storm breaks. "You think you can just slip this past me, pretending to be the innocent one."

I didn't turn around. I didn't want to. The tension between us was like a knot tightening in my chest, pulling at the fibers of every word, every action that had led me here. But the accusation hung in the air, thick and suffocating. All evidence pointed to me, and though I could tell him the truth, the truth didn't matter. Not right now. Not when betrayal had already been planted like a seed in the fertile soil of suspicion.

The silence stretched, a taut wire waiting to snap, until a familiar voice broke through the tension.

"She didn't do it, Uncle." Luca's voice was calm, deceptively so, considering the chaos swirling in the room.

I hadn't heard him approach, hadn't even realized he was in the house until that moment. He stepped into the kitchen, his figure sharp against the dimming light. His dark hair, still a little damp from the rain, clung to his forehead. His eyes—those deep, impossibly blue eyes—never wavered from my uncle's face. His stance was relaxed, but his shoulders were squared, a silent show of support that, despite everything, made my chest tighten in a way that was almost unbearable.

My uncle's glare shifted to Luca, and for a moment, I saw the old man hesitate. The air between them crackled with something—something unspoken, ancient. My uncle didn't like being questioned, certainly not by someone younger than him, certainly not by someone who had been a part of this family for less than a fraction of the time he had. But Luca was never one to cower under the weight of anyone's disapproval.

"I know you want someone to blame," Luca continued, his words measured, deliberate. "But it's not her."

I could feel the weight of their conversation, each word a delicate drop into the already overfull cup of tension between us. And still, I didn't say anything. What could I possibly say? The evidence—every whispered accusation, every stolen glance, every hurriedly turned-away face—pointed directly at me. No matter how much I wanted to fight it, no matter how much I wished I could hold onto the truth, it felt like a lie now. Like something that had been twisted beyond recognition.

"Enough, Luca." My uncle's voice cracked like thunder, but Luca stood firm, unflinching. It was in moments like these that I wondered how the two of them were even related. My uncle was like an old tree—rooted, unwavering, proud of his years. Luca, on the other hand, was like the wind. He shifted with grace, with purpose. No matter how hard you tried to hold him down, he would always find a way to blow free.

"Let's just—let's think this through," Luca continued, his voice steady, though there was something in the corners of his eyes—something that looked a lot like doubt. He wasn't as sure as he sounded. He couldn't be.

But what was there to think about? The evidence was there, hanging in the air like an unfinished sentence.

"I don't care what you think you know," my uncle spat. "You're covering for her. She's your cousin, Luca, but you're not going to make me look like a fool. Not again."

I could see the storm swirling inside Luca, his jaw tightening ever so slightly, the sharp line of his lips twitching. His loyalty was on display—raw, exposed. And in that instant, I felt both a sense of relief and a crushing weight. The relief came from his defense of me—finally, he was speaking up. But the weight... it was a double-edged sword. If he was right, if he was truly defending me, then that meant he was also implicating himself. And for someone as careful as Luca, that was not a decision made lightly.

I wanted to tell them both that it wasn't me. I wanted to scream it from the rooftops, but the truth didn't feel like something I could hold onto anymore. Not with the way everything was unraveling. The lies, the secrets, the manipulations. It felt like I was drowning in a sea of uncertainty, and the only thing that kept me afloat was Luca—his quiet strength, his steady gaze, the way he was willing to stand between me and the storm, no matter the cost.

But the storm was coming. And I could feel it in my bones.

The air seemed to thicken the longer we stood in that tense silence, each second pressing against me like an uninvited weight. My uncle's rage crackled in the space between us, more felt than seen, as if it had already transformed into something tangible—a thundercloud waiting to burst. His gaze, sharp enough to slice through steel, was fixed on me, and for the first time in years, I felt like a stranger in my own home. He used to be the one who protected me, the one who made me feel like I could trust him with anything. But trust had become a currency too expensive for either of us to afford anymore.

Luca's steady gaze was my lifeline, a rope thrown to a drowning woman in a storm. He didn't flinch as my uncle's fury turned toward him, didn't back down in the face of the looming threat. If anything, he seemed to grow taller, his broad shoulders relaxed in a way that made it clear he wasn't going to let my uncle walk all over him—especially not now, when it felt like everything had come undone.

"I'm not covering for her." Luca's voice rang out with quiet confidence, though I could tell it cost him. His words were firm, but there was an edge to them, like he was daring my uncle to press further. "I'm simply not going to let you accuse her without the facts."

My uncle's fists clenched at his sides, the knuckles turning white, but Luca didn't move, didn't take a step back. The room seemed to shrink in that moment, the walls closing in, but Luca remained unmoved—a rock against a raging river. I hated that he was putting himself in the line of fire for me. I hated it because I couldn't promise that he wouldn't get burned.

"Facts?" my uncle scoffed, his voice dripping with disdain. "The facts are right here, Luca. You're too blinded by whatever... loyalty you think you have to see the truth."

I swallowed hard, feeling the weight of their words like heavy stones sinking into the pit of my stomach. The truth, it seemed, had already been written, and I was the villain. The one who had betrayed them all. And no matter how many times I tried to speak, tried to tell them I was innocent, the story had already been written in their eyes. It didn't matter that the facts were skewed, or that the people who could exonerate me had disappeared into the shadows.

Luca's hand shot up, cutting off my uncle's tirade before it could fully take root. The tension in the room thickened, like an electrical charge just before a storm. "I don't care what you think you know," he said, his voice low but unyielding. "I'm not going to let you destroy her for something she didn't do."

My uncle's face twisted, a mask of anger and something darker, deeper. But there was something else there too—something almost... sad? I wasn't sure if I was reading him wrong, but for a brief moment, I thought I saw the flicker of doubt in his eyes.

But it vanished as quickly as it came, buried beneath layers of resentment. "You're playing a dangerous game, Luca."

The words were a warning, one that he'd said before, but this time, there was an undertone—something final, something ominous. I didn't like it. I didn't like any of this.

My uncle turned to me then, his eyes full of accusation and something else—something I couldn't place. "You think you can just walk away from this, don't you?" he spat. "You think you can hide behind Luca's words, but I see you for what you are. You always think you can outsmart me, but I'm done letting you use him as your shield."

I wanted to scream at him, to throw my hands in the air and demand that they see me for who I really was—not the villain they'd turned me into, but someone caught in the middle of a mess far bigger than any of us. But my voice faltered in my throat, caught somewhere between the need for self-preservation and the overwhelming urge to make them understand the truth. But the truth was tangled—too twisted for any one person to unearth, and certainly not something they were ready to hear.

Luca stepped closer, his presence a barrier between my uncle and me. The scent of his cologne—woody and faintly peppery—was a sharp contrast to the bitter tension filling the room. I had always been able to rely on Luca, but this... this was something else. This was a reckoning. And I wasn't sure we would survive it.

"I don't know who's behind this," Luca said slowly, his eyes never leaving my uncle's face. "But I know she didn't do it. And I'm not going to let you destroy her to save face." His words hung in the air, and I could feel my heart clenching. It was strange, really, to hear him speak with such certainty, knowing that it wasn't the truth that had sealed my fate, but their beliefs. In this house, the truth was a fluid thing, constantly shifting and changing with the winds of favor and fear.

"Then you're as foolish as she is," my uncle snapped. "You'll both learn the price of your defiance. Trust me."

There was a finality in his voice that made my stomach churn. It wasn't just the words that stung; it was the undertone of something worse—the subtle implication that the stakes had just gotten higher, and the game we were playing was one neither of us could win.

I wanted to turn to Luca, to thank him for standing beside me, but I couldn't. Not when I wasn't sure where his loyalty ended and mine began. Not when I wasn't sure if his act of defense was truly for me or simply for the sense of justice that had driven him all along. And in that moment, the weight of betrayal shifted again, the scale tipping violently in a direction I couldn't quite see, but I knew it was coming.

The weight of the room shifted, the energy crackling between my uncle and Luca, neither one willing to give an inch. The kitchen had become a battleground, and I was caught right in the center, torn between two forces that had once felt like home. Now, they felt like strangers, pushing against each other with a ferocity I didn't understand.

My uncle's gaze cut through Luca, his voice low and dangerous. "You think you can protect her? You're not even willing to look at the truth. You're blinded by whatever... foolish affection you have for her. This has gone far enough."

Luca's jaw tightened, his eyes darkening with something that wasn't just anger. It was an emotion that, if given a name, might have been closer to a quiet resolve. "I don't need you to lecture me about affection," he said, his words clipped. "I've seen the damage that lies can do. It's time you started seeing her for who she really is—before it's too late."

A silence fell between them, thick and suffocating. I could hear my own breath—ragged, uneven—as I watched Luca stand firm, his shoulders squared, the pulse in his neck a steady thrum of tension. There was something oddly heroic in the way he stood, something that made my heart twist uncomfortably. The truth was, I didn't deserve his loyalty. Not when everything pointed to me. Not when I could feel the walls closing in on me, piece by piece.

"You don't get it, Luca," my uncle spat, his voice rising now, the mask of calm slipping further away. "She's never been one of us. You're so blinded by your need to save her that you've forgotten what she is."

I felt it then, that final fracture. The moment when everything that had once been mine—my family, my place in the world, the safety of their love—slipped through my fingers like sand. What had I done? What had I really done to deserve this? The answer seemed impossible to grasp. All I could do was stand there, helpless, as the two most important men in my life turned their fury on me like a wildfire.

But Luca's gaze never wavered. He wasn't backing down.

And neither was I.

"I don't care what she was," Luca said, his voice steady despite the undercurrent of frustration that made my heart skip. "I care about who she is now. And if you can't see that, then that's on you. Not her. You're chasing shadows."

My uncle's eyes flashed with something dark—something bitter. "Shadows?" he muttered, his tone dangerous, low. "No, Luca. This isn't a shadow. This is betrayal. And the price for it is higher than you think."

I swallowed hard, the words sinking deep into my chest, where they lodged like splinters. Betrayal. That was what they thought I had done. But I hadn't. I had never betrayed them—not in the way they thought. But how could I prove that now, when the truth felt so elusive, so tangled? No one was listening. No one but Luca.

Luca took a step forward, and my heart stuttered, a rush of warmth spreading through me. But his expression was grave, his shoulders tense, his every movement radiating that quiet confidence I had always admired. He was standing in the fire for me, and I wasn't sure if I deserved it.

"I've never been more sure of anything in my life," he said quietly, his eyes locked on my uncle's. "She didn't do it."

For a moment, I thought my uncle might actually back down. But the muscles in his jaw worked, his fists clenched so tight that I could hear the leather of his gloves creak under the strain. "You're making a mistake," he warned, his voice cold, final. "I won't let you destroy everything because of her."

Luca didn't flinch. "Then destroy it," he said simply, the words so effortless, so final, that they sent a chill down my spine.

The tension in the room was unbearable, thick as smoke. My uncle's expression twisted into something darker, a reflection of the years of resentment he'd carried for me—and for all of us. He had never believed I belonged, had never truly accepted me into the fold of this family. Not really. The only one who ever had was Luca.

And now, it felt like that was all crumbling too.

I wanted to say something, anything, to break the tension, to make it clear that I wasn't some pawn in their game. But no words came. My throat was dry, my chest tight. I had been living in a world of silences for so long, I was beginning to wonder if I'd forgotten how to speak my truth.

"I don't want to do this," my uncle finally said, his voice hollow, like the last breath of someone who had long ago given up. "But I will if I have to. She'll never be a part of this family. Not again."

The finality of his words hit me harder than any slap. I had been holding onto the hope that somehow, someway, things could return to the way they had been. That I could find my place again. But that was gone now. He had made his choice.

Before I could say anything, Luca stepped forward, his hand gripping my arm in a firm, yet gentle way. His touch grounded me, but also... pushed me away, like a tether I wasn't ready to sever.

"I don't think we're done here," Luca said quietly, his voice carrying a weight I hadn't expected. There was a shift in his eyes—something that spoke of deeper things, of pasts unspoken, of a future we hadn't even begun to face. I could feel it, the change in the air, the unsaid words hanging like a fog between us.

My uncle's eyes narrowed, his lips pulling back in a grim smile. "We're not. But you'll regret this. Both of you."

And then, just like that, the door slammed behind him. The sound echoed through the house, a symbol of everything that had been shattered.

In that silence that followed, I realized something—something that felt as sharp and cold as the steel of a knife: this wasn't over. Not by a long shot.

Chapter 23: The Line Between Us

The estate had become a prison of my own making, its luxurious walls now a cage I couldn't escape. I walked the grand hallways as if in a trance, my shoes clicking softly against the polished floors, each step reverberating in the stillness of the mansion. There were no sounds of laughter or conversation here, no visitors to break the monotony. Only the oppressive silence that clung to every corner, the kind of silence that made you start questioning your own thoughts.

Luca had become my reluctant companion, though he never seemed to mind. His presence, once an irritant, had become the only thing that anchored me in this strange, gilded exile. At first, I couldn't understand why he stuck around. He was, after all, a man who had everything to lose by associating with me. Yet, night after night, he was there—silent, watchful, and somehow... patient. It wasn't until the tension between us started to shift that I realized something had changed. I had changed. The way I looked at him had changed.

He had his own quiet manner, the kind that spoke of years spent learning how to stand apart. The sort of man who knew how to hold a room with just a glance, yet remained an enigma, never offering anything too revealing. And yet, there were moments when I thought I glimpsed something behind those cold, calculating eyes—something almost human, something that made me question everything I thought I knew about him.

We were sitting in the library one night, the shadows long and creeping, the fire crackling softly in the hearth. I hadn't meant to ask the question, but it slipped out before I could stop it. My voice, quiet but laced with all the curiosity I'd kept buried for so long, hung in the air between us. "Why do you keep defending me?" I had no idea what I expected him to say, but it certainly wasn't the softness in his voice when he finally answered.

"Maybe I see something in you that you don't see in yourself," Luca replied, his eyes meeting mine, holding them just a little too long, as if daring me to see it too. His words hit me with the force of a revelation, the kind that leaves a mark long after it's been spoken. I wasn't sure what he meant, or what he thought he saw, but I felt something stir within me, something I couldn't quite name.

The firelight flickered, casting a warm glow on his face, but I couldn't shake the feeling that his words had been more than just an attempt at comfort. He wasn't offering pity. No, Luca didn't deal in pity. He was too pragmatic for that. This was something else. And for the first time in what felt like forever, I found myself wondering if maybe, just maybe, I was starting to believe in whatever it was he saw in me.

I leaned back against the leather chair, absently twirling a strand of my hair around my finger. "And what is that exactly? What do you see in me, Luca?"

He didn't answer right away, but the slight tightening of his jaw told me that my question had caught him off guard. For a moment, I thought he might dismiss it, as he had so many of my attempts to probe his thoughts before. But this time, he surprised me. His gaze softened just enough for me to catch it, like the briefest crack in his armor.

"You're stronger than you think," he said, his voice low and steady. "Most people would have broken by now. But you... you keep fighting."

I almost laughed, the sound bitter on my tongue. "Fighting for what? For you to keep locking me up in this house?"

"Fighting for yourself," Luca replied, his tone firm now. "I don't think you even realize how much you've fought to stay here, to not let this place swallow you whole. That's something worth respecting."

His words wrapped around me, heavier than the silence in the room, and I found myself grappling with them. I wanted to argue, to push back against the idea that I was some sort of warrior, but I couldn't deny it. I had fought every day since arriving at the estate. Fought against the isolation, the fear, the constant pressure to submit to this life I hadn't chosen. And now, I was fighting against the growing realization that Luca might be right.

The air between us thickened with unspoken understanding, and for a moment, I thought we might say more. But instead, we sat in that quiet, that space where words were both a comfort and a burden. Outside, the wind had picked up, rattling the windows, and the shadows seemed to stretch even further across the room. My thoughts were racing, but Luca's presence kept me tethered to reality.

It was strange, this pull I felt toward him. At first, it had been nothing more than annoyance, then perhaps curiosity. But now, it was something deeper, something unsettling. I could no longer ignore the way he made me feel—like I was something to be guarded, something that mattered. And in return, I couldn't shake the feeling that I, too, was guarding something in him, something buried beneath the sharp edges of his demeanor.

He looked at me again, his gaze just as intense as before, but there was something else there now—something raw, something that hinted at a truth neither of us was willing to speak aloud.

"I'm not who you think I am," he said suddenly, the words surprising even him. It was the first time he had ever acknowledged the distance between us so openly, and I wasn't sure whether to feel relief or more confusion.

"No one is," I whispered, barely able to form the words, my mind already racing ahead, trying to piece together the fragments of truth he'd just given me. But Luca didn't offer more, only leaned back in his chair, his eyes still fixed on me, as if waiting for something, though I wasn't sure what.

And in that moment, I realized something that both thrilled and terrified me: the line between us was no longer as clear as it had been.

I didn't know what to do with his words. The air in the room hung heavy, charged with something unspoken, and I could feel the distance between us narrowing, a sensation so sharp it was almost painful. There was something in his gaze, something that lingered even after he spoke, as if he had dropped a bomb into the middle of the room and was now waiting for the dust to settle. I wasn't sure what to make of it, or of him.

Luca leaned back in his chair, folding his arms with an air of practiced indifference, as if nothing had shifted. But I could see it. I could feel it. He was barely concealing the tension in his shoulders, the way his jaw tightened every time I dared to look at him too long. I wasn't sure if he wanted me to see it or if he was just too caught up in his own tangled thoughts to hide it completely.

"Is that supposed to make me feel better?" I said, the words slipping out before I could stop them. It wasn't entirely fair, but at that moment, I didn't care. My frustration bubbled to the surface, and the vulnerability his words had stirred up left me raw. "Because right now, I'm not sure it does."

He didn't flinch, didn't even blink, but the quiet, almost imperceptible shift in his eyes told me that I had struck a nerve. "I didn't say it to make you feel better," Luca replied evenly, his tone still measured, though there was an edge now, just a hint of something darker. "But I meant it."

We sat there for a moment, the quiet growing thicker between us. The fire crackled in the hearth, the low hum of the house settling around us, but it felt as though the world outside had fallen away. The uncertainty in my chest grew, gnawing at me, pulling me in two directions. I wanted to push him away, to keep my distance, to convince myself that the last thing I needed was to get tangled up in whatever this was. But there was a part of me that didn't want to do that. A part of me that wanted to know what he meant, wanted to understand why he kept coming back, why he kept defending me.

"I don't need your protection," I said finally, my voice rougher than I intended, but it was the truth. I had never needed anyone's protection. I had spent my life learning how to survive on my own. "I can handle myself."

Luca tilted his head slightly, considering me with a look that seemed both knowing and amused, though the amusement was quick to fade into something more serious. "No one's asking you to handle anything alone. But sometimes..." He hesitated, his fingers tapping lightly on the arm of his chair. "Sometimes, it's okay to let someone help."

The words hung there, hanging between us like a delicate thread that I wasn't sure I wanted to tug at. Help. It was an easy word to say, an easy thing to offer, but I had spent years building walls so high that asking for help had never crossed my mind. I had never trusted anyone enough to let them see the cracks in my armor.

"Help," I repeated, the word tasting foreign on my tongue. "And what exactly would that look like?"

Luca's lips twitched into a faint smile, and for the first time, it didn't seem like a calculated move. It was genuine, a small crack in his otherwise unyielding façade. "It looks like letting someone who's not you do the worrying for a change." His smile faded as quickly as it came. "It looks like giving yourself a break."

I felt a sting of something in my chest, but before I could process it, the door creaked open, cutting through the moment. A maid, her expression too apologetic for my liking, stepped inside. "Excuse me, Miss Donovan, but there's a man downstairs requesting to see you."

I blinked, my mind snapping back to reality. No one ever came to see me here. I hadn't seen anyone from the outside in weeks. "A man?" I repeated, half-expecting the maid to clarify that she was referring to one of the estate's staff, but no, she was not mistaken. Her nervous glance flicked to Luca, and I could feel the tension shift in the room again.

"Yes, Miss Donovan. He insists it's urgent. A Mr. Hollister, I believe."

The name meant nothing to me, but Luca's expression shifted imperceptibly, a shadow crossing his face, just a flicker of something I couldn't quite place. "I'll handle this," he said, his voice suddenly colder, his usual calm replaced with something more clipped, more authoritative.

"No." The word slipped out before I could stop it. I wasn't sure why I said it, but I felt an odd sense of protectiveness rise in me. "I'll handle it."

The maid hesitated, glancing between us, but Luca didn't move. He was waiting, watching me, his gaze intense.

"You don't have to," he said slowly, his voice softer than it had been, but with a finality that didn't leave room for discussion.

"I'm not fragile," I shot back, surprising myself with the snap in my tone. It wasn't a declaration of defiance, but it felt like one, a reminder to myself more than anyone else.

He gave me a look, one that was unreadable, before nodding, though the tension in his jaw was still there, pulling tight. "Fine. But if you need anything—"

"I'll be fine," I interrupted, standing up a little too abruptly, my heart thumping as I walked past him toward the door.

As I descended the staircase, I could feel the weight of Luca's gaze on me, his silent presence at my back like a shadow that wouldn't leave. I didn't know who this Mr. Hollister was, or what he wanted, but I knew that whatever was about to unfold, I was no longer as certain about my ability to handle it alone as I had once been.

I could feel my pulse quicken as I made my way down the grand staircase, each step reverberating in the stillness, a harsh contrast to the soft murmurs of the estate. The house was a maze of rooms, corridors, and alcoves that I had wandered through a thousand times, but tonight, they felt different. The air was thick, charged with the weight of the conversation I had just left behind. Luca's words were still echoing in my mind, a constant hum that I couldn't shake off no matter how hard I tried.

A part of me wanted to turn back, to retreat to the safety of the library, but my feet were already carrying me forward, down into the darkened hallway. The maid's anxious face flashed in my memory, her eyes darting toward Luca with a look of confusion, as if she had seen something shift between us. I couldn't explain it, but I knew I had to face whatever this was, whatever was coming.

The hallways felt colder now, the shadows longer. The soft light from the overhead chandelier flickered as I reached the entrance, where the man who had called himself Mr. Hollister stood waiting. The moment I stepped into the foyer, his presence hit me like a sudden gust of wind—sharp, cold, and unexpected.

He was tall, with dark, slicked-back hair and a face that seemed carved from marble, its sharp angles more striking than handsome. His suit was expensive, a shade of navy so dark it almost appeared black, tailored perfectly to his frame. And yet, there was something about him that unsettled me, something that made the back of my neck prickle.

"You must be Miss Donovan," he said smoothly, his voice low and measured, as if every word had been practiced a thousand times. He extended a hand, his grip firm when I hesitantly took it. "I'm Philip Hollister. I understand this is a... delicate situation, but I'm afraid we need to talk."

I didn't respond immediately. Instead, I studied him, trying to figure out the man standing before me. Something about the way he said "delicate" made me wary. The last time anyone had described a situation as delicate, I'd been handed a velvet-covered invitation to an afternoon tea that turned into an all-out war of secrets.

"What is this about?" I asked, my voice sharper than I intended. I didn't have time for games, not when I had no idea who this man was or what his intentions were.

Hollister's eyes flicked over my shoulder, as if ensuring no one was eavesdropping before stepping closer, lowering his voice. "You've been under house arrest, Miss Donovan. I'm here to offer a solution. Something more... agreeable for both parties." His words were smooth, but I could see the slight tension in his jaw, as if he didn't fully believe what he was saying.

I took a step back, crossing my arms, suddenly more aware of how exposed I felt in that moment. "I don't know who you think you are, but I don't need a solution from you. I'm not interested in whatever game you're playing."

Hollister smiled, though it didn't quite reach his eyes. "Oh, I think you'll find it's not a game. You see, Miss Donovan, your current... situation isn't exactly as simple as it seems. There are people who have a vested interest in seeing you remain here, far from the city, out of sight." He paused, his gaze hardening slightly. "But there are also people who want you to be... more useful to them. You're a commodity now, Miss Donovan, whether you realize it or not."

My stomach twisted at the word "commodity," a cold shiver running down my spine. I had been under no illusion that my time here was a result of some grand plan for my happiness, but hearing it spoken aloud like this felt wrong, unsettling. I stepped back again, suddenly feeling the weight of his presence like an anchor pulling me under.

"I'm not some object to be bartered with," I said, my voice steady despite the unease that was creeping in. "I don't know what your angle is, but if you think I'm just going to roll over—"

"Oh, no," Hollister interrupted, his smile widening into something almost predatory. "I don't expect you to roll over. In fact, I think you'll find that the offer I'm about to make will be rather appealing. To you and to the people you're trying so desperately to protect."

I froze. "Protect?"

He stepped forward, his presence suddenly overwhelming. "You're very naive if you think this is about you. It's about them. Your precious family. The ones you're trying to shield from all of this. But the truth is, they're not as safe as you think. Not by a long shot." His words hit like a slap to the face, and I could feel my chest tighten, panic rising in my throat.

"What do you mean by that?" My voice was barely above a whisper, but it didn't matter. Hollister's grin widened further, and I could see the satisfaction in his eyes, the knowledge that he had me on the ropes.

"I'm sure you've heard whispers, haven't you?" He was toying with me now, enjoying the power he wielded in that moment. "You've been kept away from everything, insulated from the real world. But there's no escaping the truth. If you want to protect them—your family, your loved ones—you'll have to play by my rules. And if you refuse..." His voice trailed off, leaving the threat to hang in the air like a heavy fog.

I felt my breath catch in my chest, a cold knot forming in the pit of my stomach. I opened my mouth to respond, but no words came out. The enormity of what he was suggesting hit me like a freight train.

Hollister took another step closer, his voice soft but unmistakably menacing. "Make no mistake, Miss Donovan. Time is running out."

Just then, the sound of footsteps echoed in the hallway behind me, and I spun around, my heart leaping into my throat. The door to the foyer swung open, and Luca appeared in the doorway, his eyes locking onto Hollister with a coldness that made my blood run cold.

Before I could speak, Luca's voice cut through the tension. "I think you should leave, Mr. Hollister."

Chapter 24: The Storm Within

The storm hit without warning, a furious crack of thunder that seemed to rattle the very bones of the old estate. For a moment, everything was silent, as if the house itself held its breath. The wind howled through the ancient oak trees lining the driveway, their branches clawing at the windows like desperate hands. And then, as if on cue, the lights flickered once—twice—before finally succumbing to the inevitable darkness.

I stood there, frozen for an instant, heart pounding in my chest as the reality of the power outage settled in. My fingers trembled as I reached for the old brass candlestick on the side table, the flame of the candle flickering to life with a soft pop. The dim glow cast long, shifting shadows on the walls, and the room seemed to close in around me, the air thick with the scent of rain and dust.

His voice cut through the silence, soft yet sharp, like the sudden edge of a blade pressed too close to skin. "It's just a storm," he said, though his words were more for himself than for me. I knew that. The familiar cadence of his voice, the one I had grown accustomed to in the quiet of the house, now held an unfamiliar tension.

I turned slowly, the flickering light revealing his silhouette against the darkened windows, his broad shoulders framed by the storm. But it wasn't the rain that made my pulse quicken. No, it was the unspoken words between us, the weight of them heavier than any storm could ever be.

I knew he was watching me, waiting for me to speak, and for a moment, I couldn't bring myself to. The air felt thick, oppressive even, as if the room itself was holding its breath. It wasn't just the storm that had brought us here, trapped in this house together, in the quiet dark. It was something deeper, something darker. A storm of our own making.

"You're the only thing that feels real in all of this," I found myself saying, the words slipping from my lips before I could stop them. My voice was barely above a whisper, as if saying it any louder might shatter the fragile bubble we had built around ourselves. "Everything else is... a lie."

The candlelight danced between us, casting our shadows long and distorted on the walls. His silence was a knife between us, and I felt the distance—longer now than it had ever been before. His eyes, dark and unreadable, studied me for a long moment. I couldn't see them clearly in the dim light, but I could feel them, like they were burning through me.

"And that terrifies me," he replied, his voice low, the words heavy with something I couldn't place. His hand brushed against mine, the contact electric, despite the storm outside. My breath caught in my throat. I had been so sure of myself before, so certain of the boundaries we had carefully constructed between us. But now, with the world outside raging and the power gone, everything felt... different.

His fingers lingered on mine, a tentative touch that sent a shiver crawling up my spine. I could feel the pulse in my wrist, faster now, as if it wanted to match the rapid thrum of my heartbeat. The air between us crackled with an energy I couldn't deny. The kind that pulled at the very marrow of my bones, urging me to cross that line we had both been so careful not to approach. But I couldn't. Not yet. Not when everything else felt like it was slipping through my fingers.

"I thought I had you figured out," I said, my voice barely audible over the storm outside. The wind rattled the windows again, but it was the vulnerability in his expression that made my chest tighten. "You're not the man I thought you were."

He chuckled, but it wasn't the easy sound I was used to. There was a roughness to it, a rasp that told me he had heard the truth in my words. "You've never really known me, have you?"

His hand dropped away, and the sudden absence of him felt like a vacuum, a hollow space where everything I had been holding onto threatened to spill out. I took a step back, my feet slipping slightly on the polished wood floor. The shadows twisted around us, stretching in impossible directions, as if the very room itself were trying to keep us apart.

"You've kept your secrets," I said, my voice trembling as I tried to steady myself. "And I've kept mine."

There was no judgment in my words, only a quiet acceptance. Because we both knew it was true. We had both built walls around ourselves, carefully constructed facades, pretending that we could move through this world without ever truly touching the people we held closest.

"You think I'm the only one hiding something?" he asked, his voice suddenly sharp, the words cutting through the fragile tension between us. His eyes flashed with something—anger, maybe? Or was it fear?

"I never said that," I replied quickly, my breath catching. "But you're right. I've got my own things I've never said."

We stood there, the flickering candlelight the only thing between us, the silence between our words louder than any storm could ever be. The night seemed to stretch on forever, a promise of things left unsaid, of moments we couldn't yet face. I felt the distance between us grow, then shrink, and I knew—whether we spoke the words or not—there was something between us, something that was far more dangerous than any storm.

The storm outside hadn't eased, and the air in the room seemed to pulse with the rising tension. I couldn't decide if the electricity had been sucked from the air by the storm, or if it was merely the presence of the man standing across from me, so close, yet untouchable. We stood in the half-light, the shadows around us deep and almost tangible, as though the room had become a thing of its own—a living, breathing entity feeding off our uncertainty.

I could feel his gaze on me, probing, measuring. It had always been like this, hasn't it? His scrutiny sharp enough to cut through the walls I'd carefully built. I could feel them crumbling now, brick by brick, every word from his lips, every move of his hand, a small assault on the fortress I'd wrapped around myself for years.

But in the back of my mind, there was a voice, a little too steady for my comfort, that whispered a simple truth: I wasn't the only one hiding behind a mask. Not by a long shot. He had secrets, just as heavy, just as tightly wrapped. The only difference was, he wore his mask with the ease of a seasoned actor, while I was still struggling to remember which face I was supposed to wear today.

He took a step toward me, slow and deliberate, and I couldn't stop myself from stepping back, even if only an inch. My heels clicked softly against the wood, and the sound echoed in the room like a warning bell. The air between us thickened, and I swallowed hard, suddenly aware of how the quiet could be far more terrifying than the storm outside.

"I think we both know," he said, his voice low and rough, as though he had been holding it back for far too long, "that pretending everything is fine isn't working anymore."

I didn't answer right away. What could I say? He was right, after all. Every glance, every word between us had been an act. The dinner table banter, the casual strolls through the garden, the long, quiet evenings spent with a book in hand—all of it had been nothing more than a performance. We had spent years playing our parts, each of us pretending we were someone we weren't, someone we could be proud of.

But I wasn't proud anymore. I wasn't sure I ever had been.

His eyes—those dark, unreadable eyes—never left mine as he closed the gap between us. The candlelight cast his face in sharp relief, and I could see the lines of stress around his mouth, the subtle tightness in his jaw. He wasn't as in control as he wanted to appear. For the first time, I saw it—the vulnerability that he had always hidden behind that polished mask.

"You're right," I said finally, my voice quieter than I intended. "It's not working. It hasn't worked for a long time."

His lips pressed together in a thin line, as if he were debating whether to say something more, something dangerous. His hand twitched, and before I could stop him, he reached out, brushing his thumb lightly across my wrist. The touch was barely there, but it had the effect of a spark, and I felt the heat of it pulse through me.

"You're the one who keeps pulling away," he said, his words low, like a confession, but there was no judgment in them, only a strange kind of understanding. "Every time I think we're close, you shut me out again."

I was shaking now, and not from the cold. There was a storm raging inside of me as much as outside. I wanted to argue with him, to tell him he had no idea how complicated it was, how much I had buried in order to be the woman I was supposed to be. But I couldn't, not with him standing there, his face so close to mine.

"Maybe it's easier this way," I muttered before I could stop myself. "Maybe it's easier if I don't let anyone in."

He stepped closer, his breath warm against my cheek. "And yet, you're still here. Still letting me in."

I stiffened at his words, my breath catching in my throat. It was true. I had come back, time and again, even when I told myself I wouldn't. Even when I swore that whatever this was between us would end.

The wind howled again, the trees outside swaying violently, their branches scraping the house like claws. But inside, the air had gone still, too still. My heart pounded as I struggled to push away the sudden flood of emotion that threatened to break free.

He reached for me then, his hand resting gently on my arm, and for a moment, the world outside ceased to exist. It was just him and me, two souls trapped together in this moment, in this storm.

"You don't have to be alone," he said, his voice softer now, almost coaxing, as if daring me to believe the words. "Not anymore."

My chest tightened, and I felt the familiar resistance rise within me, that instinct to pull away. But something in his voice, something in the way his fingers brushed against my skin, broke through the walls I had so carefully constructed.

"Why do you care?" I asked, the words coming out more jagged than I intended. "Why would you want to?"

He was silent for a long moment, his hand still resting on my arm. I could feel his breath, warm and steady against my cheek. And then, with a slow, deliberate movement, he stepped back, breaking the moment in a way that left me hollow and wanting.

"I don't know," he said quietly, the distance between us suddenly stretching. "I don't have the answer. But I think maybe that's okay."

The words hung between us, unfinished, hanging in the air like the storm outside—unpredictable, wild, and still far from over.

The air was thick now, too thick for words or the absence of them, a pulse that hummed between us, louder than the wind howling outside. He hadn't moved away, hadn't let go, his fingers still resting gently on my wrist, as though waiting for me to pull free, waiting for the moment I'd make my escape.

But the truth was, I wasn't sure I wanted to. That was the terrifying part, the part that clawed at me from the inside out. I had spent so long building this fragile version of myself, a version that wasn't real, a construct of what was expected, of what was easy. But here, in the dark, with him so close—his warmth, his presence—everything felt real. Too real.

I tried to swallow the lump in my throat, but it wouldn't go away. "I don't know how to do this," I finally managed, my voice cracking in a way that made me sound like someone else, someone I barely recognized.

He didn't say anything at first. Instead, his thumb traced a slow, circular path over my skin, back and forth, as though testing the waters, waiting for me to give some sign, some permission. The room seemed to shrink, the shadows crawling up the walls, folding in around us. The candlelight flickered once, twice, before settling into a soft glow, and it was as though the world outside had fallen away entirely. There was only him. Only this.

"You don't have to know how," he said quietly, and it sounded like a promise, like something he wanted to give me, but wasn't sure I would take. "Not with me. Not now."

I should've said something, anything to break the heavy silence that followed his words. Instead, I stayed there, rooted to the spot, my chest tight with the weight of everything I couldn't say.

The storm outside intensified, the wind battering the house like a thousand fists. The sound was deafening, the power of it making the old estate creak and groan, as though it, too, were trying to hold itself together. For a moment, I wondered if the house would cave in around us, if we would be swallowed by the night, trapped in this space that felt more like a prison than a sanctuary. And yet, I couldn't bring myself to move. Not when he was here, not when everything felt as though it was tipping dangerously toward something I couldn't name.

"You can't keep running from this," he said, his voice low, each word weighted with something I couldn't quite place. "You think I don't know you, but I do. Better than you think."

I laughed, but it was a bitter, hollow sound, and it didn't reach my eyes. "You think you know me? You don't know a thing about me."

He smiled then, a small, sad curve of his lips that sent a strange shiver through me. "Maybe not. But I know enough to know that you don't let anyone in. Not really."

There it was. The truth laid bare, no room for pretense or games. I felt exposed, vulnerable in a way I hadn't allowed myself to be in years.

"I never asked for anyone to get in," I whispered, more to myself than to him. "I built these walls for a reason."

"You're not the only one who builds walls," he replied, his voice barely audible. "But walls are only as strong as the cracks you let in."

I wanted to argue with him, wanted to scream at him that he had no idea how much damage I had done to myself by letting those walls fall, by allowing someone—him—so close. But the words wouldn't come. Instead, I found myself stepping closer, as if drawn by some magnetic force, my hand reaching out without my permission.

The heat between us was undeniable now, each breath we took in sync, and for a split second, I wondered if maybe we had crossed some invisible line, one that we couldn't return from.

Then, just as quickly, I pulled away, snapping back to reality. My heart pounded against my ribs, and I couldn't breathe.

"I— I can't do this," I said, my voice shaking. "I can't."

The storm raged on outside, the wind tearing at the trees, the thunder shaking the windows, but it was nothing compared to the storm in my chest. The confusion. The fear. The ache that threatened to swallow me whole.

"Then stop running," he said, stepping toward me again, his hand outstretched. "Stop running from us."

But I couldn't. I couldn't face what was between us, not when I didn't even know what I wanted. The tangled mess of desire and fear was too much to unravel all at once, too much to process in the dim light of the candle, the storm outside crashing like an unforgiving wave against a cliff.

"I don't know how to fix this," I whispered, my eyes brimming with something I couldn't name. "I don't know how to fix us."

He didn't answer right away. Instead, he seemed to search my face for something, some sign that I wasn't as lost as I felt. When he spoke again, his voice was low, almost hoarse. "Maybe it's not about fixing anything. Maybe it's just about letting it happen."

I wanted to tell him that wasn't possible. That I wasn't the kind of woman who let things happen. I wasn't the kind of woman who let herself fall without a safety net. But when I opened my mouth, the words wouldn't come.

And then, as if on cue, the lights flickered once more before plunging the house into complete darkness.

I froze, a lump forming in my throat. The sudden silence was deafening, as though the storm had stolen everything—every sound, every thought—leaving only the weight of the moment.

And then, in the blackness, a soft, familiar sound echoed through the house. The click of a door opening. Slowly, quietly, the unmistakable sound of a footstep.

I turned, my breath catching in my throat, but before I could say anything, a voice—low, cold, familiar—whispered from the shadows.

"You think you're in control here?"

Chapter 25: Broken Chains

The rain lashed against the windows, a constant roar that drowned out all but the sharp pulse of my heartbeat. I could feel the tension in the room like a thick fog, as though the air itself had become too heavy to breathe. Every drop of water outside seemed to carry with it a memory of betrayal, the cool wetness creeping into the cracks of my chest where trust had once lived.

Luca stood across from me, his face barely illuminated by the flickering lamp. His usual charm, the easy confidence that always made my heart skip, was gone. In its place was something darker, something harder. The man I thought I knew was slipping away, replaced by a stranger whose secrets now spilled into the room like that very storm outside.

The paper in my hands trembled, and I forced myself to focus on the words, the lines that had sent everything spiraling out of control. Names, dates, times—all leading back to the one person I had never suspected. I had always prided myself on knowing people, on reading them like the back of my hand, but this... this was a betrayal I wasn't ready for.

Luca took a slow step forward, his gaze never leaving mine, though it seemed to be somewhere far beyond me. He reached out, his fingers brushing the paper I still gripped too tightly.

"Is this... really happening?" His voice was barely a whisper, the disbelief still cutting through it like shards of glass. He had to ask. He had to confirm, because the reality was too absurd to accept. Too painful to bear.

I swallowed hard, forcing down the lump in my throat. "It's happening," I managed to say, though the words felt foreign in my mouth. "And you knew. You knew all along."

His jaw tightened, and for a moment, I saw something flicker in his eyes—something dark, something regretful. But that flicker disappeared just as quickly as it came, buried beneath the weight of whatever truth he was now carrying.

"I didn't know," he said, his voice rough. "Not in the way you think."

"Then why didn't you tell me?" I could feel the rawness of my anger bleeding through, but it wasn't just anger—it was betrayal, confusion, hurt. "Why did you hide this from me, Luca?"

He ran a hand through his hair, the movement tense, almost frantic. "I didn't want to lose you. Not like this."

I laughed—bitterly, without humor—and dropped the paper onto the table. The storm outside had finally breached the windowsill, and I could see the reflection of my own face in the glass. There was a time, not so long ago, when I would have looked at that face with pride. Now all I saw was a woman who had been blind to the very things that had been staring her in the face.

"You didn't want to lose me, but you've already lost me, Luca," I said softly, my voice trembling despite myself. "You've lost me in ways I can't even explain. The one thing I always thought I could count on—our partnership, our trust—that's gone. And you've taken it with you."

His eyes softened, but only for a moment. He stepped closer, his hands outstretched like he was about to offer some sort of comfort, but I pulled back. The gesture, meant to soothe, only stung.

"You don't understand," he began, his voice low and strained. "This wasn't about you. It was never about you. This... this was about keeping us safe. It's bigger than us. You wouldn't have believed me, not without seeing it for yourself."

I stared at him for a long moment, trying to make sense of the chaos swirling between us. His words didn't add up, not entirely, and yet there was something about the way he said them that made me pause. He was telling me the truth—or at least, part of it.

"And the part about you working with the person who—" I cut myself off, not wanting to say the name aloud. It was too much, too raw.

"I never worked with them," he said quickly, almost too quickly. "I just... had no choice. Do you think I wanted to drag you into this? Into all of it?" His voice cracked, and for a moment, I saw something so vulnerable in him that it nearly made my heart break.

"Why didn't you trust me?" I whispered, stepping back further into the dim light. "Why didn't you let me choose? I could have helped you. But instead, you kept me in the dark."

Luca's shoulders slumped, his eyes closing as if he were physically weighing the burden of my words. I wanted to reach out to him then, to fix it, to make everything okay again—but I couldn't. The damage was too deep. The trust was gone.

"I never wanted to hurt you," he said quietly, his voice hoarse. "I just... I thought I was protecting you. But I see now—"

"You thought you were protecting me?" I cut in sharply, a bitter laugh escaping me. "From what? The truth? Or just from being a part of your mess?"

The silence stretched between us, heavy and suffocating, until Luca spoke again, his voice filled with a quiet resignation. "The storm's not over yet, Paige. And neither is the fight. We still have time, but we need to decide what we're willing to lose."

The storm raged on outside, but I felt like it was inside me too—raw, unrelenting, and full of the sharp edges of a truth I wasn't ready to face.

The silence between us was unbearable, suffocating in its weight, as the storm outside battered the windows with an urgency I couldn't escape. Luca stood there, the lines of his face drawn taut, a man made weary by the very secrets he had kept. But those secrets were now spilling into the room, thick and acrid, suffusing the air like smoke from a fire you can't outrun.

I should have felt something—relief, even. After all, I had spent countless nights wrestling with questions, the unanswered ones gnawing at the edges of my mind, demanding to be addressed. And now, here they were, laid bare in front of me. But the answer didn't bring the resolution I had expected. No, it was just a jagged shard of the truth, one that left a bitter taste on my tongue and a coldness creeping into my bones.

"You're not telling me everything," I said, my voice cutting through the quiet with surprising steadiness. I had expected more tears, but there were none left. There was just this empty, gnawing feeling in my chest, an absence where the warmth of our shared history had once lived.

Luca's eyes darted to the floor, as if the hardwood could somehow offer him an escape. He was always so composed, so controlled. Yet in this moment, I saw the cracks forming, the first real sign that the man in front of me was just as vulnerable as I was. That was the thing about trust, wasn't it? It's not so much about knowing someone's strength as it is seeing their weakness and still choosing to stay.

"I never meant for any of this to happen," Luca finally murmured, lifting his gaze to meet mine. There was no bravado, no smirk. Just the truth in his eyes, raw and unguarded. "I thought I was protecting you. From all of this."

"Protecting me?" I repeated, a dry laugh escaping before I could stop it. "From what, Luca? The truth? You know what's worse than lies? Half-truths."

His expression faltered, and he stepped back, rubbing his hands over his face in frustration. "This isn't what you think. I didn't—"

"Don't." I cut him off before he could finish. The last thing I wanted to hear was a justification, a rehearsed excuse. He didn't get to explain this away, not after everything.

"I trusted you, Luca. I thought we were in this together. But it's like you built a wall around me, and I only just realized I've been on the other side of it the whole time."

The storm continued its relentless assault, but it felt as though the storm within me had finally broken. I was done pretending. The pieces of us, of what I had believed was real, lay scattered across the floor like shards of glass. And for all his regret, Luca hadn't reached out to pick them up. Instead, he stood there, as helpless as I was.

"I didn't want to lose you," he said again, his voice softer now, and something in it softened the edges of my own anger. "But I've been so afraid, Paige. I didn't know what to do. The people I'm dealing with... they're not who you think they are. This is bigger than just us."

"So, what? You thought lying to me was the best way to protect me?" My words came out sharper than I intended, but they were the ones I needed to say, no matter how much they stung. "How did you think this would end, Luca? Did you really think I'd just... go along with it?"

His shoulders slumped under the weight of my words, but there was something else in his gaze now. Guilt. Recognition. He had hurt me, and for the first time, he was allowing himself to see it. The cracks in his armor, ones I had been waiting to see for so long, were finally becoming visible.

"I thought if I kept you away from this world, kept you safe, I could protect you from what's coming," he admitted, each word falling from his lips like a confession. "I didn't think you'd get caught in the middle. I should have told you sooner, but I was afraid. Afraid you'd leave me if you knew the truth."

For a second, I felt the heavy weight of his words settle over me, the complexity of his motives pulling me in, even as I recoiled from them. There was a part of me—still aching, still tender—that wanted to believe him. That wanted to believe this was all some massive misunderstanding. But deep down, I knew better. The damage had been done. And the longer we stood here, wrapped in our own web of miscommunication and secrets, the further apart we drifted.

I crossed the room slowly, almost as though I were drifting through some sort of fog, and grabbed my jacket from the chair by the door. My fingers shook as I slid it over my shoulders, the cool fabric brushing my skin in a way that made everything feel so much more final than it had a moment ago. The truth had come, but it wasn't the end. No, it was just the beginning of the real damage, the aftermath that followed the storm.

"I don't know if I can do this anymore, Luca," I said, my voice tight but steady, a wave of finality in each word. "I don't know if I can just... forget. If I can trust you again after all of this."

I moved toward the door, but as I passed him, I hesitated, just for a moment. It was so stupid, but I felt that flicker of hope in my chest—like maybe he would say something, anything, that would make this all make sense again. But he didn't. Instead, Luca stood frozen in place, his eyes dark with regret and sorrow.

"I'm sorry," he said, the words barely audible, but they were the only ones left between us.

And then, without another word, I stepped out into the rain, the cold drops washing away the remnants of a love that had once been everything.

The streets of Chicago were almost empty, save for a few lone souls hurrying along, their coats pulled tightly around them, heads down, as though they could escape the storm just by moving faster. The rain had turned the city into a blur of gray and glass, the neon signs above bar entrances flickering like old, tired fireflies. I walked without thinking, each step a metronome that only seemed to amplify the pounding in my chest. The night air tasted like steel, sharp and bitter, and I couldn't quite escape the feeling that something—no, someone—was still pulling at my heart, despite the rupture that had just occurred between us.

But Luca's voice, that apology, was like a ghost at my back. "I'm sorry," he had whispered. It was a thin thing, hollow. A way to make himself feel better, I thought. The weight of his words had sunk into me, but not the way I wanted it to. Not the way it should have. It was more like being handed a bandage when you're bleeding out. How could I forgive him for keeping me in the dark? For assuming I was so fragile I couldn't handle the truth?

I needed to get out of the storm—out of my own head—and into the bright, chaotic pulse of the city. I took the next turn, seeking refuge in the warmth of a nearby bar. It was one of those dives tucked in between a tattoo parlor and a jazz club, the kind of place that only served beer and whiskey and played music that had too much soul for its own good. The kind of place where, if you sat long enough, you could hear everyone's story without them ever having to speak.

As soon as the door swung shut behind me, the low hum of chatter and the clink of glassware wrapped around me like a blanket. The bartender didn't bother to look up, already knowing the routine. The old man sitting at the end of the bar raised an eyebrow when he saw me, a flicker of recognition in his eyes, but he kept his thoughts to himself. It was the kind of place where nobody asked too many questions.

I took my usual seat at the far side of the bar, the one that gave me a clear view of the door but kept me out of the main crowd. Just another ghost, blending into the background of a city that never slowed down long enough to notice.

"Whiskey," I told the bartender, my voice steady, though my insides were anything but.

The glass came quickly, the amber liquid sloshing against the sides as he slid it toward me. I tipped my head back, savoring the burn that scorched my throat and momentarily shut down everything else. The storm outside raged louder now, but it felt so far away, as though I could separate myself from it, from everything.

Except I couldn't.

The door to the bar opened with a sharp creak, and I didn't need to look up to know who had walked in. I could feel him. The tension in the room shifted, like a ripple on a still pond. I didn't have to turn my head to know he had seen me. I could feel his presence, a weight pressing against the air. He didn't speak at first. The sound of his boots echoed softly as he moved toward me, his steps deliberate, measured.

"I thought you might be here," Luca's voice came, low, rougher than I remembered.

I didn't say anything at first, just continued to sip my drink, the bitterness of it mingling with the ache in my chest. I wasn't ready to face him again, but apparently, he wasn't giving me a choice.

"You left," he said, taking the seat beside me without asking.

"You followed," I shot back, my words sharper than I intended.

He exhaled, dragging a hand through his wet hair, the water dripping down his neck and onto the bar. "You really think I'd just let you walk away, after everything?"

I turned to look at him then, finally. His eyes, usually so composed, were worn, heavy. His jaw clenched in frustration. There was something else in his gaze now, something raw that made my heart ache all over again, even as I tried to keep it at bay.

"You think I wanted this?" he asked, his voice rough. "Do you think I wanted to drag you into this mess?"

"I didn't ask for any of this, Luca," I snapped, my temper flaring again. "You made your choices. You kept me out of the loop. And now you're here, in my space, thinking you can fix it all just by showing up?"

"I never wanted to hurt you." His voice was quieter now, filled with an exhaustion that mirrored my own. "But I wasn't given a choice."

The words hung in the air between us, too many unsaid things curling like smoke around the edges of the conversation. I leaned back in my chair, trying to create some distance between us, both physically and emotionally. But Luca wasn't done.

"I know you're pissed. Hell, I don't blame you for it. I've been a coward," he said, his eyes searching mine, almost pleading. "But there's more. There's something you don't know. Something I couldn't tell you before."

I glanced at him, my brow furrowing in confusion. "What are you talking about?"

His gaze shifted nervously, and I could feel the tension creeping back between us, thicker than it had been before.

"I didn't just work for them," he said, his voice barely above a whisper. "I am one of them."

My pulse stopped in my veins, the words landing with a sickening thud. For a moment, I couldn't breathe. I stared at him, trying to make sense of what he had just said, but the words tangled together in my mind like a knot I couldn't untangle.

"You... what?" I barely managed to croak.

"I've been a part of this from the inside, Paige. And I never told you because I didn't want you involved. But it's too late now. They've got their eyes on you."

I opened my mouth, but no words came out. My chest tightened, and the world around me began to spin. I had been walking in the dark, trusting the wrong person, and now I was trapped in a web of lies I didn't know how to escape from.

And then, just as I was about to speak, the door to the bar flew open again, and a cold gust of wind swept inside, carrying with it the unmistakable sound of sirens.

Chapter 26: The Unraveling

The apartment smells like burnt coffee and regret. I can't even remember the last time I brewed a fresh pot; I just keep the mug there, half-empty, sitting on the edge of the counter as if the act of sipping from it might somehow make the mess in my life less chaotic. It's one of those mornings, the kind that reminds you of how deep you've sunken, how much you've lost, and how little time there is to fix any of it.

Outside, the city is waking up with its usual energy—cars honking, people bustling along the sidewalks, the faint hum of a distant siren slicing through the noise. But all of it feels muffled, as if I'm submerged beneath an ocean of bad decisions, too overwhelmed to swim back to the surface. I press my fingers to my temples, trying to will away the headache that's been lodged there for days. Maybe if I don't move too fast, I can convince myself I'm not drowning in a sea of consequences.

The door slams open behind me, and I don't have to turn around to know it's Luca. His presence fills the room in a way no one else's does—powerful and sure, like a storm gathering in the distance. But this isn't the easy confidence I've come to rely on. This is something darker, something jagged.

"Amelia," he says, his voice low and urgent, like a warning. "We need to talk."

I keep my back to him, pretending to be busy with the coffee mug, as though I can delay the inevitable. But the truth is, I've been avoiding this moment for weeks. I'm not ready to hear the words I know he's about to say, but I don't have a choice. Not anymore.

"I know," I say, my voice quieter than I intended. I glance over my shoulder, meeting his eyes. The betrayal in them stings like a fresh wound. His jaw is clenched, his fists balled at his sides, and for a split second, I wonder if he's going to hit me.

He's been angry before, furious even, but this—this is different. This feels like a breaking point.

"I'm not asking you to pick sides, Amelia," he mutters, his voice thick with frustration. "But if you don't make a choice soon, you'll lose everything."

I swallow, fighting the lump in my throat. "What do you mean, 'lose everything'?" My voice is shaking, but I refuse to let him see how much this is tearing me apart.

Luca steps forward, his eyes never leaving mine. "I mean us. I mean me."

I shake my head. "I don't understand."

He lets out a harsh laugh, the kind that doesn't reach his eyes. "Of course you don't. You never do until it's too late." His words slice through the silence like a blade. I flinch at the intensity of them, but I don't look away. If I do, I might just lose the nerve to face him at all.

He paces the small kitchen, his boots heavy on the hardwood floor. "You don't see it, do you? You think this is just a game. A family squabble. A few power plays to keep the peace, and then everything will be fine." He stops in his tracks, spinning back toward me. "But it's not. It's bigger than that. And now, because of him"—he spits the word like it's poison—"you're stuck in the middle. Between me and your uncle. And I'm telling you, Amelia, I can't do this anymore. You need to choose."

The finality in his tone makes my stomach drop. I want to tell him it's not that simple. I want to remind him that nothing in life ever is. But the truth is, I'm not sure anymore. I thought I knew what was right, what was worth fighting for, but that was before my uncle's betrayal tore the seams of everything I'd ever known.

He takes another step toward me, and the rawness in his expression pulls at something deep inside of me. "You're not just in the middle of this, Amelia. You're the reason it's happening. The reason we're all falling apart."

I don't know what to say to that. How do I respond to the accusation that I'm the cause of everything going wrong? How do I defend myself when I'm not even sure where I stand anymore?

"Luca, I never asked for any of this," I finally whisper, my voice small in the face of his fury. "I didn't choose this."

He steps closer, his breath warm on my face. I can feel the tension radiating off him, the weight of a thousand unsaid things pressing in on us both. "But you're in it now," he says, his words softer, but no less devastating. "And whether you like it or not, you have to choose. Me or him."

I try to swallow the lump in my throat, but it sticks there, like a bitter pill I can't force down. I want to tell him that I've already chosen, that I've known for weeks what my answer would be. But saying it out loud would mean admitting the depth of the rift between us—and I'm not sure I can bear the consequences of that.

The silence that stretches between us is thick with the weight of everything we've lost. And as Luca stares at me, waiting for an answer I'm too afraid to give, I realize that no matter what I choose, it will never be enough.

Luca doesn't move. His gaze is like a challenge—sharp, demanding—waiting for me to break. But I don't. I can't. There's something cold that settles in my chest, a gnawing ache that twists every thought I try to form. I want to run, hide, pretend none of this is happening, but I'm done with running. It's taken everything I had just to stand here and face him.

"I never wanted this for us," I finally say, my voice steadier than I feel. "This... this mess, it's not my fault."

He lets out a short laugh, bitter and low. "Of course it's not, Amelia. You're just the innocent bystander in your own life, right?"

He takes another step forward, closing the distance between us, and I feel the heat of his anger radiating off him like a furnace.

"I never asked for any of this," I repeat, my words coming out stronger this time, but the truth lingers in the air between us, undeniable. I did ask for this, didn't I? I was foolish enough to believe I could have everything—him, the family, the loyalty—but all of it was built on shifting sand.

I've known for weeks that things weren't going to stay the way they were. Uncle Tony's betrayal was just the beginning, the spark that lit the powder keg. The family I thought I knew, the people I trusted, had turned into something unrecognizable.

And yet, standing here with Luca, with the storm cloud of his disappointment hanging over me, I don't know which is worse—the rage or the hurt that flickers beneath it. I can feel the tension winding between us like a taut wire, threatening to snap at the slightest movement.

Luca rakes a hand through his hair, a nervous gesture I haven't seen from him in a long time. His anger is real, but there's something else too—something that feels like regret, like he's as trapped in this as I am.

"I never asked you to choose between us, you know," he mutters, his voice quieter now, almost resigned. "But it feels like you're already making your choice. Every day that goes by, it feels like you're pulling away from me."

The words hit me harder than they should. I want to argue, tell him I'm not pulling away, that I'm just trying to keep my head above water. But it's true, isn't it? Every conversation, every look, every time he touches me, I hesitate just a little longer. I pull back just a little bit more. It's like I'm bracing myself for the moment when I'll lose him for good.

"I'm not pulling away," I say, my voice softer now. I take a step forward, trying to bridge the gap between us, but he doesn't move. His expression is unreadable, like a mask I can't decipher.

"I just... I can't live in this constant state of fear," I add, a harsh edge creeping into my voice. "Fear that if I make the wrong move, I'll lose everything. Fear that if I don't choose, I'll lose you."

The words land between us with a weight neither of us can ignore. Luca's jaw tightens, and I see the muscles in his neck twitch as if he's holding himself back from saying something he'll regret. His eyes are a storm—dark, turbulent, unreadable.

"You've already lost me, Amelia," he says, his voice low but sharp, cutting through the air like a blade. "Every time you hesitate, every time you look at me like I'm just a choice... you're losing me."

I flinch, the sting of his words settling deep in my chest. I want to reach out to him, pull him into my arms, tell him that I'm not trying to push him away, but that's the problem, isn't it? It's not enough to just feel something. Not anymore.

The sound of my phone buzzing on the counter breaks the silence. I glance at it, but I already know who it is—Uncle Tony.

"Answer it," Luca says, his voice barely a whisper, but the weight of the command is unmistakable. "Tell him. Tell him what you need to tell him. This is the moment, Amelia. You can't keep pretending it's not happening."

I look down at the screen, the name blinking back at me in bright letters. My uncle, the man who's shaped so much of who I am, whose betrayal has shattered everything. I want to ignore it, turn it off, pretend I'm not being forced into a corner. But I know I can't. I can't avoid this any longer.

With a deep breath, I answer.

"Hello?" My voice is shaky, and I hate it.

"Amelia," Uncle Tony's voice crackles through the speaker, smooth but with an edge that makes my skin crawl. "We need to talk. It's time you made your choice. Him or us."

My heart skips a beat, and I feel a rush of panic flood my chest. He doesn't even wait for me to respond before he continues.

"This isn't something that can be fixed with a few kind words, darling. You can't have it both ways. You've got to decide. And soon."

I don't respond immediately. I can't. I feel Luca's eyes on me, the pressure mounting between us, like a storm that's about to break.

"I'll think about it," I finally manage to say, my words clipped, unwilling to give him more than he's asking for.

"Think fast," Uncle Tony says before the line goes dead, the finality of it hanging in the air like a guillotine.

I look at Luca, who's still standing there, his face a mask of frustration and helplessness.

"You heard him," I say, trying to steady my voice, but it cracks anyway. "I have to make a choice."

Luca nods, his expression unreadable. "And when you do, Amelia, you need to be ready for the consequences."

I want to ask him what that means, but I know. I know exactly what it means. And I don't think I'm ready for it.

I sit back against the counter, the cool ceramic of the coffee cup in my hands doing little to steady my racing pulse. The air is thick between Luca and me, charged with all the words neither of us dares say. I want to scream, want to throw something, anything, to break the oppressive silence suffocating the room. Instead, I stay frozen, the weight of the decision pressing down on me like a hundred-pound anchor.

Luca is no longer standing directly in front of me, his presence now more like a shadow lurking in the corner of my vision. I can feel his gaze on me, but I refuse to look at him. To do so might make the choice real, might force me to confront what I've been avoiding all this time.

"I never wanted to hurt you, you know," I say, my voice barely a whisper, a futile attempt to bridge the chasm that has grown between us. "I never wanted any of this."

There's a long pause, the kind that's heavy with the weight of unspoken truth. Then, Luca's laugh rings out, hollow and sharp.

"Don't you see?" he says, his voice tight with a mixture of pain and frustration. "It's too late for that, Amelia. We're already in it. You've already made your choice."

His words sting, and I wish I could defend myself, explain the tangled mess of loyalty and love that's caught me in its snare. But I can't, because he's right. I have made my choice, even if I've done it unconsciously. My heart is already with him, even if my mind keeps running to safety, to the world I used to know, the one my uncle has now destroyed.

"I know," I say quietly, swallowing the lump in my throat. "I know it's too late."

Luca takes a step closer, his boots tapping softly on the floor, the sound somehow louder than the pounding in my chest. His presence is suffocating, but it also feels like the only thing anchoring me to reality.

"You're not going to walk away from this, Amelia," he says, his voice low and dangerous, a promise wrapped in steel. "Once you make this decision, there's no going back. You'll lose pieces of yourself you didn't even know existed. And you'll have to live with that."

The finality in his words feels like a punch to the gut, and I force myself to take a deep breath, willing my racing thoughts into submission. I'm not prepared for this. I never was.

"You think I don't know that?" I snap, my voice sharper than I intended, but the fury bubbling inside me breaks through. "I've already lost so much, Luca. My uncle's betrayal has shattered everything. And now I have to choose between the two people I love most in this world." I can feel the burn of unshed tears threatening to break free, but I won't let them. Not yet.

"I didn't ask you to choose, Amelia," Luca says, his voice softer now, though still filled with an undercurrent of pain. "But if you don't, you'll lose both of us. And I can't... I won't... stand by and watch you destroy yourself."

The honesty in his words cuts through me like a knife. I know, deep down, that this is the final warning, the last opportunity to make a decision that could save us both. But I'm frozen, caught between two worlds that are crashing together faster than I can comprehend.

And then, as if fate itself is playing its hand, my phone rings again. This time, it's not Uncle Tony, but my father. The phone buzzes incessantly, the sound jarring in the heavy silence of the room.

I stare at the screen, my thumb hovering over the answer button. Every instinct tells me to ignore it, to turn it off, but I know better. I know that the conversation I'm about to have with my father might be the very thing that decides my future. And no matter how much I wish I could escape this moment, I can't. I never could.

"I have to take this," I say, barely looking at Luca. He doesn't respond, his eyes now trained on the phone in my hand. The tension between us feels almost unbearable.

"Answer it," Luca says, his voice tight. "Tell him what you need to tell him. You can't keep hiding from this, Amelia."

With a deep breath, I swipe the screen and press the phone to my ear. "Hello?" I say, trying to keep my voice steady, but it cracks anyway.

"Amelia," my father's voice is smooth and calm, the way it always is when he's trying to control the situation. "We need to talk. I've been patient with you long enough, but it's time to make a decision."

I don't say anything, just let his words hang in the air. The moment feels like a stage, and I'm caught somewhere between the act and the real consequences of what's to come.

"You've known the stakes for a while now, darling," he continues, his voice calm but insistent. "This is the final call. I'm giving you one last chance to decide. Him, or us."

The words echo in my head, a twisted mirror of what Luca just said. My pulse is racing again, the weight of the decision more oppressive than ever. This isn't just about family anymore. This is about survival, about choosing the path that will leave me whole—or break me completely.

But before I can respond, I hear a loud crash, the unmistakable sound of something shattering, followed by shouting.

"Amelia," Luca's voice is frantic now, the panic in his tone cutting through the phone call like a blade. "Get out of there—now."

The world tilts on its axis as the urgency in Luca's voice sinks in. I turn to look at him, but he's already halfway to the door, his hand gripping the handle like he's about to tear it off.

"Luca—what's going on?" My voice is shaking now, a cold, clawing dread filling my stomach.

"I don't know, but you need to leave," he snaps, his eyes wild with fear. "They're coming for us."

The room spins around me, the walls closing in. My heart races as the decision I've been avoiding slams into me with the force of a freight train.

And then, just as I move toward him, the door flies open—and I hear my uncle's voice, dark and cold, calling my name from the hallway.

"Amelia," he says, his tone lethal. "It's time to decide."

Chapter 27: A Fragile Alliance

The city was a jungle of steel and glass, the sun's last rays slicing through the towering skyscrapers like blades of light. The air smelled like rain that never quite fell, thick with the promise of summer storms that seemed to hover just beyond the horizon. I stood on the rooftop of the office building, my eyes scanning the horizon, but my thoughts were anchored somewhere much closer—somewhere far more dangerous.

Luca's hand on my back was the only thing that kept me tethered to reality, to the here and now. His fingers were warm against my skin, but the tension in his grip told me everything I needed to know. We were both playing a game, one we didn't know how to win, but the stakes were high. Too high. The consequences of losing were far worse than any we'd ever faced before.

Below us, the streets of Chicago pulsed with life, oblivious to the storm brewing in the underbelly of the city. Traffic hummed, the distant honking of car horns a dull, rhythmic sound, almost comforting in its normalcy. But I couldn't shake the feeling that the city was holding its breath, waiting for something—someone—to make the first move.

"Do you think he'll show?" I asked, my voice barely above a whisper, as if speaking louder might change the fragile balance between us.

Luca's gaze never wavered from the street below, his jaw tight. "He'll show. He always does. The question is—what happens next?"

It was a question I'd asked myself a thousand times in the last twenty-four hours. Emiliano had made it clear that he wasn't interested in playing nice, but I didn't expect him to be. People like him never played by the rules. I wasn't sure what kind of game he was playing, but I was fairly certain the rules had already been bent so far out of shape that even the strongest players would lose their footing.

My phone buzzed in my pocket, its vibration harsh against the silence between us. I pulled it out, glancing at the screen. One missed call. From Emiliano. I didn't need to look at Luca to know his body had stiffened at the sight of the name.

"Are you going to answer that?" he asked, his voice tight, his eyes flicking to me with something dangerously close to impatience.

I didn't answer at first. I couldn't. I wasn't ready to face whatever Emiliano had to say, and I wasn't sure I ever would be. But the buzzing persisted, relentless, until I finally slid my finger across the screen and brought the phone to my ear.

"Emiliano," I said, my voice barely above a murmur, as though the mere act of saying his name might shatter everything I was trying to hold together.

"Meet me in twenty," he replied, his voice smooth, disarmingly calm. There was no pleasantry, no wasted words—just the unmistakable weight of authority in every syllable. "The alley by the bar on Clark Street."

I swallowed hard, my pulse quickening as the finality of his words settled over me like a heavy fog. I'd known this moment would come, but that didn't make it any easier to bear. The alley on Clark Street wasn't a place where deals were struck with good intentions. It was a place where men like Emiliano made their mark, where lives were traded like currency, and nothing was left behind except a faint trace of blood and regret.

I didn't respond at first, just let the silence stretch between us until the tension became unbearable. Then, finally, I found my voice.

"I'll be there," I said, my words as cold and hard as the city beneath me.

I hung up the phone and slipped it back into my pocket, the weight of it almost too much to bear.

Luca didn't ask what had been said. He didn't need to. He already knew. His hand was still pressed against my back, but now his fingers tightened, almost painfully.

"Are you sure about this?" he asked, his voice low, a note of concern lacing the words.

I nodded, though the truth was, I wasn't sure of anything anymore. But one thing was clear: Emiliano was the only player left in the game. He was dangerous, volatile, and untrustworthy—but without him, we were nothing. We were already halfway in the grave, and Emiliano was our last chance for survival.

"I don't have a choice," I replied, the words tasting bitter on my tongue.

Luca didn't say anything, but the shift in his posture spoke volumes. He wasn't happy about this, but he'd never been one to walk away from a fight. Not when the stakes were this high.

We stood there for a long moment, the noise of the city carrying on around us, as if life had no idea what was about to unfold in the shadows of its streets.

Finally, Luca broke the silence, his voice rough. "I don't like it. But I'll be there with you. Always."

I nodded, but the words didn't come. What could I say? That I was terrified? That I didn't know what would happen next? That everything I'd believed in, everything I'd fought for, was on the verge of falling apart?

No. Instead, I forced a smile, the edges of it strained, but still present. "Let's go. We don't have time to waste."

Together, we turned away from the rooftop, leaving behind the city's indifferent hum, knowing that the real game was just beginning.

The car was an old, beaten-down sedan, the kind that had seen too many miles to be called reliable. It reeked of stale coffee and air fresheners that tried, and failed, to mask the scent of leather that had long since lost its sheen. The tires hummed against the pavement as we made our way to Clark Street, the engine sputtering in protest with every turn.

Luca sat beside me, his gaze fixed out the window, as though the passing scenery could somehow provide answers to the questions neither of us had dared to ask. His jaw was clenched, a muscle twitching every time the car hit a pothole. I knew he was scared, and though I wasn't brave enough to admit it, I was too.

"This is insane," Luca muttered, more to himself than to me.

I didn't answer at first. He was right, of course. It was insane. The entire situation felt like something out of a bad crime thriller, the kind you watch on Netflix in the middle of the night when you can't sleep, telling yourself that you'll turn it off after one more episode. But then it gets dark. Too dark. You can't look away, even as you start to realize how far the characters have fallen.

And that's exactly where we were, stuck in the middle of something we couldn't escape, no matter how fast we ran.

"You're right," I said finally, breaking the silence that had settled like a thick fog between us. "But what other choice do we have? We either play his game, or we risk losing everything."

Luca turned to look at me, his eyes narrowing. There was a flicker of something—anger, frustration, maybe fear—but it was quickly masked by the cold mask he wore so often.

"I just don't like it," he said, his voice low. "The whole thing stinks. Emiliano doesn't do favors. He doesn't give anything without taking something in return."

I met his gaze, my heart pounding in my chest. "I know. But we don't have time to figure out what he wants. We just need to survive."

He sighed, the sound heavy with exhaustion. He was right, of course. There was no time for anything except surviving. The seconds were ticking away, and every moment that passed was one where Emiliano had the upper hand.

As the car slowed and I watched the neon lights of the city flicker into view, I could feel my nerves twisting tighter. Clark Street wasn't exactly a place for the faint of heart. The alley Emiliano had chosen was as far from the polished glamour of the Gold Coast as you could get. It was gritty, rundown—a place where even the most desperate wouldn't linger unless they had no other choice. And we were about to make it our meeting point with a man who could ruin us both with a single word.

I wasn't sure if I was more afraid of Emiliano or the way the city itself seemed to breathe around us, alive with secrets that weren't meant to be discovered. The streetlights cast long shadows on the pavement, and in the distance, a homeless man sat with his back against a brick wall, smoking something that smelled far too sweet and far too strong. The air was thick with the tang of something metallic, a storm that hadn't quite broken yet.

I glanced over at Luca, trying to read his expression, but he was lost in his thoughts. The tension between us was suffocating, and I knew he could feel it too. I reached over, placing a hand on his arm, the gesture a silent reassurance. It didn't mean much, but I needed him to know that we were in this together, whether he wanted to be or not.

When the car finally pulled to a stop, my heart leaped into my throat. We were here. It was real. I could hear my own breathing, loud and ragged in the silence of the car, and for a brief, terrible moment, I wondered if I'd made the right choice. But then, Emiliano's words echoed in my mind: You don't have a choice.

I was here because I had no other option.

Luca didn't speak as we got out of the car, his hand brushing against mine as if we both needed that small, fleeting contact to keep ourselves grounded. We made our way down the alley, our footsteps echoing against the narrow walls that closed in around us like a trap. The air was thick with the scent of wet asphalt and decay, the distant hum of traffic above us a stark contrast to the eerie stillness of the alley.

I didn't look around, didn't let myself get distracted by the shadows that seemed to reach for me from every corner. My eyes were fixed ahead, on the figure standing in the dim light of the streetlamp at the end of the alley.

Emiliano.

He was everything I'd expected and nothing like I'd imagined. Taller than I remembered, with a sharp jawline and the same piercing eyes that had once made me question everything I thought I knew about people. He was dressed in a black leather jacket that seemed to absorb the light around him, the collar turned up just enough to add to the menace of his presence. His hair was slicked back, a few strands falling into his eyes as he looked at us with that same calculating gaze.

"You're late," he said, his voice smooth, mocking, and just a little too confident.

I forced myself to meet his gaze, refusing to let him see how much I wanted to shrink away from his presence. "We're here now, aren't we?" I said, my tone clipped, though I could feel the tremor in my chest.

Emiliano smiled, a thin, dangerous thing that didn't reach his eyes. "You are. But that's not enough." He stepped closer, his gaze flicking to Luca before returning to me. "I need you to understand something, sweetheart. I'm not in the business of making friends. I don't care about your little family drama. I don't even care about you." His eyes darkened slightly, as if the words held some deeper meaning. "But you're in my way. And that's why we're here."

I swallowed hard, knowing that we were playing his game now, whether we liked it or not.

The moment Emiliano spoke, the air between us thickened. I could practically hear the weight of the words hanging in the dark, settling like a blanket over our heads, suffocating every last breath. It wasn't just that he was dangerous—it was the way he commanded the space around him, as though the entire alley, the decrepit buildings on either side, and the flickering streetlight above us belonged to him. It wasn't intimidation exactly. It was something worse. A cold, undeniable certainty that nothing was beyond his reach.

"You think you're in control," Emiliano continued, his lips curling into a smirk, "but you're not. You're playing catch-up. You're already a step behind."

I forced my hands to relax at my sides, refusing to give him the satisfaction of seeing me flinch. I could almost feel Luca beside me, tense and ready to leap into action at any sign of danger, though the danger had already been here for some time. The world had spun so far off its axis that we were barely clinging to the edges of sanity.

I didn't want to give him anything—nothing at all. Not an inch of ground, not a single concession. But in the tightness of the moment, I knew the truth, however ugly it was: I couldn't afford to push back. Not yet. Not when every step, every word we exchanged, was a gamble with stakes I couldn't fully comprehend.

"So, what do you want?" I asked, keeping my voice calm, even as my pulse roared in my ears. "I'm here. Let's get this over with."

The smirk faltered, replaced by something colder, something sharper. Emiliano took a step forward, closing the distance between us until his presence was almost suffocating. I resisted the urge to step back, to distance myself even slightly from him. Luca's hand twitched at my side, an instinctive motion to protect, but I held him back with a subtle shake of my head. We were already here, and there was no turning back.

"You think I want something from you?" Emiliano asked, his voice dropping to a low whisper. He was too close now, his breath mixing with mine in the stagnant night air. I could almost taste the bitterness in his words. "No. You're the one who needs something from me."

I swallowed hard, fighting the rising dread. "And what's that?"

A wicked gleam flashed in his eyes, the kind of look that made me shiver despite the warmth of the summer night. "I want loyalty. Real loyalty. Not just to your little family drama. I want you to prove that you're worth the risk. Because right now, you're not."

Luca's jaw tightened beside me. He didn't speak, but the way he moved, the way his stance subtly shifted, made it clear he wasn't about to let Emiliano talk down to us. But Emiliano wasn't just talking. He was manipulating, pulling at strings we hadn't even realized were there.

I forced a laugh, though it came out harsher than I'd intended. "Loyalty? You're asking for loyalty from us? The same loyalty you've shown to everyone else? You're a snake, Emiliano. And no matter how many tricks you pull, I'm not about to be charmed into following you."

His eyes flickered with something that resembled both amusement and disdain. "We'll see about that," he murmured, and in the next moment, his gaze snapped to something just beyond us.

I didn't see it at first—didn't hear the movement—but suddenly, from the shadows, a figure emerged. My heart skipped in my chest, my body tensing as the newcomer stepped into the dim light.

"Who's this?" I demanded, my voice barely masking the sudden spike of panic.

Luca, too, had stiffened. His eyes darted from me to the new figure, a tall man with dark features and a quiet presence that screamed danger. I had never seen him before, but his gaze was cold, calculating—entirely out of place here in the heart of the city's darkest corners.

Emiliano grinned, as though he knew exactly what his new pawn was worth. "Meet my associate," he said, his tone clipped, almost affectionate. "He's been very helpful in ensuring that you and I have this little chat. He's... persuasive."

My blood ran cold as I took in the new arrival, his eyes never leaving me, not even when he moved to stand just behind Emiliano, like a shadow.

The man didn't speak, didn't make a sound, but I could feel his presence like a weight pressing down on my chest. The sense of danger was palpable, and for the first time in a long time, I realized just how deeply I had underestimated Emiliano. This wasn't a simple power play. It wasn't just about loyalty or business—it was about something darker, more insidious.

"You've been preparing for this, haven't you?" I said, my voice barely audible but laced with disbelief. "This whole time, you've been playing us."

Emiliano's smirk didn't fade, but there was a sharpness to it now, a calculating edge that made me sick to my stomach. "Everything's a game, sweetheart," he said, his voice low and dangerous. "And right now, you're just a pawn. But you'll come around. Everyone does."

Luca moved subtly, a flash of movement I barely registered before I felt his hand on my arm, pulling me slightly behind him. He was ready, poised to protect me in a way I couldn't quite understand. But before either of us could react, the man behind Emiliano made his move, stepping forward with a sudden speed that took us both by surprise.

"Don't even think about it," the man warned, his voice deep, cold, his gaze unwavering. He was standing too close now, close enough for me to feel the heat of his presence. My breath caught in my throat, and I instinctively stepped back, tugging Luca with me.

And then, from somewhere in the distance, the unmistakable sound of a siren wailed through the alley, cutting through the tension like a knife. It was too far to be a real threat yet, but I could feel Emiliano's eyes narrow, his posture shifting, ready for whatever came next.

"What's this?" I asked, my heart racing, suddenly aware that we weren't alone—not by a long shot. "Did you call them?"

Emiliano's lips quirked into a grin, one that promised far too much. "I think you'll find that your problems are just beginning, sweetheart."

Chapter 28: The Final Test

The air in the room felt like it had been squeezed out of every corner, leaving nothing but taut tension. The office — or what I had tried to convince myself was a temporary safe house — was bathed in the cool, fluorescent hum of overhead lights. The scent of stale coffee and polished wood hung in the air, mingling with the faint odor of fear. Emiliano's rivals weren't the kind of people you encountered in daylight, not unless they were looking for something or someone to destroy.

Luca stood by the large window, his silhouette sharp against the grey cityscape, watching as the last traces of the afternoon sun disappeared behind a cloud of ominous smog. His jaw was tight, hands fisted at his sides as though holding onto the fragile thread of control that kept him from spiraling. I knew the look well enough. It was the same one that had appeared on his face when we first met — the face of someone who'd been forced to live in a world of chaos, and the one that still haunted him in the quiet moments when he thought no one was watching.

"We're doing the right thing," I said softly, my words barely rising above the low murmur of city traffic outside. It was a desperate attempt to reassure him, though I wasn't sure I believed it myself. His eyes flicked over to me, dark and unreadable, before he gave a slow, deliberate nod.

"I hope so." His voice was calm, but there was a slight quiver in it that I couldn't ignore. It was the sound of someone who had fought too long to keep his balance, and now the world around him was tipping dangerously to one side.

The knock on the door came suddenly, sharply, like a gunshot in the quiet tension between us. My stomach dropped. The timing was too perfect, too calculated. They were here.

"Showtime," Luca muttered, his hand brushing through his hair as he turned to face me. For a moment, I saw something flicker in his eyes — something primal, almost savage — and my heart gave a sudden jolt.

"Do we have a plan?" I asked, a smile that didn't quite reach my eyes tugging at my lips. It was an odd question to ask considering the circumstances. But if we were going to walk into a den of vipers, it was best to keep the conversation light.

Luca didn't laugh, but the corner of his mouth twitched upward, a brief moment of levity before the storm. "I'm going to handle the negotiations. You stay close. Don't make any sudden moves, and don't—" He stopped, seeming to realize how ridiculous that sounded. "Don't do anything that might get us both killed."

I raised an eyebrow. "Well, you've got a way with words."

The door creaked open before he could reply, and in stepped a man who looked like he belonged in an entirely different world. Clean-cut, with a tailored suit that screamed money and power. He was too smooth, his every movement too calculated. His eyes scanned the room like a predator sizing up its prey before he locked onto Luca with an almost predatory gleam.

"Luca," he said, his voice rich with a foreign accent that I couldn't quite place. "It's good to finally meet you in person."

The words were polite, but there was something cold behind them, like the calculated politeness of someone who had already decided how the meeting would end.

I felt an involuntary chill creep up my spine. There was no warmth here, no friendly gestures, only the tightening of the noose.

Luca didn't move a muscle, his gaze unwavering. "The pleasure's mine, I'm sure."

The man's smile was thin, but it didn't reach his eyes. "I think you know why we're here." He gestured to the sleek black briefcase in his hand, the glint of metal catching in the low light as he set it on the table between us.

I couldn't help but watch the briefcase like it was a bomb waiting to go off. It was all part of the game, I knew. But that didn't make the stakes any less terrifying.

"You have something we want," Luca said, his tone measured but edged with the steel of someone who was used to playing this game. "I have something you need. We settle this now, or we walk."

The man raised an eyebrow. "Walk?" He chuckled, low and dangerous. "I think you'll find that walking isn't really an option, Luca. Not when the price is as high as it is."

I saw Luca's hand tense, but he didn't move. There was something in the air now — an invisible weight pressing down on us, pulling the world into focus. This wasn't just a negotiation. It was a battle for survival.

I wasn't sure if he realized it, but I could see it clearly enough. They were pushing us into a corner, hoping we would flinch, hoping we would make the wrong move. And I wasn't sure if we had the luxury of getting out unscathed.

The man tapped the briefcase, the sound sharp against the silence. "You want the leverage, Luca? This is it. One decision, and everything changes." His eyes shifted to me briefly before returning to Luca. "But first, I think we need to make sure you're willing to pay the price."

Luca didn't flinch. He didn't give an inch. But I saw the way his eyes darkened, saw the storm brewing beneath his calm exterior. He had never been the type to back down from a fight, even when it meant risking everything.

I could feel my own pulse quicken, my breath coming in shallow gasps as the gravity of the situation crashed down on me. The stakes had never been higher. Not for me, not for Luca. We were standing at the precipice of something irreversible.

And then, without warning, the man smirked.

"We'll see if you're as willing to pay the price as you think, Luca."

The briefcase felt like a boulder between us, a constant reminder that nothing in this room was as simple as it seemed. I wanted to move—anything to break the suffocating tension—but every muscle in my body seemed to be frozen, held in place by the weight of the man's gaze. The polished wood of the table gleamed, almost mockingly, in the cold, artificial light. The room was too neat, too ordered for the chaos we were about to face.

Luca stood like a statue, his back straight, eyes hard as granite, but I knew him too well to believe that this meeting hadn't shaken him. There was an undercurrent of doubt, one that ran deep, just beneath the surface. And I could feel it, creeping through the cracks of his controlled demeanor. I wasn't sure if it was the stakes, the enemies at our backs, or just the weight of everything we'd been through together. Maybe it was all of it.

The man who had come to play his part in our little game—his name, I'd learned earlier, was Victor—leaned back in his chair with a casualness that was downright insulting. He was playing it too cool, as though he thought we were somehow beneath him, pawns on a chessboard that would fall into line when the time came. The truth was, he was right to think so. He had the power, the leverage, the money—and we, well, we had nothing but each other. And sometimes, even that wasn't enough.

"You still don't understand," Victor said, his voice an almost bored drawl, like he was offering a lesson to a child. "This isn't a negotiation, Luca. It's a final game. And I'm the one who gets to decide the terms."

Luca didn't react to the threat in his words, which told me everything I needed to know. He had heard those threats before, from people much worse than Victor. But still, I saw the muscle in his jaw tighten, and that quiet, dangerous calm came over him like a dark cloud, rolling in fast.

I couldn't help myself; I was drawn to that storm, even if it terrified me. I wasn't just scared for myself anymore. No, I had already signed up for that the moment I stepped into this mess. But Luca? He was different. He was everything I never thought I'd need, and now I was facing the terrifying prospect of losing him, not to some overblown game of fate, but to someone who would destroy him for the sheer pleasure of it.

Victor smiled, all teeth, and it made my stomach churn. "You're going to do exactly what I tell you," he continued, tapping the briefcase again, "and then, maybe, I'll let you walk away. Maybe. But I'll be keeping my eye on you, Luca. I always do."

I could feel Luca's eyes snap toward me then, though they didn't soften in the slightest. He didn't need to say a word; I could read him like the back of my hand. That look—sharp, knowing, and filled with that burning intensity I'd grown to love—was all I needed.

"Get ready," Luca murmured under his breath, his voice low and lethal.

I took a deep breath and fought the wave of nausea rising in my throat. "I'm not here to make deals with men like you, Victor," I said, surprising even myself with how steady my voice sounded. I glanced at Luca for reassurance. He was still motionless, unreadable. The world had a way of bending itself around him. I wanted that power. I wanted to be like him—calm, collected, unshakable. But, as always, I was just a woman caught in a web she'd woven herself.

Victor chuckled, as though my words were the faintest echo of a joke he wasn't even remotely amused by. "I admire your bravado, darling," he said, his eyes sliding over to me with a practiced, almost predatory glance. "But that won't save you. You should know that."

I wasn't so sure. I wasn't sure of much at this point. But there was something in the way he spoke, something beneath the surface, that made me think we had a choice here. A way out.

Luca's voice cut through the silence, sharp and hard. "Enough with the games. We're not here to play your little power struggles." He leaned forward then, just enough to remind Victor who held the real power in the room.

Victor leaned back in his chair again, as if Luca's words hadn't even made an impression. His smirk never wavered. "You think you have control here, don't you? You and your little lady—" He paused for a moment, as though weighing the words. "—I think it's cute, really. But no one has control. Not even you."

I wanted to shout back, to tell him that we weren't the ones under his thumb. That we had our own weapons. But something in the air—something sharp and dangerous—told me it was better to wait. I knew better than to underestimate Victor, but I also knew that Luca wasn't a man who would be cowed so easily.

Silence settled over the room, a thick, oppressive fog that seemed to pull the air from my lungs. The longer it lasted, the more I could feel the invisible clock ticking down. I wasn't sure how much time we had before things went too far, before we couldn't turn back.

Victor broke the stillness with a languid stretch of his arms, as if he had all the time in the world. "You know, Luca, I think we've come to an impasse." His eyes were cold, calculating. "There's really no point in pretending that this is anything but a power struggle. One of us will walk away. But which one? That's the real question, isn't it?"

Luca exhaled slowly, his gaze narrowing as he studied the man across the table. "You won't be the one walking away."

Victor's smile returned, wider this time. "We'll see about that."

And just like that, the game was on.

The words hung in the air, heavy and suffocating, as if they were meant to settle over us like a shroud. Luca's voice was calm—too calm, I thought. The way he said it, as if he could truly convince himself, made something stir in my chest. It wasn't a sense of reassurance. It was the understanding that neither of us had a choice.

I shifted in my seat, trying to avoid the weight of Victor's stare. He was still watching us with that unnervingly smug expression, as if everything in this room—this entire power struggle—was just a game he was playing, one where the rules had long been written in his favor. I hated that look, that sense of inevitability, the way he seemed so certain we were on the losing end.

"You think this is about walking away, Luca?" Victor's voice was almost too soft, like a purring cat about to strike. He leaned forward just a little, his eyes glinting under the harsh light. "No. You're in this now. This isn't about deals or leverage anymore. This is about survival."

His words had an edge to them that cut deeper than I expected. For a moment, I could see it—the desperation, the way his facade wavered just enough for me to catch the flicker of something darker underneath. It wasn't just about winning. Victor needed us to fall. He wanted us to break under the pressure.

"I don't think you understand the situation," Luca said, voice still controlled but laced with a new kind of coldness. His tone was razor-sharp, a warning that hadn't been there before. I felt the weight of his words sink into my bones.

Victor's smirk faltered for just an instant. He knew—he knew Luca wasn't intimidated. But that didn't stop him from leaning back, fingers tapping on the edge of the briefcase as if this was all some sort of trivial annoyance. "You really think you have the upper hand, don't you?" he asked, amusement dripping from each syllable.

"We're not here to trade insults," Luca said, his words clipped, every syllable calculated. He was reaching that point, I could feel it, where the game was no longer about being civil. It was about power. And right now, the power in this room was slipping away faster than I could track.

There was a moment, a split second, where I almost felt sorry for Victor. But then his eyes caught mine, and I was reminded of just how dangerous people like him could be. This was no longer a negotiation; it was a standoff. And as much as I hated to admit it, I knew we were both too far in to walk away without paying a price.

Victor's phone buzzed, a sharp, intrusive sound that sliced through the thick tension. He glanced down at the screen, his eyes narrowing just slightly before he silenced it. For a moment, it felt like the calm before a storm, the air thick and charged with the kind of silence that promised everything was about to explode.

"That's your last warning," Victor said, voice low, almost a whisper, but the intensity behind it made my stomach twist. "If you're not willing to play by the rules, Luca, then I'll make sure you understand what happens when you're too late."

The words were a clear threat, one that didn't need elaboration. But Luca didn't flinch. He didn't even blink. His gaze never left Victor's face, and for a moment, I was certain Luca could see right through him—through every layer of control and mask Victor had carefully built over the years.

"I'm not afraid of you," Luca finally said, his voice steady but cold, each word like a stone dropped into a lake. The ripples of his declaration spread across the room, breaking the fragile calm we'd been living under. I didn't know what to expect after that. A fight? A bullet? Some sudden, unforeseen twist that would turn our world upside down?

But nothing prepared me for what happened next.

A figure stepped into the room, completely unnoticed by either of us. The sharp click of high heels on polished wood was the first clue I had that someone else had entered. My heart skipped a beat, and I instinctively reached for Luca's hand, trying to ground myself as the new arrival moved closer.

It was a woman, tall and poised, dressed in a sleek black dress that seemed to absorb the light in the room. Her hair was swept back in a tight, perfect ponytail, and her eyes—dark, calculating—bored into mine as she stopped just behind Victor. There was something eerily familiar about her, something I couldn't quite place.

Victor looked over his shoulder at her with something close to disdain before returning his gaze to Luca. "Did you think you were the only one playing games, Luca?" he asked, a challenge lacing every word.

The woman smiled—sharp, like a knife—and my breath caught in my throat.

I knew her.

I'd seen her once before, fleetingly, in the shadows of Emiliano's office, but there had been no time to question who she was. Now, standing in front of me, with that chilling smile playing on her lips, everything about her screamed danger.

Luca's posture stiffened beside me. I felt him tense, as if this new arrival had just tipped the balance of everything. The realization hit me with the force of a freight train. This wasn't just a business deal anymore. It wasn't just power plays or threats.

We were all standing in the middle of a trap, one I wasn't sure any of us were going to walk out of.

"Who is she?" I whispered, my voice low, barely above a breath.

Luca's eyes darkened, and I saw a flash of something—something dangerous, something that, for just a moment, I feared.

"We're about to find out."

Before I could react, the woman spoke, her voice smooth and unbothered. "I think it's time for you to choose, Luca. But choose wisely. There's no going back from this."

And with that, everything went black.

Chapter 29: The Weight of the Truth

I'm not sure what hurts more—the words that slip out of my mouth, or the way his grip tightens in response. I didn't expect him to hold on, not like that, not with a force that almost feels like an anchor. I don't want to be anchored. I want to run. To scream. To tear it all apart and start over, but instead, I stand there, locked in this moment with him, feeling the weight of the room closing in.

The air between us is thick with the scent of coffee and something more. Something darker, like smoke still clinging to a fire long after it's gone out. There's blood on the floor—mine, Luca's, and too many others to count. The kind of blood that stains the soul. I'm not sure if I'll ever be able to wash it off.

"You can't," he insists, his voice low, like he's speaking to a child. Maybe I am one. A child caught in a game too big for me.

I glance up, meeting his eyes, and there's a flicker of something there, something I don't want to acknowledge. There's a flicker of guilt, of fear. Maybe even pity. But then it's gone, replaced by that impenetrable look of his—the one that hides every emotion, every thought behind a mask of indifference. A mask he wears so well, I sometimes forget it's not his real face.

The problem is, I know him better than that. I can feel the cracks in his armor, the parts of him he's desperately trying to keep hidden. He doesn't trust me, not fully. And why should he? I've been playing a part in this circus of lies and betrayal for far too long.

"I don't know how much longer I can keep pretending," I say, my voice barely above a whisper. My heart is pounding, my hands are shaking, but I try not to let it show. I've learned the hard way that vulnerability is a luxury I can't afford.

Luca's grip loosens, just slightly, and I think maybe he's finally heard me. Or maybe he hasn't. Maybe he's just trying to hold it together, like we all are. But that's the thing—none of us really know what holding it together even looks like anymore.

He looks away for a moment, his gaze drifting to the bloodstained carpet where bodies still lie, unmoving. The sound of distant sirens echoes through the night, a reminder that the world beyond these walls continues to turn, oblivious to the chaos we've created inside.

"I never wanted this for you," Luca says quietly, his voice tight with something I can't quite place. Regret, maybe? Guilt?

"But you didn't stop it, either," I reply, my words sharper than I intended. I didn't mean to lash out. But there it is. The truth, raw and unfiltered. And it's not just directed at him. It's aimed at both of us. At this life we've chosen, or maybe this life that's chosen us, without asking for our opinion.

He doesn't flinch. He never flinches. That's Luca for you. Unbreakable on the surface, while everything inside him is unraveling, piece by piece.

"I did what I had to do," he says, his tone hardening. "I didn't have a choice."

"You always have a choice," I snap back before I can stop myself.

The silence stretches between us, heavy and uncomfortable. I regret my words immediately, but it's too late. I can't take them back. The damage has already been done.

"I wish I could believe that," he murmurs, his voice barely audible. "But you don't understand. Not like I do."

I want to scream. I want to throw something at him, shatter the cool, calm façade he's so carefully constructed. But instead, I just stand there, my hands clenched into fists at my sides.

"I understand more than you think," I say, my voice trembling despite myself. "I'm not some naïve girl who doesn't know what's at stake here. I've been in this long enough to see the darkness that surrounds us. I know what it means to lose yourself in all of this.

But I also know that there's still a part of me that wants to get out. That wants something more than... this."

I gesture vaguely at the wreckage around us, at the lives we've destroyed, the people we've killed. I can see the flash of regret in Luca's eyes, but it's quickly masked by his usual implacable expression.

"I don't know if I can do that," he says, his voice strained. "I don't know if either of us can."

The words hang in the air, heavy and ominous. And for a moment, I'm not sure if he's talking about us—or about this whole damn family. The one we've built on lies, on blood, on promises we can't keep.

I want to say something—anything—to make him understand. To make him see that there's still hope, that we can still walk away from this if we want to. But I can't find the words. Not when everything between us feels like it's falling apart.

Instead, I just nod, the movement stiff and unnatural, like my neck is too heavy to hold up. There's nothing more to say, not right now. The silence is the only answer I have left.

Luca watches me for a long time, his gaze unwavering, as if he's trying to read me. To understand the puzzle I've become. But I don't know if he ever will. Because the truth is, I don't even understand myself anymore.

And that, more than anything, terrifies me.

I stand there, my body frozen in place as Luca's hand tightens around mine, pulling me closer, like he believes I'll run if he lets go. Maybe I would. Maybe it's the only thing I've wanted to do for months, but I can't bring myself to take that first step away from him, even though the pull to do so has never been stronger. It feels as if the room itself is shifting, the very air crackling with tension—like we're standing on the edge of something. And I'm not sure if it's an abyss or a breakthrough.

His breath is warm against the back of my neck as he steps closer, the heat of his body seeping into mine. I want to pull away, but I don't. There's something magnetic about him in this moment—something broken and raw beneath the mask of the mob boss he insists on being. It's the first time I've seen him like this. The hardness in his eyes has melted away, replaced by something I can only call desperation.

"You don't understand," he mutters, his lips brushing my ear, his voice barely a whisper. "None of this was ever supposed to be like this. I didn't want you involved, not this deep."

His words, soft as they are, leave a bitter taste on my tongue. He didn't want me here? Then why the hell is my name etched on everything that's gone wrong in his life over the past few months? Why has he let me crawl into this mess if he didn't want me involved? I could argue with him. I could say something snide, something clever that would remind him how much of this is his doing, but I don't.

Instead, I pull my hand from his grasp, not forcefully, but enough to make a point. Enough to make it clear that I can stand on my own, even if every part of me feels like it's crumbling.

"I never asked for any of this," I say, my voice trembling as I turn to face him. "But here we are."

He watches me, his eyes soft, like he's trying to read me, to understand what's going on behind the mask I've learned to wear. But there's no way for him to know. No way for anyone to know. Not unless they're willing to look past the surface, past the hardened exteriors we all wear, to the soft, fragile things underneath. I wonder if he sees it—if he sees how close I am to breaking.

The silence stretches out between us, thick and suffocating. It's not the comfortable kind of silence that comes after a shared moment of peace. It's the kind of silence that feels like a storm is coming, and neither of us knows how to brace for it.

"You're right," he says at last, breaking the silence, his voice still low and rough. "You didn't ask for this. I dragged you into this life."

He runs a hand through his hair, a rare gesture of frustration that I haven't seen from him in... well, maybe ever. Luca doesn't get frustrated. He gets even. That's how he's always been—cold, calculating, never letting anything shake him. But now? Now he looks like a man on the verge of unraveling.

"I should've kept you safe," he mutters, almost to himself. "I should've gotten you out of here before things got this bad."

Before things got this bad.

The words sting more than I want to admit. Because, deep down, I know he's right. He should've kept me away from this. But instead, he let me dive in headfirst, a willing participant in a game I didn't understand. And now... now we're both drowning in it.

"You're not the only one who's in too deep," I say, forcing the words out, even though it feels like they're cutting me from the inside. "I didn't just fall into this, Luca. I made my choice. And now I'm stuck with it. Stuck with you."

His eyes flash, something like anger or maybe hurt flickering behind them. But I'm not scared. Not anymore. Not by his rage. Not by anything he can throw at me. I've seen the worst of him, and I'm still standing here, still fighting to keep my head above water.

"Is that what this is?" His voice rises, a tinge of bitterness creeping into his words. "You think you're stuck with me? After everything we've been through? After everything I've done for you?"

I want to snap back, to remind him that I've done plenty for him, too. That this mess is just as much mine as it is his. But the words die on my lips, because in some twisted way, I do feel stuck. Stuck in this world of violence and deceit, stuck with him—whether I want to be or not.

"Look, Luca," I start, my voice steadier than I feel. "I didn't ask for your protection. I didn't ask for any of this." I gesture around us again, taking in the shattered glass, the broken lives, the blood that still clings to the floor. "But we can't undo what's been done. I can't erase any of it. And neither can you."

His jaw clenches at my words, but he doesn't speak. Instead, he just looks at me, his face unreadable, his dark eyes locked on mine like they're searching for some kind of answer. Some kind of sign that we're not both drowning in this mess, that there's still a way out.

"You're right," he finally says, his voice low, almost reluctant. "But that doesn't mean I'm going to let you go. Not like this."

I swallow hard, the lump in my throat threatening to choke me, but I refuse to show him any more weakness. Not now. Not after everything.

"I don't know what you want from me," I say, my voice barely a whisper. "But I can't keep doing this, Luca. Not with you. Not with any of it."

He doesn't say anything at first. He just stands there, watching me, like he's trying to decide if I really mean it. But I do. I do mean it. I'm done playing this game, done pretending that we can still come out on top. Because in this world of ours, there's no winning. There's only surviving. And I'm not sure I want to survive anymore.

The tension in the room is thick enough to cut with a knife, but the sound of my own heart beating is louder than anything else. The pulse in my ears is deafening, like it's trying to drown out the chaos that's still echoing through the hallways of my mind. It's as if my every thought is running at a breakneck speed, colliding with another, and I can't sort them out.

But there's one thought I can't seem to shake: Why the hell am I still here?

Luca's fingers dig into my palm as though he thinks if he holds on tight enough, I'll be tethered to him forever. I want to pull away. I want to tell him everything I've been hiding, every ounce of resentment I've buried, every fear that's been gnawing at me since I first stepped into this mess of a life. But instead, I just stand there, because that's what we do in this world, isn't it? We keep standing. Even when we're drowning. Even when the ground beneath us feels like it's crumbling away.

He's watching me, waiting for me to say something, to give him something—anything—but I don't. I can't. The words have become knives in my throat, and I'm not sure I want to stab him with them. I'm not sure I can.

"You don't understand," he murmurs, his voice quieter now, almost lost in the weight of the moment. "I don't want this life for you, but I can't change what's been done. It's too late."

There it is—the same excuse, the same justification. I can't change what's been done. But that's what they all say, don't they? My father said it. My brother said it. Luca says it now. Every one of them wants to claim they didn't have a choice. Well, I'm sick of hearing it. Because we all have choices. I have a choice.

"Maybe it's not too late for me," I say, my voice quiet but firm. "Maybe I don't have to be a part of this anymore. Maybe I can walk away, and you can—"

"Don't say it," Luca interrupts, his voice sharp and rough, a warning flashing in his eyes. His grip on my hand tightens again, like he's afraid I might slip through his fingers. Like I'm the only thing keeping him from falling apart.

But I've already slipped. I've been slipping for months, and he hasn't even noticed. Or maybe he has, but it's easier to keep pretending everything's fine, easier to keep me here in this suffocating cage where the bars are made of lies and blood.

"You can't just walk away," he says, his words growing more desperate, his usual composure slipping. "You're in this now. You can't just leave, not when everything is on the line."

My chest tightens, the air feels thick, like I'm suffocating. The heat of his breath on my face is too much, and I don't know how much longer I can pretend I'm okay. Because I'm not.

"You're right," I say, my voice trembling. "I'm already in it. I'm already here."

But I don't know how much longer I can pretend that I want to stay. That I want any part of this life. This isn't what I thought it would be. I used to dream of something different. Something better. But now? Now I'm not so sure there's any way out.

The tension in the room shifts, and I realize we're both holding our breath, both waiting for something—an answer, a decision, a miracle. But there are no miracles in this world. Just choices. And consequences.

His hand finally falls from mine, and I feel the absence of it like a physical ache, a hollow space where something used to be. He turns away from me then, his back rigid, his shoulders tense, like he's wrestling with himself.

"Luca..." I start, but the words die in my throat when he speaks again, his voice rougher than before, like something is breaking inside him.

"If you leave," he says, his words slow and deliberate, "I won't stop you. But you need to understand something." He turns back to face me, and his eyes are dark—darker than I've ever seen them, full of something I can't name. "If you walk out that door, it's over. There's no going back. No coming back from what's happened. And if you leave, you'll never be safe. Not from them, and not from me."

His words hang in the air between us, thick with threat, but also with something else. Something that sounds almost like a plea. Like he's asking me to stay, but he doesn't know how to say it.

I swallow hard, my pulse pounding in my ears, as if my heart is trying to escape my chest. I want to walk away. I want to say I'm done, to leave him and this whole nightmare behind. But the words won't come. And even if they did, I'm not sure I'd have the strength to follow through.

The silence between us stretches on, and for a moment, all I can hear is the distant hum of the city outside. The world is still turning, oblivious to the storm that's brewing inside this small, blood-soaked room.

And then, just when I think I can't take the silence anymore, the door behind us creaks open.

I turn just as a figure steps inside—tall, broad-shouldered, and wearing a look of cold determination. My breath catches in my throat, my heart stops for a beat, and I know, with a sickening certainty, that everything just changed.

"You shouldn't have left the door unlocked," the man says, his voice low and clipped, the kind of voice that demands attention.

Luca's eyes narrow, and I see the muscles in his jaw twitch. He recognizes the voice. Hell, I recognize the voice.

And suddenly, all I can think is: No. Not him.

Chapter 30: A Love Worth Fighting For

The sound of my heels clicking sharply against the pavement was drowned by the blaring horn of a taxi as it swerved too close to the curb. I shot a glare at the driver, but my frustration was tempered by the weight of the moment. With each step, the air around me grew thicker, charged with the residue of a day that had been anything but ordinary. The city, as vibrant as it always was, now felt more like a pressure cooker, its usual hum somehow more insistent, more suffocating.

I wanted to be anywhere but here, but that was the thing—there was nowhere to escape to, not anymore. Not when everything I had been holding together was crumbling in front of me.

Luca had always been my anchor, the one person I could rely on without question. He was steady, solid, the kind of man who never wavered—until he did. Watching him fall apart before my eyes had been a gut punch I wasn't sure I could recover from. His walls had always been high, but I had trusted him. Trusted that, despite everything, we'd never fall.

Yet here we were.

I rounded the corner into a small café, the familiar scent of roasted coffee beans and warm pastries wrapping around me like an old friend. The doorbell above the entrance jingled as I stepped inside, and I found myself instinctively gravitating toward the counter. It was one of those places that knew you by name, where the baristas remembered your usual order and always had a joke or two ready to brighten your day. It was the kind of spot I frequented when I needed a little escape from everything.

And I needed an escape today more than ever.

The woman behind the counter, a tall, wiry figure with an unruly ponytail and a half-smile that could have been mistaken for a smirk, raised an eyebrow as she prepared my coffee.

"Rough day?" she asked, pouring the dark liquid into a paper cup with practiced ease.

"You could say that," I muttered, accepting the cup but not meeting her eyes. There was something about the way she looked at me—like she could see straight through my carefully constructed exterior. Maybe it was the fact that she'd seen me more times than I cared to admit, each visit a quiet attempt at grounding myself, but I couldn't help but feel like she was sizing me up, like she knew things I wasn't ready to face.

"Want to talk about it?" she offered, her voice unexpectedly gentle.

"Not really," I replied, managing a tired smile. "But I appreciate the offer."

She didn't press me further, just nodded as if she'd heard it all before. "Take care of yourself. Whatever's going on, it's just a bad moment, not a bad life."

I made my way to the back corner of the café, the soft clink of silverware and the murmur of voices creating a strange kind of comfort in the chaos of my mind. I wrapped my hands around the warm cup, staring out the window at the bustling city outside. The streets were teeming with life, the way they always were—people rushing to their destinations, unaware of the stories unfolding just out of sight. Everyone was caught up in their own little dramas, and for a moment, I wondered if I was the only one who could feel the ground shifting beneath me.

I had never been one to run away from problems. In fact, I prided myself on my ability to face whatever came my way. But this... this felt different.

Luca's voice echoed in my mind, a memory from just an hour ago, as clear as if he were standing next to me now. "You're worth the risk."

I had almost believed him when he said it. Almost.

But that was before the world turned upside down.

The phone buzzed in my bag, and I hesitated before pulling it out. A text from Luca. I almost ignored it, but the message appeared on the screen before I could second-guess myself.

We need to talk.

The words were simple enough, but their weight was enough to make my pulse quicken. We had been avoiding talking about the things that mattered, about the things that were slowly eating away at us from the inside. The silence between us had grown thick, like a fog that neither of us could see through. But now, with his words hanging there in front of me, I knew I had to make a choice.

I could pretend everything was fine and continue hiding from the truth, or I could face it head-on. There was no middle ground anymore. And as much as I wanted to walk away, as much as I wanted to bury my head in the sand and escape, something inside me knew that I couldn't. Not this time.

I didn't respond right away, choosing instead to finish my coffee in peace. The bitter warmth settled in my chest, and for a moment, I let myself just breathe. I had been holding my breath for too long, waiting for the storm to pass, but the storm wasn't going anywhere.

It was time to make a choice.

I slid my phone back into my bag and stood up, the weight of my decision settling over me like a thick cloak. The café felt smaller now, its familiar comforts no longer offering the solace they once had. There was a moment of hesitation as I reached for the door, my fingers lingering on the handle.

I had spent so long running away from the things that mattered most, but today... today I was going to stop running.

The streets of Chicago had never felt as cold as they did tonight. The air, thick with the remnants of a late afternoon rain, hung like a blanket over the city, pressing down on everything, muffling the usual hum of the bustling downtown streets. The headlights of passing cars cut through the mist, casting fleeting shadows on the sidewalks where people hurried past, their collars turned up and heads down, eager to escape the damp chill. But me? I was moving slower, as if the weight of everything had settled somewhere deep in my bones, forcing me to take each step with purpose, despite how much I wanted to run in the opposite direction.

I passed the familiar faces of local bars and corner shops, their neon lights flickering in the gloom. Chicago had a way of making you feel at once like you belonged and like you were lost, all at the same time. But I wasn't lost—not anymore. That, at least, was something.

The text from Luca was still sitting there on my phone screen, an echo of his voice haunting the edges of my thoughts. We need to talk. I knew the conversation was inevitable. He had been distant for weeks, and I had been pretending everything was fine, too busy to notice the cracks in the foundation of our lives. But those cracks had deepened, and now they were impossible to ignore. I couldn't put this off any longer. Not when I was finally starting to feel something I hadn't felt in months—hope.

I entered a small Italian restaurant on the corner of Rush Street, the kind of place where the smell of garlic and fresh basil hit you like a wave the moment you stepped inside. The cozy warmth was a stark contrast to the damp chill outside, and I found myself drawing in a deep breath, letting the comforting aroma fill my lungs. The hostess, a woman with sharp eyes and a smile that seemed to hide a dozen stories, greeted me with a nod, her gaze flicking over my shoulder as if checking for someone else. I didn't blame her. People were always looking for someone else.

"I'm meeting someone," I said, offering her a tight smile. "A table for one, please."

She led me to a corner booth by the window, the seat facing out toward the street. The city sprawled before me, alive with movement and noise, but in this little nook, it felt like I was cocooned in a world all my own. The gentle clink of silverware, the soft murmur of voices, the sizzling sound of food being prepared in the kitchen—it was all a welcome distraction from the chaos in my mind.

I slid into the booth and set my phone on the table, my fingers tracing the edge of the glass water bottle. The waiter came over almost immediately, his dark hair neatly combed back, his apron impeccably pressed.

"Good evening. Can I start you off with something to drink?"

I ordered a glass of red wine, the deep, velvety kind that had always been my favorite. The waiter nodded and disappeared, leaving me alone with my thoughts.

I should have felt nervous about meeting Luca. After all, we had been avoiding each other for so long that even the idea of sitting down to have a conversation felt like an insurmountable task. But strangely, there was something freeing about it. Maybe it was the thought of finally letting everything spill out, of being honest in a way I hadn't been in far too long. For the first time in ages, I didn't feel like I was holding my breath, waiting for something to break.

The wine arrived, its deep color catching the light, and I took a long sip, savoring the rich taste as it spread across my tongue. The heat from the wine warmed me, not just from the inside out but in a way that reminded me of the closeness I used to share with

Luca. The times when we'd sit across from each other, laughing and teasing, our hands always within reach. It felt like a lifetime ago.

But nothing stayed the same forever, did it? People changed, circumstances shifted, and love... love had a funny way of slipping through your fingers when you weren't paying attention.

The door to the restaurant jingled as it swung open, and my heart skipped a beat. I didn't have to look up to know it was him. There was a presence about Luca, something magnetic that drew people's attention without him trying. His footsteps were slow, deliberate, as if he were weighing each step before making it. When he finally appeared at my table, I felt the rush of everything—anger, love, fear, desire—come rushing to the surface in a way that took me by surprise.

He was wearing the same jacket he'd worn the day we first met, the dark leather one that seemed too edgy for someone so effortlessly put together. His hair was a bit longer now, and the scruff on his jaw looked like it hadn't seen a razor in days. But it was his eyes that caught me, as always—deep, dark, and filled with things I couldn't name.

"I thought you might be here," he said, his voice low and smooth, the way it always sounded when he was trying to hide something. But I could hear the edge in it. The hesitation.

"Did you?" I replied, the words sharp, but they didn't come out as cold as I'd intended. "I wasn't sure I'd be here either."

Luca sat across from me, and for a long moment, neither of us spoke. It wasn't uncomfortable, but it wasn't easy either. The air between us was thick, charged with the weight of everything we hadn't said, everything we'd avoided. He reached across the table, his fingers brushing mine lightly before he pulled them away, as if testing the waters.

"I'm sorry," he said finally, his voice steady but laced with something I couldn't quite decipher. "For all of it. For everything."

I swallowed hard, the words catching in my throat. "You're not the only one who's sorry."

His gaze softened then, the usual guard he kept so high starting to lower, just a little. "I don't want to lose you."

The words, so simple and direct, hit me in a way I hadn't expected. They weren't promises or grand gestures, but something raw, something honest. And for the first time in a long while, I felt like maybe, just maybe, we had a shot at making it work.

I watched Luca as he sat across from me, his eyes softening but still holding that familiar intensity, the same one that had always made me feel like the world was smaller, simpler, when we were together. Yet now, there was a tension between us, thick enough to almost taste—an unspoken promise of something more but also something unknown. The lines of our shared history tangled around us like vines, binding us in ways we hadn't even realized.

He reached for his wine, taking a slow sip before setting the glass down with a soft clink. His fingers lingered on the rim for a moment, his thumb tracing the edges as if trying to make sense of what he wanted to say next.

"You know, I used to think I had all the time in the world," he said, the words spilling out with surprising honesty. "That everything could just... work itself out. That we'd have all the time to figure it out."

I raised an eyebrow, watching him carefully. "And now?"

His gaze met mine, the weight of his stare pulling at me in ways I wasn't sure I was ready to face. "Now? I'm realizing that time doesn't always wait for you. People don't wait forever."

The admission hung between us, heavy and thick. I swallowed, unsure whether I was supposed to respond or whether he was merely thinking aloud. The last few weeks had felt like we were both standing on the edge of a cliff, too afraid to step back but too tired to jump forward.

I studied his face, the way the dim light from the restaurant seemed to soften his features, as if the flickering candles were trying to erase the exhaustion in his eyes. But there was no hiding the truth. We were both worn out—tired from pretending, tired of carrying the weight of things unsaid.

"Do you think we still have a shot at this?" I asked before I could stop myself, the question tumbling out in a whisper. I could hear the vulnerability in my voice, a stark contrast to the coolness I had been hiding behind for so long.

Luca's lips parted, and for a moment, I thought he might say something grand, something sweeping that would make everything feel right again. But instead, his smile was small, almost sad, as though he too was trying to figure out how to put the pieces back together when the puzzle seemed so far from completion.

"I think," he started, his voice quieter now, "I think I'd be willing to fight for it. For us." His gaze dropped to the table, a flicker of uncertainty flashing in his eyes before he looked back up, meeting my gaze with a sincerity that made my chest tighten. "But only if you are."

I exhaled slowly, the air leaving my lungs in a slow, deliberate breath. It had been so long since I'd allowed myself to even think about fighting for us—about fighting for anything. I had buried my emotions under a mask of indifference, pretending I could let go without feeling the sting of it. But deep down, I knew I hadn't. I hadn't let go of him. I hadn't let go of us.

"I don't know," I said, the words feeling foreign on my tongue. I hadn't expected it to be this hard, this complicated. Maybe I had hoped that walking away would be easier. But it wasn't. Nothing ever was, especially when it came to him.

Luca leaned in a little closer, his voice dropping to a near whisper. "If you're asking me if it's worth it, then yes. I think we are. We're worth it."

My heart pounded, and for the first time in ages, the thought of choosing something—or someone—didn't feel like a burden. It felt like a possibility. But the path before us wasn't clear, not by any stretch of the imagination. The past we shared was littered with mistakes, some that could never be erased. And the future? Well, that was still as uncertain as the rainclouds hanging over Chicago's skyline.

I glanced at my phone, the screen still lighting up with the unread text messages I had been avoiding. I hadn't even realized how much time had passed until now. The hour was growing late, and with it, the pressure that had been building between Luca and me seemed to intensify.

"We can't just pretend this never happened," I said, my voice steadier now. "We can't sweep everything under the rug."

Luca nodded, his expression soft but resolute. "I'm not asking you to forget. I'm asking you to move forward with me. Whatever that looks like."

And just like that, it felt like a door opened. A glimmer of hope that I hadn't dared to entertain in months flared up inside me, only to be immediately doused by a sudden rush of doubt. The tension in the air seemed to shift, something unspoken hanging between us, thick and undeniable.

Suddenly, a loud crash echoed from the kitchen, followed by an exasperated shout from one of the cooks. It broke the moment in an instant, the fragile thread that had been connecting us snapping. Luca stood up quickly, his hand moving toward mine, but he pulled it back at the last second, unsure, hesitant.

"I think we should leave," he said, his voice tight, as if he was holding something back. His eyes darted around the restaurant, the spark that had been there moments ago suddenly dimming.

Before I could even process what was happening, the lights above us flickered violently, plunging the entire room into darkness for a brief, tense moment. The low hum of conversation stopped, replaced by the soft rustling of people shuffling in confusion. A few seconds passed, and the lights flickered back to life, but the air had changed. Something wasn't right.

And then, I saw it—through the window, just past Luca's shoulder. A figure standing across the street, watching us intently, their face hidden in the shadows.

I froze, my stomach twisting into a knot. "Luca," I whispered, my voice barely audible. "Look."

He turned, his expression immediately hardening as he noticed the figure, their presence unsettling in the way only a stranger's gaze can be. It was only a brief moment, but it was enough.

The door to the restaurant swung open again, and the figure was gone. But the unsettling feeling lingered, settling over us like a storm cloud, heavy and ominous.

And as the tension between us thickened once more, I realized that the conversation we had just begun might have been the least of my worries.

Chapter 31: A Fractured Crown

I never imagined it would come to this—the sound of my own voice, defiant and sharp, cutting through the thick, oppressive silence that fills my uncle's office. The same office where, years ago, he would tell me bedtime stories of ambition and power, tales of building empires from the ground up, always ending with a reassuring pat on the head, his smile warm and full of promise. How quickly those promises had turned to shadows.

Now, as I stand across from him, there's no warmth, no trace of the man who once made me feel like his world was built entirely for my benefit. His eyes, cold as steel, flicker with the faintest hint of recognition, but there's nothing familial in them. His hand, once gentle as it brushed my hair back from my forehead, now grips the edge of his desk with a tension that speaks volumes.

"You don't understand," he mutters, his voice low, strained, like a man on the verge of unraveling. He looks away, staring at the darkened windows, his gaze distant. "I didn't come this far to lose it all to a bunch of half-wits who can't see the bigger picture. The world doesn't wait for you to catch up."

I try not to flinch at the bite in his words, but it's hard not to feel it, like a slap across the face, as if all the years of affection were nothing more than a ruse to keep me obedient, pliable. His back is turned to me, and I can't help but notice the small, telltale tremor in his hands. It's a weakness, one he tries to hide beneath layers of arrogance and control, but it's there, undeniable.

"You think you're untouchable, don't you?" I push, taking a step closer, my heart pounding in my chest. The tension crackles between us like an electric current. "That nothing can touch you, no matter how many lives you destroy, how many allies you betray. But you're wrong."

His head snaps back toward me, eyes narrowing, lips curling into a sneer that doesn't quite mask the flicker of fear in his gaze. He doesn't say anything for a moment, and I can almost hear the wheels turning in his head, calculating, assessing whether I've crossed the line too far. The silence stretches, a taut rope pulled to its breaking point.

"You're just like the rest of them," he spits, his voice suddenly louder, sharper. "Clueless. Hopeless. All of you, pretending you know what's best, but you have no idea what it takes to keep this machine running."

I can't stop the rush of anger that surges through me. "Maybe I don't know everything," I snap back, unable to keep my voice steady, "but I know enough to see that you're tearing us apart. And for what? So you can stay in control of a sinking ship?"

His face reddens, and for a moment, I think he might explode, but he just exhales slowly, the fury simmering beneath the surface. "You think you're smarter than me? That's your problem, isn't it? You think you know better."

I take another step forward, closing the distance, my pulse pounding in my ears. I can feel Luca's warning like a weight on my chest, his voice echoing in my head. Tread carefully, he had said. But I'm beyond the point of caring.

"I don't think I know better," I say softly, the words carrying more weight than I intend. "I just know what's right."

He lets out a bitter laugh, the sound jagged and unnatural, like it hurts him to even laugh at all. "Right?" He leans forward, suddenly so much smaller than I remembered, but no less dangerous. "You don't get to decide what's right. You never did, and you never will. Not in this world."

I don't back down, though. There's too much at stake now, and if I don't push back, if I don't stand my ground, I'll lose everything. I've already lost so much. My voice comes out a little stronger this time. "You're not invincible, Uncle. You're just a man. And I'm not afraid of you anymore."

The words hang between us, a challenge, a declaration. I can see the shift in his expression, the way his mask falters just for a second, and I know I've struck a chord. But it doesn't last. His facade snaps back into place, and he straightens, his posture stiff, defensive.

"Get out," he orders, his voice low but filled with venom. "I'm done with this conversation."

I hesitate, my fingers curling into fists at my sides, but something in me knows this is the end of the road. There's no reaching him anymore. No getting back the uncle I used to know.

"Fine," I say, forcing the words through clenched teeth. "But this is your mess, not mine. You fix it."

I turn on my heel and leave without another word, the door slamming shut behind me, the echo reverberating through the quiet halls like the final toll of a bell. The weight in my chest is unbearable as I step out into the cool night air, the city sprawling around me in its indifferent, glittering glory. I want to scream. I want to break something.

Instead, I pull my coat tighter around me, my breath coming out in sharp, visible puffs. The streets of Chicago are as noisy and chaotic as always, but tonight, they feel empty, somehow. The city's heartbeat is nothing more than a dull thrum in the distance, lost beneath the fog of my thoughts.

I think of Luca. His warning still echoes in my mind, his concern a constant weight I can't shake. I knew what I was doing, but I had to do it. I had to confront him, even if it cost me everything.

And yet, as the cold air stings my cheeks and the sharp rhythm of my heels taps against the sidewalk, I can't shake the feeling that I've just made the biggest mistake of my life.

The night is colder than I expected, my breath hanging in the air like a pale ghost as I walk through the streets of Chicago, my footsteps echoing off the walls of buildings that are too tall to look at without straining my neck. This city, once a playground of possibility, now feels like an unyielding maze, each corner sharper than the last. The skyscrapers loom overhead, their glass windows reflecting the fractured world around me—a world where my uncle's empire is crumbling, and the delicate web of power he's spun over the years is starting to unravel.

I can almost hear the hum of the city's pulse beneath my feet, a steady thrum of movement, the ceaseless churn of lives moving in and out of focus. Cars whiz past, the headlights cutting through the mist rising from the gutters, and I can't help but feel the city, alive and breathing, has become a reflection of my own fractured state.

The cold sinks into my bones, and I pull my coat tighter around me, still shaken by my encounter with my uncle. I keep telling myself it had to happen, that the confrontation was inevitable. But even now, with the space of a few blocks between us, I feel that raw, jagged edge of it gnawing at me. I don't know what hurt more—the sting of his betrayal or the realization that the man I thought I knew, the man who once made me believe in something larger than myself, had become a stranger. It wasn't the loss of power that was so painful. No, it was the way he had cut ties with me so effortlessly, like a surgeon removing a cancerous growth. Family meant nothing anymore, just another piece of the empire he would gladly throw away to stay on top.

I'm not sure why I thought confronting him would somehow fix things. Maybe I wanted to believe that, by facing the truth head-on, I could restore some of what had been lost—some of the love, the care, the belief that we were still bound together by something other than blood. But now, standing here in the shadow of this city, I realize how naïve I was. Power doesn't work that way. People don't change their hearts because you ask them to.

I pull out my phone, trying to distract myself from the gnawing feeling in my chest, but the messages flashing across the screen only make it worse. Luca's name appears, and the knot in my stomach tightens. He's been texting me for hours now, asking if I'm okay, telling me to be careful. I know he's worried, but it's the last thing I want to hear right now. The weight of his concern presses down on me, adding to the suffocating feeling that has been building ever since my conversation with my uncle.

I try to ignore the ping of my phone, but the urge to answer is too strong.

Luca: You're still up?

Me: Yeah, I'm fine.

Luca: I don't believe you. Please, talk to me.

I chew on my lip, staring at the message for a long moment. I'm tempted to throw my phone into the nearest garbage can—preferably one that smells like burnt coffee and forgotten dreams—but I can't. I can't run from this, and I certainly can't run from him. Not when everything between us feels so fractured already.

Me: I'm okay. Just needed some air. It's been a long night.

Luca: I know you. Come back to the apartment. Please. Let me help.

His words are a balm, soothing in a way I don't know how to explain. I don't know if I'm desperate for comfort or if I'm just too tired to keep pretending that I don't need him, that I don't want him. But either way, I find myself texting back. I'll be there in fifteen.

I don't even realize I've started walking until I'm halfway back to the apartment. The buildings blur past me in a haze, the cold air biting at my skin. It feels like the whole city is holding its breath, waiting for something to happen, for something to change. And I realize, with a sudden clarity, that it won't. Nothing will change until I make it change. Until I choose to stop being a passive participant in my own life.

The apartment is warm when I walk in, the soft glow of the lamps casting long shadows across the walls. Luca is sitting on the couch, his body tense, eyes scanning the door as if he's waiting for me to materialize out of thin air. The moment he sees me, his expression softens, and for the briefest moment, the world outside seems to disappear. It's just the two of us, caught in this strange, fragile moment that I can't name.

"You okay?" His voice is low, careful, as if he's afraid of breaking something irreparably delicate.

I sit beside him, shrugging off my coat, feeling the weight of the day settle around me like an iron cloak. "I don't know. I don't even know what I'm doing anymore, Luca."

He doesn't answer immediately. Instead, he reaches out, his fingers brushing mine in that small, intimate way that always feels like more than it is. I turn to him, and for the first time in hours, I don't feel so lost.

"Don't say that," he finally says, his voice quiet but resolute. "You're not alone in this. You don't have to carry it all on your own."

I smile, but it's a sad one, a shadow of something I don't know how to name. "What if I don't want to carry it at all?"

He doesn't answer right away, but I feel the weight of his gaze, like he's seeing through all my walls. "Then we'll figure it out together." He leans in, and for a moment, I think he might kiss me. But instead, he just rests his forehead against mine, his breath warm against my skin. "One step at a time, okay?"

For once, the promise doesn't feel like empty words. It feels like something real. Something worth holding on to.

I wake to the sound of my phone buzzing on the nightstand, its incessant ring breaking through the fog of restless sleep. For a moment, I hesitate, curling deeper into the blankets, but the phone rings again, more urgently this time. Luca. I exhale slowly and reach for it, trying to shake the sleep from my limbs.

"Hello?" My voice is thick with sleep, rough at the edges.

"Are you awake?" Luca's voice is strained, and I can hear the undertone of panic that he tries so desperately to keep at bay. "I need you to come to me."

I sit up immediately, my heart pounding. "What happened?"

"I—" His words falter, and for a moment, there's only the sound of his breath, ragged and uneven. "Just come. Please, hurry."

The urgency in his voice stirs something deep in me, something primal. I throw the covers off and slip out of bed, the chill of the hardwood floor biting at my feet as I pull on the nearest clothes I can find. The city outside is still wrapped in the quiet of early morning, the hum of traffic just beginning to stir, but in my chest, the tension is already mounting, pulling me taut like a string.

I don't question him further, don't ask for details. I know, deep down, that something's wrong—something bigger than I've realized. The events of the night before, the confrontation with my uncle, feel like the beginning of a slow, unravelling thread, and I'm not sure how far it will stretch before everything comes undone.

The streets of Chicago are damp with the remnants of last night's rain, the air cool and crisp as I drive through the early-morning haze. The city is waking up, its skyline glowing faintly under the pale morning light. I take the usual route to Luca's place, the roads familiar and comforting in their predictability, but today, even the hum of the engine feels distant, as if the world is holding its breath in anticipation.

When I reach his apartment, the door is already ajar, and I push it open cautiously, feeling the strange weight of the moment settle on me like a heavy coat. The lights are off inside, the space eerily quiet. I call his name, my voice low, unsure, but the silence that answers me sends a ripple of fear through me.

"Luca?" I step further inside, my footsteps muffled by the thick carpet, the air still heavy with the scent of his cologne and the faint traces of coffee.

I round the corner to the living room, and my breath catches in my throat.

Luca is standing by the window, his back to me, staring out at the city beyond. There's something about his posture—rigid, tense—that sets my nerves alight. He doesn't turn when I enter, doesn't even acknowledge my presence at first. The soft hum of the city, the far-off sounds of a world too far removed from the intensity in this room, feel suddenly out of place.

I take a cautious step closer, my hand reaching out for his shoulder. "Luca? What's going on?"

At my touch, he jerks back, spinning around with a look of raw panic in his eyes. The fear there is palpable, his hands shaking just slightly at his sides as if he's holding something back, something he's afraid to say.

"Luca?" I repeat, this time more insistent, trying to close the distance between us, but something in his eyes stops me.

"I didn't want you to find out this way," he mutters, his voice low, almost ashamed. His gaze flickers to the side, as if he can't meet my eyes for too long.

"Find out what?" I ask, the unease in my stomach shifting to something colder, sharper. "What's going on? You're scaring me."

He doesn't answer immediately. Instead, he runs a hand through his hair, his jaw tightening as if he's debating whether to say the words hanging in the air between us. The silence grows heavier by the second, and I can't take it anymore.

"Luca, please." My voice cracks, barely above a whisper. "What's happened?"

Finally, he exhales a long breath and looks at me, really looks at me, like he's seeing me for the first time, and there's a moment of something—something darker and deeper than I can quite place—in his eyes.

"I'm in trouble," he says, his voice barely audible, as if the words themselves weigh too much for him to carry.

"I know," I reply, my throat tightening. "What do you mean, exactly? Is it—"

"No," he interrupts, his hand shooting out to stop me from speaking. "No, not like that. Not in the way you think."

I blink, trying to make sense of the words, but everything in my body is telling me that this is the moment—the moment where everything shifts, where the ground beneath us finally gives way.

"You're talking in riddles," I say, frustration making my voice sharper than I intend. "Just say it, Luca. Whatever it is, just say it."

"I—I can't. Not yet." He steps back, shaking his head as though he's fighting against something in his mind. "It's not just me. It's everything. It's all falling apart, and I can't protect you from it anymore."

I feel the air between us shift, like an invisible wall that's risen up to separate us. There's something he's not telling me. Something he's withholding, something he's afraid to speak into the open.

"Luca," I say, my heart pounding, "please. I'm not going anywhere. We'll face it together, whatever it is."

For a moment, I think he's going to break. I can see the battle waging behind his eyes, the vulnerability that he's trying to bury beneath the surface. And just as I step closer, as if to bridge the gap between us, the door slams open, and someone steps into the room.

I freeze. The figure is tall, shadowed in the doorway, and as I see the glint of a gun in their hand, my blood runs cold.

Luca's expression shifts, his body going rigid, and the terror in his eyes is unmistakable.

The figure steps forward, and all I can do is watch, helpless, as they close the distance between us.

Chapter 32: The Edge of Betrayal

The room feels colder than usual, the air stiff with the weight of unspoken words. Outside, the city hums, unaware of the storm brewing within these walls. The dim light from the desk lamp casts long shadows across the room, illuminating the ledger before us like some cursed relic. The names on the page swim before my eyes, each one a familiar face, a memory I'd once cherished. How had I not seen it? How had I been so blind to the web my uncle had spun, so intricate, so insidious, that even the people I trusted were caught in its threads?

Luca's silence is deafening. He's still leaning over the table, his fingertips brushing the edges of the book as if he's trying to extract some hidden meaning from the paper itself. I know what he's thinking—he's wondering if this is the moment when everything shifts, when the line between loyalty and self-preservation becomes so blurred that there's no coming back from it. His eyes flicker up to mine, and for a heartbeat, I see the weight of the decision etched in his gaze. It's in the slight narrowing of his eyes, the tightness in his jaw. Luca's not a man who makes decisions lightly. When he chooses a side, he does so with the quiet certainty of someone who has already seen the future and knows exactly what it will cost.

"Do you know what this means?" His voice is low, a rough whisper as if he's afraid the room might echo the enormity of the words. "You understand what you're asking, don't you?"

I want to look away. I want to pretend I'm not frozen in the moment, my heart pounding in my chest like a trapped bird, but I can't. Not when everything I've ever known is unraveling right before me. Not when my uncle's empire, the one I had always thought was built on honor and loyalty, is nothing more than a house of cards. I meet his gaze, steady, unflinching, because I know what this means. It means losing everything. But isn't that the price of survival?

"I'm asking for a way out," I say, my voice firmer than I expect. "A way to take control before it takes me."

Luca exhales sharply, running a hand through his hair in frustration. "You don't get it, do you? This isn't a game, Gianna. We're talking about the kind of people who don't just ruin lives—they end them." He straightens up, the light catching the sharp angles of his face, his expression now a mask of resolve. "And your uncle? He's not the only one who knows what's at stake. There's no way out once you cross him. Not for you. Not for anyone."

I know the risks, of course. How could I not? But that doesn't change the fact that every moment spent in the shadow of my uncle's empire feels like a moment closer to being crushed beneath it. I wish I could explain that to Luca—that this isn't just about survival. It's about reclaiming a part of myself that's been buried under years of deceit. But the words get stuck, tangled in my throat like something too bitter to swallow.

"I didn't ask for this," I whisper, more to myself than to him. The weight of the ledger feels unbearable now, like it's pressing down on me, threatening to crush the last of my resolve. I don't want this. I didn't ask for this. But it's too late to turn back.

Luca leans back against the wall, his arms crossed over his chest. The room feels too small, too suffocating as his silence drags on. He's thinking, I can tell. Thinking of the risks, of the consequences, of the people who will be caught in the crossfire. But I'm not going to beg him. Not for the first time, I wonder if I've made a terrible mistake in trusting him. He's always been the enigma, the one with his own hidden agenda, his own reasons for being involved in all of this. I can't pretend I understand him. Not fully. Not yet.

But there's something in the way he's looking at me now, something that stirs a flicker of hope in the pit of my stomach. It's not trust—no, trust is too fragile a thing for either of us. But maybe, just maybe, it's something else. Something darker. Something that might give us a chance at surviving this mess.

"You want out," he repeats, the words tasting foreign on his tongue. "But what if there's no out? What if the only way to get free is to burn everything down?"

My pulse quickens at the thought, the possibility of it. A part of me recoils, horrified by the thought of destroying the life I've known, the life I've spent so long trying to piece together. But that's the thing, isn't it? I never really had a life, not one that was mine. Not until now.

"I'm ready to burn it all," I say, the words tasting like ash on my lips. "I just need to know how."

Luca's eyes flash with something unreadable—something darker than I've ever seen in him. For a moment, I think he's going to pull back, to walk away and leave me with nothing but the wreckage of my decisions. But then he steps forward, the floor creaking under his boots as he closes the distance between us. His gaze is hard, almost accusatory, and yet there's a strange softness in the way he holds my stare, like he's seeing me for the first time.

"You better be sure," he says, his voice low and steady. "Because once you cross this line, there's no going back."

I nod. And for the first time in a long time, I feel something stir inside me. Something fierce. Something that might just be strong enough to keep me standing when the world tries to tear me apart.

The city never stops moving. It pulses like a living thing, restless in the night as neon lights flicker and honking horns provide an odd sort of lullaby to the night shift workers hurrying home or to some after-hours bar. A place to forget, for a little while, that the real world is always waiting to catch up. In this city, I had once believed I was in control, just another woman walking the streets, head high and hopeful. But now? Now, I'm not even sure which version of myself I should trust anymore.

The ledger sits between us, its pages heavy with secrets, its ink a reminder of how little I truly knew about my own family. As the moonlight slants through the curtains, the names leap out at me like ghosts, trailing cold fingers across my skin. Most are strangers—business partners, connections, people whose faces I'll never see, whose lives are far too tangled in my uncle's web to be anything but shadows. But some... some of the names are faces I know too well. They're the friends who've stood by me, the allies I thought I could trust. I swallow hard, a tight knot in my throat. Betrayal isn't just a concept; it's real, and it's staring me down from these pages.

Luca shifts beside me, his shoulders tense, his expression unreadable. The calm façade he wears is something I've come to expect, but it doesn't make it any easier to read. He's a man who's lived in the shadows for so long that it's hard to tell when he's playing a part or when he's simply hiding his true thoughts from the world. I want to reach out, to demand answers from him, but I know that isn't how it works with him. Luca doesn't open up easily. He never has. Instead, I look at him, waiting for something—anything—to break the silence.

"So, what's next?" I ask, my voice far steadier than I feel.

He glances at me, his dark eyes narrowing for just a fraction of a second before he nods, seemingly to himself. "Next? We start making plans." He leans back in his chair, folding his arms across his chest. "Plans you're not going to like."

I raise an eyebrow, not sure whether to be curious or cautious. "What kind of plans?"

"The kind where we get dirty," he says, the words slipping from his lips like they're nothing. "We go after the people who've been taking advantage of your family. People who thought they could just walk away without consequences. We make sure they understand that loyalty has a price."

A shiver runs down my spine, though I try not to let it show. "And what happens if they don't play along?"

His lips twitch in a humorless smile. "Then we remind them."

I stare at him, a sense of dread pooling in my stomach. "And you think I'm going to help with this?"

"Not think. I know you are." He meets my gaze, his expression hardening. "You want out, right? You want to end this, to have a life that's not controlled by your uncle's empire. This is the only way to make that happen."

It's too quiet in here, too suffocating, like the walls themselves are closing in on me. The weight of his words presses against my chest. I want to run away from all of this, to pretend I didn't see the ledger, didn't hear his plans, but deep down, I know I'm not that person anymore. I'm already in this too deep. So I sit there, frozen in place, and wait for the next move.

"You think I'm ready for this?" I ask, my voice betraying the hesitation I feel, though I'm doing my best to mask it.

Luca looks at me for a long moment, his expression unreadable. There's no comfort in his eyes, but I sense a strange respect behind them, something I can't quite place but that feels real nonetheless. He nods slowly, the decision weighing heavily on him too.

"Yeah," he says quietly. "I think you are."

I want to believe him. I want to trust that this is the right decision, that tearing apart everything my uncle has built will somehow make things better. But in my gut, I know this is only the beginning. There's no turning back now. And when everything falls apart—and it will—I'm not sure what's left. There's a chance, I know, that when the dust settles, there will be nothing but ashes.

"What's the plan?" I ask, my throat dry.

"We get in, get the information we need, and get out," Luca says, like it's the simplest thing in the world. "It's a matter of timing. We don't go in guns blazing—no heroes, no explosions. Just facts. We need leverage."

Leverage. The word lands between us like a bomb. It's clear now that Luca's not interested in playing by anyone's rules. He's not here to ask for permission or beg for forgiveness. He's here to take. And I'm standing beside him, not because I'm certain of what comes next, but because I've already crossed a line. The question is, what kind of person am I becoming in the process?

"You're sure about this?" I ask again, needing some reassurance, though I know deep down that he'll never give me the answer I'm looking for.

His lips curl into a grin that's more predatory than comforting. "Gianna, sweetheart, there's no room for doubt now."

I want to argue with him, to demand more answers, but something about the way he says it, that gleam in his eyes, shuts me down. I nod stiffly, the chill of his certainty settling in the pit of my stomach. This isn't just about my uncle anymore, or even the people who've wronged me. This is about Luca. About us. And somehow, despite all the warnings in my head, I can't shake the feeling that I'm falling into something far darker than I ever imagined.

And it's only just begun.

The city outside seems to shrink into something dark, confined within the walls of my apartment, where every creak of the floorboards and every tick of the clock feels amplified, as if the world itself is holding its breath. I can hear Luca moving behind me, the soft click of his boots against the hardwood floor, as if he's measuring the distance between us, trying to decide if the words we've already spoken are enough or if he needs to say more. But I'm not sure there's anything more to say. We're both standing on the edge now, and neither of us can pretend we're not about to fall.

The ledger is still open on the table, and I catch my reflection in the glossy surface of one of its pages—pale, tired eyes staring back at me, as if I've seen something I can't unsee. The names, the figures, the places—each one is a thread, and I'm already tangled in it. This is bigger than me now. But that doesn't mean I'm backing down.

Luca's voice pulls me back to the present. "We'll need to move fast," he says, the gravel in his tone making the air seem heavier. "The longer we wait, the harder it'll be to get out without blood on our hands."

"I know the stakes," I reply, though my throat tightens as I say it. My mind keeps returning to the faces in the ledger—the ones I thought I could trust, the ones who had smiled at me across dinner tables and shared drinks in dimly lit bars. How many of them knew what was happening behind the scenes? How many of them had turned a blind eye or worse, were actively complicit? The thought twists something cold in my chest, something that's not just betrayal, but a creeping sense of powerlessness. How could I have been so naïve?

Luca steps closer, his presence filling the space between us like a storm gathering strength. "We're not just taking down your uncle," he says, his voice lower now, more intense. "We're going to level everything. You get that, right?"

I nod, feeling the weight of his words sink into my bones. I've always known my uncle wasn't who he seemed to be. But to think I'm part of a plan to destroy it all—to tear apart everything he's built, everything that has tied me to him—it's more than just terrifying. It feels like sacrilege. Yet, I can't stop myself from feeling the smallest flicker of relief. I've been suffocating under the weight of his influence for far too long, and now... now it feels like I might finally get to breathe.

I straighten up, reaching for the ledger again, my fingers brushing over the names, trying to commit them to memory, trying to see the patterns, to understand who's who in this twisted web. "We'll need a safe place to go after," I say, turning to Luca with a determined look. "Somewhere they won't find us."

His lips curl, a faint smirk playing at the edges, as though he's already a step ahead of me. "I've got that covered," he says, pulling something from his jacket pocket—a small envelope, the edges slightly frayed, as if it's been tucked away for far too long. "I'll get us somewhere they can't reach us."

I take the envelope, turning it over in my hands, feeling its weight. "And if they find us anyway?"

"Then we make sure they regret it." His eyes meet mine, and I see a flicker of something—something not quite soft, not quite cruel, but dangerous, like a promise wrapped in a threat.

I don't ask for more details. I don't want to know what he's planning, what kinds of resources he's pulling in to make sure we have a shot at escaping this alive. Because the truth is, I'm not sure I'm ready for this, but I know there's no turning back.

I stand up, tossing the ledger aside, the sound of it landing on the floor far too final for my liking. I don't need it anymore. I don't need my uncle's secrets or his lies. I need to move forward, and I need to do it now, before the weight of what we're about to do sinks in too deeply.

Luca's voice stops me in my tracks. "You sure you're ready for this?" he asks again, though this time, there's no judgment in his tone, just a quiet, almost protective note. He knows what I'm about to lose.

"I'm sure," I say, turning to face him. My voice is firm, more certain than I feel, but I can't let him see the cracks in my resolve. "I'm not turning back."

There's a long pause, and for a moment, the world outside seems to stop. Luca regards me for a second longer, his face unreadable. Then, without another word, he reaches for his phone, sending a quick message that feels like a signal, like the first domino being tipped over in a line that can't be undone.

"You'll get what you need," he says, his voice cutting through the silence. "Just be ready. It won't take long."

My heart picks up its pace again, thumping erratically in my chest. The calm before the storm is always the hardest part, I think. But I know that once we step out of this apartment, once we start moving, there's no going back. We're playing a game where the stakes are life and death, and I can't afford to lose.

As I walk toward the door, I glance at Luca one last time. He's already looking at the street outside, the city lights catching the edges of his profile, giving him an almost ghostly quality. The man is a stranger, and yet, in some twisted way, he's the only ally I've got.

But as I reach for the door handle, a sudden noise from the hallway catches my attention—footsteps, deliberate and heavy. My pulse spikes, the sudden surge of fear cutting through the calm like a knife.

I freeze. And for the first time tonight, I wonder if we're already too late.

Chapter 33: A Whisper of Redemption

I hadn't meant to run into her. At least, I don't think I had. The rain had come out of nowhere, a thick downpour that made the city streets shimmer like slick black glass. I'd been walking through the narrow, cobblestone alleys of the older district of the city, trying to clear my head after another long day at the office. The rhythmic tap of my boots was the only sound beneath the low murmur of the world, until it wasn't.

She was sitting at one of those café tables, tucked under a pale yellow umbrella, a book open in front of her. Her eyes weren't on the pages though; they were on the world around her, like a person who had seen too much of it and was unsure if she wanted to look any longer. The jacket she wore was too big for her—soft, worn leather, its once rich hue now faded to a tired shade of brown. Her hair, long and unruly, was a tangled mess of dark curls. Despite the rain that had soaked everything, she didn't seem to mind. In fact, she barely noticed.

At first, I thought it was someone else. Someone who had walked out of a different chapter of my life, but when her gaze lifted and met mine, it wasn't recognition I saw. It was a knowing—like she had always been waiting for me.

Her eyes, dark as night and edged with a weary wisdom, narrowed just slightly as if sizing me up. I didn't stop walking, couldn't, but my body stilled for just a heartbeat. I should have kept my head down and passed by, but the slight inclination of her chin—just a flicker of acknowledgment—pulled me in. I found myself standing in front of her, unsure of whether to speak or walk away. But there was no walking away. Not from her. Not from this.

"You're Luca's," she said, her voice soft but unyielding, like the murmur of the sea just before the storm.

I blinked, trying to remember where I had seen her before. I couldn't place her face, not the woman in front of me. She was a stranger. But her words... her words cracked something in me.

"Who are you?" I asked, the question coming out more harshly than I intended. There was something in her that stirred me. The way she sat there, a delicate defiance in the way she held herself. There was no doubt in my mind that she knew far too much, but I wasn't ready to hear it.

Her lips curled into a faint smile, one tinged with something that looked like regret. "I'm the one who used to believe in him," she said simply, as though that explained everything. "Before he became the man you know."

Before he became the man you know. I couldn't say anything. My throat closed, words sticking like thorns. Luca. That name had come to mean more to me than any other. But this woman—this stranger—spoke of him as if he were someone I'd never met. And maybe, just maybe, he was.

I tried to swallow the lump in my throat. "What do you mean? What man?"

She leaned forward, her eyes glinting in a way that felt too knowing. "The one who fought for something. Fought for honor. Loyalty. The one who used to believe that some things were worth dying for. I thought he was my future." She stopped, her voice cracking for the briefest of moments, but only I caught it. She wasn't finished, though. "But then he became someone who only survived. Just like the rest of us."

I couldn't breathe. This wasn't what I had expected. This wasn't the Luca I had come to know—aloof, cold, and consumed with the weight of his own shadows. He had always been like that, a man locked in a cage of his own making. I'd accepted it. I had no choice but to accept it.

But now, this woman had given me something else—something that flickered behind his ever-present walls. A hint of the man he had once been, the man who believed in something beyond survival. The thought of it made my heart beat faster, a wild, unsteady rhythm in my chest.

"Why are you telling me this?" I asked, voice barely above a whisper.

She hesitated for a moment, and when she spoke again, her words were slow, deliberate. "Because you deserve to know that the man who loves you isn't the man he thinks he is."

Before I could ask anything more, she stood up abruptly, pushing her chair back. "But it's not my place to fix him," she added, her voice lighter now, almost as though the weight of those words had been a burden lifted. "I thought I could once. But not anymore."

She turned to leave, her footsteps barely audible in the rain-drenched silence. I watched her go, feeling the cold air settle over me like a blanket of realization.

My mind raced. What had she meant? What did she know that I didn't? And if Luca had been someone else once, was there still a piece of him left? The man she described—honorable, loyal—was nothing like the one I had come to know, the one I had come to love. But her words... they haunted me. They unraveled the image I had painted of him, replacing it with something else, something softer and far more fragile than I had ever imagined.

Luca had changed. I knew that. The weight of his past, the burden of his choices—they had molded him into something that was more about survival than living. But could there really be a man beneath that hardened exterior? Could she be right? Could he still be capable of honor, of love, of loyalty?

And if that man existed, what did that mean for us? For me?

I wasn't sure if I wanted to find out. But deep down, I knew I would. I had no choice.

The rain hadn't stopped. The sky above Chicago was a murky blanket, weighed down with the kind of clouds that promised no reprieve. It felt fitting, really. I couldn't remember the last time I'd felt anything lighter than the damp heaviness of the city. My feet hit the pavement with an almost defiant rhythm, not a single umbrella in sight—just the usual scramble of people running for cover, the blur of coats, briefcases, and the soft clack of heels on wet concrete.

I had called Luca earlier, leaving a message I wasn't sure would even be heard. The uncertainty between us had grown into a space too vast to ignore. For days now, I had tried to avoid the truth lingering at the back of my mind—the woman from the café, her words still echoing in my head. "The man who used to believe in something." I didn't know if I could reconcile the man she described with the one who existed now, the man I'd come to trust with every piece of me.

I found myself outside his apartment building, standing at the door like some kind of a nervous schoolgirl about to knock on the principal's door. The familiar dread gnawed at me—how would he react? Would he dismiss me as just another person who couldn't possibly understand, or would he let me in? I wouldn't be able to take either answer, not really.

I was almost out of excuses. The weight of what I knew—and what I didn't—was gnawing at me like hunger. I pressed the buzzer.

The muffled click of the intercom startled me, followed by his voice—low, sharp, but strangely familiar. "You're here."

"Let me up."

It wasn't a question. And he didn't ask me why I was there. There was something so inevitable about the exchange, something about it that had been brewing for far too long. He buzzed me in, and I stood there in the elevator, my mind caught in an anxious spiral, listening to the hum of the cables.

When the door swung open, I was met with his familiar gaze—intense, always searching, but this time, there was something else. A flicker of wariness, a shadow of something more fragile. I walked in without waiting for him to speak, the door clicking shut behind me.

I knew I had to say something. Something to break the tension that had been building for days, but the words didn't come. I could hear my heart beating in my throat. It had been so easy, so effortless, before—living in the quiet rhythm of us. But now... now the air felt thick with everything unsaid, and I couldn't get enough of it, but I also couldn't breathe it in.

He leaned against the kitchen island, his arms crossed. His eyes never left me. I couldn't look away. This wasn't just a man who had built walls; this was a fortress, and every part of me felt like it was trying to break through.

"You talked to her, didn't you?" His voice was so quiet, so controlled, that it felt like the calm before a storm.

I nodded, biting my lip. I wasn't sure where to begin. I had to tread carefully, like walking on glass. But I wasn't about to let him off the hook.

"Why didn't you tell me about her?" I asked, the words sharp and sudden.

Luca's jaw tightened, and for a moment, I thought he might walk away. I didn't let him. "I wasn't ready," he said. "That part of me doesn't belong to you. Or anyone."

The edge in his voice was enough to send a chill down my spine. But I wasn't going to let it deter me.

"You were someone else once. A man who cared about loyalty. Honor," I said, testing the waters. His eyes flickered, and I saw it—the briefest of cracks in his armor, a pain that was far deeper than any anger he could summon.

"That man doesn't exist anymore," he bit out, his voice thick with an emotion he wasn't willing to name. He turned away, his back to me as if he could hide from the truth just by putting distance between us.

But the silence that followed was deafening. The tension between us felt like it might snap, but instead, it settled, heavier than I had expected. I couldn't leave it there. The words were already on my tongue, and I knew I had no choice but to say them.

"I think he does," I replied softly.

Luca froze.

And in that instant, I knew I had crossed some unspoken line—one I had no business crossing. He turned back to face me, his eyes wild with something I hadn't expected. Desperation? Fear? It wasn't anger, not this time.

"No," he said, his voice low, so painfully low. "He's gone. That man died a long time ago. And you don't want to bring him back."

"Why not?" I asked, stepping closer, my voice trembling with the rawness of the moment. "Because you're afraid? Or because you don't think I can handle the truth?"

He shook his head, an almost imperceptible motion, but I saw it. And in that motion, I knew. I could feel it in the air between us.

"You don't know what you're asking for," he said, each word coming out like it was laced with regret. "You think you want the man I was, but you don't. Not really." His gaze softened, something aching beneath the hardness. "The truth doesn't make anyone stronger. It only breaks them."

I let his words settle over me, heavy like the rain outside. I understood what he was saying, I did. But somewhere deep down, I didn't care. The man he used to be was still a part of him, no matter how much he tried to deny it. And maybe, just maybe, that was the man I needed to find. Not for him, but for us.

"You don't get to decide what I can handle, Luca," I said, the words slipping out before I could stop them.

His eyes darkened, but this time, he didn't pull away. He didn't retreat into the walls he had so carefully built around himself. He just stood there, silent, as if he were waiting for me to figure it out. Or waiting for me to leave.

And for the first time, I wasn't sure which one I wanted more.

The silence between us stretched on, thick and suffocating. It was as though the words I had spoken hung in the air, waiting for him to rip them apart with the sharpness I had come to expect from him. But Luca didn't move. He didn't breathe. For a moment, I wondered if he had already slipped into a place where he could pretend he didn't care, that none of this mattered. But then his gaze flickered back to me, the sharp edge of his pain never fully masked by the cool façade he wore so well.

The air was damp, heavy with the scent of wet earth and the faintest trace of his cologne, a fragrance that had somehow become a part of the room, woven into every shadow and corner. The dim light from the overhead lamp cast a soft glow on his features, making the dark circles beneath his eyes stand out, a reminder of the long battles he'd fought within himself. And here I was, a casualty of one of those battles, standing in the middle of his carefully constructed world, wondering if there was even a place for me in it.

"You think I don't want him to be real?" His voice broke the silence, rough, almost too harsh, but it wasn't directed at me. It was a question, one that rattled through him as though he were testing the idea in the air, seeing if it might hold some kind of truth. "You think I've forgotten what that man stood for? What he meant to me?"

I hadn't expected the rawness in his words, the kind of honesty that felt like peeling back a layer of skin to reveal a wound that had never fully healed. He took a step closer, the space between us shrinking, but the tension only grew.

"No," I said, shaking my head. "I think you've convinced yourself he doesn't exist anymore. But that's a lie." The words tumbled out before I could stop them, but they felt necessary, like an anchor to hold onto when everything around us felt like it might unravel.

Luca's eyes darkened, and for a second, I wondered if he might say something that would push me away for good. His walls were always so high, built of stone and silence, and I had spent months trying to climb them, to breach the fortress he kept around himself. But even as he stood there, a wall of contradictions and sharp edges, I could see it—the flicker of something beneath the surface. A ghost of the man the woman at the café had described. The one who had cared. The one who had believed in honor.

"I don't know how to be that man anymore," he said, and his voice was quiet, almost lost in the room between us. His gaze dropped to the floor, as though he couldn't bear to face me while admitting the truth. "You don't know what it's like to let go of something that was everything. To let go of a version of yourself that you thought was all you were. That's not something you just... find again."

I felt the sting of his words, but I didn't flinch. I couldn't. I had come here for a reason, and I wasn't about to back down now.

"You're wrong," I said, my voice steadier than I felt. "You're not lost, Luca. You're just scared of remembering who you used to be. And maybe, just maybe, who you still could be."

For a long moment, he didn't respond. He only stood there, his chest rising and falling with the weight of his breath. I wasn't sure what I expected from him anymore—anger, bitterness, or something colder still. But when he finally spoke, it was with a softness that took me by surprise.

"I don't know if I can love you the way you deserve," he whispered, his words fragile, like the quietest confession. He looked up at me then, his eyes filled with something that felt like regret, like grief for something he hadn't allowed himself to mourn. "I don't even know if I deserve it."

I was too close now to turn away. Too close to let those words slip past me without doing something about them. So, I did the only thing I could think to do: I reached for him. My fingers brushed his arm, just lightly, as though testing the waters. He didn't pull away, but he didn't pull me in either. There was something in that—the way his body remained still, but his muscles were taut, like a wound too tight, ready to snap.

"You deserve love, Luca. You deserve all of it. I don't care about the past. I care about who you are now. Who you can be."

My voice was steady, sure, and maybe I was fooling myself into thinking I could fix him. But in that moment, I didn't care. What mattered was that he didn't have to be alone in this. I was willing to fight for him, even if it meant wrestling with the ghosts of his past.

His gaze softened again, just for a moment, and then the walls went back up. It happened so quickly I almost didn't catch it, the way he turned away from me, pulling himself back into the shadow of his own defense.

"I'm not the man you think I am," he said, his voice distant now, like he was speaking from somewhere far away. "And you don't know what you're asking for."

I felt the weight of his words pressing down on me, but I wasn't ready to give up yet. Not when there was still a flicker of something more between us. I stepped closer again, my voice low, but firm.

"Then show me," I said, my words carrying a weight I hadn't expected. "Show me who you are now. Let me decide if I can handle it."

There was a long pause, one that felt like it stretched into forever. Then, without warning, the door to the apartment swung open with a suddenness that took us both by surprise. A figure stood in the doorway, silhouetted by the harsh light from the hallway behind them. I didn't have to see their face to know something had just changed.

Luca's posture shifted instantly. His muscles tensed, and his eyes, once so focused on me, snapped to the newcomer.

"Who the hell is that?" I whispered, but Luca didn't answer. He just stared, his expression unreadable, as the figure stepped into the room, and the door clicked shut behind them.

And for the first time since I had walked in, I felt a cold, creeping sense of dread coil in my stomach. Something had shifted. And whatever it was, I was certain I wasn't prepared for it.

Chapter 34: The Breaking Point

The heat in the room felt almost oppressive, like the kind of humidity that drapes itself over your skin during a late summer afternoon in New Orleans. My uncle's eyes were fire, burning with questions he had no intention of letting go until they were answered. We were standing in the kitchen, the sink cluttered with half-drunk mugs of coffee and the remains of a forgotten breakfast. I had never seen him so furious, so raw. And for a split second, I wondered if I'd made a mistake. But the question of loyalty was long past its expiration date, and now it was my turn to keep the scales balanced.

I could hear Luca behind me, his presence like an anchor, holding me together despite the storm swirling in my head. The words I had said—"It was me"—felt like they were tearing at the edges of my soul, but I couldn't let the truth spill. Not yet. Not when we were so close to the edge.

"Tell me again," my uncle growled, his voice low but brimming with venom, "how did the ledger just... disappear?"

The ledger. That damned book that held everything I wished I could forget and nothing I could undo. The evidence of every deal, every shady contract, and every dark secret my uncle had buried over the years. If it was found, all of us would be exposed. I couldn't—no, I wouldn't—let that happen. Not after everything Luca had done to shield me from the chaos that had always surrounded my family.

"It was me," I repeated, louder this time, standing my ground. "I went through your things. I wanted to know what you were really up to. I'm tired of being in the dark."

Uncle Sam's jaw clenched, his hands gripping the back of the chair like it was the only thing holding him to this world. The silence between us stretched, thick and suffocating, until he exhaled sharply, his temper momentarily cooling. But only just. The man had a temper that could scorch a field and leave nothing but ashes. I could feel Luca's gaze on the back of my neck—sharp, calculating—and I refused to turn around. I couldn't bear to see his disappointment, or worse, his guilt.

"Well, I hope you're happy," my uncle spat, before slamming his fist on the table, making the mugs rattle in protest. "You think you've uncovered something? You think you know what this family's really about? You're no better than I am, kid."

His words were meant to cut, to break me down, but I had heard them all before, every cruel syllable twisted like a knife. He didn't scare me anymore. Not after everything I'd seen. I stood taller, my shoulders square, though my heart beat too loud, too fast for comfort.

"I'm better than you," I said, the words slipping from my mouth before I could stop them. "You've always used people, Uncle Sam. People who trusted you, who believed in you. But I'm not that naive anymore."

He looked at me for a moment, his eyes searching my face, as if he were trying to figure out if this was a game or if I was truly gone, lost to the same darkness that had claimed him years ago. But it didn't matter what he saw, what he believed. I had made my choice. And I wasn't about to back down.

Uncle Sam exhaled sharply, shaking his head as though trying to rid himself of the taste of betrayal. Then he turned to Luca, his gaze narrowing, every muscle in his body taut with the kind of tension that only came when a threat had been spotted. "You," he said, his voice thick with distaste. "You've been pulling the strings all along, haven't you? You've been feeding her lies, making her think she has some control over all of this. You think you're better than me too?"

I could feel Luca stiffen behind me. There was a moment, a flicker of hesitation, before he spoke. His voice was steady, but there was a harshness there that was barely contained. "I'm not your enemy, Sam. But don't ever think for a second I won't do what's necessary to protect her. I'm not the one who started this mess."

The words hung in the air like smoke, twisting between us, making everything feel like it was teetering on the brink of explosion. I had seen Luca in a hundred different situations, but never like this. Never so raw, so unhinged. And the worst part? I couldn't deny that I understood him, even as I hated the position he had put me in.

Uncle Sam's laugh was cold, cutting. "Protect her?" he scoffed. "You think you've protected her? You think this whole thing is about protection? I'm the one who kept this family together! I'm the one who made sure we didn't all fall apart. And now you're both just playing games with things you can't understand."

I stood there, the tension so thick I could practically feel it in my bones. I wanted to scream, to throw something, to get out of that room and away from both of them. But I couldn't. Not when my future—and maybe my survival—depended on the choices I made in the next few moments.

"Enough," I finally said, my voice quieter than it should have been. But there was no turning back now. "I didn't do this to hurt anyone. I did it because I'm done being the pawn. I'm done living in fear of people like you."

The words hung in the air like a challenge, and for a second, it felt as if the whole room held its breath, waiting for the next move, the next betrayal, the next lie. The world outside seemed to blur, the only thing real the weight of my decision. I had chosen this path, and now there was no going back.

The silence in the kitchen lingered long after Uncle Sam stormed out, his footsteps heavy as he retreated to his office, no doubt plotting his next move. I could still feel the weight of his gaze, the unspoken accusations that would follow me for the rest of my life. But as the door slammed behind him, I turned to face Luca, who had been standing at the periphery of the storm, a silent observer to the whole debacle. The tension between us crackled, palpable, like static before a lightning strike. He had barely moved, his gaze fixed on me with an intensity that had me wondering whether I had just committed a cardinal sin by lying to save him.

I was the one who had always been the casualty of this life—the quiet daughter in the background of a family that was a mess of secrets and lies. But now, I had stepped into the ring, and there was no going back.

The seconds stretched between us like an eternity. Finally, Luca spoke, his voice barely above a whisper. "Why?"

I wanted to tell him that it was instinct—that it had been nothing but a gut reaction, a split-second decision made in the heat of the moment. But that wasn't the truth. Not entirely.

I stared at the kitchen counter, focusing on the sink that still held the remnants of my uncle's rage, the mug he'd knocked over earlier spilling the last traces of lukewarm coffee into the drain. My hands were shaking now, and I clutched the edge of the counter to steady myself.

"Because you've done enough," I said, my voice trembling despite my best efforts. "You've been fighting battles for me from the day you walked into my life, and I can't... I can't let you take the fall for this. Not when it's me who—"

"Stop," Luca interrupted, stepping closer, his boots clicking against the tile in the quiet room. His hand, warm and firm, landed on my shoulder, and I couldn't help but flinch at the contact. Not out of rejection, but because every inch of me was wound too tight.

"I didn't do this for you to protect me. I did it because you matter. But this... this is my mess, my choice, and you're not going to carry that for me."

I swallowed hard, the taste of guilt lingering in the back of my throat like a bitter pill. "But you don't understand. If it weren't for you—if you hadn't shielded me all these years—I'd be worse than I am now. I'd be... I'd be just like him."

The words fell out before I could stop them, and Luca's eyes softened, just for a fraction of a second, before the mask of cold control snapped back into place.

"Don't," he warned, his voice low. "Don't ever think you're like him. Don't even let that thought take root."

I looked up at him then, meeting his gaze, trying to find the words that would bridge the space between us. There was so much I wanted to say, so much that had been unsaid for too long. But as the moments ticked by, my throat tightened with something—something that was part frustration, part fear.

He took a step back, giving me room to breathe. "You don't owe me anything," he said quietly. "But you have to know, it wasn't just about protecting you. It's about—"

His words trailed off, as though he were trying to find the right thing to say, and I could see the struggle in his eyes. The tension between us was thick, charged with unspoken truths that neither of us were ready to face. It wasn't the first time, and I suspected it wouldn't be the last. The connection we shared—this strange, tangled web of guilt, desire, and understanding—had become our silent language, a language neither of us was fluent in but both were deeply bound to.

I took a deep breath, forcing the words out even though they felt foreign on my tongue. "I don't want to live in fear anymore, Luca. I can't. I can't keep pretending everything's fine when it's not. And I can't keep being the one who's protected, the one who hides behind someone else's decisions. I need to figure this out on my own. I need to make my own choices, even if they're messy, even if they hurt."

The words hung in the air, unpolished and raw, but they felt more honest than anything I'd said in a long time. There was no easy way out of this mess—no clean path forward. And as much as I wanted to keep running, to keep avoiding the ugliness of what I was really involved in, there was no escaping it now.

Luca's jaw tightened, and I saw the weight of my declaration settle over him like a dark cloud. He didn't move immediately, just stood there, considering me with an intensity that made my heart race. It was as though he were weighing something important in his mind.

When he finally spoke, it was with a sharpness that cut through the fog of tension that had built up between us. "You can make your own choices, Ria. But know this: Some choices come with a price. And some prices... they'll haunt you long after you think you've paid them."

The warning hung in the air, bitter and cold, and for a brief moment, I wanted to reach out and take it back. Take back everything I had said, everything I had done. But then I remembered the ledger—the missing ledger—and I knew I couldn't. I couldn't let the past control me any longer.

"I'm not afraid of the price," I said, my voice steadier now, even though my insides were shaking. "I'll pay whatever it takes. Just don't... don't protect me anymore."

Luca's eyes darkened, his features tightening as though he were holding himself back from saying something he knew would change everything. But he didn't say it. He didn't need to. The truth between us was there, unspoken but clear: we were both too tangled in this mess, too involved in the consequences to walk away unscathed.

The air in the apartment was thick with the tension of things unsaid, a heaviness that seemed to settle into the corners of the room. We stood there for a moment, the hum of the refrigerator in the background the only sound between us. I could feel Luca's eyes on me, the weight of his gaze heavy, searching for something in me he hadn't found before. I wasn't sure what I was supposed to offer him—some semblance of reassurance, maybe, or an apology for everything that had gone wrong. But I couldn't find the words.

His voice finally cut through the silence, smooth and calculated, though there was a layer of something else beneath it. "You're really willing to go this far? For me?"

I nodded, though it felt like a declaration I wasn't entirely prepared to make. "I already have, haven't I?"

He stepped closer, and for a moment, I thought he might take my hand, but he didn't. He didn't need to—his presence alone was enough to make me feel small, to make the weight of everything press harder into my chest. "And what about you?" he asked, his tone sharper now, a thread of frustration slipping through. "What do you get out of this, Ria? What happens to you when this all comes crashing down?"

I opened my mouth to respond, but the truth was, I didn't know. Not really. What did I get from all of this? The illusion of control? The quiet satisfaction of knowing I was no longer a passive bystander to the destruction around me? Maybe that's all it was. Maybe it was the need to prove something—prove I wasn't the scared little girl anymore, cowering behind someone else's choices.

But none of that seemed like a good enough answer, not for him. Not for the man whose world I had just unraveled. So instead, I stayed quiet, letting my silence speak for me.

Luca ran a hand through his hair, the dark strands messy from the frustration that was steadily building. "I'm not the one you should be protecting," he muttered under his breath, more to himself than to me.

"But you are," I said, stepping forward. "You always have been."

He looked at me then, really looked at me, and for the first time in a long while, I saw the weight of it all in his eyes. The danger, the burden, the secrets we had both been keeping. It was there, lingering in the space between us like a storm ready to break.

"We're in this together now," I added quietly, my voice softer, but no less firm. "And there's no way out."

Luca didn't say anything at first, but I could see the internal struggle playing out on his face. He wanted to push back, to remind me of how dangerous this game we were playing was. How high the stakes had become. But he knew, as much as I did, that we were already past the point of no return.

We both turned toward the window at the same time, the skyline of Chicago spread out before us like an unfinished puzzle, each piece more tangled than the last. The city was alive, buzzing with the usual late-night energy. I could hear the distant honking of horns, the murmur of voices from the street below. It should have been comforting, but all I felt was a gnawing sense of dread.

"You're sure about this?" Luca's voice broke the silence again, steady but laced with an edge of uncertainty.

I swallowed hard, staring out into the distance. "I'm sure."

There was a long pause as the weight of my words settled between us. And then, just as I thought we might have reached some kind of understanding, my phone buzzed on the kitchen counter.

I didn't want to check it. I didn't want to see what new disaster had been set in motion. But I reached for it anyway, my fingers trembling slightly as I picked it up and glanced at the screen. My stomach dropped.

It was a message from an unrecognized number.

We know what you did. You can't hide from this. Not anymore.

The words felt like a punch to the gut, the chill running through me instant and violent. I turned the phone over, as though physically removing it from my sight would somehow undo whatever threat was looming behind it.

Luca had already seen my face change, the blood draining from my cheeks, and he crossed the room in two strides, his hand gripping my wrist before I could pull away. "What is it?"

I tried to shake my head, but the words wouldn't stop clawing their way to the surface. "It's from someone who knows about the ledger."

His grip tightened on my wrist, his gaze sharpening. "Who?"

"I don't know. But they said they know what I did. Luca, they—"

Before I could finish, the front door to the apartment slammed open with a force that made both of us jump. My heart leaped into my throat, and I froze, eyes darting toward the doorway.

There was no time to think. No time to react.

The figure standing in the doorway wasn't just anyone. It was Uncle Sam. His face was twisted in fury, his breath coming in sharp gasps as though he had been running, and his eyes locked onto me with the cold, ruthless determination of a man who had nothing left to lose.

"You think you can keep playing this game with me?" His voice was low, guttural, and it sent a shiver down my spine. "You've made a mistake. A big one."

I opened my mouth, but the words stuck in my throat. What was I supposed to say? What could I say when the truth was right there in front of us, taunting us both?

Luca stepped in front of me instinctively, his posture tense, ready for whatever my uncle would throw at us next.

And just like that, the game had changed again. This time, there would be no turning back.

Chapter 36: Shadows in the Night

The streets of Chicago are alive with a pulse that neither wanes nor rests, the kind of city that breathes in rhythm with its inhabitants. The cold wind cuts through the alleys, its bite more aggressive than usual, and the low hum of the L train in the distance vibrates through the concrete like a constant, unyielding reminder of the world just beneath the surface. The lights in the office building ahead of me flicker erratically, casting long, crooked shadows across the pavement, shadows that seem to sway with a life of their own, as if anticipating the chaos about to unfold.

I glance at Luca, his figure cutting through the fog, tall and imposing in his black coat. His eyes—dark, calculating—catch mine with an intensity that unsettles me in a way I can't quite put my finger on. Maybe it's the way he looks at me like he's weighing every word I say, every movement I make, as though every breath could shift the balance between life and death. I can feel the weight of that stare even when I look away. But I don't mind. Not tonight. Tonight, I need him more than I care to admit.

"I'm not letting you out of my sight," Luca repeats, his voice low, like the promise it is—heavy and unbreakable.

"For once, I don't mind," I reply, offering him a half-smile, the kind that says more than I ever could with words. He matches my smile with one of his own, though it doesn't quite reach his eyes. His smile is always a mask—slightly too sharp, like it's there to hide something deeper, something dangerous.

The wind tugs at my hair, sending a few errant strands whipping across my face. I push them back, trying to focus, but it's hard when everything around me seems to spin in endless circles of deceit and suspicion. The plan—our plan—has been in motion for days now, each moment of tension building toward an inevitable conclusion. There's no turning back now. We've crossed lines we can never uncross, and as much as I wish I could say otherwise, a part of me is already dreading what comes next.

I look at Luca, really look at him. There's something unsettling in the way he holds himself—this quiet, powerful presence that seems to command the air around him. His jaw is clenched, his brow furrowed in thought, but he's not lost in the strategy like I am. No, Luca is always present, always aware of everything and everyone in his orbit. And tonight, that awareness feels like a weight pressing on me. I can feel it in the air—the heat of the tension, the knowledge that there's no guarantee we'll walk out of this unscathed.

"What happens after this?" I ask, my voice barely more than a whisper, the question floating between us like smoke from a fire I can't extinguish.

Luca glances at me, his eyes narrowing. "I'm not thinking that far ahead," he says. "We get through tonight, and then we deal with what comes next."

I hate how easily he dismisses the uncertainty in my words, but I can't bring myself to argue. He's right, of course. There's no point in worrying about what we can't control, especially when what's happening in the here and now is more than enough to keep anyone awake at night.

I step closer to him, my boots clicking softly against the pavement, each step a small but significant beat in this chaotic symphony. His presence seems to pull me in, wrapping around me like an invisible force, and for a moment, I can almost forget the stakes. Almost.

"You sure you're ready for this?" I ask, though the question is more for myself than for him. I already know the answer, but there's a part of me that needs to hear him say it out loud.

Luca's lips curve upward again, but this time there's no trace of humor in the expression. "I've never been more ready for anything in my life," he replies, his voice steady, resolute.

I nod, taking a deep breath, trying to steady the rapid beat of my heart. It's hard to ignore the sense of impending doom that lingers in the back of my mind, the nagging feeling that we're not as prepared as we think we are, that something—some unpredictable twist—is waiting to turn everything upside down. But that's the nature of this world we've stepped into, isn't it? There's no room for certainty, no room for safety. Not anymore.

"How do you want to do this?" I ask, pushing away the creeping doubts, focusing instead on the task at hand.

Luca doesn't hesitate. "We stick to the plan," he says, his voice calm, reassuring. "We do what we've practiced, and we trust no one but each other."

A shiver runs down my spine, but I hide it. He's right, of course. Trust is a fragile thing, especially when it comes to people like us. But in the end, it's all we've got. And for all the scheming and betrayal, the one constant has been Luca. I can't help but wonder—how much of this plan is his, and how much is mine?

The thought lingers as we move toward the building's entrance, our footsteps blending with the pulse of the city behind us, a stark reminder that the world we're about to step into doesn't care about our plans or our fears. It only cares about survival.

Inside the building, the lights are dim, casting long, wavering shadows that stretch across the walls, adding to the tension that's been building all evening. Every inch of the place feels like it's holding its breath, waiting for the storm to break. And then, as if on cue, the elevator doors open, and we step into the unknown.

The air inside the building feels thick, oppressive, as though the walls themselves are holding their breath, waiting for something to happen. The elevator's soft chime fades into the background, replaced by the sound of our shoes clicking on the polished marble floor, sharp against the stillness of the night. The hall stretches out ahead of us, its expanse cold and unforgiving, each step echoing louder than the last. It's as if every corner, every shadow, is conspiring against us, silently pulling at the seams of the plan we've woven so carefully. But there's no turning back now. The stakes are too high, and we're too deep in this web to untangle ourselves without getting caught.

Luca's hand brushes mine as we walk, barely a touch, but enough to send a jolt of electricity up my arm. There's an unspoken understanding between us—no words needed, just a shared, unyielding determination. His presence, though always overwhelming, is strangely comforting now. I can't quite explain it, but in this moment, I feel safer with him beside me than I ever have. It's a peculiar sensation, one that makes my stomach twist in a way I can't quite decipher. Safety, in this world, is an illusion at best.

We reach the end of the hall, where the door to the office sits like a silent sentinel. The faint glow of the light from within seeps through the cracks, casting long shadows across the floor, stretching like fingers grasping for something they can never quite reach. I stop in front of it, my hand hovering just above the doorknob, the final decision hanging in the air between us.

"You ready?" Luca's voice is low, though his question doesn't carry the weight of uncertainty. He's ready. He's always ready.

I nod, but my throat feels dry. I wish I could say something—anything—that would calm the churning inside me. But the words don't come. Instead, I turn the knob, the metallic click of it louder than I expect, and step inside. The office is immaculate, coldly efficient in its design. Everything is arranged with the kind of precision that only someone with far too much time—and too many secrets—could afford.

A figure stands by the window, silhouetted against the city lights that stretch out in front of them like a million blinking stars, each one hiding a story of its own. They don't move as we enter, but I can feel their eyes on us, assessing, calculating.

"We were expecting you," the figure says, their voice smooth and neutral, like it's the most natural thing in the world to be caught in a trap like this.

Luca steps forward without hesitation, his presence consuming the room, drawing every ounce of attention toward him. His eyes, narrowed and sharp, flick toward me for a brief second, as if to ensure we're on the same page. The tension in the air thickens, the weight of the moment settling heavily on my chest.

"We're not here to waste time," Luca says, his voice smooth, like polished stone. "We have a deal, and we intend to keep it. All we want is what was promised."

I can feel the shift in the room, like the very air has changed its charge. The figure by the window turns slowly, revealing a face that I know all too well. The realization hits me like a physical blow, and for a moment, I'm frozen in place, as though my mind can't quite reconcile what's standing in front of me.

"Well, well," the figure says, their lips curling into a smile that doesn't quite reach their eyes. "I didn't think you'd make it this far. But you've always had a knack for surprising people, haven't you?"

Luca doesn't flinch. He's always so composed, so sure of himself, like the chaos of the world is just a passing inconvenience to him. But I can see it now, the tiniest flicker of something—something dark, something dangerous—behind his eyes. A hint of recognition. Of anger.

"Get to the point," he says, his voice suddenly low and dangerous. I feel the shift in the room, the tension crackling like static. The game has changed, and I can sense the new rules unfolding in front of us.

The figure doesn't speak immediately. Instead, they take a slow step forward, their eyes flickering between Luca and me. There's something almost... familiar in the way they look at me. Something that makes my stomach twist in a way that has nothing to do with fear.

"Tell me, how far are you willing to go?" the figure asks, their tone laced with an undercurrent of challenge. "How much of yourself are you willing to sacrifice for this? For your precious plan?"

I swallow hard, my throat tight. The question lingers in the air like a blade, hovering just above us, threatening to strike. But I don't flinch. I can't.

Luca steps forward again, closing the distance between them. "We're done with games. Either we get what we came for, or this whole thing ends tonight."

For a moment, everything is still. There's no movement, no sound except for the distant hum of the city below. It feels like we're standing at the precipice of something far darker than we can see, but there's no turning back now.

The figure smiles again, but it's different this time. It's not a smile of amusement or intrigue—it's the smile of someone who's just won. Someone who knows something we don't.

"You're already too late," they say, their voice soft but filled with finality. "Everything's already in motion. There's nothing you can do to stop it now."

My heart skips a beat, and I glance at Luca, searching for any sign that he has a plan. But his face is unreadable, his eyes locked on the figure with a coldness that sends a chill down my spine.

For the first time since we started this, I'm not sure if we're the ones in control anymore. And that thought, more than anything else, terrifies me.

The air inside the office crackles with an intensity that feels like it could shatter at any moment. My pulse hammers in my ears, and the faint thrum of the city outside seems distant now, as if we're encased in some unbreakable bubble. The figure standing before us knows something we don't, and it feels like we're the ones being played, the ones left out in the cold.

Luca's hand moves subtly toward his jacket, the faintest shift that sends a ripple of anticipation through my spine. He's always ready. Always. But tonight, even his unshakable confidence feels a little... fragile.

"So," the figure says, their voice smooth and dripping with something close to amusement, "you've really come this far, haven't you? All the way here, thinking you have control over the situation. But let me make one thing perfectly clear: You never had it. Not from the start."

I can hear the venom in their words, see the glint of something far more dangerous in their eyes. It's not just a game for them. This is personal.

Luca doesn't flinch. Not even a muscle twitches. "Enough with the theatrics," he says, the words clipped, harsh. He's done playing. We've all been pretending, but this—this is real. And now the real stakes are coming into focus.

I glance around the room, as though the walls might offer me some solace, some way to escape the tension choking the air. But the sterile, gleaming surfaces offer nothing but reflections of the stark, calculated danger that's closing in. It feels like we're trapped inside some sort of elaborate trap, and the walls are closing in with each passing second.

"You think you're the only ones with a plan?" the figure chuckles, a sound that feels hollow, disconnected. It doesn't reach their eyes. "You've played your part. But now, we get to play ours. You've been nothing but pawns in a much larger game."

"Stop wasting my time," Luca growls. He's always been a man of few words, preferring action over anything else. But tonight, even his patience seems stretched to its breaking point. I can see the tightness in his jaw, the way his hand hovers at his side, ready for whatever comes next. "What's the real play?"

The figure doesn't answer immediately. Instead, they step forward, slowly, deliberately, as if savoring the moment. The sound of their shoes on the marble floor is unnervingly loud, each click echoing through the space like a countdown to the inevitable. The closer they get, the more the room feels like it's closing in on me.

"I told you, didn't I?" The figure's voice is low now, almost a whisper, but the words carry like daggers in the silence. "It was never about what you wanted. You think you're the heroes of your own story, but this... this is my story. And I've been writing it for a lot longer than you've been playing your part."

The words sting, but it's not the words that frighten me—it's the implication. The idea that everything we've done, all the planning, all the risk, was never enough. We've been set up, and the realization tastes like ash in my mouth.

Luca finally moves. Fast. So fast that I don't even have time to register the shift before he's beside the figure, blocking their path with the silent menace of someone who's seen the ugliest parts of the world and doesn't flinch at the sight of them. He doesn't speak at first. The silence between them is thick, charged.

I feel the air thicken, press against my chest as though the room itself is tightening its grip on us, unwilling to let go.

"What do you want?" I ask before Luca can. The words escape me before I can second-guess them. The question is simple, but the weight of it hangs in the air like an unspoken threat. There's no room for half-truths anymore. We're past that.

The figure glances at me, their expression unreadable. "What I want?" They tilt their head, considering the question for a moment before answering with chilling calm. "I want the game to end. But it's not up to you, is it? It's up to us."

Luca stiffens beside me, and for a brief second, I swear I see a flicker of something in his eyes—something like disbelief, mixed with a kind of bitter realization. His lips press into a thin line, but his eyes don't leave the figure. "Enough," he says, his voice low, his patience gone.

I step forward, the sound of my heels on the floor loud in the otherwise silent room. My voice shakes, but I try to make it firm. "Tell us what's really going on. No more games. What is it you're after? And don't give me any more cryptic riddles."

The figure's lips curl into a smile that feels too wide for their face, too knowing. There's no joy in it—only calculation. "You'll find out soon enough," they say, turning their back to us and walking toward the desk at the far side of the room, their heels tapping like the ticking of a clock, marking time that we can't seem to slow.

Luca takes a step forward, his movements smooth, but his eyes never leave the figure. There's a tension in the way he moves now, like he's waiting for something to break.

The figure stops in front of the desk, their hands resting on the surface. The smile fades. "You think you're in control, but you're not," they repeat, their voice hardening. "You'll understand when it's too late."

Before I can respond, the door slams open behind us, and I feel the cold rush of air that sweeps in like a gust from some forgotten storm. My breath catches in my throat as I turn around to face the sudden intrusion, my heart pounding against my ribs, because I know—whatever is about to happen, it's going to change everything.

And in the doorway stands someone I never expected to see again.

Chapter 37: The Fall of a King

I didn't expect it to happen this way. Not tonight. Not with everything hanging in the balance like a delicate thread stretched taut, ready to snap. But the air in the room is thick with anticipation, as if everyone here can feel the earth shift under their feet. My uncle's estate—a monstrous thing, made of stone and glass, a fortress built on secrets—holds its breath. The chandelier overhead casts fractured shadows that slither across the marble floors, each of them twisting in the corners like memories I can't shake. There are whispers behind velvet curtains, hushed tones carried on the thick scent of expensive cigars and old scotch. The weight of what we're about to do presses against my chest, squeezing until my ribs ache, but there's no turning back now.

Luca stands beside me, his presence like a quiet storm, powerful and constant. The muscles in his jaw are tight, his eyes sharp like a predator's, scanning the room. I don't need to look at him to know he's as ready as I am. He doesn't speak, doesn't need to. We've been through too much for words to matter now. The plan has been rehearsed down to the finest detail, like a perfectly orchestrated symphony. Every note, every instrument, playing its part, meant to build and crescendo into this night—the night we take him down.

My uncle, Victor Crane, is a legend in his own mind. Ruthless, cold, and completely consumed by the empire he's built. I've spent most of my life trying to escape his shadow, to carve out a place where his reach didn't extend. But the thing about shadows is they never let you go entirely. Tonight, though, the light will shine through. Tonight, we'll end it.

The first move happens quietly. Just a few subtle gestures, a shared glance between Luca and me. The guests—an eclectic mix of old-money socialites, shady business partners, and the odd politician or two—mill about in the grand hall, unaware of the storm about to hit. I can feel the tension in the air, like static before a thunderstorm. Something's wrong. And it doesn't take long to figure out what it is.

A sudden shift. A figure, too well-dressed, too polished to belong here, steps out of the shadows, an unexpected element. A name I didn't anticipate, a face I haven't seen in years, but one I know far too well. Isabella Crane. My cousin. The one I never thought would side with us—let alone do anything that might disrupt her father's carefully crafted reign. She stands at the top of the grand staircase, her eyes scanning the crowd, and then—like a switch has been flipped—she moves.

It's like a match lit in the dark. The spark ignites, and the room explodes in a whirl of motion. My heart races, and for the briefest of moments, the world tilts, throwing everything into disarray. Luca reacts first, his hand on my arm, guiding me through the chaos. I trust him implicitly, following his lead as we push forward, each step deliberate and careful. The moment Isabella makes her move, it's as if a dam breaks—all our carefully laid plans spill out of control. But in this madness, there's an unexpected clarity. This is it.

I push through the crowd, my pulse thundering in my ears, my eyes locked on the man who has tormented me for years. My uncle. His face is cold, unreadable, but the flicker of surprise in his eyes when he sees me is all the confirmation I need. His empire is crumbling. His rule, built on manipulation and fear, is finally being torn apart at the seams.

But I didn't expect her. Isabella. She's not supposed to be here, not on our side. She was always the favored one, the one who followed in her father's footsteps, who never questioned him. She's supposed to be loyal, to stand with the very empire we're trying to take down. And yet, here she is, taking aim at the heart of everything he's built. She's holding something—a small, silver device that I know all too well. It's the trigger to the system that controls the estate's security. The very system I thought we had neutralized.

"Isabella, what the hell are you doing?" My voice is sharp, cutting through the noise like a blade.

She doesn't flinch. Her eyes flicker to me, a hint of something—fear, regret, or maybe just cold calculation—in the depths of her gaze.

"Saving us," she says, her voice low and steady, as if this were just another Tuesday for her. "Or maybe just saving myself. The old man never had any intention of letting any of us live beyond our use."

The realization hits me like a punch to the gut. She's been playing this game for far longer than I ever realized. She's always been a step ahead. Her betrayal, however quiet, has been planned. I can't quite decide if I feel betrayed or if I should thank her for finally pulling the rug out from under Victor's feet.

Luca moves closer, his hand gripping my wrist. His eyes lock onto mine, his silent question clear. What now? The plan is spiraling out of control, but there's no room for hesitation. If we don't act now, everything we've fought for will be lost.

We spring into action together. The seconds stretch long, filled with the sound of hurried footsteps and muffled voices. Luca moves like a shadow, slipping through the chaos, while I take a different route, weaving through the room, feeling the eyes of everyone on me—everyone except my uncle. He's too busy trying to regain control. It's now or never.

I finally reach him, my heart hammering in my chest, my hand steady on the small concealed weapon at my side. The moment I've waited for. The final confrontation.

"Victor," I say, my voice cutting through the air, steady and sure. "It ends here."

His eyes narrow, the years of power and control flickering behind them. For a moment, he looks vulnerable, as if he's finally realizing how fragile his empire truly is.

"You think you can destroy everything I've built?" he sneers.

I take a breath. "You've already destroyed it yourself. All I'm doing is cleaning up your mess."

The moment I speak, I realize there's no turning back. There's no second chance to rewrite the past. In the dim glow of the estate's grand hall, the words hang between us like the delicate weight of a drawn sword. For all the years I spent avoiding this confrontation, hoping for some other escape, some other way to take my life back, here it is. The point of no return. I feel it—his power slipping away, the moment when all the blood, sweat, and years of planning culminate into one single, fragile heartbeat.

Victor laughs, low and mocking, the sound bouncing off the cold stone walls like an echo of his arrogance. "You think you're the first to try and end this?" He steps closer, the anger in his eyes momentarily flickering beneath the layers of control. "This empire is mine, and it will never fall. Not to you."

I meet his gaze, steady and unflinching. "Empires crumble. They always do."

His hand twitches, just slightly, but it's enough. A flicker of panic flashes in his eyes, quickly masked by his usual mask of disdain. I don't give him the satisfaction of flinching.

I'm done with him. Done with the chains he placed on my life, with the twisted games he played to make me into his pawn. Tonight, I'm the one with the power. Tonight, I take back everything he stole.

Behind me, the tension grows thicker. I hear Luca's movements, sharp and calculated, as he circles the room, covering every exit. I can almost feel the pulse of his focus, the quiet intensity in his actions. His presence is like a storm cloud, a dangerous calm before the inevitable crash. I can't help but admire how seamlessly he works in the chaos, how everything around us seems to bend to his will. He doesn't look at me. He doesn't need to. There's an understanding between us, something deeper than words. It's our strength and our weakness.

Victor shifts, his attention back on me, a wicked smirk playing at the corner of his lips. "You think you've outwitted me? You're just as naive as your mother was."

The mention of my mother stings more than I want it to. The wound is still fresh, buried beneath years of anger and sorrow, and yet he's always known how to twist it, how to reopen it when it suits him. "Don't speak of her," I say through gritted teeth, the words heavy with restraint.

He laughs again, a jagged, cruel sound. "What, you still think she was some kind of saint? She was just another woman who couldn't handle the power. Just like you."

Something inside me snaps. I take a step forward, my heels clicking sharply against the floor, cutting through the haze of anger and adrenaline that has enveloped the room. I want to throw my entire life in his face, every sacrifice, every broken promise, every lie he's ever told me. But I don't. Instead, I meet his eyes, steady, unblinking, and let the silence stretch out.

"You're wrong about her," I say softly, the calm in my voice like ice. "And you're wrong about me. I'm not here to be your pawn anymore."

There's a brief moment where I think he might reach for something—anything—but the moment passes. He knows. I know. This is it. The end of his reign.

The room goes eerily quiet, a strange stillness overtaking the place as if the estate itself recognizes what's about to happen. It's as if all the walls are waiting to see which way the winds will blow. For a moment, everything seems suspended, caught in a timeless space, and then—chaos.

Everything shifts in the span of a breath. Isabella. That traitor cousin of mine, who until this moment had been nothing but a shadow at the edge of my world, steps out into the open, her hand raised. The sharp click of the device she's holding reaches me first, like the snap of a twig underfoot. My heart skips a beat.

I barely have time to react before everything goes sideways.

She presses a button. The lights flicker, then go out entirely. A mechanical hum fills the air, and then a flash of red lights dances across the walls, cutting through the darkness. It's like a nightmare. The estate's security system comes to life—locking doors, sealing windows, trapping everyone inside. It's exactly what I was afraid of.

"I never thought you'd have the guts to do it," she says, her voice like ice, smooth and cold. "But then again, you never did know what kind of game you were playing."

Her words hang in the air like smoke, drifting through the confusion. I don't have to look at her to know the betrayal is as sharp as a blade to the gut.

I don't have time to dwell on her treachery. I can feel the pressure in the air as the seconds slip away. The security system has triggered lockdown procedures—everyone in the room is now a hostage, and I'm not sure whether I'm more angry at Isabella for this twist or at myself for missing it. The truth stings. All those years I spent thinking I could outsmart Victor, and it's my own blood who's pulled the rug out from under me.

Luca's voice breaks through the chaos, low and urgent, cutting through the tension like a knife. "We need to move. Now."

I don't hesitate. I can't afford to. The game has changed, but I've always been good at adapting. We sprint toward the nearest door, the world around me spinning in a blur of motion and panic.

My thoughts race—how do we get out of here? How do we end this?

A door slams open ahead of me, and for a split second, I think it's my escape. But then I see him. Victor. Standing at the far end of the corridor, his face twisted in something between fury and satisfaction.

"You're not going anywhere," he says, voice cold as steel.

I freeze. A cold hand wraps around my heart, but I won't show fear. Not now. Not when we're so close. Not when everything's falling into place.

The standoff in the corridor feels like it lasts an eternity. The air is thick with tension, the hum of the estate's security system still echoing in my ears, its presence a reminder of how much we've lost control. But I refuse to let that shake me. This is my moment, and I've fought too long to let fear or hesitation cloud my judgment now.

Victor stands at the far end, his back straight, his arms crossed, as if he's the one in control. His smug expression does little to hide the flicker of uncertainty in his eyes. For a moment, I wonder if he can feel it too—the end approaching. The clock ticking louder with every passing second. The walls feel like they're closing in. He's not the god he thought he was; he's a man, vulnerable in the face of what's coming. I might have taken my time getting here, but I've learned everything I need to take him down. This, I know.

"You really think you can walk away from this?" he sneers, his words like venom dripping from his lips. "Do you know how many people have tried to take me down, only to end up buried in the dirt?"

I step forward, my heels clicking with purpose, cutting through the heavy silence. My eyes never leave his. "You know what I've learned, Victor? The higher you climb, the harder you fall."

A flicker of anger flashes across his face, but I see the hesitation. He's starting to question it. To doubt his position.

"I should have taken care of you when I had the chance," he mutters, stepping closer, his voice growing more menacing. His words, filled with bitter regret, only remind me of all the years of misery he's inflicted on me. On all of us.

Behind me, I can hear Luca's movements, his steps light, calculated, always just out of my line of sight. He's circling, waiting for the moment when things finally break open. I trust him to make the right call. The plan is a living thing now—shifting, evolving in real time, and I won't let it fall apart. Not now.

"You've had plenty of chances," I retort, my voice steady despite the roar of adrenaline inside me. "And every time, you failed. All you've ever done is let your empire rot from the inside."

He clenches his jaw, eyes narrowing as if he's about to strike, but something stops him. Maybe it's the realization that the tables have turned, or maybe it's because he knows what I'm about to do. There's no going back for him now.

The tension crackles like static in the air, every second drawn tight, stretched thin, until the silence is unbearable. My heart pounds, but my mind is clear, focused. I can almost hear the familiar rhythm of Luca's breathing, feel the solid presence of him behind me. We've done this before—fighting side by side, two halves of a whole, each one knowing exactly what the other will do next.

Victor takes one more step toward me, and this time, I don't back down. I stand my ground. I'm done running. Done hiding. The power he had over me, over all of us, is nothing more than smoke now. His reign is crumbling, and he knows it.

"You've failed, Victor," I say, my voice unwavering. "It's over."

His eyes flash with a mix of disbelief and fury. He reaches inside his jacket, and for a heart-stopping moment, I think he's going to draw a weapon. But instead, his hand emerges empty, his posture stiffening, his arrogance turning to something almost like fear.

And that's when I hear it. A soft click. A sound I recognize too well.

The security system. The backup protocol.

I turn just in time to see a figure dart from the shadows, Isabella. She stands at the far end of the hall, the device in her hand gleaming in the dim light. She smiles, a cruel, knowing smile.

"I did warn you," she says, her voice a low purr that sends a chill crawling down my spine. "You were always one step behind."

Her words are like a punch to the gut. Betrayal stings deeper when it comes from someone you thought you could trust—someone you thought was your ally. I'd trusted her, maybe even in a small way. And now, she's a traitor. A piece of the puzzle I never even saw coming.

"What are you doing?" I demand, my voice rising.

She laughs softly, her eyes gleaming with something dark and dangerous. "What I should have done from the beginning. Taking control. Taking what's mine."

The click echoes again, and the doors at the far end of the hallway slam shut with a force that shakes the entire house. Panic begins to ripple through the estate, muffled cries from the party downstairs filtering in from the other side of the locked doors. It's over. The plan has collapsed into chaos.

"Isabella," I say, the weight of the word heavy on my tongue. "You've sealed your fate."

"You think I care about fate?" she snaps, her grip tightening on the device. "I've waited my whole life for this."

The tension is unbearable. I can feel it tightening, like a noose around my throat, each moment dragging us closer to the inevitable. I know Luca is still moving in the shadows, but I can't afford to look away from her now. There's no telling what she'll do next.

Victor's voice cuts through the air, thick with an anger I've never heard before. "Enough. Let's finish this. All of you."

The words barely leave his mouth before Isabella's finger presses down on the device.

The lights flicker, and for a moment, I think it's a trick. Then the walls begin to rumble, the sound of metal grinding against metal filling the air. The floor beneath my feet shifts, and the reality of what's happening crashes into me like a tidal wave.

I barely have time to brace myself before the ground beneath us cracks open.

Chapter 38: The Cost of Victory

The city hums with the kind of feverish energy that only comes when everyone's pretending to have it all together. As if, somewhere just beyond the glitter of streetlights and the buzz of bar conversations, everything is still intact. But I know better. I feel it in the stale air of my apartment, where the curtains hang limply, too tired to catch the sun. The same air that clings to my skin when I wake up to an empty bed next to me, the only reminder of Luca's absence, the ghost of what used to be.

I move through the morning like a shadow, half-aware of the cars honking below, the clang of distant subway trains. The city feels like it's holding its breath, waiting for something — anything — to change. The streets are packed, the usual cacophony of life unchanged, but I can't escape the silence inside me. It's as if the universe knows. It always does.

The coffee shop on the corner smells like burnt espresso and faintly sweet pastries. I lean against the counter, trying to remind myself that this is my life, these people, these small comforts. But I'm too tired to pretend. The barista hands me my latte, the whipped cream on top an ironic gesture of cheer, and I take it with a tight smile.

Behind me, a voice murmurs my name.

"Ella?"

I turn. It's Cara, one of the few people who hasn't turned away. We've known each other since college — back when everything was easier, before the world got messy and tangled in secrets. She has the kind of face that lights up a room, even when her own life feels as though it's stuck in neutral. But today, her usual radiance is dimmed, something unspoken hanging between us.

"Hey, Cara," I say, trying to keep my tone light. "How's it going?"

She glances around the room, clearly wanting to pull me aside. I follow her out into the narrow alley beside the shop, the sound of distant laughter from a group of tourists floating out from the nearby park. It's surreal — like life outside is still moving forward while I'm caught in some sort of standstill.

"Look," Cara starts, her voice low, "I don't know what's going on with you and Luca, but I need to say this. You've been... different. And it's not just the usual stress." She fidgets with the strap of her purse, avoiding my gaze. "People talk, you know. About everything that happened."

I press my lips together. The weight of her words settles in the pit of my stomach. "What people?"

She meets my eyes, something flickering behind her own. "People who don't know the whole story. And people who do. There's a lot of rumors, Ella. A lot."

I want to tell her it doesn't matter. That it's all over now, the dust settling in a way I wish I could say was final. But something in her face tells me it's not over. Not yet.

"You know, you can't just walk away from this," Cara continues. "I don't know what happened between you two, but... if you think Luca is going to let you slip away without some kind of reckoning, you're wrong."

The words hit me harder than I expected, a cold chill sweeping over my skin. I swallow, trying to shake off the unease creeping through my chest. I should have known this would happen. The world doesn't forgive easily — especially when it comes to people like us.

"I didn't ask for any of this," I say, my voice steady but raw. "I didn't ask for any of it."

Cara stares at me for a long moment, her lips parting as if she's going to say something else, but she doesn't. Instead, she nods slowly, like she's made a decision, and without another word, she turns and walks away, leaving me alone with the buzzing hum of the city.

The rest of the day drags. I try to focus on work, but my thoughts keep drifting back to Luca. I can feel him out there, somewhere, his presence both distant and all-consuming. It's like he's everywhere and nowhere at once. The last time I saw him, he was standing in the doorway of my apartment, his expression unreadable. He didn't speak, just looked at me with eyes full of questions I didn't have answers to. He left without a word, and I haven't seen him since.

By the time the evening rolls around, I'm pacing the apartment, my nerves fraying. The phone sits on the counter, silent, daring me to pick it up. But I don't. The last thing I want is to open that line again — to hear him say things I'm not sure I can handle. To listen to the apology that feels too late. The silence between us feels like it could swallow me whole.

I hear a knock at the door.

For a moment, I stand frozen. My heart beats a little faster, a little heavier, as if it knows what's coming. I take a deep breath and walk slowly to the door, my hand trembling ever so slightly as I reach for the handle.

I open it, and there he is. Luca.

For a moment, neither of us speaks. He's standing there, his face weary, his usual confidence now an almost brittle shell. He doesn't look at me directly at first, his gaze drifting over my shoulder to the empty space inside.

"I'm sorry," he says, the words coming out thick, almost as if they cost him something. "I know I'm the last person you want to see."

I open my mouth to respond, but nothing comes out. Instead, I step aside, letting him into the apartment. The door clicks shut behind him, sealing us both in this strange, fragile moment where everything hangs in the balance.

"I don't know how to fix this," he murmurs, his voice barely audible. "I don't know if I can."

I lead Luca into the living room, and the quiet that falls between us is suffocating. The space feels smaller, somehow. The walls — once full of warmth, laughter, and too many long nights of plans and promises — now seem like cold witnesses, indifferent to the weight of the world we've both carried into it. I want to sit, to break the tension, but I can't. Instead, I hover near the couch, arms folded, as if that alone will keep the rawness of this moment from fully consuming us.

Luca shifts, his fingers skimming the edge of a throw pillow on the couch, his eyes catching the dim light from the streetlamp outside. For a moment, I think he might say something, might finally shatter the silence between us. But then he exhales, slow and low, as though giving up on the very idea.

"I didn't want this," he says quietly, his voice cracking just enough to make the words sting. "Not like this."

I force my gaze away from him, staring out the window, at the blur of cars zipping down the avenue, people bustling through the night like everything is still normal. They have no idea what's been lost, what's been broken — that the world is suddenly a far more complicated place than it was just a few weeks ago. A place I don't know how to navigate anymore.

"We never wanted it," I answer, my voice barely above a whisper. "But we were part of it. From the very start."

The sound of his breath fills the space between us. I feel it as if it's my own, pressing against my chest. I want to reach out, to comfort him, but there's something blocking me. Something I can't explain, not even to myself.

"You're right," he says after a moment, finally turning toward me. "We've been in this mess for so long, I forgot what it felt like to stand outside it."

I finally turn to face him, crossing the room with slow steps. My hand hovers near his shoulder, but I can't quite make the leap. His eyes, dark and full of secrets, search mine for something, anything, to hold on to.

"I don't know how we got here," I admit. "I just don't."

His lips curl, a bitter, half-hearted smile. "It's the thing no one talks about, right? How we get here. How we're forced into places we never thought we'd be, and then... well, then we start asking ourselves if it was worth it."

I bite the inside of my cheek to keep from saying what's already swirling in my mind. The truth. The truth that none of us is free from our choices, no matter how much we wish it were otherwise. The truth that there's no way to undo the damage we've done, no magic reset button that would make it all go away. The wreckage is too deep, the fallout too wide.

"I think..." I pause, hesitating. "I think it's too late to go back, Luca. But maybe that's okay. Maybe we have to face what we've done before we can figure out what's next."

His gaze hardens, the weight of my words sinking into him like a stone. I feel it too, that crushing certainty that there is no easy road ahead. But even then, there's a flicker of something — something that might be hope, or just the exhaustion of a battle too long fought.

"I don't know if I can face it," he mutters, running a hand through his hair. The gesture is tired, weary. It's not the Luca I used to know, the one who could walk into any room and take charge, no questions asked. Now he looks... defeated. As if the fight has drained him dry.

"You don't have to do it alone," I say quietly. "But you do have to face it. Whatever it is. And so do I."

His gaze flickers to mine, and for a brief moment, there's an understanding between us, something unspoken, but understood all the same. Maybe it's a fragile thing, something that could break as easily as it was made, but it's there. A thread connecting us in the midst of all the destruction.

"I wish it didn't have to be like this," he whispers. "I wish we had a different choice."

"We didn't have a choice, Luca." The words are like a slap, but they're the truth. The undeniable truth. "We made it, and now we deal with it. That's how life works."

The silence stretches, heavier now, and I can feel the pull between us. It's like the ground beneath our feet is shifting, tilting, threatening to swallow us whole. But we stand there, in the quiet chaos, unable to turn away.

After a moment, he moves, his hand brushing lightly against mine as he reaches for the bottle of whiskey on the coffee table. His fingers graze mine, a simple gesture that feels more intimate than anything else could right now. He pours two glasses without a word, handing one to me before settling down into the worn armchair across from me.

I take the glass, feeling the burn of the liquor slide down my throat. The warmth spreads through me, but it doesn't reach the cold, aching parts of my heart. No amount of alcohol will ever fix this, no matter how many glasses we drink.

The taste lingers on my tongue, sharp and bitter. Much like everything else between us.

"So," Luca says, breaking the silence, his voice steadying with the familiar bravado he wears like a second skin. "What now?"

I look at him, trying to read him, but there's too much distance now. Too much weight in the space between us. "We keep going," I say quietly. "We take it one step at a time. We try to figure out what the hell we're supposed to do with all the pieces we've broken."

He nods, but his eyes are distant again, as though he's already somewhere else, lost in thought. I wish I could follow him, could dive into that quiet part of his mind and understand what he's thinking. But instead, I sit there, watching him, feeling the distance grow even wider.

The city outside continues to hum, uncaring, oblivious to the cracks forming in my life. The lights flicker as they always do, the traffic never slowing, the world spinning onward — just as it always has. But I know, deep down, that nothing will ever be the same again.

The evening drags on with the kind of heaviness that makes everything feel slow and suffocating, like we're moving underwater, unable to escape the pull of what we've created. I watch Luca out of the corner of my eye as he stares into his glass of whiskey, the amber liquid catching the dim light, glowing with the same dull fire that burns behind his eyes. He's a man on the edge of something — I'm not sure if it's clarity or destruction, but I can feel it, like static electricity in the air. We've crossed so many lines, and yet, somehow, the worst one still feels like the one we're about to cross.

The city outside feels like a distant echo of normalcy, the hum of cars, the faint laughter of people strolling down the street. It's like the world forgot how deeply fractured the lives inside this apartment have become. A world that spins without concern for those of us stuck on the edges, watching it all go by without being able to touch it.

I think about the lies we've told, the deals we've made, the people we've hurt along the way. It's like we've built this empire of fractured glass, one small misstep away from everything shattering. And now we're here, in this room, in this silence, with the wreckage of everything we thought we could control.

"What are we supposed to do now?" I ask, my voice a little too sharp, cutting through the thick air between us. My hands tremble, just slightly, but I refuse to let him see it. The whiskey in my glass sloshes as I take a sip, the burn crawling down my throat and spreading into my chest, trying to drown out the feeling that threatens to choke me.

Luca shifts in his seat, the chair creaking under his weight. He sets his glass down on the coffee table with a clink, and for the first time in a long while, he looks at me — really looks at me. His gaze is intense, almost desperate, and I can feel the weight of everything we've both been carrying pressing down on him, too.

"I don't know," he says, his voice low, cracked, like he's not entirely sure of the words coming out of his mouth. "I wish I could tell you I had the answer. But... I don't."

The honesty of it makes my chest tighten. He's always been a man of certainty, a man who's made decisions with the kind of confidence that could move mountains. To see him falter, to hear him admit that he doesn't know what comes next, feels like a punch to the gut.

"What does that mean for us?" The words slip out before I can stop them, and I instantly regret it. What does it mean for us, after everything? After the lies, after the choices that have led us to this point? Can we even come back from this? Can I come back from this?

Luca stands abruptly, his movement jerky, like he's been startled out of a trance. He runs his hand through his hair, the frustration radiating off him in waves. "You don't get it, do you?" His voice rises, and I feel a flare of something—anger? Hurt? Maybe a little of both.

I don't flinch. Instead, I meet his gaze head-on. "I get it. I get that we've crossed lines that we can never uncross, that the consequences of our actions have been more far-reaching than either of us expected. But that doesn't change the fact that we're standing here, looking at each other like strangers, trying to figure out what the hell happened."

There's a long pause, and for a second, I wonder if we've said everything we needed to say, if the conversation is over and done with. But then Luca opens his mouth again, his voice softer this time, almost hesitant. "I don't want to be a stranger to you. I never did."

My heart stutters at his words, and for a moment, I'm back to when things were simple — back when his touch was all I needed, when his presence was a balm for every scrape and bruise life gave me. But that was before we made choices we couldn't take back, before everything became complicated.

"And I don't want to be a stranger to you," I say, my voice barely above a whisper. "But I can't ignore what we've done. And I don't know if I can live with the consequences of it."

Luca runs his hand over his face, his jaw clenched tight, as though the words he's about to speak could somehow break the silence that's settled over us. "What if... what if we didn't have to live with the consequences?"

I raise an eyebrow. "What are you talking about?"

He takes a step closer, and I feel the air shift around us. It's like the whole room holds its breath as he drops his voice, the words hanging heavy in the space between us. "I've been working on something. A way out. For both of us. Something that could make all of this go away."

The words land like a bomb in the quiet of the room, and I stare at him, unsure if I've heard him right. "A way out? What does that even mean, Luca? You think we can just erase everything we've done?"

His expression is unreadable, his jaw tight as he looks at me, his eyes flickering with something — fear, maybe, or hope? It's impossible to tell.

"I'm saying we don't have to carry this burden, Ella," he says, the desperation creeping into his voice. "We don't have to pay the price for all the choices we made. We just need to take control. Take a different path."

I shake my head, the words not making sense. "You're talking about running. Hiding. You really think that's the answer?"

Luca steps back, his hands running through his hair again, agitation clear in every movement. "It's not running. It's surviving."

The weight of his words crushes me, and for a moment, I don't know which way is up. What does he expect from me? What does he want me to say? That I'm willing to take this final step into something even darker, something I'm not sure I can come back from?

And then, just as quickly as he's spoken, he stops, his eyes widening. A sudden noise from the hallway, a sharp knock on the door, cuts through the tension like a knife.

Without thinking, I move toward the door, my pulse hammering in my throat. Luca looks at me, his face pale.

"Who the hell—" he starts, but I've already reached for the door handle.

When I open it, I freeze.

Standing in the doorway is someone I never expected to see again.

Chapter 39: A New Beginning

The city hums beneath my feet, a constant undercurrent of sound, like a heartbeat that never falters. It's the kind of place where the mornings begin with a hint of coffee wafting through the cracked windows of dusty shops and end with the sharp bite of the night air, biting back the heat of the day. In a way, it's a reflection of me—always busy, always changing, always masking the deeper turmoil beneath. I never thought I'd be the one in charge. But here I am. The mantle of responsibility draped awkwardly over my shoulders, like a coat two sizes too large, and I am expected to wear it with grace.

Luca stands next to me, his broad frame a reassuring presence against the skyline. The sun, half-dipped in the horizon, throws a muted golden glow that seems to stretch for miles, casting long shadows on the cracked sidewalk where the city's pulse is felt most acutely. I'd always been able to see the world in fragments—snippets of conversation, flashes of emotion—but now, it all feels so much more connected, like one giant puzzle. And I'm expected to be the one to piece it together.

"You don't have to do this alone," Luca says, his voice steady but tinged with something I can't quite place—something like hope, maybe. Or maybe it's just the weight of his own uncertainty pressing down on him. Either way, his words hit me in a way I don't expect.

I glance up at him, my thoughts still racing, still trying to make sense of it all. He's always been there, in the background of my life, a constant that I could lean on when the rest of the world fell away. But this? This is different. This is more than just helping with a flat tire or offering a shoulder when the world gets too loud. This is about rebuilding something—no, everything—from the ground up. And while Luca's steady presence makes it easier, it doesn't make it simple.

He's never been a man of many words, but when he speaks, I listen. I have to. He has a way of cutting through the noise of my thoughts, like a knife through butter, and suddenly, everything feels clearer. His dark eyes meet mine, his gaze softening as though he can read the chaos unfolding inside me.

"You're not alone," he repeats, stepping closer, the warmth of his presence washing over me.

I laugh, but it's hollow, like I'm trying to convince myself as much as him. "I'm not alone, huh?" I repeat, turning away to look at the street, at the cars rushing by, the neon signs flickering in the distance. "Well, that's a relief. I was starting to think I was going to have to rebuild this whole damn thing by myself." My voice is sharp, tinged with a frustration that I hadn't realized had been building up inside me.

Luca doesn't flinch. He never does. Instead, he nudges my shoulder, a playful gesture that feels strangely out of place, given the weight of the situation. "You don't have to," he says simply, his words not just a reassurance but a promise. It's not the first time he's said something like that, but today, I actually believe him. Maybe because I know that with each passing moment, I'm learning that I don't have to shoulder the weight of the world alone anymore.

But there's something in his eyes that makes me pause. It's a look I haven't seen before, and I'm not sure I'm ready to confront it yet. It's a glimmer of something deeper, something more than just the steadying presence of a friend. It's... vulnerability. Or maybe it's hope. Either way, it unnerves me. Because in a world that's already spinning out of control, I don't know if I'm ready for the mess that comes with hope.

We walk side by side in silence, the sound of our footsteps a rhythmic echo in the growing darkness. The city has a way of swallowing up the light, turning the streets into a patchwork of shadows and neon glow, where everything feels just a little bit more surreal, like nothing is quite what it seems. And I'm not sure if it's the city or if it's me that's changed. Maybe it's both.

The sound of a door creaking open breaks the silence, and I glance up to find the familiar shape of Aunt Jeanette standing in the doorway of the old brownstone. Her face, lined with the years of hardship, softens when she sees me, and for a brief moment, I feel like maybe, just maybe, I'm doing the right thing.

Luca tilts his head toward her, his voice low. "She's waiting for you."

I nod, but there's an unfamiliar lump in my throat, one that seems to have appeared out of nowhere. I take a deep breath, steadying myself before stepping forward, knowing that the hardest part of this whole mess is just beginning. Because once I walk through that door, there's no going back.

"I guess we'll see if I'm cut out for this after all," I murmur, more to myself than to him.

Luca's response is nothing more than a soft grunt, but I can feel the weight of his words settling between us. He doesn't need to say it—he's already shown me that, with him by my side, I'm never truly alone. And for the first time in a long time, that thought doesn't terrify me. Instead, it gives me a strange sense of peace, as if, maybe, this could work. Maybe we could rebuild.

I turn toward the door, ready to face whatever comes next. But this time, I'm not just walking into the unknown—I'm walking with someone who believes in me.

The door creaks shut behind me, a sound that seems to echo through the empty hallway, as if it's reverberating inside my chest. Aunt Jeanette's old brownstone, with its worn wood floors and faded wallpaper, feels as empty as I do. The weight of the world hangs thick in the air, a reminder of everything that's been lost—and everything that must be rebuilt.

Luca's voice is still in my head, his words like a lifeline I hadn't realized I needed until they were offered. *You don't have to do this alone.* A statement so simple, yet carrying with it an ocean of unspoken things. The door closes, but his presence is still here, behind me, steady as always.

I find Jeanette at the kitchen table, hunched over a cup of tea like she's trying to escape the world in front of her. Her fingers are wrapped tightly around the porcelain, knuckles pale with the pressure. Her hair, once as dark as mine, now hangs in silver strands that she's never bothered to tame. She looks up as I enter, and for a split second, there's a flicker of hope in her eyes—like maybe, just maybe, I'll be able to fix all of this. But the hope is fleeting, and the weariness takes over again.

"You came," she says, her voice raw, the years of stress and grief heavy in the tone. There's no accusation in her words, but the expectation is there, hanging between us, invisible but undeniable.

I nod, taking a step forward. "I couldn't leave it like this."

Jeanette sets the cup down with a soft clink, her fingers tracing the rim as if lost in thought. She's always been a woman of few words, but the silence between us now feels like a chasm, one we're both too stubborn to cross.

"Your uncle wouldn't have wanted this," she says finally, her voice quieter now, as if admitting it out loud might make it all too real.

I know she's right. Uncle Frank had a way of sweeping things under the rug, pretending that everything would sort itself out in the end, even as the storm clouds gathered. It was part of his charm—always the optimist, always the one who insisted that the next project, the next deal, the next thing would fix everything. And maybe for him, it did. But for me? I'm not so sure.

"I know," I say, my voice steady, though I can feel the uncertainty building up inside me. "But now, it's up to us, isn't it?"

Jeanette sighs, looking away, like she's trying to avoid the truth of it. "You don't have to take this on alone. I've got the space. I've got the knowledge." Her voice trails off, but there's an unspoken challenge in the air.

I cross the room and sit down across from her, meeting her gaze. There's a moment, just a fleeting one, where I see her as she once was—a woman full of fire and resolve, not the ghost of someone who's lost everything. I wonder if that woman is still in there somewhere, or if time and grief have eaten her away like rust on an old coin.

"I know you do," I say softly. "But it's not just about having space or knowledge. It's about having a vision. And right now, I don't know where to even begin."

Jeanette's lips press into a thin line, and I can see her fighting the urge to lecture me, to tell me that I'm wrong, that I have everything I need. But instead, she just looks at me, and in that moment, I see the reflection of the uncertainty I've been hiding from everyone—especially from myself.

"You're not alone," she repeats, her tone more of a statement than a reassurance. And then, before I can respond, she adds, "But you've got to stop pretending that you're fine. That you can do this all by yourself."

I stare at her, the weight of her words sinking in. She's right. I have been pretending. Pretending that I'm okay, pretending that this whole mess doesn't terrify me. Pretending that I can somehow just pull all the broken pieces together and make it work.

"I'm not fine," I admit, my voice a whisper. "I don't know if I can do this. I don't know if I can rebuild what's been broken."

Jeanette doesn't respond immediately. Instead, she takes a slow breath, her eyes softening as if she's finally letting go of the last thread of her own control.

"Then don't," she says simply. "Don't try to rebuild everything at once. Start small. One thing at a time."

I nod, the idea settling over me like a blanket, warm and comforting in its simplicity. For the first time today, I feel a flicker of something that might resemble hope. It's not much, but it's enough to keep me from drowning.

Luca, I think. His steady presence. His belief in me. Maybe, just maybe, he's right. I don't have to do this alone. Not when I have people who still see something in me, even when I can't see it in myself.

We sit there for a while, the only sound between us the clink of a spoon against a teacup, the world outside moving on as if everything was still normal. But inside this kitchen, a subtle shift has taken place. The cracks that ran through our lives—the ones that seemed to widen every time we tried to ignore them—are finally starting to close. It won't be easy. It never is. But it's a beginning. And sometimes, that's enough.

The night falls over the city like a blanket, heavy and filled with a quiet intensity that mirrors the thoughts swirling in my head. I stand at the window, my fingers lightly grazing the cool glass, watching the neon lights flicker in the distance, painting the streets below in muted blues and oranges. There's something about this place—the way the city feels like it's holding its breath—that makes everything feel like it could go either way. Maybe that's what's so unnerving about it. I'm no longer waiting for something to happen. It's happening now. And I'm supposed to be the one steering this ship.

Luca stands behind me, his presence a constant in the corner of my vision. He hasn't said anything since we left Aunt Jeanette's, but

I can feel him there, grounded, solid in a way I haven't felt in ages. There's something in the way he watches me—like he's waiting for me to take the next step. He's always been good at waiting. I'm not so patient.

"You should get some rest," Luca says, his voice low but firm, pulling me out of my thoughts. "You've got a big day tomorrow."

I turn to face him, his silhouette framed by the dim light spilling from the streetlamps outside. There's something in his eyes—something softer than I'm used to seeing—that makes the air between us feel charged, like something unsaid is lingering, waiting to be acknowledged. But I don't ask him what's on his mind. Maybe it's better that way. We both have too many things to figure out.

"I'll be fine," I say, my voice betraying me with a crack that I quickly disguise with a cough. "I've got this."

Luca takes a step closer, his brow furrowed as he looks at me. "I don't doubt that. But you're human. And even humans need to recharge sometimes."

I bite back the urge to snap, because I know he's right. I do need to rest. But there's no time for rest, not now. The foundation of everything I've built—the pieces of my life, my family's legacy, the people who still depend on me—feels fragile. It could all slip through my fingers if I don't keep pushing, keep moving forward.

"I'll sleep when this is over," I say, trying to force the words to sound more confident than I feel.

Luca doesn't respond right away. Instead, he steps forward, closing the space between us. He looks at me for a long moment, his gaze unwavering, as if he's trying to see past the defenses I've built, the walls I've erected to protect myself from... whatever this is.

"You don't have to carry all of this by yourself," he repeats, softer this time, a hint of something unspoken in his tone.

I open my mouth to say something, to tell him that I'm fine, that I've got everything under control, but the words get stuck in my throat. Because, in this moment, I'm not sure what the truth is anymore. I do need help. But I don't know how to ask for it. And the more I try to convince myself that I can handle everything, the more I realize I'm just fooling myself.

Luca's hand reaches out, his fingers brushing mine in a gesture that's so small, so simple, that it's almost easy to miss. But I feel it, deep in my chest—a spark that lights something inside me, something that's been dormant for too long.

"I'm not going anywhere," he says, his voice steady, unwavering. "And neither are you."

I nod, my throat tight with a thousand unsaid words. The tension between us is palpable, a line drawn in the sand that neither of us is willing to cross—at least, not yet.

"Thanks," I whisper, my voice barely audible in the stillness of the room.

Luca's hand lingers for a moment longer before he pulls away, and I feel the absence of his touch like a breath I didn't realize I was holding.

"You should sleep," he repeats, though his tone is gentler now. "I'll be here when you wake up."

I nod again, but I don't move. I can't shake the feeling that the storm is far from over. And no matter how many people stand by my side, no matter how much they say they're here to help, it's still up to me to steer the ship through the rough waters ahead.

The bed is cold when I finally crawl under the covers, the sheets crisp and unfamiliar against my skin. It feels strange to sleep in this house again, strange to lie here in the room I used to retreat to when life got too loud. But everything's different now. The walls seem to press in on me, the weight of the past and the uncertainty of the future too much to ignore.

I close my eyes, willing my mind to quiet, but it refuses to cooperate. Thoughts—fragments of conversations, half-formed plans, a million "what-ifs"—tumble through my brain like a chaotic symphony, each note louder than the last. I toss and turn, the silence of the house a stark contrast to the storm inside me.

Suddenly, I hear it. A sound, faint at first, but growing louder. Footsteps, slow and deliberate, approaching my door. My breath catches in my throat as I strain to listen.

The door creaks open, just a crack, and I hold my breath, waiting for the intruder to reveal themselves.

The shadow in the doorway doesn't belong to Luca. It's too tall, too broad, and the figure doesn't move like him.

I reach for the lamp on the nightstand, my fingers trembling as I fumble for the switch. But before I can turn it on, the door opens fully. A familiar voice cuts through the darkness, sending a chill racing down my spine.

"We need to talk."

Chapter 40: The Ghosts We Carry

The coffee shop smelled of burnt caramel and aged wood, its air thick with the hum of quiet conversations, clinking mugs, and the occasional hiss of the espresso machine. I sat across from Luca at a table near the back, where the faded red bricks of the walls were covered in artwork—splashes of color, broken frames, and scribbles that looked like they belonged on the back of a napkin rather than a gallery wall. The dim lighting cast shadows on his face, accentuating the sharp angles of his jaw and the weariness in his eyes, as if he had carried the weight of the world in a way I could never quite comprehend.

I had known him for weeks now, and yet, there were parts of him I had never dared to touch. Until tonight. The words spilled from his mouth in a low, almost haunted voice, like a confession he had been holding onto for far too long.

"You think you've done things that are unforgivable," he started, swirling the remnants of his coffee in the cup, "but you have no idea what it's like to lose everything. Not just once, but over and over again. I didn't get the luxury of keeping my hands clean."

I watched him, my heart tugging, not because I felt sorry for him, but because I understood. I had my own ghosts—ones that had followed me long before he'd walked into my life, sitting quietly at the edges of my thoughts, always waiting for a moment to pounce.

"You don't have to explain yourself," I said, even though the words didn't come out as smoothly as I intended. "I get it."

He gave me a sidelong glance, eyebrow quirked, a silent challenge in his gaze. "Do you, though?" he asked, leaning forward. "Really? Because I don't think anyone gets it. Not unless they've lived it."

I paused, a thread of uncertainty pulling at my chest. The truth, the real truth, had always been easier to hide in the dark. But here, with Luca staring at me with that intensity I couldn't quite shake, it felt like it might finally be time to let go of some of it. Maybe he wouldn't judge. Maybe.

I took a deep breath, the bitterness of my own past still lingering on the tip of my tongue, tasting of things I had long since buried. "You ever just get tired of fighting your own mind?" I asked. "Like, no matter how hard you try to outrun it, your past keeps catching up with you, slapping you in the face when you least expect it?"

Luca didn't answer immediately. Instead, he just stared at me with a strange mix of understanding and curiosity, as if trying to piece together what I had just revealed. The sound of a chair scraping across the floor nearby broke the moment, and a couple in their late twenties shuffled past, laughing too loudly for a Monday evening. I didn't mind the distraction, though. It gave me a second to gather my thoughts.

"I've spent so much of my life pretending it's all fine," I continued, my voice quieter now, less certain. "Like if I just act like everything's okay, eventually it'll be okay. But it doesn't work like that, does it?"

Luca shook his head slowly, his lips curling into a grim smile. "No. It never does. You think you've outrun it, and then—bam—it smacks you upside the head when you least expect it."

I nodded, my fingers tracing the rim of my coffee cup absentmindedly. "I used to think I could control it, you know? Like if I just kept everything bottled up, kept all the messy parts hidden, no one would ever have to know. But the thing about scars is... they never really heal. They just fade. And that's not enough sometimes."

He leaned back, studying me now, his eyes still locked onto mine, as if trying to see past the walls I'd built up. The kind of walls that had been carefully constructed over years of hurt, disappointment, and self-preservation.

"You think your scars define you?" he asked, his voice soft, almost too gentle for a man like him.

I didn't answer immediately. The question hung there between us, sharp and raw, but I couldn't look away from the depth in his eyes. "I think they shape who you are," I finally said, my voice barely above a whisper. "And I don't know how to move past them."

The silence stretched out like an old, worn-out thread that was about to snap. The barista behind the counter was humming quietly to himself, lost in his own world, and outside, the sounds of city traffic flowed past in an endless stream of noise.

For a long time, Luca didn't speak. He just stared at me, the weight of his gaze heavier than anything I had ever felt. And then, almost reluctantly, he broke the silence with a question I wasn't prepared for.

"Do you want to keep hiding, then? Or do you want to try and do something about it?"

It hit me like a wave, crashing over me, drowning out everything else. I hadn't realized it, but I had been hiding. Hiding behind my sarcasm, hiding behind my distractions, hiding behind my own carefully constructed walls. But there was something in his voice, something raw and vulnerable, that made me feel like maybe—just maybe—I could let go.

I swallowed, my throat tight, the weight of the decision pressing down on me like an anchor. "I don't know," I admitted, my voice trembling slightly. "But maybe it's time to stop running."

He smiled, that small, knowing smile that made me want to believe him, that made me feel like for the first time in ages, someone might actually understand. "Then maybe it's time we both stopped."

The city was quieting down for the night, the pulse of its energy slowing just enough to catch a breath, but not quite enough to rest. The streets of Brooklyn never really stopped moving, but there was something about this corner of the neighborhood that made it feel like a secret, tucked away just beneath the surface of the urban sprawl. The neon signs of dive bars flickered in their tired stupor, casting pools of harsh light against the damp sidewalk. A group of teenagers, too young to be out so late and too old to care, walked by, their laughter tumbling through the air like confetti. Their voices were sharp and high-pitched, full of the same unwarranted confidence that only youth could afford. But I didn't pay them much attention. Instead, I focused on Luca, his silhouette a dark shadow in the booth across from me, the dim glow of the streetlights tracing the curve of his features. He still hadn't said anything since I'd spoken.

For a moment, I wondered if I'd overstepped, if maybe I'd laid too much of myself bare too soon. But then, Luca's voice broke through the silence, smooth and deliberate, like he was testing the weight of the words in his mouth before releasing them into the space between us.

"Isn't it funny?" he asked, the question lingering in the air like a half-formed thought. "How we can go through life thinking we're the only ones carrying our ghosts around, like we're the only ones who've ever felt this heavy." He leaned back in the booth, the worn leather creaking beneath him, and for the first time since I'd met him, I saw the faintest flicker of something raw—something real—beneath his usually guarded exterior.

I didn't respond right away. I didn't know how to, really. I hadn't ever really been good at talking about things that mattered. Things that weren't wrapped up in sarcasm or hidden behind a veil of humor. But Luca wasn't letting me off the hook that easily.

"Because I'm not," he continued, his voice quieter now, almost vulnerable. "I thought it was just me, carrying all the things I've done, all the people I've failed. But here you are, sitting across from me, with your own set of ghosts." He paused, studying me in a way that made me feel like he could see through the flimsy armor I'd worked so hard to build around myself. "And now I'm wondering... how many other people are out there, just like us? Carrying around things they don't talk about, things they can't even bear to think about for too long, because it's easier to pretend they're not there."

There was an honesty in his words that made my stomach twist. A rawness that I hadn't expected, not from him, not from anyone. It was too much, and yet, it wasn't enough. How could it ever be enough, when the weight of the world sat so heavily on both our shoulders?

"I don't know," I muttered, my fingers tracing patterns on the table, anything to avoid looking at him directly. "Maybe it's just part of the deal. You're born, you do your best to make it through, and you leave with a little more baggage than you came in with."

"Yeah," Luca said softly, "and in the meantime, we're all just trying to figure out how to carry it. Some days it feels like too much to even hold up, but we keep going anyway, right? Even when it seems like no one else understands the weight we're dragging behind us."

I finally met his gaze, a sharpness in my chest as I realized that for the first time in a long while, someone else understood the quiet suffering that I had been carrying. Not in the way of a therapist or a well-meaning friend, but in the way that only someone who had been through the fire could. The way that makes your skin feel like it's been seared and the scars never really fade.

"I don't know if I'll ever let go of mine," I said, almost to myself. "The mistakes. The people I hurt. The ones who hurt me. It's like they're tattooed on my soul, you know?" My voice faltered a bit, and I hated how vulnerable I sounded, but I didn't take it back. Not this time.

Luca was quiet for a beat, and for a moment, I thought I'd said too much. But then, he reached across the table, his hand brushing against mine in an unexpected gesture. It wasn't anything grand or dramatic. Just a fleeting touch. But somehow, it felt like more than enough.

"I don't think you're meant to forget your ghosts," he said, his voice steady, like he had come to terms with this truth long before I ever would. "I think they're just... part of who you are. A reminder that you survived. And maybe, just maybe, they help you grow. Help you see things you couldn't before."

I exhaled, a soft laugh escaping me, though it wasn't from humor. It was from the absurdity of it all. "That's a nice way to spin it. Maybe someday I'll believe it."

"You don't have to believe it right now," he replied with that wry smile of his that always made my heart skip a beat. "Just take it one day at a time. You might not be able to outrun your ghosts, but you can choose how you deal with them."

I let out a breath I hadn't realized I was holding, feeling a strange sense of relief. It wasn't a magic cure, not by any means, but there was something in the simplicity of his words that made me believe for a second that maybe—just maybe—I didn't have to carry this burden alone. I looked down at my hands, at the scars I had tried to hide, and wondered if there was a way to stop running from the parts of myself that had been broken, and just... accept them.

"Maybe you're right," I said, my voice softer now, quieter. "Maybe I don't have to carry this alone."

Luca's smile was small but sincere, and for the first time, I felt a glimmer of hope that maybe, just maybe, this moment was the start of something different. Something real. Something that didn't need to be buried in the past.

The barista's tired humming filled the quiet gaps between our words, a familiar song I barely noticed anymore. Brooklyn's nights were an eclectic mix of grit and grit polished just enough to pass for charm—just enough for the rest of the city to notice. Yet, here in this little corner, where the cracked concrete met mismatched chairs and half-empty glasses, there was something soothing about the quiet that wrapped around us, like an unspoken truce.

Luca's words hung between us, heavy and raw, not looking for sympathy, just a place to land. I wasn't sure why it felt so much easier to hear him than anyone else, why his voice felt like it could carry my own burden without breaking. But I didn't have time to wonder about that—because my brain was still trying to figure out what had just happened. We had slipped past the polite small talk and into something else entirely. I could see it in the way Luca was looking at me, that rare softness in his eyes that made my pulse quicken.

I cleared my throat, trying to shift the weight in my chest. "You think it's possible," I asked, my fingers tapping a rhythm on the chipped edge of my mug, "to just... stop carrying the weight? To walk around without feeling like you're always looking over your shoulder for something you've done wrong?"

He smiled, a quick flash of something familiar and comforting. "If it were that easy, I'd have stopped carrying mine a long time ago." His smile faded, his eyes turning inward for just a moment. I could see it—like a shadow passing across his expression, something lost in the deep blue of his gaze.

"You get good at pretending, though," he continued, "at making people think you've got it all together. Even when you're just one wrong glance away from falling apart." His voice softened, almost as if he were saying it more to himself than to me. I felt the unspoken invitation hanging there, like an open door to a room I didn't quite want to enter. But, like an idiot, I walked right through it.

"What happens when you can't pretend anymore?" I asked. My own voice sounded like it was dipped in something sharp, something that stung when it left my mouth. "What happens when everything you've been running from finally catches up?"

Luca's expression didn't change, but something about the tension in his shoulders told me he understood exactly what I was asking. "Then you stop running," he said simply, his eyes finding mine with a strength that almost felt like a dare.

I didn't answer immediately. What could I say? I hadn't stopped running. Not once. I had always been too busy moving forward—picking up the pieces, putting on a mask, and hoping the cracks wouldn't show. I wasn't sure I knew how to stop. Hell, I wasn't sure I wanted to.

But Luca, with his easy smirk and the quiet weight of his words, made me think for the first time that maybe it was worth it. Maybe standing still long enough to face what I'd been running from wasn't the worst thing I could do.

The words got tangled in my throat as I shifted in my seat. I had to ask—if only to get it out of my system. "What if I can't? What if I've spent so much time hiding, so much time pretending, that I've lost myself in the process?"

He leaned back in his chair, the worn fabric creaking under his weight, and for a moment, I thought he wasn't going to answer. I almost wished he wouldn't. What if he said the wrong thing? What if his answer was some clever throwaway that made me feel more empty than I already did?

But instead, his gaze softened even further, a little disbelief threading his tone. "You think you've lost yourself?" He shook his head slowly, like he couldn't quite understand the concept. "No one ever loses themselves. Not really. You just forget where you put the pieces."

I swallowed hard, my chest tightening. That wasn't what I expected him to say, but it was exactly what I needed to hear. Something about it cracked open the knot in my throat. I hadn't been thinking about it in the right way. Maybe I hadn't lost myself. Maybe I was just buried under all the dust and detritus of my own survival tactics, just waiting for someone to knock the rubble away.

I opened my mouth to respond, but before I could, a loud crash echoed through the small café, rattling the mugs on the counter. My heart jumped into my throat as I snapped my head toward the sound, instinctively standing up from the table. A young man in a dark hoodie had knocked over a stack of chairs, the legs screeching against the floor as he hurried toward the door, his breath shallow and uneven.

It all happened too fast. The barista called after him, but the man was already gone, the door slamming behind him. I couldn't stop the unease from creeping up my spine, the feeling that something didn't quite add up.

Luca's hand reached out, steadying me before I could take another step. "Don't," he murmured, his voice low, a note of warning threading through it. "It's not worth it. Let it go."

I hesitated, my instincts screaming at me to do something—anything—but his grip on my wrist was firm, and something in his expression told me this was one of those moments where I had to trust him. But trust was a tricky thing. It was like sand slipping through your fingers when you thought you had a good grip.

As the sounds of the city filtered back into the café, I let out a breath, slowly lowering myself back into my seat. My fingers were still trembling slightly, but the unease in the pit of my stomach had twisted into something else—something colder. Something that didn't feel right.

And then, before I could make sense of it, I heard the faintest noise. A soft scuffle, barely perceptible. My heart lurched in my chest, my mind racing, my pulse quickening.

The door swung open again, and a shadow fell over the table. This time, the person who stepped through wasn't running. They were standing still, watching us. Their face hidden by the brim of a baseball cap, but the dark eyes... the dark eyes locked onto mine with a haunting familiarity.

And that's when I knew I wasn't alone in this anymore.

Chapter 41: The Ties That Bind

The morning fog clung to the streets of Chicago like an unwelcome guest, its fingers creeping into the corners of our lives, spreading an unease that none of us could shake off. It wasn't just the weather—it was the tension that had been building over the past few weeks, thickening with each whispered rumor, every sidelong glance at the dinner table. Luca had warned me that the calm before a storm never lasted long, but I hadn't expected it to come so suddenly, so violently. I stared out the window of our apartment in the Gold Coast, the skyline barely visible behind the mist, and tried to ignore the gnawing sensation in my gut. We were exposed, vulnerable in a way I had never imagined, not with the empire we had built, not with the strength that had once flowed through these very walls.

"I don't like this," I muttered, turning from the window. The soft click of my heels echoed in the quiet room as I approached Luca, who stood by the desk, his back turned to me. He was absorbed in the papers sprawled out in front of him, his jaw clenched tight as if he could will the problem away with sheer force. It didn't work like that.

Luca didn't respond immediately, his fingers tapping a rhythm against the wood, each beat echoing the rapid pulse in my chest. When he finally looked up, his expression was unreadable, but I could see the weight in his eyes. The kind of weight that made even the toughest men question their decisions.

"They think they can take what's ours," he said, his voice steady but laced with an undertone of something darker, something far more dangerous than anything I had ever seen in him before.

I nodded, stepping closer, trying to absorb the full weight of what he was saying. A rival family, one that had been lurking in the shadows for years, had finally decided to make their move. We had always known they were out there, circling like vultures, waiting for a moment of weakness. And now that we were facing the fallout from our recent battles, it seemed they had finally decided that this was the time.

"The Martinez family?" I asked, though I already knew the answer. There was no one else with the resources or the audacity to challenge us so openly.

Luca didn't need to say a word; his clenched fist told me everything. The Martinezes had been a thorn in our side for years, a family that had always been content with their own slice of the city's underworld, but the whispers had grown louder in recent months. They wanted more. And they thought we were ripe for the taking.

"We can't let them do this," I said, my voice stronger now, tinged with the kind of determination that had always carried us through the hardest times. But Luca wasn't convinced—not yet. His gaze drifted back to the papers in front of him, his fingers brushing over the edges as if searching for an answer that wasn't there.

"They'll come at us from all sides," he murmured, almost to himself. "We've got enemies we haven't even thought about yet."

I watched him, feeling the weight of his thoughts pressing down on both of us. The walls of our empire, which had once seemed unshakable, now felt like they might come crumbling down at any moment. Every decision we'd made, every alliance we'd forged, was now under scrutiny, and the stakes had never been higher.

"But we're stronger than they think," I said, my words firm, determined. I reached out, placing a hand over his. The simple contact grounded me, reminded me that we weren't alone in this. "We've fought worse battles."

Luca met my eyes then, his expression softening, just for a moment. There was a flicker of something—hope, maybe? Or was it simply the exhaustion that had taken root in both of us? I couldn't tell. But I knew this: We couldn't back down now. Not when we were so close to having everything we'd ever dreamed of.

"I'll take care of it," Luca said, pulling his hand away. He stood straighter, his posture rigid with the weight of the decisions ahead of him. "I'll make them regret this."

"No," I replied, my voice cutting through the tension. "We'll take care of it. Together."

His eyes searched mine, as if weighing the truth of my words. He was used to bearing the burden alone, the kind of man who didn't share his struggles with anyone. But I had never been content to stand on the sidelines, to watch as he fought for us without me. I had fought for this life, for this family, just as much as he had. And if we were going to face down the Martinezes—or anyone else who thought they could tear us apart—then it would have to be together.

He didn't argue, though I could see the resistance in his eyes. But there was no room for pride in this battle. It wasn't about who held the reins or who made the final call—it was about survival. And survival meant playing our cards right, no matter what.

"I can't let you get involved in this," he said after a long silence. "It's too dangerous."

"Everything we've done has been dangerous," I shot back, my voice steady. "You think I'm just going to sit back and let them tear apart everything we've built?"

His gaze hardened, his jaw tight with frustration. "I'm trying to protect you."

"I don't need you to protect me," I retorted, stepping closer. "I need you to trust me. Trust that I know what I'm doing."

The room felt smaller, the air heavier, as the tension between us reached its peak. For a long moment, we simply stood there, the weight of the world pressing in on us from all sides. And then, finally, Luca nodded. It wasn't a victory, not yet, but it was a step forward. The first step in what would undoubtedly be a long, bloody road.

"Together," he said, his voice low and steady, but with a fierce determination that mirrored my own.

I nodded, feeling the weight of that promise settle over us both. Whatever came next, we would face it. Together.

The afternoon sun barely made it through the thick, lingering fog that clung to Chicago like a damp blanket. Even the skyline, usually so proud, seemed subdued under the weight of it, as if the city itself was bracing for what was to come. I ran my fingers through my hair and paced the length of the room, the sharp click of my heels against the hardwood floor echoing in the silence. My thoughts swirled, tangled in the same knots that Luca had been trying to untie for days.

"This doesn't make sense," I muttered to myself, half to the mirror, half to the empty air around me. The Martinezes were playing a game far too dangerous, and it wasn't the first time they'd tried to pull this stunt. But this time felt different. The pressure was mounting, the walls closing in with each passing moment. We couldn't afford to lose—not again. Not after everything we'd fought for.

I turned toward the door, about to find Luca again, when I caught sight of myself in the mirror. The reflection staring back at me looked different—tired, yes, but also determined in a way I hadn't seen in a while. The soft makeup I'd carefully applied that morning had long since melted away, leaving my skin pale and raw. My clothes—once sharp, polished—felt stiff, the edges worn, as if they were carrying more weight than they were meant to. I ran a hand over my shirt, smoothing the fabric, and inhaled deeply, steadying myself.

There was no room for hesitation now.

The sound of the front door opening broke through the tension in the air. Luca. Always punctual, always the one to close off the world and retreat into his own thoughts when it all became too much. But I was no longer the kind of woman who would let him shoulder everything alone.

"I thought you were going to handle this on your own," I called out as he walked in, letting the sharpness of my voice cut through the stillness. I tried to make it sound casual, but the truth was, I was both relieved and frustrated—relieved because I didn't want him fighting this alone, frustrated because he still hadn't seen that we were in this together.

Luca looked up at me from the doorway, a faint smirk tugging at the corner of his lips. "You know me too well." He closed the door behind him with a soft click, his expression still guarded, but I could see the flicker of recognition in his eyes. He knew what I was doing—challenging him, pushing him. It was something we both did when the stakes were high.

"You didn't think I'd just sit around, did you?" I shot back, crossing the room to stand in front of him. I knew his temper—knew how easily it could flare when things weren't going according to plan—but I wasn't afraid of him. Not anymore.

Luca's gaze softened, his jaw tightening briefly as if he were trying to suppress whatever emotions wanted to rise to the surface. "You should have stayed out of this," he said, his voice barely above a whisper. There was something in the way he said it, though—something that made me think he was trying to convince himself as much as me.

"And let you face them alone?" I laughed, though the sound was humorless, more a release of pent-up frustration than anything else. "You don't get to do that. Not now. Not ever."

He ran a hand through his hair, exhaling sharply, as if he was mentally preparing himself for a battle, one we both knew was inevitable. "You don't understand, Zara. This is bigger than us."

"I understand more than you think," I replied, stepping closer. "I know exactly what they want. They want control. And we're not going to let them take it."

The tension in the room was palpable, thick as molasses, but underneath it, I could feel something else—a shift, a realignment. Maybe we weren't as far apart as I thought. Maybe we were closer to figuring this out than either of us had realized.

"We're not just fighting for what we have," Luca said, his voice low, intense. "We're fighting for everything we've built. And we can't afford to lose."

I nodded. "I know. But we won't lose. Not if we don't let them break us apart. Not if we fight together."

He met my gaze then, his eyes dark and heavy with all the things he hadn't said. But in that moment, I saw it—the trust. The acceptance. The understanding that we were in this together, and we would fight for it, no matter what it cost.

"Alright, Zara," he said, his voice steady now, more resolute. "Let's fight."

The city outside had fallen into a tense quiet as we began to make our plans. The weight of our choices hung over us like a storm cloud, threatening to burst at any moment. But we were no longer just preparing for the inevitable. We were ready to face it head-on, to take the fight to them, to show them that we were not to be underestimated.

The Martinezes had underestimated us once before. They wouldn't make that mistake again.

We spent the next few hours, too many glasses of whiskey between us, plotting every move, every countermeasure. Luca leaned over the table, his brow furrowed as he studied the maps, the connections, the weak spots. His mind worked like a machine, every calculation precise, but I could see the weariness beneath it all. The toll it had taken.

"You're exhausted," I said, pushing the glass of whiskey away from him and meeting his eyes. "We'll figure this out. You don't have to carry it all by yourself."

He looked at me, a brief flicker of vulnerability passing through his eyes before he masked it again. "It's not about me," he said. "It's about us. About making sure we don't lose everything."

And for the first time in a long while, I believed him. He wasn't just fighting for himself anymore. He was fighting for us, for the life we had built—and that meant I had to fight too.

I smiled, just slightly. "We won't lose, Luca. Not if we don't let them win."

And together, we would make sure they never did.

The night had fallen hard, the streets of Chicago dim and slick with rain. The air smelled of wet concrete and the sharp scent of metal, a reminder that the city was never really asleep—always humming with a quiet, restless energy. As I stepped onto the balcony of our penthouse, the cool breeze ruffled my hair, but I didn't mind. There was something oddly comforting about the sharpness of the city at night—the way it seemed to sharpen your senses, make you more alert, more alive. I wasn't sure what it was that had me so restless, but tonight, every sound, every shadow, felt like it was bearing down on me, as though the storm we'd been trying to outrun was finally catching up.

Luca stood behind me, leaning against the doorframe. I didn't need to turn around to know he was watching me—his presence, steady and unyielding, filled the room. We'd fought side by side before, in ways that most people would never understand. But this time felt different. The stakes were higher. The weight of it all pressed in from every direction, and I couldn't shake the feeling that we were just waiting for something to break.

"You know they'll come after us," I said, my voice low, barely above a whisper.

"I know," Luca replied, his tone sharp but calm, like it had been rehearsed a thousand times. He stepped closer, his body heat warming the cool air around us. "They think we're weakened, but they've underestimated us before."

I felt the pull of his words, a thread of reassurance threading its way through my chest. But it wasn't enough to dispel the tightness in my gut. Not when the Martinezes had made their move so boldly, with such calculated intent. They wanted control, and they were coming for everything we had built. I wasn't foolish enough to think they'd back down after one failed attempt. They were ruthless. And worse, they knew us. Knew how we fought. Knew the cracks in our foundation.

"They're not the only ones who think we're vulnerable," I said, turning to face him, my gaze unwavering.

Luca gave me a hard look, his lips pressed into a tight line. "What are you thinking?"

"I'm thinking we can't wait for them to come to us. We need to take the fight to them."

His eyes narrowed slightly, and I could see the gears turning behind them. "You want to strike first?"

I met his gaze. "They won't expect it. It's the only way we can take control back."

The room was thick with silence, the kind that made every heartbeat feel like it was pounding against the walls. Luca's jaw tightened as he considered it, the weight of the decision bearing down on both of us. This wasn't a matter of business or strategy.

It was personal. The Martinezes had crossed a line, and I was done waiting for them to make their next move.

"We move tomorrow night," Luca said at last, his voice steady, the decision final.

I nodded, feeling the tension in my body ease slightly as we both settled into the rhythm of what was coming. There was no turning back now. But even as the plan began to take shape, I couldn't shake the feeling that we were missing something—something crucial.

The sudden ringing of my phone shattered the moment, and I didn't need to check the screen to know who it was. My heart skipped a beat as I answered, the voice on the other end cutting through the night air with an urgency I hadn't expected.

"Zara, you need to get out. Now."

I froze. The voice was familiar, one I'd never expected to hear on the other end of a call like this. It wasn't one of our allies, but someone who knew the business—the game we played—and had been out of sight for too long.

"Ramon," I whispered, feeling my stomach twist with a mixture of disbelief and fear. He was a ghost, a shadow from the past who had always kept his distance. "What's going on?"

"I'm not going to waste time, Zara," Ramon said, his voice tight with urgency. "They've already moved. Your enemies—They've set a trap. The Martinezes have already targeted your building."

My chest tightened, the air around me seeming to grow colder by the second. I could hear the muffled sounds of the city outside, but they felt distant, unreal.

"Wait, what? How do you know?" I demanded, struggling to grasp what he was saying. My mind raced to catch up with his words, but they felt like a puzzle I couldn't quite piece together.

"There's no time to explain. You need to leave, now. Get out of the building. Don't trust anyone. Not even your own people." His voice dropped to a whisper. "Especially not your own people."

The words hit me like a freight train. My breath caught in my throat. I didn't have to ask what he meant. Betrayal had a way of showing up when you least expected it, and I could feel it creeping closer now.

I glanced at Luca, who had gone still beside me, his eyes locked on mine with a mix of concern and something else—something darker.

"They're already here," Ramon's voice cracked through the static. "Get out now."

Before I could respond, the line went dead.

I stood there for a moment, frozen, my mind struggling to process the warning. I glanced over at Luca, who had already moved, his hand on the door as he pulled it open with swift precision.

"Get your things," he said, his voice sharp as steel. There was no question in his tone, no hesitation. This wasn't a drill. We weren't just facing a threat anymore. We were staring it down, face-to-face.

And as I turned to grab my bag, my phone buzzed again. But this time, when I looked at the screen, it wasn't a number I recognized. The text that appeared sent an icy chill down my spine:

You don't get to run. This is where it ends.

I could feel Luca's eyes on me, but I couldn't tear my gaze from the words. A promise. A threat.

And as the door slammed shut behind us, I realized with a sickening certainty that we were walking right into the storm we had tried to outrun.

Chapter 42: The Strength of Us

The city hums in the early morning, a low, almost imperceptible murmur that feels like it's woven into the very fabric of my skin. New York has always been like this—the pulse of it, a constant companion, steady and insistent. But today, there's something different in the air. It's not just the crispness of the October breeze or the way the sun kisses the skyline just before it starts its descent, casting long shadows across the streets. No, today, it feels like the city itself is holding its breath.

I glance at Luca, the man who was once my enemy, and wonder how we ended up here. How, after all the lies and the years spent circling each other like wary animals, we became this. Together. I study his face, trying to decipher the expression that flickers across it—the soft tension in his jaw, the way his hand rests on the back of his neck as though holding something back. Something I know is as much a part of him as the shadows that dance across his brow.

We're standing in the middle of a quiet street in Brooklyn, where the city feels more like a neighborhood than a giant beast waiting to swallow you whole. The trees here haven't quite let go of their summer leaves, and they hang heavy with the scent of damp earth and the distant echo of a life lived outside the confines of boardrooms and high-rise buildings.

Luca shifts, his eyes catching mine, a flicker of something unspoken passing between us. He's different now, no longer the man who thought playing the game was everything, the man whose ambition stretched like an endless river, cutting through anything and anyone who got in his way. I can't help but wonder if it's me he's changed for or if he's done it for himself—if the pieces of him that were always so hard to understand are finally starting to fit together, if he's figuring out who he really is in the wreckage of all the things he used to believe in.

I take a step closer, the air between us crackling with a tension that neither of us knows how to name. "You sure about this?" I ask, my voice betraying the uncertainty that I feel deep down, curling like a ball of cold fire in my chest.

He doesn't answer immediately, and I can tell that he's weighing something. His eyes flick to the far-off horizon, where the last of the day's light clings to the rooftops, the warmth of it slowly beginning to fade. Finally, he turns to face me, his gaze sharp but soft at the edges, like a blade sheathed in velvet.

"I've never been more sure of anything in my life," he says. His voice, usually so commanding, is almost a whisper now, as though the weight of the words is too much to bear. "This... us. It's not a mistake, Tess. It's never been a mistake."

There's a rawness to his words that makes my heart stumble. I don't know what to say. I never thought we'd be here, standing on the precipice of something that feels as inevitable as the sunrise. When I first met Luca, I never imagined I'd be the one he'd look to for reassurance, never thought I'd be the one to stand by his side, fighting for the things we've yet to understand.

The wind picks up, carrying with it the faint scent of roasting coffee from a nearby café. The city smells like possibility, like stories waiting to be told, like dreams half-formed in the shadows of the buildings around us. And in the midst of it, I can feel something deep inside me shift—a quiet but sure turning of the tide.

"I never thought I'd find this either," I admit, my voice a soft tremor as I close the distance between us. I touch his arm, my fingers brushing against the worn fabric of his jacket, and something shifts within me too, as though I'm letting go of all the things that once seemed so important. The anger, the mistrust, the resentment. All of it is falling away, piece by piece, until there's nothing left but the two of us, standing on the edge of something so much bigger than either of us had imagined.

Luca's hand finds mine, warm and sure, and for the first time in a long time, I feel like maybe we have a chance at this. At whatever this is. I don't know how it'll end—if it'll end at all—but I know one thing for certain: it's the only thing that feels real right now.

He leans in, his breath warm against my ear, and the words he says are soft but sure. "I've got you," he whispers, and it feels like a promise, as though everything that came before was leading us to this exact moment.

The world falls away, and for the briefest of seconds, there's nothing but the two of us, the city's pulse syncing with the rhythm of our hearts. In this moment, I can almost believe in us, in what we could be.

The night falls slowly over the city, stretching its inky fingers across the horizon like a blanket, pulling the world into its quiet embrace. The hum of traffic, usually so constant, is muffled now, as though the city is holding its breath in anticipation. The streetlights flicker on one by one, casting soft halos of yellow light on the pavement, and the distant sound of laughter and music drifts up from a nearby bar, mixing with the scent of hot pretzels and the salt of the sea air that lingers just a few blocks away.

Luca's hand is still warm in mine, and I find myself not wanting to let go, as though doing so would break something fragile between us. We're standing at the edge of a quiet park in downtown Manhattan, the skyscrapers towering above us like silent sentinels, the shadows of their glass and steel reflected in the streets below. I've always loved this part of the city—the way the old world meets the new, the way history presses up against modernity, leaving traces in the air, in the cobblestone streets, in the brick buildings that have stood for over a century. But tonight, the world feels a little smaller, a little more intimate, as though the space between us has shrunk to something we can finally understand.

"You ever think about how much this city's changed?" Luca asks, his voice low, almost to himself, as his eyes sweep across the scene before us.

I laugh, the sound a little too loud in the quiet night. "Are we talking about gentrification or the fact that every new building seems to eclipse the last one? Because both are equally terrifying."

He chuckles, and for a moment, I forget about the heavy weight of what we're about to face. The tension in my shoulders melts away, and I let myself get lost in the sound of his laughter. It's strange, this feeling of ease that has settled between us. Strange, and—dare I say it—comforting. We're on the verge of something, but for the first time in a long time, it doesn't feel like it's rushing at us like a runaway train. It feels... steady.

"I meant the way it feels different now," Luca says, his eyes turning back to meet mine, the intensity of his gaze sending a ripple of something deep and unexpected through me. "The way people live, what they want out of life... Hell, even how they love. You ever think we're all just pretending to be something we're not?"

I frown, unsure of where this conversation is going, but intrigued nonetheless. "Are you telling me this is some sort of philosophical 'what is life?' moment? Because I don't know if I'm ready for that deep dive, especially not in the middle of a city that can't decide if it's a tech hub or an overpriced zoo."

Luca's smile is wry, but there's something softer in the way his eyes linger on me. "No. I'm asking if you ever think about what it means to be real. Not the version of you that shows up in meetings or posts perfect Instagram photos, but the version of you that exists when you strip all of that away."

The question hangs between us, and for a moment, the world seems to tilt. There's something about his honesty—about how he's always worn his ambition like a shield, and now he's letting it fall—that pulls me in. The vulnerability in his voice is like a thread, delicate and unexpected, and for the first time since we started this strange journey together, I realize that maybe we're both looking for the same thing: a version of ourselves that's raw, unfiltered, and... real.

"I think," I say carefully, "that maybe we're all just trying to survive long enough to figure out what real even means. Sometimes it feels like I'm chasing it, but I'm not sure I'll ever catch up."

Luca nods slowly, his fingers tightening around mine as though to reassure both of us. "I think I get it. But what if we don't have to chase it? What if it's already here? What if it's just about... seeing it for what it is?"

I open my mouth to respond, but before I can, a car screeches around the corner, the tires burning against the asphalt, and my heart leaps into my throat. The world shifts back into focus with a jarring suddenness, and I instinctively take a step closer to Luca, my body tense, all the calm that had settled between us evaporating in an instant.

The car slows as it nears us, the headlights momentarily blinding, and I catch sight of the familiar black SUV. My pulse spikes, and I know, without a doubt, that this is not a coincidence.

"They're here," I whisper, the words tasting like ashes in my mouth.

Luca doesn't flinch. He doesn't even blink. His hand slides into his jacket pocket, fingers brushing against something cold and metallic, and my stomach clenches with the familiar rush of adrenaline.

"They're here," he echoes, but his voice is steady. Too steady.

I don't have to ask who he's talking about. We both know. The fight we've been preparing for—this quiet war that's been waging in the shadows for months—is about to spill into the streets. And I'm not sure either of us is ready for it. But as the SUV comes to a halt in front of us, the door swings open, and I realize that maybe, just maybe, the real fight isn't outside—it's in here. In this strange, fragile thing we've found between us.

The SUV's engine growls as the vehicle idles, its headlights piercing the night like two relentless eyes. The weight of it presses against me, almost suffocating in the way it transforms the world around us into something tense and unforgiving. I can't shake the sensation that everything is about to shift, that we've crossed a line from which there's no turning back. The city, which had felt like a haven just moments ago, now feels like a labyrinth of concrete and shadows, a maze from which there's no escape.

I feel Luca's presence beside me, solid and unyielding. His fingers still clasp mine with a strength that both grounds me and stirs something else, something deeper, in the pit of my stomach. I should be scared, shouldn't I? But instead, there's a curious calm that seeps through my veins, a strange sense of inevitability. We've been fighting this fight for so long, it almost feels like destiny now.

The door to the SUV creaks open, and a figure steps out, tall and imposing, his silhouette just visible in the glow of the streetlights. My stomach twists. The man standing in front of us is someone I know all too well, someone I hoped I'd never see again.

"Didn't expect to find you here, Tess," Marcus says, his voice dripping with that same arrogance that used to make my blood boil. His eyes flicker to Luca, and I can almost hear the unspoken judgment. It's the same old game, the same old dance of power and dominance. But tonight, something's different. I'm not the same person I was when I first crossed paths with him.

"Didn't expect to be here either," I reply, my tone laced with a wry edge I don't quite recognize. "But it seems life has a way of surprising us."

Luca steps forward, placing himself between me and Marcus, the space between them thick with unspoken tension. His posture is stiff, his jaw clenched, but there's something behind his eyes that betrays the calm he's trying so hard to project.

"Move along, Marcus," Luca says, his voice low and controlled, but there's a bite to it, like he's daring Marcus to challenge him. "We've got no business with you."

Marcus's lips twitch into a smirk. "Is that right? Because I seem to recall a time when you couldn't keep your hands off Tess. Funny how things change." He looks me over, the gleam in his eyes unmistakable. "I always thought you'd be smarter than this. A little ambition can make even the best people do stupid things."

The words sting, but I don't flinch. Not this time. Not with Luca standing next to me. The old me might have let Marcus's words slice through me like a blade, but now? Now, I know better. The life I'm building with Luca—the one we're carving out in this city, one that's just beginning to take shape—is stronger than whatever poison Marcus tries to feed me.

"I've learned a lot," I say, stepping closer to Luca, my voice steady and unwavering. "And one thing I've learned is that ambition doesn't mean sacrificing everything. Not anymore."

Marcus's smirk falters just slightly, but he quickly recovers, his eyes narrowing. "You think you can take this city from me?" His voice drops, low and dangerous. "You think you can walk away from everything I've built?"

Luca's eyes flash with something sharp, something I haven't seen in him before. "We're not here to take anything from you, Marcus. We're here to take back what's ours."

The words hang between us like a challenge, a spark ready to ignite. For a long moment, no one moves, the silence thick enough to taste. Then, without warning, the sound of footsteps breaks the stillness—heavy, deliberate steps that echo down the street. I turn my head, and my heart skips a beat when I see who's emerging from the shadows.

It's him.

David.

I barely recognize him at first. His clothes are darker than I remember, the lines of his face harder, more defined. There's something about him that feels off—something that makes my stomach churn. But it's his eyes that freeze me in place. They're cold, calculating, the eyes of a man who's lost something essential, something human.

"Didn't expect you to be working with him, Tess," David says, his voice thick with disdain. He's looking at me like I've betrayed him, and the weight of it lands heavy on my chest.

"I'm not working with anyone," I reply quickly, my voice firm despite the knot of uncertainty forming in my stomach. "I'm just trying to survive."

David's lips curl into a smile, but it's the kind of smile that feels more like a threat than anything else. "You think you're the only one who's been fighting to survive? You think you're the only one who's been playing the game?"

The words hit harder than I expected, like they've come from a place deep inside him that I don't recognize anymore. And then, as if on cue, he steps aside, revealing the figures standing behind him. There are three of them, men dressed in dark suits, their eyes scanning us like hunters eyeing their prey.

Marcus smirks, clearly enjoying the shift in power. "I was wondering when you'd show up," he says, his voice almost too smug.

Luca's jaw tightens, his hand curling into a fist at his side. But he doesn't move. He doesn't speak. I feel the weight of his decision hanging between us, and for the first time, I realize the depth of what's at stake.

My heart pounds in my chest, and the realization hits me like a cold wave. This is it. The moment that will define everything.

The fight isn't just outside, it's in here. Between us. The tension thickens, and I know that nothing will ever be the same again.

I glance at Luca, his gaze meeting mine, and in that split second, I know exactly what we're both thinking.

We're not backing down.

Not now.

Not ever.

And then, the world explodes.

Chapter 43: A Battle Worth Fighting

The alley was quiet, too quiet for my liking. The only sound was the distant hum of the city, the kind of low thrum that fills the spaces between heartbeats. A few raindrops splattered against the cracked pavement, but the storm hadn't arrived yet—just the anticipation of it, hanging thick in the air. I hated that feeling, the weight of something coming. Luca, his sharp eyes scanning the shadows, was just as alert as I was, though he'd never show it. That's the thing about Luca: he was always three steps ahead. Even now, standing close enough for our shoulders to brush, I could feel the tension in his stance, the quiet before the storm.

"Ready?" I asked, my voice barely a whisper.

Luca's lips twitched in a way that almost passed for a smile. Almost. "If we're not, it's too late now."

His words were blunt, but that's the way he was—no sugarcoating, no unnecessary words. I'd learned to appreciate it. In a world where everyone wore a mask, Luca never did. He didn't have time for pretense, and neither did I. Our lives were too entangled in the kind of mess that didn't allow for anything but raw, unfiltered truth.

"Here they come," I murmured, eyes narrowing as the first shadow slipped into view at the far end of the alley. The sound of boots hitting the wet pavement was almost comforting, like the beat of a drum signaling the start of a fight we'd been waiting for.

We'd been preparing for this moment for months, ever since the rival family had begun to make their move. They didn't understand the kind of game they were playing, not really. But we did. And we knew the price of losing.

I reached for the hilt of the knife strapped to my thigh, fingers brushing the cool metal, and drew it with a smooth motion. Luca was already ahead of me, his own weapon in hand, eyes locked on the approaching group. We were a perfect unit, in sync in a way that could only come from years of fighting side by side. His presence next to me wasn't just a comfort; it was a guarantee.

The first figure emerged fully from the shadows, tall and broad-shouldered. His eyes were cold, calculating. There was a familiarity to him, a haunted recognition, but I couldn't place it. Not now. I could already feel my heartbeat picking up speed, adrenaline flooding my veins as the others followed.

Luca didn't wait. He surged forward, his blade flashing in the dim light, striking with the precision of someone who'd fought battles long before me. There was something about the way he moved, something raw and dangerous, that made the air feel heavier, like even the city itself was holding its breath.

I followed suit, my steps quick and determined, my blade a silver streak through the night. The first attacker lunged at me, but I sidestepped with a fluidity that had become second nature. I wasn't just good with a knife—I was fast. The second attacker didn't even see me coming. One swift slash and he was down, eyes wide in disbelief.

Luca was already engaged with the third, his movements a blur of controlled chaos. I could hear the grunt of his opponent as he blocked a strike, but Luca's smirk didn't falter. "You'll need more than that," he called, his voice loud enough to carry over the sound of metal clashing.

The moment felt surreal, like something out of a fever dream. Here we were, surrounded by a dozen or more men who had come to tear us down, and yet it felt like we had the upper hand. We knew their moves before they made them, anticipated every strike, every jab. But it wasn't just our skills that kept us in control—it was the trust between us. Luca knew my every move, and I knew his. It was a bond that couldn't be broken, even in the heat of battle.

But just as quickly as it started, it all came crashing down.

A scream sliced through the chaos. It wasn't the usual sound of someone getting hit, but something more desperate, more familiar. I turned in time to see one of our own, a young guy who had only joined us recently, caught by one of the rival family's leaders. His hands were shaking as he held a knife, his eyes wide in panic.

Before I could react, Luca was there, as always, moving faster than I could think. He knocked the knife from the kid's hand with a brutal efficiency, throwing him behind him and taking the attacker down in the same fluid motion. But not before the leader's blade found its mark.

Luca's breath hitched, just for a moment, and in that fleeting second, I felt the world shift. He was human. He wasn't invincible, no matter how much he tried to be.

The tension snapped, and suddenly, I was there, fighting with everything I had. I could hear Luca's breath, heavy and strained, but I couldn't look at him. Not now. Not with the way the enemy was closing in, their numbers growing despite our initial advantage.

I ducked under another swing, my blade flashing as I countered. One after another, our attackers fell, but it wasn't enough. They were relentless. And just as I thought we might finally break through, the ground beneath us trembled, the sound of heavy footsteps approaching louder than anything else.

My heart sank. Reinforcements.

I turned to Luca, our eyes locking for just a moment. "This isn't over," he muttered, his voice low, but with the same fire that had always driven him.

I didn't answer. I couldn't. The words felt useless, heavy in my mouth. All I could do was fight.

The scent of rain mingled with the faint, acrid tang of sweat and blood in the air, a sharp reminder of the battle that had just raged through the alley. The city, that ever-bustling, concrete jungle, had swallowed the conflict like it swallowed everything—no regard, no hesitation. We were still standing, but barely. I could feel the weight of exhaustion creeping into my bones, but I refused to let it show.

Luca stood a few feet away, his back to me, his shoulders tense as he surveyed the aftermath. I wasn't sure if it was the adrenaline still pumping through my veins or the way he stood there, so unyielding, but I could feel the shift in the air. Like the calm before another storm.

"You good?" I asked, keeping my voice light.

Luca didn't answer immediately, his gaze sweeping the alley. It was quiet now, but the kind of quiet that felt like a setup, like the universe was just waiting to hit play again. When he finally turned to me, there was no smile. No reassuring nod. Just those dark eyes, clouded with something unreadable.

"We won, but it's not over," he said, his voice low, his words carrying the weight of a thousand unspoken promises. "It's never over, not in this world."

I knew what he meant. The rival family, they were relentless. A loss like this would sting, but it wouldn't stop them. It would only make them angrier, more determined. We'd have to stay ready, stay sharp.

I wiped the blood from my blade, the cool metal gleaming under the streetlights. "I don't plan on waiting for the next round."

Luca's lips twitched, just the smallest hint of a smile. It was the kind of smile that made your heart skip, because you knew it wasn't given lightly. When Luca smiled, it meant something. It meant we were still in this together.

He reached for his phone, his fingers quick and efficient as he scrolled through the messages. "I'm calling in the others. This isn't a fight we can handle alone."

I couldn't argue with that. The rival family had made their move, but we had our own people, our own team. I'd spent years building this—building us—and now, when the world seemed like it was ready to fall apart, I wasn't about to let go of it. Not without a fight.

Luca's eyes flicked up from his screen, meeting mine. "You're sure about this?" he asked, his tone suddenly sharp, almost cautious.

I didn't have to think twice. "I'm not afraid of them."

It wasn't bravado. It wasn't some attempt to sound tough. I meant it. I had seen what those people were capable of, and I'd felt the sting of loss before. But I'd also seen the power of loyalty. Of unity. Of standing together, no matter the odds. And in that moment, I knew that Luca and I were the strongest we'd ever be. Together.

"We'll be ready," I added, my voice steady, even though my heart was still pounding in my chest.

Luca nodded once, his expression hardening again as he focused on the task at hand. But there was something in the way his gaze lingered on me, a brief flash of something softer, something almost vulnerable. It was the quiet between the chaos, the understanding that we were both in this—whatever this was—together.

The sound of tires screeching against wet pavement cut through the stillness, pulling me from my thoughts. I looked up just in time to see a black SUV sliding into the alley, the headlights cutting through the darkness. The door swung open before the car even fully stopped, and out stepped two of our people—Jace and Maria, both of them looking as sharp as ever, despite the late hour and the chaos that had unfolded in the last half hour.

"Did we miss the party?" Jace asked with a grin that didn't quite reach his eyes.

I shook my head. "Just in time for the aftermath."

Maria scanned the scene, her gaze lingering on the bodies scattered across the alley. Her eyes narrowed, calculating. "You two okay?" she asked, her tone sharper than usual. I could see the concern in her eyes, even though she tried to hide it.

"We're fine," Luca answered before I could, his voice clipped. "But this isn't over. We need to move fast."

Jace cracked his knuckles, a mischievous glint in his eyes. "You know me. I'm always ready for the next round."

Maria didn't share his enthusiasm. She was more practical, always thinking two steps ahead. "What's the plan?"

Luca took a deep breath, his gaze turning towards the heart of the city. "We hit them first. We take out their leadership. Once we've done that, we send a message they won't forget."

It was a solid plan, the kind of direct approach that Luca was known for. But I could see the hesitation in his eyes. Even he wasn't sure how this would play out. The rival family had their own strength, their own numbers. And taking down their leadership wouldn't be as simple as it sounded.

"Let's move," I said, stepping forward. "No time to waste."

The group quickly fell into step, the sound of our boots on the pavement a rhythmic reminder of what was at stake. We moved with precision, no wasted energy, no unnecessary words. We knew what needed to be done.

But even as we walked, the knot in my stomach tightened. The weight of the night, of everything that had happened—and everything that was still to come—pressed down on me. This wasn't the world I had imagined for myself. But it was the one I had to live in.

And if I had to fight for it, fight for everything I cared about, then so be it.

We were ready. But whether or not it would be enough—that was the question that lingered, heavy in the air between us all.

The night had begun to feel more like a dream—one of those dreams where you can't quite remember how you got into the mess, but you're already too deep to wake up. Our group moved like shadows, quick and deliberate, through the veins of the city that felt more like a labyrinth than the place we called home. The streets of Chicago had a rhythm all their own; even now, in the early hours of the morning, they thrummed with life, albeit the kind of life that felt dangerous and unfamiliar. The usual hum of traffic was replaced by an eerie silence, broken only by the distant echoes of sirens and the faint hiss of an incoming storm.

I could see the storm in Luca's eyes as he led the way, his posture rigid, shoulders set in the way I knew meant he was carrying more than his share of the burden. He'd always been like that, taking on the weight of the world and making it look effortless. But I knew better. He wasn't as invincible as he tried to appear, and tonight, I could see the strain etched into the lines of his face. We'd won the fight in the alley, but that wasn't the end of it. Not by a long shot.

"Hold up," Maria called from behind us, her voice low but firm.

Luca didn't slow his pace, but I did, glancing back over my shoulder. Maria was at the rear, scanning our surroundings with the same sharp eyes she always had. She didn't trust the quiet either. None of us did.

"We're too exposed here," she said, her eyes flicking nervously to the rooftops above us. "They know we're coming."

I could hear it in her voice—just a hint of doubt, the first time I'd heard it from her. Maria was solid, always had been, but she wasn't immune to the fear that seeped into the cracks of even the toughest walls.

"Then we don't stop," Luca said, his voice steady, but his words were tight, controlled. "We move fast, we stay sharp."

It wasn't the kind of reassurance I was looking for, but it was the only kind he could give. I felt the familiar flutter of tension in my stomach as we kept moving, my mind running over every possible scenario in rapid succession. Luca's plan was solid, but I knew the moment we made our move, it would trigger a chain of reactions. The rival family wouldn't go down easily. And we'd have to be prepared to handle whatever came next.

We cut through the alleyways, the familiar scent of pizza and exhaust fumes in the air, reminders of our city's pulse. There was something about the way the buildings loomed overhead, casting long shadows over the streets, that made me feel as if we were playing a game we didn't quite understand. One thing was for sure: I didn't want to lose. Not now, not after everything we'd been through.

We reached the building—an unmarked, nondescript structure that looked like any other in the industrial stretch near the South Loop. But I knew better. I could feel it in my bones. This was their base. The heart of the operation. The kind of place where you went to make decisions that would change everything.

Luca didn't hesitate. He didn't even flinch when he pushed open the door with a quiet force that matched the steel in his resolve. I followed close behind, my senses on high alert, every nerve tingling. Inside was just as I expected—cold, sterile, and silent except for the hum of fluorescent lights. It felt wrong, like the calm before the storm, or worse, the moment just after it.

"Luca," I whispered, my voice a thread in the tense air, "something's not right."

He paused, his head tilting slightly to the side, the muscles in his jaw tightening. "I know," he said softly, but the warning in his tone was unmistakable. "They've already moved. We're too late."

Before I could respond, a sound echoed from the far end of the hall—soft at first, then growing louder, more distinct. The unmistakable click of a safety being released.

"Damn it," Maria muttered under her breath, already pulling her gun from its holster with a fluid motion that spoke volumes about her training.

"Get ready," Luca said, his voice almost a growl.

I barely had time to react before the world exploded in a storm of gunfire. The walls around us shook with each impact, and I ducked instinctively, feeling the rush of air as a bullet whizzed by my ear. The loud bang of the shots echoed in my skull, and for a moment, all I could hear was the ringing in my ears and the frantic beating of my own heart.

"We need cover!" Jace shouted, pulling me to the side, his hand gripping my arm with the kind of strength that left no room for argument.

We scrambled for safety, ducking behind a row of metal filing cabinets that didn't offer much protection, but it was all we had. I could hear Luca's voice cutting through the chaos, giving orders, his presence commanding as always. But I could feel the tension in the air, a razor-sharp edge that told me this was no longer just a fight for survival. It was personal.

"What the hell do they want?" I hissed to Jace, my voice shaking with a mixture of anger and disbelief.

"Doesn't matter," he said, eyes scanning the room, watching every movement. "What matters is how we get out of here."

I couldn't argue with that, not with the way the bullets kept whizzing past us. But as I looked around the room, trying to formulate some kind of escape plan, something shifted in the air. A figure appeared in the doorway—tall, imposing, and dressed in all black, their presence filling the space with an unmistakable heaviness.

Luca froze, his hand tightening on the grip of his weapon. "You," he said, the word more of a growl than anything else.

I followed his gaze, my breath catching as recognition hit me like a punch to the gut. There, standing in the doorway, was someone I thought I'd never see again. Someone I'd hoped was long gone.

Chapter 44: A Love Unbroken

I leaned against the kitchen counter, the scent of freshly brewed coffee swirling in the air like some unspoken promise between us. Outside, the city hummed, alive with a rhythm I had long since learned to ignore. But this morning was different. The light spilling through the window felt warmer, almost as if the sun had taken it upon itself to linger a moment longer, just for us. It was funny how I could still be surprised by things like that—by the way life still found the power to shift when you least expected it.

Luca stood by the stove, his back to me, the dark silhouette of his body framed by the steam rising from the pot of oatmeal he was stirring with a casual ease. I'd never seen him cook before, and though I had no intention of being a domestic goddess, it was a small gesture that felt important in ways I couldn't quite explain. I found myself watching him more than I should have, as though studying his movements could somehow give me the answers to the endless questions swirling inside my head.

I took a sip of my coffee, the warmth of it spreading down my throat, grounding me. I could hear him humming under his breath, some old tune I couldn't quite place, and it made me smile—a small, quiet thing that only I could feel. There was something about the way he moved, something almost familiar, like a song I'd heard a thousand times but had never really listened to.

"You're quiet," Luca remarked, without turning. He must've felt me watching him. I didn't respond at first, unsure of what to say. The air between us was thick with newness—an invisible thread connecting us, fragile yet undeniably present.

I took another sip of coffee and set the mug down on the counter with a soft clink. "I'm thinking."

"Dangerous territory," he teased, finally turning around to face me. His eyes were soft but intense, the kind of eyes that could unravel you with a glance and then stitch you back together with a touch. He set the spoon down, wiping his hands on the towel slung over his shoulder, and leaned against the counter beside me. The tension between us crackled, but there was no rush to break it. We had time now, didn't we?

"I was just wondering," I began, the words coming slower than I intended. "How we got here."

Luca raised an eyebrow, a sly smile tugging at the corners of his mouth. "You mean to the part where we're standing here, together, and I'm making you oatmeal in a half-hearted attempt to win you over?"

I rolled my eyes but couldn't help the laugh that escaped. "That's exactly what I mean."

He crossed his arms, clearly amused by my sarcasm. "Well, if you must know, it wasn't a straight path. But I like to think it was all worth it."

My breath caught in my throat as I studied his face. His words, simple as they were, carried weight I hadn't expected. The memory of how we had collided into each other's lives—how love had arrived like a thunderstorm, unpredictable and impossible to ignore—flashed in my mind. Every twist, every argument, every misstep, had brought us here, to this moment in time, standing in the kitchen of a cramped apartment in the heart of the city, where nothing was certain, but somehow everything felt right.

"You know, you're impossible," I said, my voice quieter than I intended.

"That's part of my charm." He grinned, a look in his eyes that could only be described as mischievous.

"You should really stop using that as an excuse."

"But it works," he said, his grin widening. "At least, I like to think it does."

I glanced out the window again, feeling the weight of the city pressing against the glass. The streets below were a blur of movement—people rushing to jobs they hated, others stumbling into cafes for their first cup of the day, all of them oblivious to the small world Luca and I had carved out in this corner of the city. For all the noise, there was a stillness here—between us, in the spaces we hadn't yet filled, in the things we hadn't yet said. But the silence was comfortable now, the kind that didn't demand anything more than simply being.

Luca's voice broke through my thoughts. "You know, if you'd let me, I'd make this life worth living every single day."

The words hung there, heavy in the air, almost too much to bear. I could feel my heart thudding in my chest, a soft but steady rhythm that matched his words more closely than I cared to admit. This wasn't the kind of declaration I'd expected from him—then again, nothing about Luca had ever been what I expected. And that was part of why I couldn't let him go. Because somehow, despite the chaos, despite the pieces of us that had yet to come together, he felt like home.

I met his gaze, my voice coming out stronger than I felt. "You're the only thing that makes this life worth living, too."

His smile softened, and for a moment, I thought he might reach for me. But he didn't. Instead, he simply looked at me, his eyes searching mine as though he was trying to piece together a puzzle that had no answers.

"We'll make it," he said, almost as if he was reassuring himself more than me.

I nodded, but the doubt I'd been carrying around—the kind that whispered of what ifs and how long—lingered in the back of my mind. It wasn't gone, but somehow it didn't seem as loud. Maybe it was the warmth of the coffee, or maybe it was the way Luca was standing beside me, as if he was waiting for me to decide what came next. Either way, I knew that today wasn't the day for doubts. Today was for possibilities. And for the first time, the future seemed less like a distant shadow and more like something we could reach for, together.

The sun hung low in the sky as the city started to buzz, the evening rush barely a whisper against the hum of the weekend crowd. A few blocks down, a barista yelled someone's name out in a cadence that felt both a little too loud and strangely comforting. I smiled as I picked up my purse, the soft leather cool under my fingers. The weight of the day had melted away, leaving behind the soft glow of anticipation. There was something in the air tonight—a hint of possibility that whispered through the city like a secret.

Luca was waiting for me outside, his posture easy but his gaze fixed, as though waiting for something he couldn't quite name. He caught my eye from across the street, and the smile that bloomed on his face was the kind of smile I never thought I'd see aimed at me. It was effortless, warm, and it made the tightness in my chest loosen just a fraction. Maybe that's what it was—he made the impossible seem simple.

I had spent years thinking that love was this monumental thing that you had to work toward, something built brick by brick, each moment carefully constructed until the walls of it were high enough to withstand anything. But with Luca, I was starting to wonder if it was more like something that found you when you least expected it—when you stopped pretending to have it all figured out. Maybe it wasn't meant to be something you built. Maybe it was something you let happen, like a flood, sweeping everything else away.

I reached the curb just as the light turned green, and Luca was beside me in two long strides. He grinned, brushing a strand of hair away from my face. The motion was so casual, so familiar, that it made my heart skip. "You look like you're thinking deep thoughts again," he said, his voice a little too knowing for my liking.

"I was," I admitted, laughing lightly. "I think I've spent most of the day thinking about how to avoid thinking too much."

He chuckled, and there it was again—the easy way we fit together, like two puzzle pieces that had been jumbled up in a drawer for too long and finally managed to click. It should have been more complicated than this. It had to be. And yet, with him, it wasn't.

"So," he started, drawing the word out like he was testing it in the air before committing. "I was thinking we could take a walk through the park. The one by the river."

I raised an eyebrow at him, giving him a playful once-over. "You don't exactly strike me as the 'spontaneous walk through the park' type."

"I'm full of surprises." He grinned, his eyes glinting with the kind of mischief that made it impossible to say no.

"Alright, but only because it's a beautiful evening, and I'm convinced you might actually be telling the truth for once."

We made our way to the park, the city noise fading into the background as we crossed the familiar bridges, the old wooden planks beneath our feet creaking with each step. The park was quieter than usual tonight, the last remnants of daylight softening the trees into shadows. I could feel Luca's presence beside me, steady, like an anchor to a ship I hadn't realized had drifted out too far.

"I thought you hated this place," I said, glancing at him sideways. "You used to complain about the smell of the river."

"I do," he said without hesitation, shoving his hands into his pockets, his tone light. "But you like it here. And I'm beginning to think I could get used to it."

I stopped walking, a small laugh escaping my lips. "That's a hell of a confession, Luca. Is this your way of saying you've made peace with the fact that you're spending your weekends here?"

He looked down at me, eyes unreadable, his jaw tight, but there was no denying the warmth in his gaze. "Maybe. Or maybe it's my way of saying that I'll follow you anywhere, even to places that stink."

I blinked, caught off guard by his words. "And if I took you somewhere else?" I challenged, stepping forward so I was inches away from him.

He paused, considering. "I think you'd be surprised by where I'd go next."

The words felt heavy in the space between us, and suddenly, there was no laughter in the air, no teasing. Just a quiet, unspoken promise. The kind that made everything feel a little more fragile but also a little more real. There was a part of me that wanted to keep it light, to brush it off, but I knew better. With Luca, you didn't just play games; you threw yourself in. Headfirst, no hesitation. And something told me that if I hesitated, I might miss it—whatever "it" was.

"What if it's not a place that's easy to get to?" I asked, my voice quieter now, unsure of where my words were leading.

Luca studied me for a long beat, and I swore I could feel the air shift around us, growing thicker with every passing second. "Then I guess we'll find our way. I'm good at getting lost, you know. But I'm better at finding my way back."

I swallowed hard, feeling the weight of his words settle deep inside me. There was no pretense with Luca. No sugar-coating. Just the truth, however messy it might be. And for once, I didn't want to run from that truth. I wanted to dive into it, to see where it would lead.

"Just don't get lost," I said, my voice almost playful, despite the tangle of emotions in my chest.

He raised an eyebrow, and I could see the flicker of something dangerous—something that made the air crackle with electricity. "If I get lost, will you come find me?"

I didn't answer right away. Instead, I took his hand, letting the warmth of it remind me that there were no guarantees, no promises. Only us. And that, in itself, was enough. For now.

The night felt like a whispered promise as we strolled deeper into the park, the muted glow of the city's lights casting long shadows across the winding paths. I could hear the distant hum of traffic, but it seemed so far removed from the world we had carved out for ourselves in the quiet. The air was heavy with the smell of damp earth, mingling with the faint scent of jasmine blooming somewhere off in the distance. I had always been one to appreciate the small things—the texture of a cool breeze against my skin, the flicker of a streetlamp in the distance, the way the world felt just a little bit slower after the sun went down.

Luca's hand, warm and steady in mine, anchored me in this strange new reality I was still trying to wrap my head around. He was the kind of person who made the ordinary seem extraordinary, as if every moment shared with him could be the start of something new. He didn't need to say much; his presence alone was enough to shift the balance of things.

"You know," he began, breaking the comfortable silence, his voice quieter than usual, "I never really thought I'd end up in a place like this."

I tilted my head, glancing up at him. The moonlight made his features look softer, but there was something in his eyes—an undercurrent of something deeper, more vulnerable—that made me pause.

"A place like this?" I asked, my voice light, though my curiosity piqued.

"Yeah," he said, his gaze not leaving mine. "With you. A place where everything's... right. Even though it shouldn't be."

The words hung in the air, heavier than any of the weight I had been carrying. I didn't know how to respond. The vulnerability in his voice made the ground beneath my feet feel a little less stable. But I couldn't afford to second-guess everything he said. Not now. Not when I had already started to believe the impossible was possible.

"I think you're overthinking it," I said after a moment, squeezing his hand. "We're here. Right now, that's all that matters." I tried to make my voice sound light, but the truth was, I wasn't sure how much longer I could keep pretending that everything between us was easy.

Luca stopped walking, turning to face me fully. His expression was unreadable, a mixture of determination and something I couldn't quite place. The look in his eyes was enough to make my heart skip a beat.

"Do you really think it's that simple?" he asked, his voice low, almost as if he were daring me to contradict him. "Do you think that after everything we've been through, it's just a matter of walking away and pretending nothing happened?"

I felt the sharp bite of his words, more cutting than I had expected. A part of me wanted to pull away, to retreat back into my shell where things were safer. But that was the last thing I wanted. Not with Luca. Not when the possibility of something real, something enduring, was finally within reach.

"No," I said softly, taking a step toward him. "I don't think it's simple. But maybe that's the point. Maybe it's not supposed to be."

Luca's jaw tightened, and he let out a breath, the kind of breath that felt like a confession. He reached out, his thumb brushing against my cheek in a way that made everything inside me pause, like the world had stopped moving just for us.

"I'm not good at this," he admitted, his voice rough around the edges. "I'm not good at letting myself want things I'm not sure I can keep."

I wanted to argue, to tell him that we all had our flaws, our hesitations, our moments of doubt. But I knew it wouldn't help. Instead, I closed the distance between us, placing my hand over his and holding it there, steady.

"You don't have to be good at it," I said, my voice steady but soft. "We can figure it out. Together."

He stared at me for a long moment, as though searching for something in my eyes. His hand slid from my cheek, down to my wrist, where his fingers wrapped around it gently, like he was afraid I might disappear at any second.

For the briefest moment, I wondered if we were already too late—if the walls we'd built around our hearts were too high to climb. But the thought was fleeting, replaced by the weight of his touch. There was something in that simple gesture—something that told me we still had time.

I took a deep breath, pushing aside the worries that had started to claw their way back into my thoughts. "Let's not overthink this. We'll take it one step at a time. No rush. Just... this."

He nodded, the tension in his shoulders easing ever so slightly. "You're right," he said quietly. "Maybe I just need to let go."

I smiled, not because I had the answers, but because the uncertainty was starting to feel like something we could embrace, not something to fear.

But as the night deepened, a subtle shift in the atmosphere caught my attention—a sensation that something was coming, something neither of us had prepared for.

I heard the sound of footsteps approaching from behind, steady and deliberate. We both turned instinctively, the hairs on the back of my neck prickling. The figure emerged from the shadows, its features indistinguishable in the half-light. My heart thudded in my chest as the figure stepped closer, its presence an unsettling interruption to the fragile peace we'd found.

I could feel Luca stiffen beside me, his hand slipping from mine as his stance shifted into something protective. The figure drew nearer, and as it stepped into the dim light, I gasped, my breath catching in my throat.

It was someone I never expected to see again.

Chapter 45: A Kingdom of Our Own

I sat back in the worn-out armchair, the leather creaking beneath me as I took in the sight of the empty room. Sunlight filtered through the cracked blinds, casting soft, uneven lines on the hardwood floor. The old clock on the wall ticked away, its steady rhythm the only sound in the room, punctuating the silence like the ticking of a countdown I wasn't entirely sure I was ready for.

Luca was in the kitchen, his back to me as he rummaged through the cabinets. I could hear the soft clink of mugs, the occasional sigh of frustration. I smiled to myself, though the corners of my mouth didn't quite reach my eyes. It had been weeks since we'd decided to move back to the old house—the house that had been more of a symbol of failure than anything else for years. But now it was different. We were different.

"You're making coffee, right?" I asked, my voice breaking through the stillness, though I didn't really need to ask. The scent of the beans was already wafting over to me, wrapping around my senses like an old, familiar blanket.

Luca didn't answer right away. I could tell he was concentrating, trying to measure out just the right amount. He always did that, even with something as simple as coffee. It was one of those quirks of his that drove me mad when we first met. And yet, now, it felt like a tiny bit of magic in the chaos of everything else.

"Mm-hmm," he said, his voice laced with the deep hum of contentment that seemed to have settled in him ever since we decided to make a go of this, whatever "this" was. It wasn't just about rebuilding the family anymore; it was about rebuilding us, too. "Coffee's brewing. Don't get your hopes up. I'm not a barista."

I leaned back further into the chair, letting the heat of the sunlight warm my face. It wasn't a hot day, not by any stretch of the imagination. The air was crisp, autumn creeping in like a lover's whisper. Still, I felt the heat from outside, the sun's touch lingering on my skin, mixing with the quiet joy of knowing I didn't have to navigate this alone anymore.

It wasn't that I hadn't always been alone. In the early years, my life had been a whirlwind of activity, of people and plans, a never-ending stream of things to keep me occupied. But it was the kind of loneliness that you don't recognize until someone offers you a place to sit down and take a breath. That was Luca's gift to me—quiet, steady, and unwavering.

I heard the coffee machine click off in the kitchen. A moment later, Luca appeared, holding two mugs. He didn't say anything, just placed one in front of me before settling into the chair next to mine. His jeans were faded, the hems frayed in places where he'd worn them through the years. There was a soft scrape of his boots against the floor, the kind of sound that told you someone had been on their feet for too long.

"You're looking at that chair like it's going to bite you," Luca said, his voice teasing, but there was a softness in the words. A knowing.

I glanced over at him, raising an eyebrow. "It's not the chair, it's the room."

"Ah," he said, a grin pulling at his lips. "The room. You mean the place that nearly swallowed you whole the last time we were here?"

"Not quite," I muttered, taking a sip of the coffee. It was strong, far stronger than I liked it, but it was warm and grounding. "But I'm getting there."

He chuckled, settling deeper into the chair. "You're stubborn, you know that?"

"Tell me something I don't know," I replied, meeting his gaze. He was still looking at me like he could read me, and it made me uncomfortable in a way I couldn't explain. "We're getting there," I said again, more firmly this time. "We'll make it work."

He nodded, his expression shifting, his eyes darkening with something unspoken. "You've been saying that a lot lately. What does it mean to you?"

It was a simple question, but it made my stomach tighten. What did it mean? Rebuilding, reworking our lives, putting things back together? I didn't know. Not really. But I did know this: for the first time in a long time, the thought of moving forward didn't feel as terrifying as it used to. Not with him beside me.

"I don't know," I admitted after a long pause, feeling the weight of the honesty settle between us. "But whatever it is... it's enough for now."

Luca took a slow sip of his coffee, his gaze never leaving mine. There was a flicker of something in his eyes, something unreadable that made my heart do a little flip.

"Well," he said, setting the mug down on the table between us, "whatever comes next, we'll face it together." He leaned back in the chair, crossing his arms. "And we'll win."

I felt the weight of his words sink in, the certainty in them almost more than I could handle. But there was a quiet strength in his voice that I couldn't help but believe. For once, it wasn't just bravado. It was belief.

I leaned forward, my fingers curling around my mug. "You know, you're really annoying sometimes," I said, the words playful, even though the truth of them was a little harsher than I intended. "But for once, I think you might actually be right."

His smile was slow, easy. "I like hearing that."

I snorted, but the warmth in my chest made me forget to add a retort. Maybe it was true. Maybe, just maybe, we were going to win. Together.

I don't know when it happened—the exact moment when everything shifted. But as I watched Luca leaning against the doorway of the kitchen, his shirt sleeves rolled up to reveal those familiar, calloused arms, I could almost pinpoint the moment everything changed for me. Not in a dramatic, life-altering way. It wasn't an epiphany or some grand revelation. It was subtle, like the dawn creeping over the horizon without a fanfare, yet unmistakable.

I was home. And I had been, for some time.

It wasn't just the house—creaky floors, faded wallpaper, and the kitchen that always smelled like burnt toast no matter how hard I tried to avoid it. It was the fact that, with Luca by my side, the cracks and bruises of my past had started to heal. The doubts, the insecurities, the constant fear that something would fall apart—that I would fall apart—were quieter now. Maybe even gone.

"You planning to stare at me all day, or are you going to come over here and help with lunch?" Luca's voice was low, teasing, but there was an undercurrent of something serious there too. A challenge. His eyes narrowed slightly, the corners of his mouth lifting just enough to hint at a smile.

"Depends," I replied, raising an eyebrow as I stood from the chair. "What are we having?"

He turned toward the stove, pulling a pan from the cabinet. "It's a surprise."

I didn't ask any more questions. In the beginning, I would've insisted on knowing everything—down to the smallest detail. I didn't trust that things could unfold without me controlling the situation. But with Luca, I had learned to let go. To allow things to fall into place, even if I didn't have a roadmap. The food would be good, I was certain of that. Even if it was a surprise. Especially if it was a surprise.

The quiet rhythm of his movements in the kitchen soothed me as I walked over to the counter to grab a cutting board. The scent of garlic, onions, and tomatoes filled the space as he sliced vegetables with a sharp, practiced ease. There was something impossibly calming about the way he moved—his every action, from the careful way he placed the knife down to the methodical stirring of the sauce, felt like a promise. A promise that no matter how messy everything was outside of this space, within these walls, things would be okay.

"So, what's next?" I asked, breaking the silence between us as I set the cutting board down with a soft thud. "We finish lunch, we eat, and then what?"

Luca paused for a moment, his back to me. His hand stilled over the chopping board as if he was mulling over my question. Then, he turned to face me, his eyes serious, though the glint of amusement in them was hard to ignore.

"We fix the fence," he said, like it was the most logical thing in the world.

I blinked. "The fence?"

He nodded, motioning to the backyard through the window. "It's been falling apart for weeks. We should probably do something about it before it completely caves in."

I glanced out the window, then back at him. "I thought you said you'd get a professional for that."

"I did." Luca shrugged, a playful grin spreading across his face. "But then I realized, why hire someone when we can do it ourselves? It'll be good for us. We'll fix it together. Like everything else."

There was a warmth in his words that I hadn't expected. The fence—something as simple as fixing a fence—had become a metaphor for our lives. Everything had been broken, in need of repair. But we weren't just patching things up. We were building them anew. Together.

"You're absolutely insane," I muttered, shaking my head. But there was affection in my voice, a soft chuckle bubbling up despite myself.

Luca grinned, the mischievous glint in his eye giving him an almost boyish quality. "That's why you love me."

I opened my mouth to retort, but then I stopped myself. Was it really that simple? Could it be? Had I really come to a place in my life where I no longer feared the future, where I no longer doubted my choices? A place where I could finally admit that maybe—just maybe—I did love him? The thought was like a weight being lifted from my chest, freeing me in a way I hadn't expected.

"Yeah, I do," I said softly, my gaze softening as I met his.

Luca seemed to sense the shift, and for a moment, everything between us seemed to pause. His eyes darkened just a little, his expression unreadable. The playful banter, the teasing, the constant back-and-forth we had always shared—it all seemed to fade for a heartbeat. And in that silence, I saw the truth of it. The truth that had been there all along, buried just under the surface, waiting for me to notice.

"Well," he said, finally breaking the moment with a smile, "now that we've established that, you should probably get a move on with that fence. I'm not doing all the work myself."

I rolled my eyes, but there was something soft in my laugh. "You're unbelievable."

"You wouldn't have it any other way."

And just like that, the moment passed, but the truth remained. I loved him. It wasn't some grand gesture or a sweeping declaration—it was in the little things. The way he made me laugh, the way he made everything feel less heavy, the way he never once let me back down from my own doubts. In all of that, I found a kind of peace I didn't know I was looking for. A peace that didn't require perfection. Just honesty. And maybe, just maybe, that was enough.

"I'll go get the tools," I said, breaking the silence, already moving toward the door. "But if we're doing this, I'm picking the paint color."

Luca groaned. "You are not picking a color."

"Oh, I'm absolutely picking a color," I called over my shoulder, already feeling the weight of the day shift. "And you'll like it."

I heard him mutter something that sounded suspiciously like, "I'll be the judge of that," but I didn't care. As I stepped outside into the cool breeze, I felt a strange sense of calm wash over me. The fence would be fixed. The house would be made whole again. And for once, I wasn't afraid of what came next.

The tools were scattered across the yard, haphazardly tossed around like toys after a particularly enthusiastic game of catch. A shovel here, a rusty wrench there, the electric drill resting idly on the cement like it had given up on the world. I could hear Luca moving around inside, the faint scrape of his boots against the floor as he found whatever else he deemed necessary for our little backyard project. It was absurd, really. Here we were—two grown adults, both equally stubborn, equally aware of the fact that this house had far too many problems to deal with in one sitting—and yet we were acting like this small, broken fence was some kind of noble cause.

But there was something undeniably appealing about it. About him.

I glanced at the mess, the crooked picket fence that had stood as a silent testament to all the things left unresolved in my life, and found myself strangely pleased. It wasn't perfect, not by a long shot. But it was ours now. My heart clenched a little at the thought.

Luca appeared on the porch, holding a can of paint, its red label peeling at the edges. He didn't say anything, just handed it to me. His eyes were narrowed in that way of his, like he was trying to figure out if I was going to balk at the task. He knew me too well.

"Are we painting the fence now?" I asked, twisting the cap off the can with a little more force than necessary.

"I thought we might as well," he said, not breaking eye contact. "We're already here, aren't we?"

"Yeah," I muttered, setting the can down and grabbing a brush from the pile. "Sure, why not. Let's add some color to the chaos."

The paintbrush glided over the weathered wood, its bristles biting into the rough surface as I worked, slow and deliberate. The house had been full of moments just like this one, full of unfinished conversations and projects half-done. But this? This felt different. It wasn't about finishing something for the sake of completion. It was about making a choice to be here. To be present.

"I'm still not convinced this is going to hold up," I said, eyeing the fence with skepticism as I ran the brush over another picket. "Seems like every time I fix something, it falls apart again."

Luca chuckled softly from behind me, his voice warm and familiar. "Nothing stays perfect. Especially not us."

I froze for a second, my hand hovering midair. His words lingered like a secret I hadn't been expecting him to share. The unspoken truths between us had always been there, tucked away under layers of laughter and sarcasm. But this time, it felt different. More real.

"We're getting there, though," I said, my voice quieter than I intended. "And maybe that's enough."

Luca didn't answer right away. I could feel his gaze on me, sharp and steady, the weight of his silence both comforting and unnerving. When he finally spoke, his words were softer than usual.

"You're not alone, you know that, right?"

I met his eyes, swallowing the lump that had formed in my throat. For a moment, I wasn't sure if I could respond. The vulnerability in his voice, the rawness of it, caught me off guard. He wasn't the type to open up unless it was absolutely necessary. And yet, here he was, laying his cards on the table without so much as a hint of hesitation.

"I know," I said after a beat, my voice cracking just slightly. "It's just... hard, sometimes. To believe things can change."

He reached for the paint can, his fingers brushing against mine as he took it from me. There was an understanding in his eyes, something we'd both learned the hard way. Change didn't come easily. It was more like a slow, steady erosion of everything we thought we knew—until one day, you woke up and realized you had rebuilt yourself from the ground up.

"We'll face it together," Luca said, his words like an unspoken promise. "Whatever comes next, we'll face it."

The sound of a car engine interrupted the moment, a sharp contrast to the quiet tension between us. I turned instinctively, my heart picking up speed as I saw the dust cloud rising in the distance. It was a familiar car, a sleek black sedan that I hadn't expected to see today.

It was John.

He hadn't shown his face around here for weeks. Not since the night things had gone sideways with my family, and I couldn't bring myself to think about it. John was a constant in my past, a man I had grown up with, the kind of person who knew far too much about me for comfort. His presence was never a welcome one—not now, not after everything that had happened.

"What the hell is he doing here?" I muttered under my breath, the paintbrush trembling in my hand as I stepped away from the fence.

Luca's expression darkened, his jaw tightening. He took a slow step forward, his eyes fixed on the approaching car like a predator watching its prey.

"I don't know," he said, his voice quiet, dangerous. "But he's about to find out it's a bad time."

The car pulled into the driveway, the engine cutting off with a sharp sputter. John climbed out, his casual stance at odds with the weight of the situation. He adjusted his jacket as if he hadn't just appeared uninvited, like he wasn't about to stir up all the old chaos we'd been trying so hard to leave behind.

"Luca, are you sure you want to—" I started to say, but the words died in my throat. I didn't know if I wanted to stop Luca from confronting him, or if I wanted to hide from the tension already brewing between them.

John's gaze locked onto mine as he made his way toward us, the faintest of smirks playing on his lips. His eyes flicked from me to Luca, a silent challenge in his posture. And that was when I realized something. This was no coincidence. Whatever he wanted, it wasn't just to check on me. It was to stir something up.

And I wasn't sure I was ready for it.